THE APRIL
OF HER AGE

To Slim: All my Love,

–Always,

Steve

THE
APRIL
OF
HER AGE

◆   ◆   ◆

John Cummins Mebane

WINDWARD PUBLISHING CO.

Copyright © 1994 by John Cummins Mebane
All right reserved
Published by Windward Publishing Company
1939-C Kaiwiki Road
Hilo, Hawaii 96720
(808) 961-5796

Book cover illustrated by Paul Marciel Souza
Santa Fe, New Mexico

Photographs courtesy of Hawaii State Archives

Designed by Doug Behrens Design
Honolulu, Hawaii

LIBRARY OF CONGRESS CATALOGING-IN-PUBLICATION DATA

But Love is a durable fire
In the mind ever burning;
Never sick, never old, never dead,
From itself never turning.

—Sir Walter Raleigh

◆ ◆ ◆

And without partiality, a woman of
sense and manners is the finest and
most delicate part of God's creation,
the glory of her Maker, and the great
instance of his singular regard to
man, his darling creature, to whom he
gave the best gift either God could
bestow or man receive.

—Daniel Defoe

◆ ◆ ◆

The life of man upon this world of
ours is a funny business. They talk of
the angels weeping; but I think they
must more often be holding their
sides, as they look on.

—R.L.S.

Princess Victoria Kaiulani

Robert Louis Stevenson

ACKNOWLEDGEMENTS

It would be impossible for me to create a novel unless I were completely captivated by its chemistry beforehand. Therefore, let it be known that I was lured, trapped and held hostage by *The April of Her Age*. The story is my attempt to deal with the labyrinth, the tentacles, the teasing mysteries that closed in on me. My captors: Princess Victoria Kaiulani and author Robert Louis Stevenson. An enchanted trail had been baited, leading to buried treasure; a lure was set one hundred years ago. Sooner or later, someone would have stumbled on it. I've never stopped to ask: 'why me?' Once on the trail, I was magnetized by hints that at first were elusive, then downright electrifying.

An innocent series of occurrences started it off: little things: why was I living in an antique Victorian house on Kaiulani Street in Hilo, Hawai'i? Big things: Kaiulani's haunting portrait. She had me spotted! She looked right at me! Tantalizingly expressive. Commanding. Victoria invaded my life without cease. The beautiful young princess had something to say. "Tell my story," she charged, each time I entered her sphere. Then, an amazing event: clearing a site on the slope of Kilauea Volcano, a rickety little bulldozer unearthed an old, rusted strongbox with an assortment of papers, a journal, and several Stevenson poems. A tarnished bit of silver—an intertwined hibiscus and thistle completed the collection. Like someone driven by Madame Pele's lava flows, I plunged after the lure. The terms of my release were all too clear. "Tell my story," she directed.

There were gaps in Victoria's story. At first, her brief life seemed to deny me any sense of her depth, or her significance. I embarked upon extensive research, and stumbled into Robert Louis Stevenson, and one amazing finding after another. Finally, deep into my explorations, my princess seemed to say, "You have enough! Now use your imagination!" And so I have. She sounded the trumpet: possibilities far beyond the printed page sparkled upon the glow of the canvas.

The foundation for *The April of Her Age* is the historical and literary material available to me. There is much I am grateful for in numerous historical works. These were my picks and shovels as I unearthed the story, the buried treasure of Kaiulani and Stevenson. I am indebted to many people.

First of all, Kristin Zambucka for the wealth of information about Kaiulani in *Princess Kaiulani. The Last Hope of Hawai'i's Monarchy.*

Shoal of Time, a History of the Hawaiian Islands by Gavan Daws was a source of fascination for me long before this book was undertaken. Daws enabled me, as faithfully as the novel form permitted, to track the friendship of Kaiulani and Stevenson against the turbulent background of Hawaiian history.

The Royal Torch by Billie Beamer revealed the plight of the Hawaiian people as historical events carried them from a primitive island society, through a brutal era of priest-chieftains, to a status as commoners under a unified monarchy.

Joseph Feher's *Hawai'i: A Pictorial History* reconstructs for our century a picture of Hawai'i, and especially Honolulu in the 1880's and 1890's.

John F.G. Stokes *Heiau of the Island of Hawai'i, A Historic Survey of Native Hawaiian Temple Sites* provided rich detail for the encounter of Kaiulani and Stevenson at the City of Refuge. In the same vein, William D. Westervelt's *Hawaiian Legends of Old Honolulu* contains an intriguing account of *The Ghost Dance on Punchbowl.*

Emmett Cahill's *Yesterday at Kalaupapa* is a valuable recent publication which provides a vivid background for Stevenson's experiences at the Molokai Leprosy Settlement.

The year 1993, a century after the overthrow of the monarchy, yielded an outpouring of valuable material such as Russ Apple's fascinating columns, *Mo'olelo na Apu,* in the Hawai'i Tribune Herald. Honolulu Magazine published historical writings about Robert Wilcox, the *Stone-eating Song,* and *Hawai'i's first Christmas.* Michael Dougherty's *To Steal a Kingdom* is a provocative probing of Hawai'i's past based upon archival sources and material never before published.

Sister Martha Mary McGaw gave me a wealth of material about Stevenson's visits to Hawai'i. Virginia Fettes, reference librarian at the Hawai'i Medical Library provided insights into the remarkable life of Dr. Phillippe Trousseau.

Victoria Kaiulani's benign haunting bestowed upon me a deep love and respect for Robert Louis Stevenson. I had known him most casually, superficially. *Treasure Island* was almost the extent of it. The treasure trail I followed brought me to Stevenson's extensive writing about the South Seas. The complexities of Stevenson's character have been well set forth in Hellman's *The True Stevenson*, Mackay's *The Violent Friend: The Story of Mrs. Robert Louis Stevenson*, and Hinkley's *The Stevensons, Louis and Fanny.*

Prodded I was, to study Stevenson in his short stories, novels, and most of all—his poems. Stevenson's devotees will recognize that I have paraphrased and excerpted from his works here and there, borrowing the unique richness of his expressive genius.

Finally, there is my profound respect, gratitude, and love—for Victoria—the wellspring of this work, whose presence was always there, breathing inspiration into my words.

Dr. Paul Weisser made many helpful suggestions in editing portions of the manuscript..

And what of my captivity? I realized that, after all, a better term would have been 'bonded!' —to a lifelong enchantment.

♦ ♦ ♦

TABLE OF CONTENTS

PROLOGUE

The vast Pacific ocean floor is a dwelling place of creative magic. During eons of time the workings of the earth's crust, galvanized by volcanic fire, have thrust upward a chain of islands, and Earth's most isolated archipelago has emerged. The natives of these islands, drawing on ancient wisdom as deep as the ocean itself, would declare this to be the work of the Master God, Kane, and of his goddess of fire, Pele.

In the fullness of time, those great sailors, the ancient Polynesians, came to this uninhabited garden that we now call Hawai'i. A hybrid people, their long journey began in southeast Asia and, over three centuries, extended to the central Pacific. By 200 A.D., they had reached the Marquesas, Tahiti, and Easter Island. In the next two hundred years, they settled the Hawaiian group. Life for those pioneers in the next half-century came close to our notion of an island paradise. These early Polynesians thrived under a benign community code. They shaped an agricultural and fishing society free of class subjugation and the threat of tribal war. This—not what came later—was the virgin, inviolate Hawai'i.

In 1100 A.D., there occurred the first grievous violation of this community: the invasion by Tahitian Polynesian priest-chieftains with fleets of warriors. Divine leaders established a new ideology, surrounding themselves with a retinue of priests, chiefs, and obsequious commoners. Eight hundred years of human abuse ensued, with the common people under constant threat of violent death or enslavement. They were objects, beasts of burden to supply the needs of the elite. Anyone unproductive, aged, or handicapped—even women and infants—were eliminated. We tend to think in more modern terms of violations imposed by Caucasians, Japanese, missionaries, whalers, merchants, and planters. These came much later, each to add their own spin to the frenetic gyrations of the Garden. Billie Beamer, in *The Royal Torch*, with bitter irony, describes this as a golden age—but only for the favored few. The chiefs in their feathered capes destroyed any hope of paradise for the people. Their methods of persuasion were cruel: smashed heads, gouged eyes, branding, drowning, strangulation, decapitation, burial or roasting alive. In the years from 1100 to 1800, there were no traces of Eden for the commoners of Hawai'i. Their history is a dark one—an account of people oppressing their own kind for the glory that power allows.

Chiefs and warriors of the four major islands—Hawai'i, Maui, Oahu and Kauai—once daring explorers of the Pacific, now were content to fatten on the indulgences extracted from the conquered commoners. Inevitably, they fought among themselves for dominance. In the middle of the eighteenth century, amidst rich prophecy, Kamehameha the Great was born in Kohala on the island of Hawai'i. In fiercely successful battles, he unified the islands and stabilized his rule. Picture a time two hundred years ago when these ravaged islands existed in a primitive Stone Age. With plentiful slave labor in the islands, there was little incentive for rulers to view human energy and creativity, let alone commoner existence and welfare, differently.

Then another invading force arrived from the outside world. This was even more complex and bewildering in its impact on the arrested, contorted Garden. Enter the world at large: foreign cultures, religions, customs, and ideas of government. The new invaders brought with them their quest for trade, acquisition, and dominance—and their diseases. Captain James Cook, the English explorer, with his ships, his "floating temples," the *Discovery* and the *Resolution*, appeared out of the sea in 1778. The tall white sails were to the Hawaiians a god-like manifestation of advanced technology and craftsmanship. Kamehameha was quick to avail himself of foreign tutors and advisors, rewarding them richly with land, slaves, and wives. With the expertise of these foreigners, he assembled ships and firepower to slaughter any remaining domestic resistance. He accumulated great wealth from his control of trade, supplying ships with food, water, and women. Still, the people shared none of the wealth. Three decades after Cook, the British economic impact on the islands was so extensive that Kamehameha ruled Hawai'i in imitation of a British colony. The silks, the Windsor uniforms of the Court of St. James, the plumed helmets and gold-braided European cloaks were a lasting badge of Hawaiian royalty. The Union Jack flutters even today, superimposed upon the red, white and blue stripes of the Hawaiian State flag.

Kamehameha the Great had many wives and children, which should have guaranteed a lasting monarchy. But as foreign oppression and disease progressively diminished the Hawaiians, the royal lineage failed to multiply. In succeeding generations, Kamehameha IV (Alexander Liholiho) and Queen Emma produced a child, Albert, only to lose him to spinal meningitis. Alexander died the following year, at twenty-nine, of grief and asthma. Brother Lot, Kamehameha V, never married. As he struggled against massive currents poised to erode his rule, he revived ancient hula and kahuna rituals and was the last great chief in the old tradition. Lot passed from the scene at the age of forty-three. King William Lunalilo succeeded, only to die a year later of tuberculosis and alcoholism. Faced with this frailty of its blood, the royal family called upon the skills of foreign advisors to rule a rapidly growing foreign population. Still, to succeeding generations of Hawaiian royalty, the pattern ingrained by the Tahitian Polynesian chief-priests clung relentlessly: their world-view outside themselves was meager; they neglected the land; and the displaced and dispossessed common people barely survived, while the royals lived in extravagant abundance.

Then a new, vastly different influence burst upon the scene: on March 31 1820, a contingent of Protestant missionaries arrived from Boston aboard the brig *Thaddeus*. Beamer graphically depicts the distance that Hawai'i had fallen from the earliest Eden: decadent port towns were filthy havens of crime, towns answered to no god, and drunken orgies played out daily in the open theater of the harbors. It was a dramatic quagmire of drunks, opium dens, criminal scavengers wheeling and dealing, and native women soliciting. Honolulu had become a hectic port of lasciviousness, the hell hole of the Pacific. Greed was king, and the King himself was the leading consumer. Not all the vices were foreign. Unrestrained sex was part of the primitive native culture of work, eat, sex and war. But now these indulgences became organized businesses available to all. The commoners squandered whatever they could steal and sought to emulate the foreigners in every way. Women paraded about town in the adornment they had earned from their bed partners.

The missionaries, highly educated for their time, introduced a new and startling idea: each person—king and commoner alike—had a soul worth saving. Their goal was to share their experience of civilization. They learned the language, opened schools, ministered to the sick, and called for protective health laws and social controls. This small group of men and women set about to free the natives from their birth-incurred bondage. Unlike the Biblical David, who danced in the procession of the holy covenant, the missionaries were deeply serious, even joyless. They had little understanding of the rich portion of Hawaiian emotional life.

Nevertheless, the influence of the missionaries' religious beliefs permeated royalty and leadership and may have added in a paradoxical fashion to the continuing attrition of the Hawaiian population. But the devastating impact of gonorrhea and syphilis on Hawaiian reproductive capacity was undoubtedly greater. The missionaries sought to encourage marriage and to discourage fornication. In 1827, their pressure on the Hawaiian monarchy was largely responsible for a law against adultery that featured punishment by imprisonment in irons. In subsequent months, the prohibition extended to include even fornication.

Western visitors in the 1830s noted that Hawaiian children were scarce. There was an unusually large number of childless women, and the practice of suckling pigs and puppies at their breasts had become common. To avoid punishment, unwed lactate women were turning to animals as substitutes for the babies they had lost through abortion or infanticide.

Then, in 1865, the mission withdrew from the islands. The entry of Catholic, Mormon and Episcopalian missionaries diluted the influence of Calvinism. The excitement of the great awakening had died down, Christianity had become a workaday religion, observed as a matter of convention. The total victory of Puritanism for which the American Board had hoped was not to take place. Still, they left a legacy that touched every aspect of life. An extensive network of schools came under the control of the government. The commoner now had some possibility of survival in this vastly changing world. Threatening to the native Hawaiians, however, was the torrent of immigrant laborers who poured in to work the extensive sugar plantations established throughout the islands. The Chinese had long been in Hawai'i, and to their ranks now were added Japanese, Portuguese, Filipinos, and Puerto Ricans who settled and made the islands their home.

The wrenching human struggle of the powers now in the islands heightened. It was a battle of the old ways versus the new, ebbing and flowing, sometimes shooting off on wild tangents. The political scene was a relentlessly advancing storm. Thunder and lightning marked Hawai'i's entry into the last quarter of the nineteenth century.

The year 1874 began the Kalakaua dynasty, seventeen years of resurgence of Hawaiian culture under the encouragement and commanding will of a bright and gifted family. Kalakaua's reign was a constant tug of war between royal privilege and representative government. Kalakaua and Queen Kapiolani remained childless. So did sister Princess Lili'uokalani, who bestowed instead a rich musical heritage. Again fate stepped in, taking away brother William Pitt Leliohoku, dead at twenty-two of rheumatic fever.

On October 16, 1875, Princess Miriam Likelike, wife of Scotsman Archibald Cleghorn, and sister to Kalakaua, gave birth to Princess Victoria Kaiulani. They named her after the English Queen in the hope that she would someday become Queen of Hawai'i. Victoria entered a world of great joy and rejoicing. Bells pealed throughout Honolulu and cannons fired salutes throughout that memorable day.

◆　◆　◆

THE APRIL of HER AGE is a story of the time when the mighty line of chiefs and chiefesses who had ruled Hawai'i for centuries had dwindled to this one princess. The desperate hope of continuity for the Hawaiian throne rested upon this delicate flower. Kaiulani became the final remaining dream of the Hawaiian Monarchy.

For compelling personal reasons, Kaiulani became for me the object of a quest: she was a flame that brightened a dark time. Poised between embattled political ideologies, she might have offered a compromise to a bitter conflict. Kaiulani was herself a union of East and West, a Royal Hawaiian-Scottish maiden, bright, articulate, an international beauty, adored by her people. The political convulsions of that era in Hawaiian history thrust her aside, then tragically deprived her of the promise of a truly remarkable life. The broad outline of her life is known, but Kaiulani herself has remained a mystery. Surely, there is more to be salvaged of her life. In pursuing my quest, I discovered that I might know Kaiulani only by delving into the life of another meteoric and star-crossed person: author Robert Louis Stevenson. The crossing of their paths was a ray of hope.

Stevenson and Kaiulani were linked in life. That is firmly historical. But were they mysteriously bonded as they pursued their destinies? I found much that pointed unmistakably to this. It called for a closer look.

One morning, breakfasting with friends on Tantalus, high above Honolulu, a copy of Kristin Zambucka's *Princess Kaiulani — the Last Hope of the Hawaiian Monarchy* caught my eye. Turning the pages, I stumbled upon Kaiulani's "incidental" friendship with Stevenson. I learned that they spent many hours together beneath the huge banyan tree at Ainahau. This suggested a relationship of some intensity. The history books record that it flourished during a brief six months. Kaiulani then sailed for England to complete her education and prepare for royal duties. Stevenson resumed his voyages in the South Seas.

Zambucka described Stevenson as *enthralled* by the beautiful young princess; he found her more beautiful than the fairest flower. She, in turn, felt *spellbound* by the man known to the South Sea Islanders as "Tusitala, Teller of Tales." Surely this was a magical moment, and at last I sensed an opportunity to fathom this hauntingly mysterious Hawaiian Princess. There must have occurred a rich sharing. Was there beyond that perhaps something more enduring along the paths toward their tragic fates? Their hours together blended with critical moments in the history of the Hawaiian Kingdom. How did that play into their relationship? Most confounding of all, and adding even greater weight to this relationship, was my discovery that Stevenson, a prodigious letter writer, wrote nothing afterward of this relationship, beyond venturing a farewell poem. In that disconcerting way I have come to expect of Polynesians, Kaiulani also was totally silent. Yet, they were mutually "*enthralled*," "*spellbound*." I couldn't walk away from such expressions. I was certain that Kaiulani and Stevenson could not, either. What could have happened to the transcending energy born of this enchantment and fascination? The story of the princess and the poet beckoned insistently.

Chapter I

HONOLULU HARBOR

In the pre-dawn darkness of a January morning in 1889, a Kona wind, ominous to Hawaiians, whipped and lashed with unrelenting fury. Amid the salvos of a tropical downpour, the Harbor Master's longboat lurched and rolled. Dr. George Phillippe Trousseau hunched over the flailing tiller, cowering from the driving gusts. In the blackness, the oarsmen struggled for a semblance of rhythm as they groped their way back toward Honolulu Harbor channel. With a craft and a storm of separate wills, the boarding party slid, shuddered and veered in the deluge.

Trousseau wondered how, under the best of circumstances, such an inappropriate word as *party* could be applied to his miserable little group. The wretched night was fully in keeping with his thankless duties as physician for the Port of Honolulu. He had ample reason to know, having already held this position for three years, back in the 1870s. With keen misgivings, he'd let himself be persuaded to handle the operations again. He wiped his face and pondered his constant inability to say no. The pressure of needy people and this needy community that was now his home— these were always on him. Trousseau had a way about him that impressed the islanders. They never forgot the episode at Kalihi Receiving Hospital when a suspected leprosy patient leaped at him with a loaded gun. A quick duck, a good tackle and the situation was under control. That led to his appointment as physician to the Insane Asylum!

The longboat lurched violently in a swell, digging the tiller into Trousseau's belly. There were so many satisfying things in life, but pitching about in the middle of a storm-ridden night outside the Honolulu channel was definitely not one of them. There was his private practice to tend—not neglect—while he foundered among public services. Important things were happening. From the windows of his office, he could follow the progress of the new hospital that King Kamehameha IV and Queen Emma had worked so hard to create. The word *micro-organism* had crept into the medical vocabulary. A blast of spray across the bow hit the first corresponding secretary of the Natural History and Microscopical Society full in the face.

The sopping blasts of a Kona storm had whipped Honolulu for two long days. This deluge had swept up the leeward side of the Hawaiian chain, as powerful wind and rain battered the arid shores, dropping incredible amounts of moisture. Amid the whistling gusts and the strain of the creaking, whining oars, Dr. Trousseau ground his teeth in frustration. Miserably seasick, he cursed the *S.S Mariposa.*

Down the channel, through the sheets of rain, the lighthouse blinked. The stern lights of the unmindful steamer *Mariposa* were fading away toward the harbor. The *Mariposa*—that was what this nightmarish mission was all about. All ships entering Honolulu harbor had to submit to boarding and inspection for disease. The *Mariposa* had slipped by them in the storm, heedless of the vigorous hail of the longboat's crew. Trousseau wrestled with the tempest and mounting questions about his role in many things Hawaiian. For seventeen years, he had directed his considerable energy to the perils of the dwindling Hawaiian population. The ravaging diseases of the world outside this most isolated archipelago had descended in full force.

Trousseau knew as much about epidemics as any medical man alive. He'd dealt with outbreaks in the French army in Algiers and northern Italy. He was a knight in the Imperial Order of the Legion of Honor: this for services rendered during several epidemics. Now here he was, soaked to the marrow, nauseated in extremis, throwing up in the middle of a storm-tossed night in Honolulu channel. What would be next? Cholera? Whooping cough? Smallpox? Leprosy? This was Hawai'i's disastrous record in the first half of this nineteenth century: three-fourths of the native population had vanished in virulent visitations from the outside world. A drenched Trousseau sat shivering, ruminating in the gale. There was word from Europe of some sort of device to look inside the human body! At last, Honolulu was planning a sewage system. What was he doing here?

Thank God for his crew! How they could maintain humor in such a storm was beyond him. This was especially true of Kalamake, his right hand man. Kalamake was pure Hawaiian, of the best blood in Molokai and Maui, yet fair. His hair, when not wet, was the color of dry grass. He joked and poked fun at Trousseau, shouting loudly, though often the gusts swallowed his words and blew them away. Kalamake looked over his shoulder, laughed to the mates, bolstered their spirits, and bellowed some cadence to their rowing.

"Eh, Doc! You get them *Mariposa* basta'ds good, by'm bye, eh?" Glancing at Adam in the bow for confirmation, "An', Doc! Your beard—bettah you wring 'em out. Adam say we startin' to sink in the stern!" Kalamake pulled a few vigorous strokes to correct their course, then: "What you think do wit' dem *Mariposa* guys? Lock 'em up in the Fort?"

Trousseau spit over the side, mopped his beard with both hands, waved an arm toward the distant shore and shouted over the wind: "Kalamake! Unless you put more muscle to starboard, we shall do nothing! The *Mariposa* will be at Samoa before you get us into port!" He ducked from another shower of spray. "But this I can tell you— there will be one day of quarantine for every sore throat on that ship. The *Mariposa* will lay to with a yellow flag. And as for the Port and the merchants, they will wait!"

Adam whooped and tugged at his oar; "An', Doc—what about the grog shops an' the women? You make them wait, too?"

♦ ♦ ♦

The sky was at first light east toward Diamond Head. The angry clouds were in tatters when at last the longboat threaded its way to the pier through the thicket of tall masts and yardarms, steamships, and sailing schooners. Wringing wet, squeaking in his boots, Trousseau hurried along the rain-swept, deserted pier to the Harbor Master's office at the foot of Nuuanu Avenue. The debris of the storm littered the desolate street. At least there would be regular cleaning crews now, thought Trousseau. He'd had something to do with establishing that. Above the town, the palms braced against the wind, their fronds in an agitated dance toward the west. The forlorn stores, grog shops and offices along the harbor huddled under their overhangs like rain-soaked cardboard boxes.

Trousseau's troubled mood turned from the storm and the duties of harbor physician. There was another reason for gloom. The town had been on the edge of grief. A schooner, a very special one, the *Casco*, was long overdue, presumed lost. Honolulu anxiously waited for word of this sailing ship. On board were the famous author Robert Louis Stevenson and his family. Everyone had been ready to celebrate. For once it wasn't a French or British warship arriving to make trouble for the islanders, or the conniving, lawbreaking Americans out to redress some grievance of one of their drunken citizens or hatching new schemes to overthrow the monarchy. Honolulu had been eagerly awaiting a friendly visit from a widely read author who had been voyaging among the Pacific islands. Hawai'i was experiencing troubled times involving warring governmental factions. How refreshing it would be to greet someone with a genuine interest in the island people!

During this period of anxious waiting, Trousseau had spent much time with Belle Strong, Mrs. Stevenson's daughter. Belle and husband Joe had been residents of Honolulu the past six years. They had come to Hawai'i to paint the Royal Court, and their art and photography were having a favorable impact on the town. They were a delightful couple who had quickly found a place among the royal crowd. Trousseau was fighting a losing battle to reassure Belle that there might still be hope for her family. The tropical winter was so unpredictable and threatening, even more so now with the present storm. Belle had begun to isolate herself as the vigil dragged on. The *Casco* had become a deadly subject. People ceased to speak to her about it.

Then there was Victoria, Trousseau's little princess, niece of King David Kalakaua and heir to the throne of the Hawaiian monarchy. Trousseau's gift of Stevenson's *Treasure Island* and *A Child's Garden of Verses* had whisked her into a fervor for the author's visit. She, too, was sad and dispirited. Trousseau was royal physician to King Kalakaua and his family, and traced an intimate path through their lives. The young princess was most special of all to him. With growing relief, he'd watched her slowly emerge and blossom in the two years since her mother's bewildering death. Victoria and father Archie had plunged into pain and shock after the loss of Princess Miriam. At last, Trousseau felt he was beginning to see sparkles of a delightful child-woman, an intriguing blend of her Scottish father and her royal Hawaiian mother. "*Little* princess? Well, hardly!"

Trousseau turned up Fort Street. Between the buildings, he could see a pallid sun spotting the mountains at Punchbowl and Round Top. To the west, the marine semaphore on Telegraph Hill above Waikiki would be visible soon. Patches of the palisades glowed an emerald green as he stomped off the dampness and entered the Port Dispensary. It was early for sick call, but an assortment of seamen brooded about the reception room in various postures of pain, discomfort, and inconvenience.

There stood Kumulipa, bright and beaming, a sun banishing the tail of the storm. She filled the doorway to his consulting room, her smile as wide as the transom above her flower-bedecked head. Kumulipa and Kalamake—a rare couple, man and wife of many years, blessed with many keikis, gifted with an intuitive sense that baffled Trousseau, and with hearts as great as their generous Hawaiian bodies. Kalamake was always where the doctor needed him. Kumulipa ran his dispensary with the canniness of a combat surgeon, triaging the sick, wounded, offish, and ailing with rare aplomb. Trousseau had brought Kumulipa into Victoria's life several months ago. He pondered the change he'd seen in the girl. Now his own intuition told him that Kumulipa's broad smile had something to do with Victoria.

"Doctor! What news! Guess! The *Casco*! They've sighted her off Kona! The *Kilauea* spotted her on the way out. Hurry! The kelepona! Your princess—she's waiting—she already knows. She told us! The *Casco*'s off Waikiki!"

Trousseau caught his breath. Then his face broke into a quick gasping smile of relief. In tickled agitation, he paced the waiting room, clapping his hands. He, too, had given up hope for the *Casco*. In his excitement, he lapsed into French exclamations and roared with laughter at the response of his audience. Trousseau surveyed the scattering of seamen with a deafening voice: "Who could be sick on such a beautiful day!"

Kumulipa intercepted his excited movements. "Doctor, the kelepona!" She stood at the wall before the mounted oaken box of the newly installed telephone, waving impatiently with the ear piece. "Come! Come!" Kumulipa began to crank the handle on the transmitter.

♦　♦　♦

Princess Miriam Likelike and Archibald S. Cleghorn

Chapter II

A CHILD OF AIR

It was dawn at Ainahau— "cool land" of Waikiki, "place of the hau tree." This bountiful parcel fronting the beach once belonged to Victoria's godmother, "Mama Nui", Princess Ruth, one of the last high chiefesses of Old Hawai'i. Mama Nui died in the Spring of 1883. Greatly missed, she had lavished affection and gifts on Victoria and was fiercely generous and protective toward those she loved. She was equally formidable toward those she disliked or mistrusted. Ainahau was an exquisite area, one of many gifts to Archibald Cleghorn and his family. Like his father before him, Archie had a flare for gardening, a landscaping vision that embraced the early barrenness of Oahu and fashioned its most beautiful estate. Abiding trade winds descended to this cool land from the northern mountains and from the fragrant nest of Manoa Valley.

At this early hour, the weather at Ainahau was no less blustery than at the harbor. Offshore the sea churned upon the reef under heavy purple rain clouds. The wind gusts were at last moderating, and pools of pale sunlight began to spot the southern ocean. Except for the intermittent rattle of the palm fronds, there was a hushed mood on the beach. The peacocks were stirring after two days huddled in the undergrowth, but the usually noisy birds were oddly silent.

At the water's edge, a slender figure in fluttering white leaned against the gusts, gazing intently out to sea. Victoria kicked her dark boots at the sand restlessly. In her mind's eye, a stage curtain waited to be drawn from the vast watery horizon. The tempest of the past few days could be the overture—but to what? One hundred years ago, it would have been Captain George Vancouver who anchored his ship directly offshore, then walked through the grounds to meet with the

High Chiefs of those times. The omens of recent days were so conflicting. A wedge-shaped cloud had hung over the palisades before the
storm, suggesting that something was coming, but *what?* An angry
shark had gotten itself trapped inside the reef. Victoria interpreted
this as a favorable sign, recalling the legend of Ka-ehu, a shark who
befriended surf-riders.

Archie's retainers hadn't missed the signs. They had gone about
their duties quietly. A century of contact with the *haole* [foreign
whites] had taught them to treat such matters discreetly—but
Victoria was always privy to their observations. They shared a way of
thinking totally beyond her father's world. Archie might dig and plant
about the estate with his big Scot's hands. He could yield wonders of
tropical foliage. Ainahau was covered with mango, teak, cinnamon,
rubber, camphor, and palm trees, their varieties nearly beyond counting. Multicolored hibiscus waved and danced everywhere. For
Victoria, though, the soil itself, the sea, the stars, the movements of
the air were all *alive and could speak and feel.*

Victoria played tag with a little crab in a brief distracting game.
The wind tossed her dark curls. The crab, defeated, retired to his hole.
Victoria searched the horizon, then gathered her skirt and sank down
on a hulk of wood embedded in the sand by the storm. That dark, billowing curtain beyond the reef—England was out there somewhere.
And Scotland, the home of her father's people. Victoria sighed. In a
year, she would be in England—to be educated for royal duties.

There had been a dramatic and very disturbing episode to which
Victoria's thoughts repeatedly returned in the years since Mama
Likelike's death. With the profundity of one departing this life, with
her dying breath, Mama had murmured that Victoria would be away
from her islands for a very long time. Even more disturbing, in
Mama's last moments she sighed that Victoria would never marry,
never be queen! How puzzling!

How could Mama know these things? Victoria rejected them
vehemently. In October she had celebrated her fourteenth birthday.
She was on-going witness to the breath-taking twists and turns that
life could take. In pain, she had learned that life was more than mysterious—it was precious. Each year, each day was as fleeting as the
delicious scent of the jasmine lei resting about her shoulders. She
thought of the Hawaiian people, of their losses, of the losses within

her own family. Mama Nui, Uncle Leleiohuku, Mama Likelike—half of the *Na Lani Eha*, the "Four Sacred Ones," had departed. Was it all part of some unfathomable plan? The fate of the monarchy appeared to be bearing down on her. How ironic! The queen of the Hawaiian Islands would be half Hawaiian, half Caucasian! What kind of queen would she be? How to relate to her people in a world that was finding ever more reasons to reject royalty?

Physically, Victoria was every inch a princess. She was tall, beautiful, gracious, high-spirited; at times—not often—hot-tempered. There at the water's edge, staring out at the horizon, she would have made a wonderful subject for a sculptor. Dark, penetrating, amber-flecked eyes. Delicately formed face. Dense Polynesian curls. Full, sensuous lips. Classic nose, strong like Archie's, but gracefully softened. Her neck a slender, stately curve. Her chin stalwart. Her smile quick and sly.

Looking back at the past few years, Victoria now realized there had been a turning point for her. A seemingly casual event that turned out to be a mustard seed. It was a morning, very clear in her mind, that started out in dark, dismal shades. She'd been confined at home, tucked away in bed nursing a winter cold. Congestion in her chest and head that day were nothing compared to her desolation after Mama Likelike's death. The house was empty, the servants busy outside. Father Archie was off on Maui on business. Much as they loved each other, and desperate as their need was to comfort each other, they were too depleted. Each had withdrawn in mute numbness. Victoria lingered apathetically between governesses. Archie, grieving, buried himself in A.S. Cleghorn & Company. The dry goods stores at Queen and Ka'ahumanu Streets in Honolulu and on Maui, Molokai and Hawai'i absorbed his heartache. Then, too, his closeness to the Royal family provided a welcome excuse to be drawn into government affairs as well.

A stirring at the bedroom door had roused Victoria. Peeking out from her covers, she saw Dr. Trousseau peering in, smiling, tapping lightly on the panel. Over his shoulder she recognized Kumulipa, unsmiling, her dark eyes boring into the room, her hands gently propelling Trousseau forward.

"Bonjour, ma petite. And how is our princess feeling today?"

Victoria shrugged and forced a pallid smile. "Oh, Dr. Trousseau,

Kumulipa. How nice. Please come in." She sat up wearily as the doctor felt her forehead with his broad hand and raised a curtain to view her better. She smiled up at him as he searched for, and failed to find, swollen glands in her neck, no redness in her throat or eyes. Her smooth skin was clear and cool.

Throughout the examination, Dr. Trousseau reminded Victoria of a feeling which had always been a part of their relationship. There were the professional, physical things, examinations, tests—but more than that. In his warm Gallic fashion, somewhat shyly, he always seemed to be looking, puzzling his way into her deepest self. Somewhere in her reading she had run across the term *kindred spirit*. She knew that was what they were to each other.

Trousseau motioned to Kumulipa who moved a chair up to the bedside and sat close beside Victoria. "I am reassured, Princess. Your cold is clearing." He glanced out the window toward the beach. "There's a warm sun waiting for you out there, ma cherie, and a restless pony. I heard your peacocks complaining as we came in. They were asking where you were?"

Kumulipa had watched their interaction patiently, and had settled comfortably beside Victoria in contrast to Trousseau's restless movements.

Victoria looked distressed. "I'm sorry you had to come all this way. I'll be fine. I told father so. I'm sorry he dragged you both from town."

Trousseau mocked her expression with jovial humor. "Dragged? Not at all, ma cherie. We know you are going to be fine. We stopped by for a social call on our Princess. Well! Your father! We'd have to scour the islands and the government buildings to find *him*!"

Kumulipa gave a signaling glance to Trousseau. "Doctor, you have a 10:00 o'clock meeting at the hospital. You won't be needing me. I will stay here and visit with our princess."

Now, gazing out to sea, and thinking about that first visit with Kumulipa, Victoria's expression was faraway. That had not been a social call. As she visited with Kumulipa she realized that her fellow Hawaiians, with their typical elaborate preparations, had been waiting for this moment of opportunity in what had previously been Victoria's carefully regulated life. Kumulipa opened a door with her warm, reassuring manner, overflowing with the excitement of living.

That was the beginning: a kahuna nui, whom she came to know as *Uncle*, highest of the ancient order of craftsmen-priests, entered her life. Kumulipa had been very specific in her instructions to Victoria about the first meeting with Uncle. She was to go alone, in secret, on a particular day and hour, to windward Oahu where she would find him in a special, holy place.

Victoria, a muddle of anxiety and excitement, had almost turned back. She went, a frightened little girl, shaking in the saddle, supported only by her recall of Kumulipa's promising smile.

Uncle was waiting for her in a quiet glade beneath palms on the windy shore. The crumbling ruins of an ancient heiau [temple] were clustered facing the sea. He was alone, a very large, muscular figure clad only in a malo [loincloth]. Turned away from her, he was sitting on an immense stone remnant of the heiau. As he turned to greet her, Victoria was astonished to realize that she knew him. On this occasion there was a different, arresting dimension to this powerful figure which overshadowed and made totally different, the person she had known.

"Aloha, Princess. My heart overflows with your coming. I have waited a long time for you. Whatever ways you have known me before, put them aside." He was then silent for several minutes, searching her face deeply, studying her as one might deliberate the beginnings of a canvas or a sculpture. His expression was analytical, but warm and reassuring. "Are you afraid, Victoria?"

Victoria's fear had vanished. She was fascinated, already absorbing something energizing from the man's study of her. "Kumulipa said that you would be my uncle." She smiled brightly, "No, I'm not afraid now. I'm with family."

Uncle smiled slowly, and grasped her shoulders firmly with large, gentle hands. "Do not be put off by my silence at times. You will be learning to feel and sense, you will use your mana, your life force, not words and thoughts. You will break through many barriers. There will be a reckoning, but it will be well worth it."

Victoria was a gifted student under Uncle's tutelage. Quietly, passionately, she applied herself to the ancient lore of the earth, sky, sea, and all living things. It was a quest pursued in secret. Uncle was insistent on this. She had many questions for Uncle as the months went by. The stars of the crystalline Hawaiian skies both thrilled and troubled her. Which was her guiding star? Where would it take her? In her initiation, the poetry and art of her Polynesian ancestors were her greatest joy. True to her Kalakaua blood, lyric and song were the tissue that formed this living vessel that was Victoria Kaiulani. The vessel enclosed a vastly growing, submerged pool of knowledge. A studied part of Victoria's rigorous discipline and training was in her countenance: her distant expression was a cover for the fermenting inner world of excitement, for the awareness of the unity of all things, for the mystifying surges of joy within her. There was a dark side, too, very distressing for Victoria. She spent much time with her fellow Hawaiians, painfully witnessing their poverty and poor health. She ruminated unhappily at the contrast between her life and that of her sturdy, resourceful, and somehow buoyant and lyrical people.

Victoria had not been entirely successful in concealing her secret from everyone. Her kindred spirit, Doctor Trousseau noticed something rather quickly, always observing her closely in that bashful way of his, always looking to brighten her days. In the autumn of 1888, Dr. Trousseau introduced something startling into Victoria's life. On the surface it seemed another casual sort of event. As it turned out, it added and built powerfully upon the world view that Kumulipa and Uncle had given her.

Victoria was riding in her father's carriage down Queen Street that day, when she recognized a familiar, bearded figure, medical bag in hand, scurrying across the street toward the hospital.

Victoria waved, calling. "Dr. Trousseau! Dr. Trousseau! Over here!" She ordered the carriage halted and ran to him.

Trousseau, jolted out of his preoccupation, paused in the middle of the street, turned, arms outstretched, recognized Victoria and, stopping traffic, greeted his princess.

"Victoria!" With bustling enthusiasm he took her by her arm and led her back toward his office building. "How fortunate! I've been wanting to see you. I have something for you. It will take just a moment. Come up to my office."

Trousseau's second-floor office was up a long staircase and down a hushed, high-ceilinged hall. As he opened the glass-fronted door and ushered her through the empty waiting room, Victoria found herself in a large, bright room, more like a combination of laboratory and library. Cigar smoke scented the air. Anatomical charts and pictures of men of medicine covered the walls. A jumble of heavy books over-flowed the cupboards, and invaded mirrored cabinets filled with spec-imens, bones, skulls, beakers, and flasks. A telescope and microscope stood proudly before a window looking out toward the harbor. Beside it was a human skeleton beneath a shelf on which stood an approving bust of Aesculapius. The gleaming luster of a soft leather examining table seemed out of keeping with Trousseau's old, squeaking desk chair. Trousseau, bustling about, shifted a stack of journals to clear a place for her. "Please, sit down, ma cherie, while I find this."

Trousseau rummaged about impatiently among his papers, glanc-ing curiously at Victoria from time to time. "You are looking very well, Victoria. How pleased I am. Kumulipa keeps me informed of your progress." He paused, puzzled, not sure of wanting to pursue this further. He was a scientist. Kumulipa baffled him. Now Victoria was taking on a glow he couldn't understand. At last he remembered a bottom desk drawer and brought forth two books triumphantly. "Aha! Here we are! Now, Victoria, the island is going to have a visitor, a famous author. Have you heard of Robert Louis Stevenson? He was born in Edinburgh, like your father. He's written some things that are very popular, especially these two which I got for you."

Victoria's eyes sparkled as she read the titles of the two volumes. *Treasure Island* and *A Child's Garden of Verses*. Trousseau had always encouraged Victoria's love for poetry and these gifts of Robert Louis Stevenson's work delighted her.

That afternoon, relaxing under the great banyan of Ainahau, she met Stevenson for the first time. Inside the little volume of poems, he had spoken directly to her:

> *As from the house your mother sees*
> *You playing round the garden trees,*
> *So you may see, if you will look*
> *Through the windows of this book,*
> *Another child, far, far away,*
> *And in another garden, play.*
> *But do not think you can at all,*
> *By knocking on the window, call*
> *That child to hear you. He intent*
> *Is all on his play-business bent.*

He does not hear; he will not look,
Nor yet be lured out of his book.
For, long ago, the truth to say,
He has grown up and gone away,
And it is but a child of air
That lingers in the garden there.

Now, weeks later, standing there on Ainahau's beach, scanning the horizon, Victoria recalled how deeply that poem had moved her. It defined a feeling she had about herself. She, too, was a child of air. Was Mama Likelike now a child of air? Stevenson's poem wafted Victoria to happy times at Ainahau, playing under the banyan tree, pausing in her games to glance toward the wide porch facing the sea. There, rocking contentedly, would be Mama Likelike, smiling down at her, laughing to hear Victoria's fertile dialogue with her unseen playmates.

That exciting announcement from Dr. Trousseau: the poem's "child of air"—Stevenson—was sailing in the southern seas bound for Hawai'i! Victoria was thrilled! Perhaps that child, a real person, could shed some light on the mysteries in her life. Was it possible to lure the child out of the book of poems? It was this inspiring news, heralded by Stevenson's verses, that started Victoria on her vigil. By day on the beach, looking out to sea, she devoured his poetry. Riding about Waikiki on her white pony, Fairy, she searched the horizon tirelessly for a small, white, two-masted schooner and longed for the day when she would see it sail triumphantly past Diamond Head.

Then the winter storms attacked. Rumors kept arriving, brought by ships and mariners from the southern ocean. Stevenson's ship capsized in a violent storm in the Marquesas, they said, and all aboard drowned. Frantic and in despair, a mingling of hope and fear, Victoria clung to her newfound inner voice that reassured her and gave her stamina to resist another loss.

The wind was shifting and ruffled the curls against her cheek. A broadening band of blue sky had split the distant bank of clouds. Now a full sun swiftly transformed the sea. The surf flashed in brilliant patterns of gold and white. Victoria leaped to her feet. A joyous smile, a deep, fulfilling gladness rose within her. The sun had revealed the answer to her prayer. Far out beyond Diamond Head, a little white schooner rose in the swells.

Chapter III

HONOLULU BOUND!

Dawn was breaking through somber clouds off the *Casco's* stern, banishing the deeper shades of night and sharpening the contours of scattered storm clouds to the west. Louis Stevenson had sandwiched himself into the red velvet cushions in a corner of the mirror-lined salon, a writing tablet on his drawn-up knees.

The passage up from Tahiti had been crisis-filled. It had allowed Louis occasions to write, but his mood was more reflective than creative. During the cruise, writing and reflecting competed with each other like shifting breezes. He was not one to discourage this. As he assembled his thoughts, he munched on the last salt beef and biscuit aboard, savoring the scent of wet rope in his fingers and the saltiness of the meat. A chain smoker, he balefully eyed his dwindling supply of cherished black tobacco. Safe arrival at Honolulu seemed assured, and the family could gorge themselves after that. For forty-eight gratifying hours, the *Casco* had rested in the lee of the Kona coast of Hawai'i Island while crew and passengers cast about to regain their composure.

Casco was a mere seventy tons, small for an oceangoing schooner. She was ninety-five feet long with two lofty masts, clean lines, gleaming brasswork and a spotless deck. She had a mirror-lined cabin with velvet-cushioned salon chairs. She had been an exciting sight when the Stevensons departed San Francisco's Golden Gate in June 1888. The *Casco* was histrionic for an inanimate craft and revealed her true capricious self as the cruise progressed.

The Stevensons had elected to sail from San Francisco to the Marquesas Islands, westward to Tahiti and then north to Hawai'i. What a see-saw it had been! They floated or were blown through unlighted, badly charted waters. Nightly, they lived in haunting fear of unmapped islands and unidentified rapid and variable currents. In Tahiti the cruise came to an abrupt halt when they discovered both masts were rotting away.

The past thirty days since departing Tahiti on Christmas Day, 1888 had been a run of calms and squalls, head seas, water spouts, rotten masts, and sprung spars. When a hurricane breathed hard astern, the Captain faced a dilemma. They could lie-to and hope to ride it out with rickety replacement masts installed at Tahiti, or risk a run before the wind, which might mean being swamped by a following sea. When the equal dangers were stated to Louis, he consistently responded, "Go for it!" The hands then lashed themselves on deck, the best helmsman was stationed at the wheel, and the passengers were forbidden to leave the cabin. Up and down swooped the little white yacht between precipices of foam.

On another stormy occasion, as Louis came on deck, he found the sea rushing over the cockpit coamings and down the companion like a torrent. Just then, the foresail sheet jammed, and the Captain had no knife. Louis leaped into the crisis like a Trojan, judging the possibility of a lung hemorrhage better than the certainty of drowning. Afterward, the whole ship's company were as white as sheets, from the captain to the cook. It seemed to Louis, the semi-invalid, that poor health was a thing of the past. In spirits, renewed interest in life, and refreshed capacity for work, he had found the cruise to be a wise folly. He was exhilarated: for fourteen years he had not had a real day's health. He had wakened sick and gone to bed weary, done his work unflinchingly, written in bed, and written out of it, written in hemorrhages, written in sickness, written torn by coughing, written when his head swam with weakness.

Their first sighting of Hawai'i, two days ago, had been hair-raising. The wind was fair but very strong. The *Casco* was carrying jib, foresail, and mainsail all single-reefed, flying with her lee rail under water. Louis rubbed his knees and smiled to himself. He'd been at the wheel and felt he'd done nobly—or been very lucky. The swells, biggest he'd ever seen, at least fifteen feet high, came tearing after them. At times it seemed they must surely be swamped, but the swells would miss somehow. Only the sprays came over the quarter-deck and turned the little outside lane of deck into a deep millrace. He couldn't remember anything so delightful and exciting.

They'd been warned about the towering mountains of Hawai'i Island. Rather abruptly, the *Casco* lay absolutely becalmed. Captain Otis never confessed that he'd deliberately put them in this haven under Kona's lee, but when accused, he smiled. What a dangerous race it had been!

Louis looked up from his writing pad and scanned his surroundings. What a crew they were! Four deckhands—two Swedes, a Russian, and a Finn—and a Chinese steward-cook who chose to pass himself off as Japanese. Some were stirring about the ship now as dawn advanced. Louis surveyed their random activities—no one anticipated breakfast—then covered his face with his long fingers and grinned again. He recalled that stormy, wave-tossed night when the pumps failed and they had to bail frantically. Their sailors were adequate for most occasions, but during that black and blustery night everyone pitched in, straining to keep afloat. It was quite a retinue: Louis's wife Fanny, stepson Lloyd, now twenty-one, gawky, bespectacled, dreaming of a writer's career; Louis's mother, Margaret Isabella Balfour Stevenson, whom they all called Maggie, prim, gentle, pious, frail—always with a Victorian starched widow's cap, even that night in the storm. Finally, there was Maggie's maid, Valentine Roch, who had become a part of the family. The women had quickly adopted the garments of the tropics: the *holoku*, a long, loose gown flowing waistless from a yoke; and underneath, a *muumuu*, a straight full chemise with a flounce around the hem. Louis prized his simple, striped flannel pajamas. Unlike the rest who went barefoot, Maggie Stevenson clung to her shoes and stockings.

Captain Albert Otis, a man of fierce temper, had growing respect for Louis as the cruise progressed and the semi-invalid blossomed in the southern clime. At their first meeting, however, a quick inspection of Louis gave the Captain elaborate doubts about him. None of that escaped Louis; he was accustomed to even the most subtle reactions at first meetings. At thirty-nine, now a world-renowned literary figure, Louis was one whose image beckoned for colorful description: a stumbling skeleton with a grotesquely gay air; a slight man, always with a coat of velveteen, ninety-eight pounds, and long dark hair that framed his narrow face with its blue-veined forehead; a fine long nose, good chin and smiling mouth. The glory of his face lay in his glowing dark eyes which burned as though they looked out from an inner fire that was consuming him. Louis's bombastic friend Ernest Henley—the inspiration for *Treasure Island's* Long John Silver—had described him in a sonnet:

> *Thin-legged, thin-chested, slight unspeakably,*
> *Neat-footed and weak-fingered: in his face—*
> *Lean, large-boned, curved of beak, and touched with race,*
> *Bold-lipped, rich-tinted, mutable as the sea,*
> *The brown eyes radiant with vivacity—*
> *There shines a brilliant and romantic grace,*
> *A spirit intense and rare, with trace on trace*
> *Of passion, impudence, and energy.*
> *Valiant in velvet, light in ragged luck,*
> *Most vain, most generous, sternly critical,*
> *Buffoon and poet, lover and sensualist:*
> *A deal of Ariel, just a streak of Puck,*
> *Much Antony, of Hamlet most of all,*
> *And something of the Shorter-Catechist.*

Louis glanced across the salon at Fanny and followed her movements. She didn't return his gaze, but he knew she had eyes in the back of her head. He was never out of her view, certainly in social situations, where, with clinical scrutiny, she would assess the demands people placed on Louis. She would quietly conduct her daily assessments of his health and struggled, with mixed results, to keep his bursts of enthusiasm within bounds. The cruise had not been easy for her. She was frequently seasick, and they'd lost a baby through a miscarriage since leaving San Francisco. Fanny had formidable resilience and a rich sense of humor. When they left the ship and lived alone among the natives, she got on very well. But shipboard for her was a different matter. The demands of keeping house on a ship were all directed to her. When she was deathly seasick, the cook would ask to go over menus for the next few days. Food would have to be inspected. Weevils would get into the biscuits. Would she please smell the pork, which seemed pretty strong? What directions were there for making a pudding with molasses? And what was to be done about the bugs? In the midst of dangerous weather, with Fanny lying on the floor clutching a basin, down would come the mate with a cracked head, and it would be Fanny who cut off his blood-matted hair and washed and dressed his wound.

Frances Mathilda Van de Grift Osbourne—Fanny—had grown up in the frontier hamlet of Indianapolis in the 1840's. Her years on the frontier were an education in resourcefulness. She was observant in a manner totally different from Louis. He could never identify any tree. Fanny knew them all, as well as the herbs, vines, plants, nuts, and fruits. She was an inspired gardener with a fancy for tiger lilies—a fact that had earned her the nickname "Tiger Lily." In those frontier days, she was a tiny tomboy, dark as a gypsy, and swift as a hummingbird. She always felt that her hair was too dark. She had no idea that she was pretty, with her clear olive skin, regular features, and sparkling eyes.

The *Casco* heeled over a bit in the freshening wind. Fanny turned and smiled at Louis, scribbling away in his corner of the salon. The prospect of being ashore in Honolulu was beckoning brightly.

Leisurely intervals on the cruise, in between the crisis times, allowed the Stevensons to immerse themselves in the lives of native people, and they lived and shared with them in the Marquesas and the Tuamotus. Intermittently, Louis had fretted and gnawed away at a novel, *The Master of Ballantrae*. He had reluctantly contracted with *Scribner's* Magazine to write this for serialized publication. Earlier chapters had already appeared, and Louis scored himself for agreeing to be put under such pressure. The outlines of his story had long intrigued him, as far back as his stay in a sanitarium at Lake Saranac in New York. It was to be a deep tragedy about a good younger brother tormented into hatred, madness, and death by his wicked elder brother. Louis pictured a tale of an unattractive good man destroyed by a fascinating evil one. It was placed upon a broad historical and geographic canvas and constituted a tantalizing challenge after the disappointing critical reception to Louis's recent efforts. It had seemed quite possible to bring the novel off, but he hadn't conceived a satisfactory ending. How wearisome this project had become over the last two years! Life was going so well, was so invigorating, so exciting. How could he deal with this bothersome novel?

Fanny moved across the cabin, braced herself against the bulkhead behind Louis and examined his writing tablet. "And what is with *The Master* this morning, dear?" She asked.

Louis looked up at her ruefully and tapped himself on the chest.

"*This* Master—meaning me—is very distracted. But in such a pleasant way. The other *Master*—on the page here—he's freezing in upper New York State. And so are my ideas, I'm afraid. Hungry?"

Fanny eyed his tobacco. "I could survive on just one more cigarette."

The *Casco*, too, drifted in desultory fashion about the Hawaiian group over the next few days, tacking here and there with different faint slants of wind. It was a strange experience to see the distant lights of Honolulu, go to bed hungry, rise again in the morning and find themselves, not nearer, but farther off. But at last, they were making brisk time, sailing west along Alenuihaha Channel toward the southern coast of Maui. Jagged little Kahoʻolawe and the bulge of larger Lanaʻi slumbered in the mauve morning mist off the port beam. Peaceful Mount Haleakala loomed to starboard, wispy morning clouds gathering speed over the dormant crater. With the wind fresh off Maui, the rhythmic surge of the swells upon the hull was pleasurable. Flying fish had discovered the *Casco* and were flitting along her bow, like skipping flat stones over the blue water. A pod of whales, winter visitors, played in the distance dead ahead in the Lahaina Roads of Maui. The saltiness of the breeze carried a new freshness of earth and blossoms. Far in the distance, almost lost in the hazy dawn, lay Molokai akina, "gray" Molokai, the leper colony—and Father Damien, whom Louis planned to visit.

Salt beef and biscuit gone, Louis chomped on his pen. Any consistency in his life—there hadn't been much—had vanished among the South Sea islands. During the cruise, he kept digging within himself for reference points. Far to the South, in the watery world of the Marquesas, he had witnessed an ancient, primitive past confronting unrelenting jeopardy from the outside world. Still, he found that the Pacific remained a strange place where the nineteenth century existed only in spots. All around was a no-man's-land of the ages, a melange of epochs and races, barbarisms and civilizations, virtues and crimes. He could see powers stirring that made his personal worries seem trifling. Louis long ago had entrenched within himself an attitude of minimizing personal problems. That was the "valiant in velvet" that Henley pictured in his sonnet. But worries there were. And homesickness as well. Often Louis's mind drifted to Scottish scenes—windblown moors, flowering highlands, mists and biting cold—but now in an unsettling, detached way. As he groped for feelings and movement in his *Ballantrae* characters, Pacific Island perspectives kept disrupting his concentration, and he struggled with the story like a galley slave.

Louis's first landfall, Nukahiva in the Marquesas, had been spellbinding. The schooner had crept toward shore in a breezeless drift. Birds sang in the hillside, and the scent of a hundred fruits and flowers flowed forth to meet them. Soon they spied a native village upon a curve of beach under a grove of palms. The surf growled and whitened on a concave arc of reef. Louis found a deeply meaningful saying in the South Seas, where the coco palm and the island man live intimately with the surf: "The coral waxes, the palm grows, but man departs," says the sad Tahitian proverb.

Their mark of anchorage had been a blow-hole in the rocks, near the southeasterly corner of the bay. Helpfully, the blow-hole spouted. The *Casco* turned upon her heel, and the anchor plunged. It was a small sound, but for Louis, a great event. His soul went down with those moorings, and he knew that no windlass, nor any diver, would ever fish it up. From that hour he knew himself to be a bond slave of the isles.

Louis's need for travel and exploration was not purely a result of his perpetual struggle for health. There were other strong motives going back to life with his family in Scotland. He had to distance himself from the Edinburgh outlook, from his father, and the family's dour Calvinist religious stance. Louis knew now the insight he lacked as a youth. In those times, if he couldn't separate himself physically from the family's unyielding religious attitudes, he could carouse in the forbidden places of the riffraff of Edinburgh. In this he was encouraged by his over-animated cousin Bob. They went through ten years of flouting social standards, and this was a time of reckless sexual excess. It had not yet become a geographic split; rather, it was a painful emotional and ideological split, because he deeply loved his family. How to compromise? The views he developed came gradually, but they were agonizing in their inevitability. He knew he had damned the happiness of the two people in the world who cared for him.

Louis had been a fragile, only child raised with much tenderness. Cummie, his nurse, read him poetry and psalms in the long nights of coughing and wakefulness. In his youth, frailty and the care it required carved unique patterns in his character and relationships with others. He was not the vigorous kind of child who could be popular with his peers. He endured more than his share of humiliation. There were no friends, and except for Bob, his numerous cousins merely tolerated him. His education was intermittent and, except for Latin, he was an affliction to his tutors. The buffeting of his teens, the keen mind that looked deeply into itself and others, and the frequent nearness of death forged in Louis a toughness—a tempered steel beneath the velveteen jacket. Such an amalgam shaped his mind to draw the last ounce of energy possible from his reluctant body.

The wrenching break with his family—how else might he have viewed them? What more agreeable perspective of human life might he have found? How to attune himself to the rapid changes he saw in his world? His family's values smacked of self-righteous Christianity, condemning others and clinging to what he felt were stale, threadbare points of view. Who was good and strong? Who was bad and weak? Louis agonized about winners and losers, victims and victimizers. He drew many of his persuasions from intimacy with the borderline scraps and shreds of humanity in the bars and brothels of Edinburgh. The shadows of those people, their turmoil, needs, hates and fears— and their collisions with the established world of his family—focused the swirling ideas in his writer's mind. He always had two books in his pockets—one to read and one to write in. His father's success as a marine architect held no attraction for him. A law degree seemed for a time a possible outlet for his rejection of established attitudes, until the experience of a single day in court left him shaken and defeated. But the day when he first expressed his ideas about people in writing, he knew his life's true quest.

A wry smile turned the corners of Louis's mouth. What a great source of amusement he'd been to Bob—but not to himself. Louis couldn't resist falling in love. A free-and-easy girl of Edinburgh in those days could fire him to peaks of ardor and poetry. He was Lancelot resurrected. Bob called him "The Champion!" He teased Louis for his courtesy and loyalty to such people. And most of all, to Kate Drummond. What a battle raged between Louis and his father about her. It was then that Louis suffered his first tubercular hemorrhage.

Louis pushed the lamp aside, got up, and paced the salon. *Ballantrae*—he had to get cracking on it. What unseen hand had drawn him westward? God knows, from his early days in Edinburgh, his susceptible lungs were a barrier to a scheduled existence. All his life, Louis had defied the hovering specter of death. The accursed relapses placed a premium on rest, on rural settings and warmer climes. Extended times in France, at length, were no longer maintaining his health, but France brought Fanny into his life.

Louis rubbed his cheeks, stretched and glanced at the distant hills of Maui across the sun-tinged water. Fanny. He first glimpsed her at Madame Chevillon's Inn. It was at Grez in the forest of Fontainbleau. Louis was just twenty-six then, and had just come down from Paris. A friend had warned him that this male-dominated artists' paradise, this setting of carefree summers and poetic wanderings, had changed. There were now two women painters, Americans, at Chevillon's! Louis had exclaimed in mock dismay. It turned out that they were mother and daughter, though they looked more like sisters. Louis arrived at Chevillon's just after dark and paused outside the lighted window of the dining room. He saw the merry crowd inside, a delicate face among them, a cluster of dark locks. Her direct dark eyes turned on him with a sort of surprise. He fell in love with Fanny at that moment.

Fanny was a married woman eleven years Louis's senior. For months he agonized over his family's anticipated attitude about this relationship. Fanny returned to San Francisco to divorce Sam Osbourne. Louis's emotions erupted in a headlong plunge across ocean and continent. More alone than ever before, Louis crossed the Atlantic one step above steerage on the Anchor Line's *Devonia*. He was like an iron filing drawn to the magnet of Fanny and California. With massive dedication, he spent sick, lonely months on the beach at Monterey waiting for Fanny. He was out of funds, and he'd given no word of his plans to his family.

Louis studied Fanny as she moved about the salon, busy, keeping matters shipshape about the *Casco*. Fanny was a person of many talents, of extraordinary energy and industry. When she chose, she had a gift for making friends. She was a woman of deep and strong emotion. Her genius was her tenacity. Her perceptions could be curiously odd, primitive, and intriguing to Louis. Beneath her ready talk, friendly and frank, she was shy. Flawlessly courageous, she had yet a certain timidity. In the summer of 1875, Louis found her most appealing. She was thirty-five, but looked ten years younger. She was a small woman with a flair for clothes. The beauty of her face bore the refining touch of mastered pain. She had acquired skill in knowing when to be timid and when to be bold, when to use a gentle look, and when her sword-like glance. Such Fanny was when she gathered up her three children, left a faithless marriage, and, for the sake of her daughter's gift and her own, followed the star of art across the sea.

Louis fought his inner battle about Fanny for many months in great turmoil. He'd never earned a cent in his life. He was a chronic disappointment to his parents. In 1875 he had hardly a glimmer to suggest that he could—of all things—support a ready-made family. Was marriage his last, best chance to grow up?

There had been another Fanny in Louis's life a few years earlier. He had worshipped her as his Madonna. This was Fanny Sitwell, twelve years his senior, a bluestocking minister's wife who had separated from her husband. Fanny Sitwell was well-connected with literary circles in England, and she saw something special in this clever, expressive, emotional young man. She was the one who made him believe in himself as a writer. Louis would have married her. He suffered deep depression when it became clear that she preferred his friend, Sidney Colvin, a teacher at Cambridge and a figure in the literary world.

Lancelot, the champion—that driving force in Louis's makeup—overcame his self-doubt and despair in loving Fanny Osbourne. One factor loomed large in the evolution of their relationship. While in Paris, the year before they met, Fanny had lost her youngest son, Hervey, to tuberculosis. She came to Grez wrestling with the first great sorrow of her life. She was physically and emotionally depleted, but she drew on courage, which had not failed her in the past. She took up her art studies again with Belle. She worked harder than ever, but she had grown thin, pale and silent. Louis and Fanny formed a bond on long walks in the forest, during the rich outdoor after-dinner talks at Grez and the balmy summer hours of canoeing on the Loing. They healed each other. Each brought the other onto a new shared stage in life. At Grez, Louis had plunged into her life, a leader in the social sports and conversations. He radiated that charm his friends had freely advertised to Fanny.

Louis grinned to himself at a remark of Belle's that Fanny confided to him. "He is such a nice looking ugly man, and I would rather listen to him talk than read the most interesting book I ever saw."

That winter Louis was a constant visitor at Fanny's flat up four flights of stairs in Montmartre. His friends regarded his restless dashing about England and France as the silliness of an inspired schoolboy. He was productive and wrote some successful short stories. On a crucial decision-making canoe trip in Belgium, he wrote "Inland Voyage." Most significant of all were the thoughts he formulated in an essay, "*On Falling in Love.*" Louis's struggles with his complicated love for Fanny had at last brought him to an integration within himself. He could see the intimate relationship between joy and pain, beauty and ugliness, life and death. He could see it now in all the visible world.

Louis shifted his weight and rubbed his fingers. The reflections in the mirrors about the salon were brightening in the swift tropical dawn. He lapsed back into musing again. The days in Monterey. Jules Simoneau's restaurant, a nondescript barber's shop and bar, with a little kitchen and a *salle-a-manger.* Across a courtyard was the town's adobe prison. Those were days of waiting, being deathly sick, hungry, stone-broke, yet always hopeful.

"Perhaps," Louis thought, "at my core I am a chronic wanderer. I look backward and can count my special inns like a rosary. There is something so warm and reassuring about arriving at sundown at one inn or another in some corner of the world. To unsling my knapsack, descend from my omnibus, and dine there by the chimney where the snowwind whistles, to have breakfast with open shirt under the green trellis at the garden end. Out of all my private recollections of inns and restaurants, one particular house of entertainment stands forth alone and unrivaled: Simoneau's. I'm grateful, indeed, to many a swinging signboard, to many a rusty wine-bush, but not with the same kind of gratitude. Some were beautifully situated, some had an admirable table, some were the gathering places of excellent companions; but take them for all in all, not one can be compared with Simoneau's at Monterey."

Louis discovered later that the nightly circle at Simoneau's had chipped in to provide the meager salary his scribblings brought from editor Crevole Bronson and that losing proposition, the Monterey *Californian.* Along the way, Louis met Charles Warren Stoddard, writer and poet, whose "eyrie" on San Francisco's Rincon Hill overflowed with artifacts from his trips to the Pacific Islands. The idea of a cruise through the South Seas grew slowly in Louis's mind, and thoughts of a voyage in the realm of the noble brown savage kindled his romantic yearnings.

Louis roused and moved across the salon toward Fanny. Gently, he stroked her close-cropped hair, and stepped out onto the deck. A bright morning sun warmed the trade wind blowing past his cheek. Diamond Head on Oahu was showing mistily in the distance.

Louis felt a sense of anticipation, a glow of happy feeling. It called to mind a moment traveling through the mountains of Southern France with his donkey, Modestine. He had moved in an atmosphere of pleasure, and felt light and quiet and content. Suddenly, it was as though someone were thinking of him in another country. A beautiful thought, as though a god suddenly opened a door, gave one smiling look into the house, and sped away forever. Was it Love with folded wings, he'd wondered? He felt once again that peace and pleasure in his heart.

◆ ◆ ◆

The Cleghorn household was in confusion. Archie, just sitting for breakfast, saw his daughter burst through the living room with her scarf, straw hat, and ribbons trailing and heard her excited shouts. Victoria had run from the beach, pounded the front steps, and rushed through the house. There was only time for a hasty kiss and, against his ear, a husky "The *Casco*! Stevenson! He's here, Father!"

She raced to the stables. "Limu! Quickly! Help me get Fairy ready!" Victoria's young groom, a broad and lurching Buddha-like figure, scrambled about excitedly, saddle under one large arm, coaxing her pony into the yard. "Oh, thank you, Limu! You heard? Did you see the schooner out there?" Limu, half bowing, half nodding, tossed the saddle like a leaf onto Fairy's back. Grinning broadly, he handed Victoria into the saddle, stepped back, and admired his contribution to the start of the day.

Limu had washed ashore on Oahu four years ago when his father was sent to Molokai with leprosy, and his mother went along as *kokua* ("helper") to nurse him. Victoria found him wandering on the beach one day, a lost boy. The Cleghorns promptly made him a part of Ainahau, naming him Limu ("seaweed").

Limu clung to Fairy's reins. "Miss Victoria, now just hold on while I saddle up Kimo, and I'll be right along." But there would be no waiting for this princess. She wheeled her horse, dug her heels into his ribs, and dashed off down the lane through the tall palms to Waikiki Road.

Archie rushed from the house, biscuit in one hand, napkin in the other. "Limu! You stay with her. Hurry up! Be sure you watch those furious riders on King Street!" Archie watched anxiously as Victoria disappeared among the palms. His worried frown emphasized the deep lines about his eyes. "I'll be along in the carriage. Look for me at the wharf! Limu! You stay with her!"

A ride down Waikiki Road was an enduring delight for Victoria. The trade winds had returned, and the sun was high over her left shoulder. Above the palisades, thin, fast-moving clouds laced the blue sky. Beyond the broad marshy plain of rice fields, the mountains beckoned, dipping and rising, valley and peak.

The white schooner was distinct now and closer to the beach. Sails reefed, she tacked sharply toward the harbor. Victoria pulled up and fished a telescope from her saddle bag as Limu, with big gray Kimo snorting and splashing through the puddles, lumbered up to her. Squinting through the eyepiece, Victoria found the schooner. Figures in the bow were waving to a welcoming boat approaching from the harbor. "It absolutely must be the *Casco!* Oh, Limu! Isn't she handsome?"

Below Round Top they hurried west onto King Street at a trot, Victoria impatient with the hindrance of the four miles to the harbor. At Punchbowl they passed the cluster of American missionary houses and Kawaiahao Church. There was now a fair amount of bustle on King Street: mule-drawn hacks, carriages, an occasional party of brightly clad women on horseback, cantering up and down, blossom leis of crimson *ohia* and orange *lauhala* falling over their costumes, their *Pa-u* silks streaming behind them.

More slowly now, they passed the grounds of Iolani Palace. In the distance, the volunteer militia was drilling at Iolani Barracks. Victoria took solace in this, admiring the way they handled their rifles so smartly and with such authority. She sent a grateful smile in their direction and waved to the Royal Household Guards at the Palace Gate. But beneath her smile she felt a lingering fear. This island—her home—was so vulnerable. The militia was a meager thread of protection.

The bustle and excitement of an open market roused Victoria from her unsettled thoughts as she and Limu turned seaward down Merchant Street. Men and women were thronging among the straggling stalls. They were a brilliant, laughing, joking crowd. Their jaunty hats were trimmed with fresh flowers. The women's *holokus* were dyed every imaginable color. The stalls were piled up with wonderful fish that could hardly be seen for the crowd.

Victoria remembered the king's fiftieth birthday just three years ago. It had been a jubilee: parades, tableaux, illuminations, aerial fireworks, a harbor regatta, public lu'aus, hula dancing and horse racing at Queen Kapiolani Park. Everyone was so happy in all the noise and fun. It was so delightful. They called Papa Moi the "Merrie Monarch." In one of the parades the king and queen had worn their headdresses from the coronation of six years ago: crowns fashioned of small golden taro leaves encrusted with pearls, diamonds, rubies, emeralds, and polished black *kukui* nuts. The people had so very little, but how they loved such bright, tumultuous, and colorful spectacles. The American missionaries stood aside. There was a deep gratitude the people felt for their helpfulness, for their concern about the everyday native. It was so puzzling that they were unable to share in such happiness.

So much had changed—so much was changing. She could see why she had become so caught up in Stevenson's visit. Everyone seemed so eager for a touch of lightness.

Victoria urged Fairy past John Cummins' supply store to a two-story wooden lookout. Reining in Fairy, she squinted in the bright sunlight at the figures leaning out from the top. "The white yacht out there—is she the *Casco*?" A man leaned down from a mounted telescope, studied her, and cupped his hands in a shout. "Yes, ma'am! It's the *Casco*! Yes, indeed! They say it's the writer, the *Treasure Island* man. Just anchored. Passengers bein' brought in to the wharf!"

Fairy, ever attuned to Victoria, wheeled, doubled back to Fort Street, dodged a tramcar, drew a bead on the lighthouse, and cantered past James Robinson & Company down to the seaward edge of the harbor. Along the Esplanade, a crowd was gathering at the wharf to greet the Stevenson party. Captain Henry Berger's Royal Hawaiian Band was hastening into place at the landing.

Below Victoria, a launch glided by as the sounds of the band swelled to strains of "*Aloha O'e*." Among the smiling passengers she saw a gaunt man in a velveteen jacket, his hair quite long. He was very animated, waving gaily to the crowd. Then he waved to a young princess on a white pony—who waved back, a bright Royal Stewart tartan fluttering in her grasp.

♦　♦　♦

King David Kalakaua

Chapter IV

MODESTINE

The Stevenson party, astonished at such an imposing reception, disembarked from the cutter and trudged up the damp, uneven wooden ramp on rubbery sea legs. A new test awaited: a human wave to buffet them at the edge of the wharf. The Royal Hawaiian band had struck up a greeting tune, quite martial and stirring, the crowd responding with cheers, shouts and whistles. Sweating newspaper reporters and photographers lugged their bulky equipment through the crushing throng. Louis, belabored by photographic flashes, greeted them warmly, attempting to respond to questions about his plans, his new writing endeavors, his views of the Pacific. Fanny, struggling to stay close, recruited Belle and Joe to keep Louis moving toward a carriage waiting beside the Custom House. Amid the battering and roar of this multitude, Louis saw the young woman on horseback pacing them slowly at a distance.

Suddenly there was an abrupt outcry, then a gasp from the throng. Louis felt his head yanked to the side with a rough, twisting jerk of his long hair. Stunned, he grasped his head in pain and turned in the squeeze of the crowd to see a native man retreating rapidly. Joe Strong yelled excitedly and pushed after the man, shouting as the fellow melted away in the clamor of the crowd and the rumpus of the band. Louis, bewildered, saw the young woman signal to a husky young rider beside her, who spurred his horse through the crowd in pursuit. At the same moment, a massive Hawaiian boomed out a command above the pandemonium. With his vigorous approach, the crowd yielded and fell silent. It was Kalamake—and behind him, Dr. Trousseau. Louis was dazed, close to fainting. Kalamake quickly caught him and supported him to a bench by the Custom House.

"Some fine aloha, Mister Stevenson! Here! This is Dr. Trousseau. Let's have him take a look." Trousseau quickly examined the area of Louis's swollen scalp where a fistful of hair had been torn away. Fanny, Belle, Lloyd, Joe and Maggie had gathered in a semicircle about him. Louis looked up at them woefully, scanned the crowd cautiously, and shook his head. He took a deep breath, straightened up, and then, a slow grin at Dr. Trousseau.

"Well, Doctor, Are we safe? I've traveled through Indian country in the western plains, had fights with my father where I fully deserved such treatment, but never before have I been scalped."

Trousseau smiled ruefully, relieved at Louis's quick recovery. "This is a terrible thing, Mr. Stevenson. So regrettable." He shrugged, "Well, just hair, no scalping." He turned to Kalamake. "What do you think, what's this all about?"

Kalamake surveyed the crowd standing outside their semicircle, curious, friendly, offended by what they had seen. "Not so good! That kane (man)—I think he want some of Mr. Stevenson's hair. You're somebody special."

Louis rubbed the back of his neck and pursued a brighter approach. "Well, what can he do with hair? I would gladly autograph one of my books for him!"

Everyone chuckled with relief except Kalamake. "We'll find the man. Hard to hide in the islands. Don't you worry. The Princess, Limu—they saw him. I think he got away for now. We will find him."

Archie Cleghorn burst belatedly into the semicircle. His touch of Scottish burr was fresh reassurance to Louis. "Mr. Stevenson! How horrible! I just heard! Are you all right? What a terrible way to greet you and your family! Do you feel up to a carriage ride to the hotel?" Archie looked about at the family, still struggling to regain their composure. "The police are already looking into this. I think we'll have Dr. Trousseau ride along with us." Then, agitated and embarrassed, Archie shepherded them off to the carriages.

◆ ◆ ◆

The next several days blurred with activity for the Stevensons. They left the wharf carefully guarded by their new friends. Belle, mindful of Louis's health problems, had made some arrangements for the family, accommodations held through the fearful days when everyone believed they had been lost at sea. She'd witnessed Louis's near-death episodes in France and California before moving to the Islands. But this was a shocking event that none could have foreseen. Typically, Louis was the least upset, and teased them out of their anxiety. The party stayed briefly at the Royal Hawaiian Hotel, where they made up for several days of lost meals. Then they moved in with Belle and Joe at Mrs. Caroline Bush's home on Queen Emma Street.

Louis and Fanny paid off the *Casco* and went in search of a setting favorable to Louis's unresolved *Ballantrae* struggle. They came at last across Frank Brown's Manuia Lanai on the beach at Waikiki. This was a straggle of low buildings, including a grim little shanty, as Louis described it, which would serve as his bedroom and workroom. With his usual humor and generosity, he accepted co-tenancy with cockroaches, spiders, scorpions, mosquitoes, and a friendly mouse. Quickly the family embellished the walls with South Sea curiosities: war clubs, idols, pearl shells, stone axes. It rankled Louis to find in his mail a critical review of early chapters of *Ballantrae*. The review termed his work a valiant effort to enter the capital of his kingdom. It noted that he did introduce a woman, and that he confronted problems of love as well as fraternal hatred. Louis ruefully acknowledged his inability to please himself with any of his woman characters. "Well," he ruminated, "perhaps there was *Olalla*."

Oahu was much too civilized and Honolulu too cold for Louis. He felt oppressed by all the electric lights, the creeping growth of civilization. Even his cottages on the beach were connected through that abhorrent device, the telephone, with the shops four miles away in Honolulu. Waikiki was a suburb of rice paddies; a marshy, lazy scattering of thirty or forty summer houses among the coconut palms along a fringe of beach. It afforded mule-drawn tram cars for the hour-long drive to Honolulu. A walk along the wooden causeway brought one to Kapiolani Park, where a horse and hack could be hired for twenty-five cents an hour.

Louis and Fanny waded through seven months of accumulated correspondence waiting for them at Honolulu, but found nothing in the way of money forwarded from his writings. There were many days of suspense and frustration before a bundle of mail turned up, bringing news that his work was selling well. Louis fretted greatly over their lack of funds. This was his keen-felt responsibility in his marriage. Fanny could make anything grow, but she couldn't produce money. Now, with Belle and Joe added, there was an even greater retinue to think about.

Joe was a good photographer, but Louis recalled from France and California that he didn't know the meaning of money. Joe had been in severe difficulty in the months before the Stevensons arrived, suffering from over-indulgence in alcohol and opium to the point of a nervous breakdown. It was a mixed picture indeed. Having Belle and Joe around meant involvement with the "royal crowd," the gay stratum of society that clustered about King David Kalakaua and Queen Kapiolani. King Kalakaua was Belle's admiring patron and the Strongs were on familiar terms with all the island aristocracy—brown, white, oriental or half-caste. Belle and Joe appeared at such occasions as the coronation and its evening ball in the palace gardens, and were part of a scene of magnificent costumes, the ladies with trains, bustles, jewels, and feathers. Much as Louis enjoyed such distractions, his money worries, responsibilities, and need to keep writing—not to mention his health and available energy—gave him cause to view his situation with some worry.

Formal presentation to King Kalakaua was an early event. Louis and Lloyd arrived at Iolani Palace for a breakfast meeting armed with letters of introduction from California. With his Scottish penchant for royalty, Louis basked in the king's warmth and friendly informality, delighted with word that His Majesty had already read *Treasure Island* and *Dr. Jekyll and Mr. Hyde*. Included at the breakfast, and becoming a fast friend, was the king's brother-in-law, Archibald Cleghorn, Collector General of Customs, a former resident of Edinburgh. Considering his recent experiences in the South Seas, Louis found much to ponder about in Kalakaua, this "Merrie Monarch."

Kalakaua traced his descent back to Keawe, a great ancient chief in Honaunau on Hawai'i Island. He was elected king after a bitter struggle with dowager Queen Emma in the stormy election of 1874. Kalakaua's victory over Queen Emma was paid for at a haunting price. His election required the support of the business and missionary community, and this support was forthcoming with Kalakaua's willingness to seek a sugar reciprocity treaty with the United States.

Kalakaua secured this treaty in Washington, but only by giving up Pearl Harbor to the United States. Kalakaua was tall, broad, stately, mustached, a hard-drinking monarch. On state occasions, he wore operetta-like uniforms. Known as "First Gentleman of the Pacific," he was a man of culture and achievement—a poet, scholar, and musician. He interested himself deeply in native lore and arts and translated many Hawaiian myths and chants into English. He was the first King of any nation ever to circumnavigate the globe. Kalakaua recruited Captain Heinrich Berger from Prussia to form the unique and already historic Royal Hawaiian Band. When he returned from his round-the-world trip to visit foreign royalties, including Queen Victoria at her Jubilee, he modeled his little tropical capital on European courts. It had an opera house with red velvet, gilt, electric lights, Italianate scenery, and a royal box. His Majesty was the center of elegant riding picnics, court banquets and balls, and parties on visiting men-of-war.

But Kalakaua was running against the massive tide of history. He wished to restore personal rule, to establish Hawai'i as a sovereign nation, to be primate of a Polynesian League. He ruled over eight thousand Hawaiians and part-Hawaiians, twenty-four thousand Europeans, and forty-seven thousand Asian laborers. Frightfully lacking in a power base, he nevertheless had a grasp of power politics. Germany, the United States, and Britain were in a three-way struggle for dominance in the Pacific. Kalakaua recognized that Japan, with its powerful navy, would be an impressive ally. The United States already had too much control of economics and politics in Hawai'i, and there was a real danger of usurpation. Prince Komatsu, a nephew of the Emperor of Japan, impressed Kalakaua. So much so that he broached the idea of a royal marriage to Princess Kaiulani. This never developed, since Komatsu was already betrothed. Kalakaua's world-view and hopes for a sovereign Hawai'i left him vulnerable to self-seeking adventurers, whom he appointed to high places in the government, men who provoked strong reform movements and over time discredited his rule.

The high-water mark of the Polynesian League was "Kalakaua's Navy," the *Kaimiloa*. This star-crossed effort was a converted guano trader with four brass cannon, two Gatling guns, a chronically drunk skipper, and a crew made up largely of boys from the Honolulu

Reformatory School. The king launched his "Navy" to give added weight to the Hawaiian program of primacy in the Pacific. Alas, the great powers could not think of Hawai'i as a serious imperialist. Mutiny and embarrassment followed, and thus the end of the short and melancholy life of what wry observers came to call the Empire of the Calabash. Not long after, the Bayonet Constitutional Crisis left Kalakaua with only a legislative veto.

Louis found much to enjoy in Kalakaua's warm and intelligent nature, and the two quickly formed a rich friendship. Kalakaua often dropped in at Manuia Lanai, followed by his chamberlain under a load of books. He loved to talk to Louis about the South Seas and fascinated him with Hawaiian history and archeology. Through his encouragement Louis studied the native language, and the king tried hard to persuade the Stevensons to settle in the kingdom. Louis found the court a charming center of music and culture. It amused him greatly that the king strung Oahu's first telephone line between Iolani Palace and the Royal Boathouse where hula girls and poker tables were featured attractions.

◆　◆　◆

Settled at the beach at last, Louis, clad in flapping pajamas, contended with the problematic Lords of *Ballantrae* each morning. His characters had moved on from Scotland and India to New York State. Louis's mind ranged everywhere else but on the plot and its worrisome characters. If that did not constitute enough of a problem, all Honolulu society flocked to call on the newcomers. The gentlemen dressed in white duck or flannel with bands of shells or peacock feathers on their straw hats. The ladies were elegant in morning attire of Mother Hubbards trimmed with lace or ruffles, under wide-brimmed hats with ostrich plumes and gay little parasols. In the afternoon, they appeared in waspy European dresses, bowling along behind liveried coachmen. Smart riding parties in white linen reined up in front of the gate and sent in their cards. Fanny and Louis adopted the expedient of having a regular "day" when they "received," to avoid continual callers.

◆　◆　◆

It was a languorous time after the stressful sea voyage. Fanny, lighthearted to see her two boys so happy, frequently went off with Belle on painting jaunts. Lloyd, mimicking his step-father, spent his time sorting out the groundwork for a short story. Maggie was often left napping on the verandah while the others, even faithful, attentive Valentine were off exploring Honolulu and Oahu.

On one such afternoon Maggie roused from a reverie with a thought about *Ballantrae* which might help Louis. She yawned behind a dainty hand, shook off her lassitude and walked over to Louis's little shanty with its surrounding tall fence.

"Louis!" Maggie called. She stepped inside the bedroom-workroom arrangement, slapping at mosquitoes, to find Louis's usual clutter. But her son was not there. She called again, loudly for such a delicate matron, and heard a mumbled response from next door, the cottage where Fanny did her painting and Lloyd his writing.

"Oh, Lloyd, is that you?" Maggie called impatiently. "Where in the world is everybody?" Maggie wandered into the cottage. Lloyd, girded with a lava lava, sat at a table, a pad in front of him, biting on the end of a pen. He looked across at her vacantly and stretched back in his chair.

"Everybody's gone, thank heaven! I can't get my mind going when they're all bustling around here. All these creative geniuses, interrupting you with their brilliant ideas." Lloyd's frustration softened. "Thank you, Maggie, for just being you." He sighed and pushed away from his writing. "The truth is, I put Joe up to carting them all off to town. Not Louis—he's probably out on the beach. Joe's very good at distracting them. But I hope he doesn't leave them in a ditch somewhere. Belle sure has her hands full with him."

Lloyd put down his pen and turned toward Maggie with a sly grin. "Maggie, if you'll deign to take off your shoes and stockings, I would be honored to take you for a walk on the beach!"

♦   ♦   ♦

Afternoons, now only occasionally ruminating over the violent theft of locks of his hair, Louis laid his writing tablet aside for walking, wading and swimming along the beach.

One afternoon, somewhat late, with the sun dipping into mauve clouds beyond the Waianae range, Louis strolled along the water's edge. He was piping a thoughtful tune on his flageolet, pausing now and then to gaze out to sea, to crunch his toes into the sand, to feel the trade winds at his back, to watch the wind flicking the edge of the curling surf.

He recalled a prophesy, a meditation of a friend from his days in the forbidden parts of Edinburgh. He was seventeen, she was a drunken Highland pleasure-seeker. She said he was to be very happy, to visit America, and to be much upon the sea.

Louis's stroll brought him to the edge of the garden at Ainahau. On the broad lawn, several peacocks grazed beneath a majestic banyan directly in front of the wide porch. This was Louis's first view of Ainahau, unmistakable with its massive tree, of which Archie Cleghorn was so proud. It was father to all the noted banyans in Honolulu. Louis reclined nearby at a comfortable spot against a palm tree, yawning and stretching luxuriously. The remarkable figure of the woman on horseback at the Esplanade kept returning to his thoughts. In all that confusion, he recalled Kalamake referring to a princess. Indeed she was! He'd never seen anything like her: poised, in command, recognized by the throng with a friendly deference, beautiful in those indescribable essentials that set Polynesian women apart. Such women occupied a very special chamber in Louis's gallery of perfection.

Lying on the sand, Louis became drowsy and could prevent slumber no longer in the warm, waning hush of afternoon surf and gentle breeze. Unnoticed, a figure in a flowing white lace-trimmed holoku approached, stepping slowly through the sand toward the water. A ponderous sea turtle lumbered after her greedily.

Victoria came upon Louis as he dozed off. She carried a loaf of bread in one hand, her ukulele in the other. The bread was for Honu, her pet turtle. The ukulele would fulfill her afternoon ritual of song at sunset. It had been a full but typical day in the life of a young princess: a morning visit to the sick at Queen's Hospital, an afternoon playing guitar with the boys from the Reformatory School.

Victoria moved softly over to Louis and sank down on her knees in front of him. She studied him slowly and in detail, pleased with such a singular introduction to her fellow "child of air." As she settled back on the sand and waited, she thought, "His hair's much too long. He's so thin."

A ponderous crunching and rustling in the dry carpet of lauhala fronds behind Louis's palm tree signaled Honu's impatience for an evening snack. "Hush, Honu! We have a sleeping guest!"

Louis roused, opened drowsy eyes, and sat up in surprise. He drew his knees up, steadied his chin on the flageolet gripped between his fists, and returned Victoria's deliberate, beguiling gaze. His eyelids crinkled in a slow smile.

"Aloha! I am Victoria Cleghorn, Mr. Stevenson." She nodded toward Honu. "I apologize for my noisy turtle—he's hungry. Oh, but you looked so peaceful! Were you dreaming? I would not have wanted to interrupt *that*."

Louis rubbed his face. His expression was quizzical. "In truth, I *was* dreaming—about a fairy princess in a far-off land. I take my dreams very seriously." He tapped his brow. "You see, I have these 'little people' who give me dreams—and then I do my best to write them down. Some of my best ideas." He gestured with pleased surprise. "But here you are—a *real* Princess, full of life, and far exceeding any words. I've been looking for you, young lady. You were one of my rescuers at the wharf. I believe I've met several thousand people since we arrived—and saw you the very first of all of them on your white steed at the pier. Where have you been?"

Victoria flushed and hunched her shoulders in a gesture of helplessness. "I'm at quite a loss. I didn't want to seem a schoolgirl coming to you to autograph my copy of your *Garden of Verses*. It's so awkward—like being introduced to someone you—how can I say it? I feel you're someone I already know." She sat back, reached out, and framed him with her open palms. She shivered slightly and sighed a half smile. "What a strange feeling!"

Louis leaned forward and considered Victoria's eloquent eyes. "Look at you! Victoria! You are Scotland and Hawai'i blended so marvelously in one person. How perfectly splendid! Already I've had the pleasure of meeting your father. I know a lot about you, you see. And also Doctor Trousseau. Oh, you see, I really have a head start! You and I have much to talk about. Well, now—my little book of verse—did you enjoy it?"

Victoria bubbled over. "Oh, yes! Do you know we are both 'children of air?' You said so many things I've felt and thought. I've devoured your verses and everything else I've been able to get my hands on. But, you have no idea what a fright you gave us. Until you arrived, everything had become so horrid. We were convinced you'd been lost at sea."

"What? Miss this delightful meeting—and I just now sleeping my way through it? Certainly not! Those verses—did you know they came to me lying in bed for weeks on end in a darkened room? I couldn't see. I scratched them out on a huge tablet. No, Victoria, it would take more than a few hurricanes or a snapped mainmast to do me in."

Victoria paused, pursed her lips quizzically. "Of all your verses, which one is your very favorite?"

Louis clapped his hands and laughed mischievously. "That's easy!" He paused and looked thoughtfully out to sea. His expression became whimsical:

> *When I am grown to man's estate*
> *I shall be very proud and great,*
> *And tell the other girls and boys*
> *Not to meddle with my toys."*

Victoria laughed and rolled her eyes. "I hoped it would be that one!"

Louis tapped Victoria's ukulele. "I see you have one of those little instruments the Portuguese brought to the Islands. I'm no master of this"—he flourished his flageolet—"but sometime we'll have a concert, you and I. Could I ask you to play something for me now?"

A gust of seawind swept in upon them from offshore. Victoria quivered slightly, looked sharply out to sea, and grasped her forearms. There was a long silence, and she seemed suddenly distracted and embarrassed.

"Forgive me. I—I was interrupted. Did you feel something? Are you familiar with—we call them our aumakua? We in the islands believe we have spiritual ancestors who are always with us, somewhere in the background. But they often enter into our daily lives." Victoria's eyes could not conceal a precautionary flashing glance. "Good heavens! Promise you won't tell Father?"

Louis studied her, puzzled, and shrugged the thought away. He nodded. "Yes. I know. The people in the southern islands have the same belief. A different name. They think of this—whatever it is—influence as some sort of intermediary to help them. Sometimes to warn of some danger or misfortune."

Victoria continued more confidently. "Even more. It isn't always some deadly serious matter. Our aumakua can comfort, give advice. They even get in a mischievous mood and play tricks. I think my aumakua is in that sort of mood right now. True, there is also the belief that the aumakua can punish or possess someone. The Hawaiians see them as a guiding star. If we please them during life, we will join them after death."

Louis retreated within himself, preoccupied, and ran his fingers through his long hair. He grinned wryly: "People have been telling me I should be on guard—that some harm will come to me from that lock of hair that was grabbed out of my head at the wharf. They look very glum and expect me to worry. It seems preposterous. Do you believe this?"

"It worries me," Victoria acknowledged. She thought back to Princess Miriam's death and the rumors that were flying: she was being prayed to death by a powerful kahuna. Such fearful beliefs ran deep among the people. Others named a huge school of small, bright red local fish, *aweoweo*, seen about that time off Hawai'i, as a harbinger of death for a member of the Kalakaua family. "It's puzzling. Who knows? The American Reformists aren't very happy to have such a popular representative of Britain visit us." Victoria narrowed her eyes in a frown. "But if there has been a curse, we have ways to return it, I assure you. We shall see. Enough of that! Oh! But here's a nice thing. You asked me for a song, and—well, there you are—just then my aumakua sent me an affectionate touch of breeze and a message." Victoria smiled happily. "That gust from the sea carried my mother's favorite scent. So I shall sing for you her own very special song. I wish you could have known her. She was such a special lady. Graceful, so very stylish. She could be imperious and haughty—she was a princess—but she was so thoughtful and considerate of everyone. This song—*Kuu Ipo Ika Hee Pue One*—she composed for her singing club. In English it means 'The Tender Touch of Love.'"

Victoria sang with a lilting sweetness about quiet kisses, as warm as the tropic sun. Even without understanding the words, Louis was mesmerized. When Victoria was done, they sat quietly in the sunset for several moments. In healthy times it was rare for Louis to be serious or silent. But at this moment neither felt a need for conversation. The sea was darkening. The Hawaiian moon was rising through lacy clouds over Diamond Head crater. Honu had been waiting patiently, drowsing beside them like a rock sculpture, and now renewed his bid for sustenance.

Louis surveyed Honu's bulk as Victoria offered generous portions of bread. He was truly a huge animal, with a towering shell that surely could have borne them both easily. "You know, Honu reminds me much of someone I knew in France. Together we took a walking tour in the highlands, the Cevennes. Is Honu a boy or a girl?"

Victoria broke the breadloaf into pieces, which Honu munched unceremoniously. "She's wahine—a girl—look at her short tail."

"Even better. My friend's name was Modestine. I owned her for a few delightful weeks."

Victoria drew back in feigned shock. With a sly glance, Louis leaned back against the palm tree, looked up at the moon, and hugged his knees thoughtfully. "Yes, I wanted someone cheap and small, who had a stolid, peaceful temper."

Victoria wrinkled her nose. "I can well imagine. And you found her?"

"Indeed, I did. She had a kindly eye and a determined under-jaw. Unlike Honu, there was something neat and highbred about her. Now, perhaps I'm not being fair to your turtle friend. She had a Quakerish element that hit my fancy. So I bought her—just like that—right on the spot for sixty-five francs and a glass of brandy. I baptized her instantly—Modestine."

Victoria's mouth dropped open. She pressed her cheeks in disbelief. "Do all writers have such an imagination?"

"No, no! It's *true*. We walked together up hill and down dale from Le Monastier to St. Jean du Gard. Sometimes we slept in the fields, sometimes at an inn. Well, that is, I slept in the inn. Modestine slept in the yard or the stable."

Victoria laughed and flicked a resounding ukulele discord. "Ah, sir, you've been misleading me." She pointed at him with a canny grin. "She was no poor enslaved woman! Modestine was a donkey!"

"Yes, yes! A donkey, yes!" Louis rolled his eyes and laughed. "Oh, but she was so slow, just like Honu." He ambled his fingers across the sand in imitation. "She had such a sober, finicky gait. I'd apply my whip—mind you, it goes against my conscience to lay my hand on a female—three quicker steps. Then, if I dropped a few steps behind her, Modestine would halt instantly and begin to browse. Can you imagine?"

Victoria looked at Louis thoughtfully, then gazed out past the reef where the moon was splashing silver on the wave crests. "Yes, I *can* imagine ...." Her eyes widened in wonder. "Because—Oh!—Because I was *there*! We left Bleymard you and I, didn't we? And at the top of the woods, we struck a path among the pines, until we hit on a dell of green turf. A streamlet made a little spout over some stones to serve us as a water-tap. The trees grew thickly around the glade. There was no look-out except straight upward to the sky. This was our encampment, secure and private. Night fell, lightly, with stars and dews and perfumes."

Louis stared in amazement, spellbound. Then, aroused from his wonderment, he leaned close to Victoria. "You *saw* it! *You*—! But how? *How* could you know?" He sat back, gazing intently at her. "You read my book, *Travels with a Donkey*?"

"No!" Victoria breathed a lingering, bewildered sigh of confusion. "I haven't read your book, Louis. It's so very strange. You remember I told you—I, too, am like the child of air—the child in your poem. Like your little boy—you—in your poem. Oh, this takes my breath away! You said some words—and I was there! I've been told of this, even told I should look for it, expect it. ..."

Louis scooped handfuls of sand and pitched them back and forth in his fingers, awed. "How *eerie*! Yes—! At times while I was traveling, I felt a presence—not just Modestine."

Victoria's expression was strained, perplexed. "Oh, my! Should I go on? Louis, a thought crossed your mind. Do you remember? 'To live out of doors with the woman a man loves—'"

Louis spoke softly, slowly, as if from a trance: "—is of all lives most complete and free."

There followed a long silence. Then he roused, stretched, rose, and gestured to the far horizon. "I felt—as I do now—I was in some-one's debt for such bountiful entertainment. When we left the next morning, do you recall that I threw coins on the turf as we went along until I had left enough for my night's lodging."

"*Our* night's lodging, Louis. Why was I so much a presence apart? Was Modestine an aumakua, a spirit ancestor? Think of your own memories of departed loved ones. How Modestine must have empowered you! True, you fed Modestine, but you goaded her, and it hurt." Victoria winced in the growing twilight. "But—worst of all— didn't you overlook something unequaled?"

Louis rubbed his face, slow to find words. "You move me to tears, Victoria. Modestine and I—we had our last meal together—a snack upon the top of St. Pierre, I on a heap of stones, she standing beside me in the moonlight and decorously eating bread out of my hand. She—forgive me, I was going to say, 'poor brute'—seemed to have a sort of affection for me. And, yes, this I knew I would soon betray."

Victoria injected quickly: "Before noon the next day, you sold me for thirty-five francs. And you thought you had bought freedom into the bargain!"

Louis paced about in the sand. "Poor soul! She came to regard me as a god. She loved to eat out of my hand. I pushed away the feeling of never seeing my companion again. I felt a stark sense of forever-ness....Later, traveling alone in the coach, Victoria, my emotions *did* pour forth."

Honu, satiated, stirred heavily and moved off into the crunching shadows of the lauhala. In the bright moonlight, Louis watched her thoughtfully. Then, with an expression of enchantment on his face, he slowly considered Victoria.

"Well, Princess, it seems your turtle has had enough for one night. I, alas—or rather, happily—have not. You've brought Modestine back with your breezes, your scents, your aumakua. She—you—are still with me, after all. I doubt my little book about our journey gave proper honor. And you, Princess, have goaded *me*—and for that, too, I thank you. It occurs to me that I require a certain amount of that or I shall fall victim—no, no!—not to the curse of the stolen lock of hair—but to a certain soul-swallowing publishing machine." Louis turned away, a slender figure against the glittering moonlit sea. "But more of that tomorrow...."

Victoria nestled her ukulele against her as she sat back pensively in the sand. "France. Why was it in *France*? I should much rather be with you in Scotland, Louis."

Louis looked down at her whiteness against the shadows of the Ainahau garden. "I shall charge my little people with that delectable task, Victoria."

"Please do, Louis. Aloha. Pleasant dreaming."

Louis's response was exuberant. "Indeed it shall be. Aloha—Modestine!" As he disappeared in the shadows down the beach, a shooting star flashed through the heavens. Victoria shuddered. Was it Akualele, the dreaded flying god, bent on an errand of destruction?

♦ ♦ ♦

The following morning, a servant brought Victoria a package that had been delivered earlier by a young man in a striped blazer, Louis's stepson, Lloyd Osbourne. The envelope was addressed to: "Princess Victoria Kaiulani, Mistress of Ainahau." Inside was a note in Louis's handwriting: "Allow me to introduce 'Ballantrae,' the depressing, soul-swallowing project that returned to plague me at the moment of my departure last evening. Until our happy meeting, I had despaired of ever pulling off the confounded ending to it. As you read it, you will find me stuck somewhere between the deep sea, the wilderness and an open grave. May I entreat you kindly to direct your vision to my travail's inner parts?—RLS."

Robert Kalanihiapo Wilcox

Chapter V

THE STONE-EATING SONG

February advanced swiftly. For Louis, the softened flow of the southern islands seemed far astern. Honolulu was reminiscent of those tropic sites, but he felt pervasive tension and uneasiness in Hawai'i. It twisted its way into his pores. In startling, charming contrast to the dismaying erosion he found in Pacific island life, the entry of Victoria into his own life was astounding. She offered a healing antidote for the unsettled feelings he absorbed in Honolulu. Their friendship flowered in delightful hours spent "talking story," as the Hawaiians would say, under the huge banyan tree. Ainahau had become a magical enclave for Louis. In Victoria's presence, even the blades of grass and grains of sand appeared to come alive. The peacocks strutted and fanned about her with a delicate fussiness beyond any human attendant's capacity.

Victoria's inventive way of seeing things tantalized Louis. Modestine—how uncanny! She'd quoted him chapter and verse of his writing that she'd never seen. It was not simply the words: she'd captured his own feeling of joy and sorrow from a distant time. With great amusement, she taunted him that his first literary female was a donkey. She needled him about *Ballantrae* and the timid Alison—wife of the indestructible evil brother and later to wed the good Lord of Durrisdeer.

Louis in offhand moments felt uncannily transported. Could Victoria be the *Olalla* of his dreams? Ever since the dalliances, the love affairs, the sexual involvements of those troubled years in Edinburgh, Louis had scanned the clamoring elements of his deepest self. It was a tangled, bewildering search for the woman who was the mate, the other half of his restive, agitated soul. He thought he had found her in the world outside several times. Kate, who gave of herself so warmly, freely, unquestioningly. Fanny Sitwell, his Madonna, who breathed life and substance into his creative genius. Fanny Osbourne, who made him feel needed, who inspired him to adult responsibility—and who kept him alive!

And now, Victoria. Quietly insinuated, then suddenly, breathtakingly, accelerating into the turbulence of his life. Was she *Olalla*? Olalla was an enchantress, a sublime woman. The little people had brought her to him. Shaken to the bursting point, half-awake, he had written the story of Olalla. From that time on, she took her place as a recurring, haunting image.

Louis's creative chemistry mellowed in Victoria's presence. They laughed together in merry conversations that blew away the dark shadows. No kindred spirit among Louis's wide range of friends was the measure of Victoria. She was a vibrant treasure chest of royal purple, of gleaming gems, softly glowing, dazzling. An hour with Victoria provided substance—at times jolting insights—for the characters of a dozen stories. She gave things a breathtaking spin that sent Louis's literary senses reeling. He was in a state of exhilarating suspense with Victoria. Her surprises were unremitting, with something always in store for him. *Ballantrae* became a less turbulent creation, a safer topic—good for banter, even to stirring Father Archie's interest in the unfinished novel. Archie got into the manuscript and to him Lord James Durie was a devil, but he swore that Durie could have learned a few malicious tricks from Lorrin Thurston's political manipulations in the islands.

Each departure from Victoria carried for Louis a sense of anticipation. They'd been exchanging ideas about *The Sire de Maletroit's Door*, about the young cavalier, Denis de Beaulieu, hiding from the troops of Burgundy and England, stumbling through a door to what he hoped would be a safe haven—not a compromising situation with a woman. At one point, Victoria's eyes flashed. "Oh, Louis! Would you like to go through a door like that? I mean *here*? I could show you something like that door. Wait! Not long. Just a day or two!"

◆　◆　◆

Louis and Dr. Trousseau became quick friends. Fanny had badgered Louis into a medical checkup, even though he'd been feeling exceptionally strong, quite recovered from the serious bout in Tahiti a few months earlier. Louis visited the doctor at his office on Punchbowl Street across from Queens Hospital. Dr. Trousseau listened to Louis's accounting of his endless struggle with "Old Man Virulent," thumped and auscultated his chest carefully, and cheered him with cautious encouragement. The roentgen ray had not yet made its way to the Pacific, but the passionate doctor spoke of it with great enthusiasm. One day the lungs and the entire body's interior would be as visible as the skin. Trousseau's enthusiasm sent Louis into a fit of laughter. What, then, would be the human condition? Where would literature be? Would all the hues and subtleties in life be stripped away by an electrical beam? Both were versed in Sigmund Freud's studies of the human unconscious, and Louis especially, from his friendship with Henry James had delved extensively into the work of his psychologist brother William James. Trousseau, eyes twinkling with prime amusement, teased Louis about the searchlight he'd beamed into the human soul in *The Strange Case of Dr. Jekyll and Mr. Hyde*.

Trousseau and Stevenson met often in the weeks that followed. Victoria was a recurring topic. Trousseau was gratified by the friendship Louis and Victoria had formed. Still, he felt uneasy about the intensity of this relationship. He had done much to initiate it. This Scot was a glib character—charming, indeed! Victoria's bewilderment and sadness in the wake of Miriam's death were so recent. Now she was so joyful, but how genuine was it? What disturbing complexes lay buried inside her? Had she felt undeserved guilt? Until recent months, Trousseau had seen unremitting feelings of unworthiness, doubt, and fear in the girl. She had been joyless, sad, afraid of growing up. Victoria had not had a governess the past few years. Archie was often away. This left only the family retainers to offer the princess what comforts they could. The doctor knew Victoria traveled the island for unexplained periods of time. She was much on her own, and this disturbed him—and her father as well. There had never before been reason to mistrust this usually steady girl.

Where did the worldly Stevenson fit into this? Trousseau was a man of action, of control. From the day *Casco* reached Honolulu, he felt an elusive something slipping away from him, some indefinable force stirring his princess and the famous author. Some catalyst. Was it the bewildering array of chemical or physical forces this age of science had unleashed upon the world? Whatever it was, it was asserting itself, and the medical scientist fumbled uncomfortably with his thoughts. It set him on edge, curious, cautious, but feeling left out— much the same puzzlement he felt about two others he was very fond of: Kalamake and Kumulipa.

♦   ♦   ♦

Early twilight. A few streetlights in distant Honolulu were shimmering in the waning heat of the day. Louis was traveling by hack into Honolulu to share an evening with Scottish friends at the Thistle Club. Albeit reluctantly for him, Louis had sent off letters to the *London Times* stating his views of the political struggles in the Pacific islands. They were evident elsewhere but intensifying in Hawai'i. Giant America loomed large on the horizon, an emerging world power. The Sandwich Islands were a floating morsel in America's geopolitical spoon, as were Samoa and Spanish holdings in the Philippines and Cuba. American business interests, especially the sugar planters in the islands, were fueling the fires of annexation. When Louis studied the editorials in the annexationist Honolulu newspapers, his rueful thoughts drifted to Long John Silver and his pirate crew. It promised to be a lively evening to be shared with the many Scots in Hawai'i who reveled as much as he in the tropic climate. The horse, a large black, was moving along at a pleasant trot down Waikiki Road. Louis and his drowsy driver, becalmed in the scented evening hush, passed through dense, gnarled *hau* trees clustered on both sides. The bright yellow blossoms he'd seen that morning were now dark red and scattered on the ground. So short a life for the *hau* blossom. He shivered, drew his jacket about him, and envisioned Polynesian legends of birth, blooming life, and deepening, plunging darkness. The night before, he'd had another dream. It seemed a fading, farewell dream of Olalla. His emotions in these past few days were like crisp, brittle kindling.

There could be no further doubt. Victoria was Olalla! At last! The pale saint of his dreams had vanished forever. In her place he beheld this maiden on whom God had lavished the richest colors, the most exuberant energies of life. Active as a deer, slender as a reed, in her great eyes He had lighted the torches of the soul. The thrill of her young life, vibrant as a wild animal's, had entered into Louis. The force of soul that had looked out from her eyes had conquered his, had mantled about his heart and sprung to his lips in song. She passed through his veins: she was *one* with him!

Louis was suddenly aware of a change in the rhythm of the big black's gait. The horse's ears abruptly cocked backwards and he lunged forward, bolting out of his driver's grasp. Clutching the sides of the hack, Louis twisted and saw two mounted figures bearing down upon them at a gallop. Louis helped the driver haul mightily on the reins, but the big black lowered his head and flew down the dusty road. Amid the rush of air, clouds of dust, and pounding hooves, the two riders at last drew abreast on either side of the big black and slowed him to a walk. With astonishment and great relief, Louis recognized Victoria and Limu. Mopping his brow, glaring at the big black, Louis thanked them profusely for their rescue.

Big Limu laughed excitedly: "No thank us! I think we scare your horse—he run off!" It was then that Louis noted that the two had an additional saddled horse in tow.

Victoria dismounted and held the big black securely. "I'm so sorry, Louis! How frightful—running you down on the road like this! We called for you at the beach—you had just left." She turned the hack reins over to the driver and brought the riderless horse forward. By now, Victoria could strum Louis's love for adventure like a musical instrument. With a sly grin, she gestured to him: "Come! Here's your horse. I have something for you to see."

Without a word, Louis leaped down from the hack, straightened his hat, brushed the dust from his sleeves, came to attention, saluted smartly and leaped upon his horse. He shielded his eyes theatrically and peered off into the distant twilight. "Lead on, my lady. The forces of Lancaster are positioned just beyond yon distant moor! The—ah—rice fields."

Enjoying the suspense, Louis waited for Victoria to explain this ambush. She led them off the barren stretch of Waikiki Road, onto a path through the rice fields, and followed a stream bed for a half mile below Round Top. Darkness was falling rapidly now, and cool air moved steadily down from the mountains. Beside the path, a large family of mynah birds in a huge banyan were noisily sharing the day's activities and nesting down for the night. As the three riders slowly picked their way, Louis looked up at the moist, swiftly drifting mists whistling through the ironwood pines on the slopes, shivered, and hoped the mountains were not Victoria's destination. Then Limu moved into the lead, and they turned their horses westward along the foothills. Offshore the stars glistened with growing brightness. Victoria pulled Fairy back to ride beside Louis.

"Princess, we have vanquished the Lancastrians down on the plain. What orders have you now for your troop?"

She spoke in a hush, deliberately. "Louis, this is something I've been wanting to share with you. You tell me I've been mysterious. I have—even to myself! Forgive me. Bless you for being patient. I know that you and Father and Dr. Trousseau worry about me. Those two hover over me constantly. I've felt their worry so keenly—I was in such torment after mother died. They both try so hard to help me. I'm afraid I've made them feel like complete failures."

Victoria lapsed into silence, and they rode slowly on, listening to the trudge of the horses' hooves in the soft trail, the squeak of the saddles, feeling the rhythm of the ride under the stars. "Things have happened. Certain people have come into my life—before you, I mean.... And then, *especially* you. Somehow, you've opened up something, set something in motion."

Louis leaned across and touched her hand, trying to make out Victoria's expression in the darkness. "And your father? What does he know of these things? These people?"

"Some. Well, really very little. I love him dearly, but I don't believe he would understand. Louis, I was born a Hawaiian princess. Many things, though, that are more Scottish or British crowd in on me. The past few years—since mother—have been bewildering. Finally, for the first time, I've found my Hawaiian nature. Louis, it's been so—so—I can't find a word! *Kupanaha.* Yes, *kupanaha*—surprising! Strange! Extraordinary! Marvelous! But never to be discussed outside the *kapu.*"

"Oh? And the *kapu*—am I within it?"

Victoria's voice surged in the darkness, full and happy: "Oh, Louis. You are on the *sacred* side. With me. Surely, you must already know that!"

Louis felt a rush of warmth in the evening coolness. He formed the word softly: "*Kupanaha?*"

"Yes, *kupanaha*! There is a person very special among the Hawaiians. I'll call him 'Uncle.' He lives among the very poor, although perhaps 'poor' is the wrong word. He's so far from the royal crowd—and that's all you've seen since you arrived. I've spent a great deal of time with Uncle. He's wise beyond all imagining—magical! He's enabled me to feel whole, perhaps for the first time. The child in your poem: Uncle helped me find that deepest self inside me. He put me in touch with the mana within me—you understand? It's a fountain of energy that opens up the world! It sorts all our experiences, our memories and gives them meaning. Louis, you've told me that in far-off Scotland you've been blessed with your little people who give you ideas in your dreams—tell me you understand!"

Louis cleared his throat and chose his words cautiously. "Princess, I come from a family of engineers. I've been trained in the law. I grew up surrounded by every element, every influence possible to negate what you are saying. Even to the belief that such happiness as you describe should not be expected in this life. Why? How should I understand?" Victoria felt her heart sink. "But, I've been poised at death's door so many times.... I can't help seeing things on both sides of that door, not with fear but with wonder. I tried to say something like that in *Sire de Maletroit*. But *kapu*—how sad for such things to remain secret."

"I think Uncle would say that our deepest self is something so personal that no one else could possibly understand. So we live in it quietly once we've discovered it. Within us, he says, we unfold to a superior consciousness, to wisdom and beauty, truth, justice—and humor! Oh, Louis, I have laughed so much with you!"

In the shadows up ahead, Limu guided his horse onto a road leading up the furrowed side of Punchbowl crater. By now they had adapted quite well to the darkness. As they climbed they could distinguish the scattered lights of Honolulu below them; and beyond, the sea and the vast ocean of stars. Now, immediately below they heard the oncoming sound of horsemen, moving swiftly and closing in. Save for the muffled rumble of the horses' hooves, all was remarkably still. Victoria called ahead to Limu, and the three drew off to the edge of the narrow road, out of the way. A uniformed man rode briskly in the lead, with some two dozen riflemen trailing after him. As the horsemen drew alongside, the leader called out a sharp halt, stopped, and studied the trio in the darkness. He recognized the bulky Limu immediately and quickly deduced that the woman on the white horse was Kaiulani.

"Princess! How happy I am that you have joined us!" He moved closer and peered at Louis cautiously. "And this gentleman accompanying you—?"

Victoria's voice was wary, deliberate. "This is Mr. Stevenson—a visitor from England. Louis, this is Robert Wilcox."

"Of course! Stevenson!" Wilcox seized Louis's hand enthusiastically. "How very fortunate, sir! Every report that has come to me affirms that you are a friend of Hawai'i and would defend us in these troubled times." The man's commanding presence intrigued Louis as he acknowledged this charismatic and impetuous rebel, about whom he had already heard so much.

Wilcox signaled his men to continue on, and he himself rode beside Louis. Victoria remained polite but reserved in the presence of this man the Hawaiians referred to as a charming rascal, bold, flamboyant, romantic—very much one of their own.

Wilcox gestured broadly: "Those men riding up ahead—they're my Kamehameha Rifles. Hawaiians! We need them! The Reformers, sir, have a well-drilled army, the Honolulu Rifles. Oh, they deny it, try to stay out of sight, but we know they're plotting. Here tonight, we must be very alert. They plant their spies among us, even for something peaceful. We cannot trust anyone, Stevenson, but your support for our cause is well known." Wilcox's voice rose eloquently as he waved a gloved fist. "Tonight is a peaceful remembrance—but soon we will clash! And then power will be restored!" He waved his fist and thumped it forcefully against the saddle. "Restored, sir! To a new monarch!"

Nonplused by these words, Louis looked questioningly to Victoria. She spoke sharply: "Robert! You said this was to be a peaceful remembrance. Kindly keep it that way!"

The towering rim of the crater loomed before them. Victoria leaned toward Louis and spoke softly. "Louis, the passage across the crater rim through the rock wall ahead—it's the door I spoke of. Into something very different. Stay close to me."

The night air over Punchbowl had a crispness that set Louis on edge. The misty wind blowing down off the palisades rustled in bleary groups of ironwoods and *keawe*. Thin clouds moved swiftly overhead—softening, hiding, then revealing the stars in sudden brilliance. The horses wound single file through a narrow passage that twisted suddenly down onto a level, grass-covered, brightly lit area.

Leaving the stillness of the trail, a surprised Louis found a multitude of people gathered quietly in a circle enclosed by flaming torches. As his group entered, a ceremony was beginning with the hushed sound of drums and soft chanting. Louis, Victoria, and Limu tethered their horses in a grove of *keawe*. Taking Louis's hand, Victoria led him into the circle and approached a woman in native dress, seated on a raised platform. Beside her, attendants held tall *kahilis*, symbols of her royalty. Victoria knelt ceremoniously, and an austere Princess Lili'uokalani admitted Louis gravely and motioned him and his companions to join the circle. They walked about the circle, Victoria displaying Louis, extending her arms in a greeting of friendliness to all, signaling the importance of the slender man who accompanied her.

Settled among the others, Victoria whispered to Louis: "Robert Wilcox—he's a very angry man. He hates Papa Moi. I know he's trying to turn Aunt Lydia against him. Aunt Lydia—I don't know why—lets him stay in her home in Palama. I wonder. I don't like it! Wilcox has a grudge. He thinks Papa Moi sent him to military school in Italy to get him out of the way. Perhaps that's true. He's such a hothead. Be careful with him. He has a tremendous appeal with the people. His mother was a Chiefess on Maui. They think of him almost like the demi-god Maui."

Louis glanced back at the riflemen ranged in the shadows outside the circle and smiled to himself: Wilcox was his kind of man of action. Softly, in Victoria's ear, he said: "You know, I can't help but like him! Right or wrong, Victoria, Hawai'i is ripe for people like Wilcox. This political scene beckons someone like him."

"He's so fiery, Louis. He frightens me. Yes, he makes the people feel strong—and hopeful. He claims Papa Moi broke up his marriage. When he was forced home from Italy by the Reformers, he said Papa Moi ignored him, didn't make him Commander of the Royal Guard as he'd promised. I don't know how much is true. Papa Moi wouldn't have had the power to appoint him then, even if he'd wanted to. They say Robert's wife—she was an Italian countess—thought he was royalty. I guess having a Chiefess for a mother doesn't count in Europe. Anyway, she left him and went back to Italy. Poor thing. They say he's brokenhearted. He wants to be a hero like the revolutionists in Europe. He hates America. He rants about how they practice race hatred, slavery, lynch law. He makes passionate speeches in the legislature. He says America is filled with crime and corruption and hatred of aristocracy."

The rhythm of the drums gradually intensified above their whispering. The chanting had now become plaintive, insistent. From the shadows, several dancers in native costume appeared, swaying slowly, the movements of their bodies conveying a graceful message. Louis studied them intently for clues. In the glow of the torches, the dancers' faces were reflective, deliberate. Victoria rose, shed her outer garments, and drifted slowly into the group, swaying gracefully, gesturing in rhythm with the drums. To Louis the hula seemed to express peace and aloha, but something ominous as well. The drumbeat grew more assertive, as though proclaiming a mighty event about to occur.

Chain-smoker that he was, Louis could sit passively no longer. He rose quietly and drifted back out of the circle, lit a cigarette, and looked for Robert Wilcox. The latter, standing with a group of riflemen among the tethered horses, called to him: "Stevenson! Over here!" Louis shared his cigarettes with the Rifles and looked for an opening to talk with Wilcox. They were all well briefed about Louis and eager to talk, especially Robert.

Wilcox gestured with his lighted cigarette: "Can you guess what you are seeing?" Louis smiled and threw up his hands in a helpless gesture. Wilcox continued: "In the indefinite long ago, Kakei was the *moi*, the high ruling chief of Oahu. He was brave and enterprising, and he had gathered about him all the restless young chiefs of the districts. Kakei set them a challenge—an expedition of conquest—and sent them off to their districts to make elaborate preparations—for what, he didn't tell them. They understood there would be a voyage, a battle, great victories, and spoils."

As Wilcox spoke, the rhythm of the dance became agitated and excited. New dancers, warriors, entered the hula. Louis recognized the commanding figure of Kalamake. The drums beat powerfully, and the chanting was shrill and imperious.

"Then one evening, Kakei's great flotilla was launched, the sails set, the young chiefs brilliant in their bright red and yellow war capes, hideous with their war masks. The winds of the seas and the strong arms of the oarsmen vied with each other in hastening the fleet toward—as it turned out—the island of Kauai." The Rifles followed Wilcox intently as he recited the ancient legend. Louis, enraptured by the drama of this scene, harmonized the dancers' movements with the images evoked by Wilcox's words.

"At dawn the army assaulted the village of Waimea. The battle was short and decisive. Very rapidly many people were killed. The thatched houses were set on fire, and great destruction was wrought. Kakei ordered his warriors to seize the canoes and the women and children and whatever plunder in calabashes, mats, *kapa* cloth, stone implements and feather cloaks could be had. They filled their canoes and safely returned to Oahu."

The hula had become frenetic, depicting the scene of combat, death, and burning, and the kidnapping of the families. As Victoria glided among the dancers, she began now to fulfill an Olympian role of overseeing, witnessing the tragic event, comforting, directing, reassuring in the midst of the battle and destruction.

"At home now, Kakei saw the beach covered with his new riches and the captive women and children. He ordered a great feast on the slopes of Punchbowl. Kakei and his victorious warriors gathered around the *poi*-bowl, while the hula girls danced most joyously before them." Wilcox paused, stepped forward to face Louis and the riflemen, and gestured dramatically: "Suddenly, the earth shook under them, the *poi*-bowls rocked as if tossed on the waters of the sea, the feast that had been spread before them moved from place to place as if made of things of life. The rocky cliffs of Punchbowl began to separate and come crashing down the hillside in great masses. The people fled in every direction, leaving a part of their number crushed under the falling stones."

Wilcox pointed to the dancers, who, in rhythm to the thunder of the drums and the piercing shrill of the chanting, depicted the disastrous scene. "Then came another mighty earthquake. The side of Punchbowl opened, and a flood of lava poured out, mixed with clouds of steam and foul gases. Down poured the fire over the place where the feast was spread on the luʻau mats. The feast became the food of the fire-goddess. Then a wonderful thing appeared above the flowing lava!"

Their narrator paused abruptly, hands clenched tightly together. His eyes peered intently toward the torchlit circle and the frenzied dancers. Above them, on top of a crown of perpendicular rock, the night air suddenly burst into flame. A dazzling, wrathful torrent of fire poured forth like a waterfall down the face of the pile. The swift flow struck the crater floor, sending up clouds that hovered over the dancers and drifted among the torches. Abruptly, the dancers vanished. Out of the swirling cloud, a new group emerged in a solemn and stately rhythm.

"The *aumakuas* of Kauai appeared. Back and forth they moved to the rhythm of steady peals of erupting gases. The clouds swayed to and fro, while the ghosts moved back and forth among them. The spirits of the ancestors had come to protect the women and children. It was the ceremonial, sacred dance of the spirits, to be followed by swift punishment of those who had brought such great injury to Kauai. While the ghosts continued their awful dance, the terrified king and his warriors hastily prepared a propitiation. The captured women and children were called to the beach. All the plunder brought from Waimea was hastily collected and placed in the hands of the captives. The *kahunas*, the priests of the king, were sent to the slope above Punchbowl to cry out to the *aumakuas* that all the reparation possible would be made at once."

Louis recognized Victoria's slender figure leading forth the captive group of dancers, in rhythmic fury reprimanding the terrified warriors as they placed the captives and their goods in the canoes and started back to Kauai.

Wilcox turned to Louis gravely, gesturing to include his men: "And thus, sir, have you seen a re-enactment of the ghost dance on Punchbowl. As the canoes with their captives and goods passed out of sight on their way to Kauai, the earthquakes ceased. No longer was there the thunder of imprisoned gases leaping to liberty. The fires died away, and the flood of lava cooled. The *aumakuas* had accepted the offered repentance of the king and his warriors. And it is said that the fire never again returned to the crater or to the island of Oahu." Wilcox looked about at his riflemen, then returned his gaze to Louis. "What does this teach us? The ground upon which we stand in these islands, in the midst of this vast ocean, has its own wisdom, its own sense of justice. It will defend those who love this land."

Meditatively, Wilcox and his riflemen drifted into the gathering within the torchlit circle now swelled by the dancers and performers. The drums were soft and set a slow, graceful rhythm. Victoria appeared beside Louis and searched his face, her eyes glowing. She took his hand, and Louis found Kumulipa also beside him, joining him to others in the circle. Princess Lili'uokalani looked to those about her in the circle and began to sing. Quickly the others joined her, singing in Hawaiian, a melody unfamiliar to Louis. They sang with profound feeling, at times seeming bitter. Yet the melody that emerged was light, even lighthearted.

One by one the torches died out—all but one that was prominently situated beside Lili'uokalani. As the light faded, the people moved off and began to leave the crater, singing softly under the stars as they wound their way through the steep crater rim and down the slope of Punchbowl toward the city.

Victoria broke their thoughtful silence. "The song we were singing—it's the 'Stone Eating Song,' a patriot's song. It refers to a time when Kamehameha the First and his warriors were on windward Oahu and ran out of food. There's a place in Kailua called Kawai Nui. One can gather mud there—*lepo'ae'ae*—it's edible, and it sustained them. The song is about the mystery, spirit, and power of the land. Even in the blackest night, if we love the land we stand firm. It protects us, even transforms us."

As they reached the foothill, Victoria and Louis found Robert Wilcox and his riflemen waiting for them. Silently, the group ranged themselves as an escort and they made their way into the center of Honolulu. It was quite clear that Wilcox had much more to say to Stevenson, despite Victoria's coolness. He expounded on the faults of the new reform constitution, which excluded most of the native Hawaiians from voting rights. He was furious about Pearl Harbor and taunted Victoria, "Princess, admit it. If Lili'uokalani had been here, instead of away in England, she would never have allowed her brother to sign away our land."

Victoria flared at his treatment of Papa Moi. "Robert, you don't know what you're talking about. The King has done everything he could think of to make us feel proud to be Hawaiians. He has blocked the Reformers at every step, but he can't do it all by himself. The Chiefs have failed him—and so do you, with such talk!"

They were coming under the street lights on Fort Street. Wilcox cut a dashing figure as he sat astride his horse in his Garibaldi uniform with its gold epaulets. Victoria continued vehemently: "You come back from Europe and talk of revolutionary overthrow! And with *what* will you replace the meager foothold the Hawaiians have now? You should have spent more time in England, where a monarch and her people reign together. What are you doing to help that cause?"

Louis rode silently beside the two articulate, forceful young people. In his mind's eye, he pictured Kalakaua on the day of that long, oppressive session when he had yielded power under a new constitution. Was there no middle ground? Had the world grown too small to accept the uniqueness of Hawai'i, whatever her form of government?

Wilcox was undeterred. "We are doing a great deal, Princess. Our committee is about to petition the King for a new constitutional convention. We're not going to be ravished by that milk-sucking dog, Thurston. We'll get the vote for the Hawaiians—just what the reformers don't want. They'd like to see us merely 'annexed' to America. If Hawai'i were a State, it would mean equal rights for us *kanakas*. The Reformers would never tolerate that."

Victoria, regarding their mounted escort, bristled: "I think you provoke armed warfare! Surely you can't think you would win? And now you try to involve my dear friend, Mr. Stevenson!"

"Mr. Stevenson well knows that he's already involved. His letters in the British press prove that. I caution you, the Reformers are after your scalp, sir! That ruckus on the wharf the day you arrived—what do you think that was all about? A warning, believe me! My Rifles have since been instructed to protect you." Wilcox wheeled his horse, flashed a broad smile, and saluted Victoria. He rode off with a parting: "And you as well, Princess, if we can ride swiftly enough to catch up with you!"

A light, misty rain had begun to drift in from the sea as Victoria, Louis, and Limu turned their horses eastward onto King Street toward Waikiki. Waiting for them in a hack drawn up on Palace Square were Kalamake and Kumulipa.

"Eh, Princess! You and Mr. Stevenson need a ride home. It's so late! We hear Mrs. Stevenson has a search party out looking for you, and if you get home soaking wet, it just be more trouble. Climb in! Limu will take the horses back!"

Louis settled back in the cushions and savored the evening's events. Kumulipa studied him and noted the excitement in Victoria's face. "I think we got you a whole new book tonight, Mr. Stevenson: full of earthquakes, lava flows and—"

"—And edible mud!" Louis said with Puckish delight. "Kalamake, turn the hack around! The Hawaiian Hotel! We're starving!"

◆　◆　◆

The Royal Boathouse

Chapter VI

PLEASURE APPROACHED

The morning flowed like a mountain brook for Victoria, bubbling its merry way down the pali. A warm sun smiled through breeze-rustled fronds of the date palms along Ainahau's main drive. She was approaching the gate astride jaunty Fairy, reining back to allow Limu time to saddle and catch up with her. Then she laid the reins slack upon the horse's neck.

"Fairy, dear, what shall it be today?" The horse looked back at her mistress, confused by the absence of any signal. "Shall we go to Sans Souci? What would you think about Manoa Valley? You decide!"

Fairy's ears flicked backward as Limu approached. She turned toward Diamond Head.

Victoria laughed happily and patted Fairy's neck. "Such a wise pony! You're exactly right! We shall visit the Stevensons and pay a call on poor Louis!"

The night at Punchbowl had set Louis back, triggering a touch of fever and congestion. Dr. Trousseau ordered him to bed for a week to prevent his respiratory symptoms from burgeoning into something more alarming. Victoria kept in touch with the household by telephone. The news was good: the fretful, now recovering Louis was making everyone miserable, agitating to resume his activities. Victoria hadn't talked with Louis (his distaste for telephones was prodigious), but Belle and Fanny pleaded with her to make a distracting visit. Louis had been well enough to add material to *Ballantrae*, and Victoria was eager to hear about it.

Dusty Waikiki Road had somewhat more than its usual number of mule-drawn hacks and barking dogs as Victoria and Limu ambled along under the silvery candlenut trees toward nearby Manuia Lanai.

Limu leaned across to hand Victoria a letter.

"Please, Miss Victoria, this from my mother. You read fo' me?"

Squinting in the flicker of the bright sun, Victoria unfolded the pages and narrated for Limu his mother's account of life at the leper colony. In the process, reaching over and pointing out words, she fashioned a reading lesson for him. Limu had been waiting several months for permission to visit his parents, thus far to no avail.

"But, you know," Victoria said, "Mr. Stevenson plans a trip to Molokai soon. He'll visit your mother and father and take things to them. Perhaps he hasn't mentioned it. He has to get permission, too. He wouldn't want to disappoint you."

"*Mahalo*, Miss Victoria. I go too, mebbe?"

"Dr. Trousseau is afraid of any more exposure for you. He thinks you are fine now, but he wants to keep checking you for awhile. Sorry, Limu."

"You think safe Mr. Stevenson go there?

Victoria frowned, shaking her head slowly. "I doubt we could stop him. I worry. This visit is most important to him. You see, he's suffered so much himself that he feels great pity for the people on Molokai. He was terribly disappointed that Father Damien died before he could visit him. I do hope it will be safe. Uncle says it will be all right."

They turned in toward the beach and Manuia Lanai. Limu held the horses while Victoria called out and went inside. Fanny and Belle, delighted with her visit, emerged blinking from the dark room where they were fussing with a stereopticon, reviewing pictures for a lecture at one of the women's clubs. Louis was sequestered in an adjoining wooden bungalow, coerced by Dr. Trousseau's orders to avoid any opportunistic germs. But he was well within earshot, and bellowed out a beleaguered greeting.

Victoria positioned herself where Louis could hear and announced that the Cleghorns of Ainahau requested the honor of their presence at a Scottish-Hawaiian dinner party. She promised there would be delicious *kaukau*. Victoria's presence had drawn the rest of the family—Maggie and Lloyd—from their various activities. They all embarked upon an animated visit, interrupted frequently and vigorously by blustering protests from the prisoner in the bungalow. At last, with a long-suffering sigh, Fanny took

Victoria by the hand, led her over to Louis's quarters, and presented her with mock ceremony.

Louis sat propped up in bed in rumpled striped pajamas, his hair
in disarray. A corner of mosquito netting drooped over his brow, and
a copy book was on his knees. He looked up in joyful relief, the tyran-
ny of his confinement visibly easing away.

"Thank God! Here's a princess to ransom me out of this brig!
Fanny, did you tell Victoria about the Lords Durrisdeer?"

"Dear Louis, I've saved that for you."

Long saturated with the *Ballantrae* novel, Fanny smiled dolefully
at Victoria. Moving toward the door, she reflected momentarily upon
the change in Louis's mood, directed a swift appraising glance at
Victoria, hesitated, and then quickly departed.

"Well, my lady! You'll never suppose what I've done! It's finished!
The two lords—guess what? I did them both in. I drove one crazy and
let the other one freeze to death. Tidy! Much as they hated each other,
I even deposited them in the same burial plot. Merciful heaven! Never
again for any serialized novels!"

"And what about Alison, that faltering little wife? And Mackellar,
your narrator?"

"Mackellar! Thank God I don't have to speak in his slavish tongue
any more. I abandoned him in New York. Alison—I don't even
remember. Who cares?"

"Alison and Modestine—both donkeys! Really, Louis! What
next?"

"Next is Scottish *kaukau* at the Cleghorns!" Louis smacked his
lips. "I presume the dinner will feature the procession of the *haggis?*"

"Ah! You'll see! Don't forget your flageolet and tell the family to
bring all of their musical instruments."

Louis waved expansively, overjoyed to be in circulation again. "I
shall even bring that obstreperous *kelepono* bell!"

◆ ◆ ◆

The days before the dinner party passed swiftly for Victoria. She
spent many happy hours with Louis. Nevertheless, there was a relent-
less backdrop of loneliness and foreboding whenever her thoughts
turned to leaving home. There were ruminations that invaded her

sleep and swirled like a whirlpool about to engulf her. Louis spoke often of England and Scotland in reassuring tones. Victoria listened keenly and asked many questions, but these conversations saddened her. Perhaps Louis couldn't know how aware she was that his own homesickness lurked just under the surface. She loved it when he lapsed into Scottish dialect: his face and entire bearing changed, and he sent her into gales of laughter.

The approaching banquet at Ainahau offered welcome distraction. Victoria had developed into an experienced and skillful hostess in the years after Miriam died, and Archie took delight in her inventiveness. She had a keen eye for detail and an infectious knack for creating enthusiasm among the retainers. Papa Moi and Queen Kapiolani would be there. Also Auntie Lydia—Princess Lili'uokalani—and husband John Owen Dominis. And, of course, typical of Victoria, there would be surprises.

Sunday afternoon arrived enjoyably cool. Trade winds lofting over the palisades comfortably balanced the bright sun. Showers dispersing over distant Manoa Valley yielded rainbow after glistening rainbow. The Ainahau garden ruffled pleasantly, bowing to the banyan landmark standing cathedral-like before the lustrous blue sea. Victoria and Archie attended church at Kawaiahao. Aunt Lydia played the organ that day. The music was buoyant, surging with power. The sermon paralleled thoughts Victoria had expressed to Uncle with growing urgency. The minister spoke of those who wait upon the Lord: they would renew their strength; they would mount up on wings like eagles. The Bible said this came through the holy spirit; Victoria and Uncle called it *mana*. She saw little conflict between these Biblical teachings and Uncle's penetrating insights. Uncle would smile reassuringly and remind her that mana was everywhere, but people didn't see it. Since Louis's arrival, Victoria had experienced it in brief, exciting bursts, but how to direct it? These were the burning questions she pressed upon her Wise One. How to break the bonds, to mount up on wings? Uncle said she would discover the way, that one day she would find it within herself. That morning in church, she wished so much that Louis could have been there beside her.

◆ ◆ ◆

Louis could hardly have been further from a church pew that morning. Fanny brought the king's chamberlain to his bedroom-shack, just as he was putting pen to paper, going through the initial motions of a creative whirl. The King had a different whirl in mind for his Scottish friend. Louis was expected at the Royal Boathouse!

Fanny looked uncertainly at Louis, then at the chamberlain, and shrugged her shoulders with a grimace. Louis was speedily out of bed, throwing on his clothes. He sighed, stifled his excitement, and gave Fanny a meek smile. "Well—it must be something very important." He turned to the chamberlain, as he pulled on his shoes. "Did his majesty say? Was it anything very serious?"

The chamberlain smiled, gestured for Louis to hurry, and gave Fanny an apologetic but reassuring glance. "His majesty just said, 'Have Mr. Stevenson come. Straight away!'"

From the doorway, Fanny paused and assumed a posture of wariness. "The Royal Boathouse? On Sunday morning? Some affair of state that will be! Well, just remember that his royal highness—and you, Louis Stevenson—are expected at the Cleghorn's at five o'clock this afternoon!"

Clutching his straw hat and fumbling with his shirt, Louis hurried out to the royal coach. With the crack of the coachman's whip, he and the chamberlain sped down Waikiki Road in a swirl of dust, horns honking, trams and riders scattering before them. Louis had not been uninformed about this violation of a quiet Sunday morning. In fact, everything was going pretty much as planned. A regatta would be underway at the harbor, and the king had made it quite clear that an enjoyable time was in store.

In the swell of traffic as they neared the harbor, the chamberlain shouted and honked more vigorously than ever. A surging, colorful crowd, lively and laughing, on foot, horseback, or carriage, cheered the royal coach as it threaded its way toward the waterfront. The Royal Boathouse loomed before them, a huge, multi-storied structure, on pilings in the harbor, extending long boardwalks toward the shore. Flags were beating in the wind, banners were everywhere, and the brassy voice of the Royal Hawaiian Band soared above the clamor of the festive throng.

The king had just arrived, and was standing at the head of the boardwalk, laughing and joking with the crowd. He waved a greeting

King David Kalakaua and Robert Louis Stevenson

to Louis, coaxed him impatiently up the ramp, and, because it was too noisy for speech, raised Louis's arm in introduction to the crowd. Then they made a hasty rush down the long ramp and up the stairs, with the chamberlain running interference.

A large gathering—all male, Louis noted—was milling about. Several bars were briskly employed. Huge punchbowls, well patronized, adorned tables groaning with food. The deck resounded with boisterous shouting, exchanging of bets, and loud toasts to the Hawaiian rowing crew. For Louis it was a spectacle that was well worth the sacrifice of an inspired day of writing.

Kalakaua and Louis followed their ushers to the royal dais overlooking the racecourse. As they took their seats, champagne glasses instantly materialized from waiting servants. Louis reached across and, clinking glasses, observed that he and the king each had an assigned servant, standing attentively nearby with a full bottle at the ready. Kalakaua stood for a moment and waved to the crowd as the band gave him a musical salute.

Sitting down, Kalakaua held out his hand. An attendant quickly furnished field glasses. "Now, Louis, you've got to see this. This is the big race of the year. You know, I told you—we've got the best rowing crew in the Pacific. Ha! What a bunch! Can you make them out? The boys with the striped shirts? Third boat from shore? Two American ships think they can beat us. Ha! Challenged us! The *Tuscarora* and the *Portsmouth*. I don't know which is which. They're out there getting lined up. A British crew from the *Tenedos* is out there, too. I think there's also a crew from Spain. Anyway, it doesn't matter. We just passed the word around that we'd take on all comers!"

There was a thunderous cannon boom, a crescendo of boat whistles, and cries from the audience. The boats in the distance were underway, the water thrashing about their frantic oars as they vied desperately for the lead. The course was a measured mile, and with each stroke of oars, the excitement grew. The railing shook with spectators, all of one voice, speeding the Hawaiian crew.

Kalakaua sat quietly, self-assured amid the pandemonium, following the race through his field glasses. "Watch, now," he instructed Louis. "They'll hold back a bit at the start—let the others get overconfident. Then you'll see—about mid-course—*there*! Now they're *really* pulling!"

Indeed, the Hawaiian boat seemed to rise out of the water, pull abreast of the leaders, and lunge powerfully toward the finish line. Louis and Kalakaua leaped to their feet and pounded the railing, as the Hawaiian boat dispatched its rivals and raced past the finish flag. The crowd went wild with joy. On the landing below, men leaped into the water and swam, waving and shouting with excitement, to congratulate the panting crew.

The hours that followed were a slowly blurring scene for Louis. The glass he clutched from the time of his arrival was never allowed to empty. Well, he sighed, truly, he could tell Fanny he'd had one glass of champagne, and never finished it. Kalakaua beamed like the sun. Mingling joyfully and boisterously, he seemed to be everywhere at once. The crew arrived amid an uproar of acclamation. Hula dancers poured into the ballroom to the wild beating of drums, and the boathouse rocked with revelry and jubilation. In the crowd, Louis recognized Joe Strong, intoxicated with drink and the affections of the pretty hula girl who had drawn him out on the floor. Louis was not neglected, either. In the gathering haze of the afternoon, he danced so much that his legs were numb, and the girls collapsed with laughter at the leaping contortions of his Highland hula.

Here and there were windows of awareness and recognition. Dr. Trousseau appeared at one point, and the two spent a moment on the deck while Louis caught his breath. Trousseau seemed unhappy, restless, quick to refill his glass.

"The race—I hear it was a good one. Such a bad morning at Receiving. Another boatload of lepers will be shipped to Molokai at daybreak. *Mon dieu*! How I hate this! Families wretched with grief— how can one console them?" He scanned the gyrating community of the boathouse, and gulped his cognac. "Well, I suppose I've come to the right place. I wonder how many of these people I'll be seeing off on the ship to Molokai someday?"

Louis tipped his glass to the doctor. "Thank God you can do more for *me*!"

The hula dancers drifted about, their soft, eager eyes ever attentive. Trousseau's mood abruptly lifted. A slender Polynesian, graceful, lusciously scented with *pikake*, joined them. She greeted the doctor with a kiss, and as she embraced him she placed her lei about his neck. Louis watched them, suddenly lonely. They were clearly not strangers, these two. Then again, few were strangers to Trousseau. Still—. The girl was lovely. "What was it about these Polynesians?" Louis mused. He was a wordsmith, but their aura was beyond his description. Before any introductions, the girl reached out and plucked a passing dancer from the milling celebrants. She smiled at the girl, nodded at Louis, and, with a warm "*Aloha*," she drew the doctor away.

The celebration, the dancing, the soaring spirits rolled on, untiring, building unyielding momentum. The rival boat crews, loaded down with cases of whiskey, joined the party. Their elaborate, imaginative excuses for losing the race prompted catcalls and roars of laughter that shook the boathouse. The girl Trousseau's friend had recruited for Louis lingered quietly by his side. She smiled, laughed easily, and met his gaze in a direct, curious manner. Louis expected her to drift away. She didn't.

"I am *Loke*," she said with a shy smile.

"*Loke*—'Rose'—how lovely!" Louis began dredging up words from his newly acquired Hawaiian vocabulary.

The girl's eyes danced with delight. "Yes—Rose! How *'auli'i*! You speak Hawaiian!. You honor us! You are *'a'ala*."

Louis's expression was quizzical. "High rank? Me? Well, hardly!"

Loke was irrepressible. She deftly drew her long, dark locks aside, lifted a rose lei from about her neck and placed it on Louis with a kiss. "High rank? Yes—but *'a'ala* also means—" She paused for accent, "—sweet smelling, fragrant!"

Beneath Loke's lei was a necklace that caught Louis's eye. "What a pretty necklace! *Puka* shells, aren't they?"

Loke looked at him with feigned sadness, and fashioned a melancholy look. "Yes, each shell has a *puka*—a hole in it. Poor little shells! Tossed about in the surf 'til they're worn away. I call this my 'lonely hearts necklace.'" She gave a downcast shrug. "For times when I feel lonely."

Louis cast caution to the winds. "Lonely, Loke? Surely, with all this excitement, all these handsome young sailors—"

She measured Louis with a calculating glance beneath the crinkle of her smile, and gestured disparagingly at the crowd. "This is just an *'aha inu*—drinking party." She fingered the rim of her glass, then looked up at him inquisitively. "Dr. Trousseau told me you are a great *haku mo'olelo*."

"'Great author,'" Louis thought. "Wheels within wheels." He smiled to himself. He ought to know by now, without surprise, these multiple interconnections and roles of the island people. "Oh? You know the good doctor?"

"Indeed, yes. He is my professor—at the Queen's Hospital. I am studying to be a nurse."

Louis tipped his glass to her. "Ah! Dr. Trousseau asked you to look after me? To be my *kahu maʻi?*"

Loke gestured at the boisterous crowd around them, "No! Please! For you? Not a nurse! He said he was afraid you might—" She made a whirlpool motion with her fingers— "*Hoʻopalemo!*"

Louis shook his head, grinning. "I don't *drown* that easily, I assure you, Loke. Instead, how about you *hoʻokipa* me?"

Loke clapped her hands in enthusiasm. "Entertain you? Oh, yes!" She slowly raised her glass to her lips, sipped, and gazed at him appreciatively. Something about his bright, piercing eyes, his manner, his keen attentiveness: "You—if you like—I would even take to *Pali-uli!*"

An avalanche was building inside Louis. The rumbling reverberated from the distant, grimy cobblestones, the black labyrinths and garrets of Edinburgh, resurfacing through time and space. It stunned him. Louis drank in this smiling, provocative beauty who stood shimmering before him. *Pali-uli*—the legendary land of plenty and joy....This maiden indeed knew the way. She induced the image of Victoria. It flowed into and merged with her, staggering Louis's senses.

Loke drew in her breath, grimaced and sighed apologetically. She fumbled for an end to the sudden silence between them. "Forgive me! Sometimes I am very *hawawa!*" Louis was also groping, trying to find a focus.

Loke wriggled and forced a smile. "But, my! How skillful you are with our language! How much Hawaiian have you learned? I know! I shall give you a test!" Loke reached out to an attendant and filled Louis's glass. "Now, then, are you ready? Let's see: what is *hapa haole?*"

Louis grinned, on safer ground, warming to a contest. "Easily answered! Someone who's part-Hawaiian!"

Loke pirouetted before him, her colorful sarong swirling. "Exactly so! Like me—Hawaiian, English, Spanish and Porto Rican! From Laupahoehoe on the Big Island! Did I turn out pretty good?"

Louis bowed and grinned his assent, "You are truly a *pohaku makamae!*"

"A gem? Ah, sir!" The girl was exciting, vibrant. Her giggle was infectious. "Now! Another! Let me think!" She bit her lip and grinned. "What is *hinuhinu?*

Louis shook his head in puzzlement. Loke laughed with pleasure. "That means bright, shiny—like my necklace. Too bad! You missed that one! Now you must empty your glass!"

Louis complied without hesitation. "It's my turn. You, dear miss, are *hone!*"

Loke responded coyly with a sidewise glance. "'Teasing?' Yes, but *hone* also means sweet, and soft. Surely, you meant *that*! You lose again! Drink your champagne." She looked at him boldly, challengingly. "Now, one for you: *hamo!*" The word breathed softly from her lips. She moved close to him, held him by the shoulders, and then stroked his face. "*Hamo*—it means 'I caress you.' It's the very beginning of *hana aloha*—love magic," she whispered. Loke nestled against him, radiating a yielding glow. The warmth of the girl's presence ionized him. Here was *Pali uli....*bursting through his champagne haze. He lost all sense of time.

The blare, the ribaldry of the boathouse, faded, trance-like, into the background. Loke led him away, vaguely conscious. "For a *hiamoe iki*—a little nap," she said. A secluded room, a soft futon, pillow whispers, then Louis's towering sensation of pent-up energy exploding. Emerging at last out of the drowsy flow of images was Loke, leaning over him. "*Hiamoe*," She whispered. "Rest!" She unclasped her necklace and placed it beside him. "To cure the lonely times," she said. "*Mai poina 'oe ia'u.*" Louis sank into deep slumber, suspended, timeless, weightless.

Real time returned with Kalakaua and his chamberlain. They roused Louis, prodding him with strong coffee, convulsing with laughter. Later, he recognized Archie, standing at the doorway, worried, solicitous, looking at his watch.

♦ ♦ ♦

Ainahau, if not Louis, was all in readiness. The Scottish-Hawaiian evening had been prepared down to the last detail. Victoria was incandescent in a flowing ruby gown. Her dark curls were piled high and framed by a wreath of flaming poinciana. Dinner would be served in the spacious Ainahau living room. The *mauka* side of the room flowed onto a broad landing that provided an elegant stage. Victoria had plans for that. Flowers—bursts of orchids, rich and colorful anthuriums—were in abundance on the low dining table. Plumeria garlands festooned the chandeliers, and potted palms brought the garden to the guests.

Soon the carriages arrived. Each lady greeted warmly with a delicious *pikake* lei; each gentleman, with sweetly scented *maile* from the mountain forest. The Stevenson family, reassured by telephone that Louis would meet them, strolled along the beach to Ainahau, arms laden with leis for Victoria and Archie. They knew that champagne would flow in abundance anywhere within the shadow of King David, but brought along a few bottles of Scotch whiskey as an appropriate touch.

Dr. Trousseau arrived a bit late, his carriage bouncing to a stop as he gingerly balanced a basket of eggs brought from his ostrich farm in nearby Kapiolani Park. His ranchers had chased the big birds as far as Waialae Avenue in Kaimuki that afternoon to harvest their feathers, and there was much merriment as he tripped about, distributing a huge bundle among the ladies.

Louis slipped in quietly by a side door, with a barren hope it would seem he'd been there for some time. Confronted by Fanny's prompt inspection, he assumed a weighty expression, brushed his sleeves, and made wry comments about his majesty's affairs of state, and the traffic on Waikiki Road. The grinning Kalakaua brought him a glass of champagne.

Dinner was served at a wide, low, and very long table supplied with cushions for the guests. King Kalakaua and Queen Kapiolani sat at one end. Louis and Maggie, the revered kupuna of the Stevenson clan, sat beside them. The Hawaiian flag, with a red stripe for each island, and a superimposed Union Jack, was draped from the ceiling behind the king. A less substantial table would have sagged in despair beneath the array of serving dishes, calabashes, platters, cups, glasses, and seltzer bottles whose contents were emptied and replaced endlessly during the feast.

The conversation at dinner flowed in high-spirits. Maggie's prim

Victorian widow's cap became a challenge for Lloyd, who insisted on adding a bright ostrich feather as a decorative touch. There were many toasts, much banter, talk of travel, distant lands, the sea, and the Stevensons' perilous cruise.

Louis, emerging from the perils of the day, found some amusing similarities in reflecting on their cruise. "You know, I've had this strong belief that I shall die by drowning." He winked at Kalakaua. "Perhaps, even on land!" He shrugged with a wry smile. "Yet, I love the sea, for all its hazards."

John Dominis, slender, bearded, stolidly sober, nodded and raised his glass to the Stevensons in deference. "I was at the harbor yesterday. Took a ride out to look over the *Casco*. My father was a sea captain, you see. Sailed the world, and what stories he had! But that little *Casco*—the chances you've all taken!

Louis shrugged his shoulders. "It's the highest form of gambling. I love the sea and I always thought I hated gambling. The sea is a world always beautiful; air that's better than wine; always exciting. Surely, there is no better life."

Kalakaua added connivingly, "Well, the *Casco* gave you a bit more than a family cruise on a Sunday afternoon—with some Sunday afternoons excepted, of course!"

Fanny, stifling her irritation at these references to the earlier part of the day, echoed Louis's words. "A positive risk is so—well—wholesome. Much more so than a negative one." She ventured a cool stare down the table toward Louis. "We seem to have built our lives around that. I make the arrangements—most of them, that is," another cool look down the table, "and Louis writes about the consequences."

Maggie joined in harmoniously. "Much as we detest rocking about on the ocean, we do so love the tropic weather, and the island people—"

The dinner party was suddenly punctuated by the shrill skirl of bagpipes. *The Bluebells of Scotland!* From the main entrance, two bagpipers entered in full regalia, escorting two kilted chefs who bore on their shoulders a large koa tray. The haggis: a meaty mound of Scottish lore, the scent wafting memories of Robert the Bruce, and the bloom of heather on the Highlands. Delighted, everyone stood and applauded. Archie, tears in his eyes, offered a toast.

"Your majesty, this is a salute to Scotland, and to you, as well, for

Kalakaua's Racing Crew

our beautiful home in the tropics. You have made so many Scots, no longer shivering in that northern clime, feel very welcome and useful!"

The haggis was sliced, served and disappeared rapidly while the bagpipers continued their concert. With a signaling glance to Fanny, Louis rose and they took their places on either side of Kalakaua.

Louis raised his glass to the king. "Your Royal Highness, this delectable evening with the Cleghorns, the reminders of Scotland, the music, have lofted us to the very stars. Thoughts of such jewels in the Hawaiian sky have brought Fanny and me to a pleasureful presentation."

Louis drew from his pocket a beautiful golden pearl that he held up for all to see. "We have a poem to accompany this jewel of the sea, a humble offering which I know will make the gift even more pleasing by contrast."

Fanny, in thespian tones, recited:

> *"The Silver Ship, my King— that was her name*
> *In the bright islands whence your fathers came—*
> *The Silver Ship, at rest from winds and tides,*
> *Below your palace in your harbor rides:*
> *And the seafarers, sitting safe on shore,*
> *Like eager merchants count their treasures o'er.*
> *One gift they find, one strange and lovely thing,*
> *Now doubly precious since it pleased a king.*
>
> *The right, my liege, is ancient as the lyre*
> *For bards to give to kings what kings admire.*
> *'Tis mine to offer for Apollo's sake;*
> *And since the gift is fitting, yours to take.*
> *To golden hands the golden pearl I bring:*
> *The ocean jewel to the island king."*

Kalakaua rose, beaming with pleasure to accept the Stevensons' gift. "I am very strongly tempted," he looked down at Queen Kapiolani, "and this is after consultation with her highness, to invoke one of my few remaining powers." He pounded his fist into his palm for emphasis. "That would be," and he paused dramatically, "to confine you to our islands forever. Not that you would be our prisoners. You and your family have already made prisoners of us. The beauty of this pearl will always attest to our *aloha*."

"Your majesty," Louis replied, "I would gladly live out my life on your glorious islands—except, as I said, for this premonition that I shall die at sea."

"No more of that, Stevenson. We shall all drink a toast to your long life—on *land!*"

Raising a glass to his own health, Louis winked knowingly at Dr. Trousseau, who was sitting across from him beside Princess Lili'uokalani. The princess was vibrant and startlingly different, Louis thought, from the evening on Punchbowl, when she had seemed otherworldly, in touch with elements so far removed from the tone of this charming evening at Ainahau.

Dinner concluded, Victoria rose, eyes sparkling, and encompassed her guests with a wide and gracious smile. To Louis, she seemed to convey a highly amused manner. Laughingly, she hoped that everyone had enjoyed the Scottish blend of this Hawaiian feast, and that the demands of state functions at the royal boathouse had not dulled anyone's appetite.

"Father and I have chosen this opportunity for a formal welcome to our guests of honor, the Stevenson family. You have become so much a part of us that tonight we shall seal our *aloha* in the most lasting way we know. There is only one thing that will take us deeper into your hearts than any other." Victoria paused, watched their puzzled faces, and laughed. "Surely you know? It's our *music!*" She moved to Princess Lili'uokalani, and placed her hands affectionately on her Aunt's shoulders. "Tonight, you are surrounded by a musical family."

Again, she teased them. "Oh, we know how musical the Stevensons are—Louis with his flageolet, Belle with the piano, Lloyd with the violin. But Hawaiian music is filled with *aloha*. You won't be filled with our *aloha* until you absorb our music. Now, it's Aunt Lydia's turn."

Princess Lili'uokalani rose and saluted the Stevensons with a toast. "*Aloha nui loa!*" She looked at Victoria admiringly. "My niece, as you can see, is a picture simply waiting to be set to music. I must do something about that, Victoria." Animated and colorful in her gestures, Lili'uokalani described the fluidity of the Hawaiian language in a way that was music in itself: "Our lyrics are like a stream wandering down a mountain: a twist here, a pause in a quiet pool, a sharp drop there. Musical anagrams with many meanings! Listen, tonight, to the heart of our Hawai'i."

Lili'uokalani turned to group of smiling faces peering from behind the palms in the mauka hallway. The members of her glee club filed onto the landing. They were an impressive group, the ladies in long white lace holokus, the men, tall and dignified in formal white, scarlet sashes about their waists. All wore garlands of *kukui* nuts. Their songs swept the dinner guests off on a musical tide of rolling swells of the vast Pacific, bathed in its sunny warmth, its blue clouds, its tender breezes.

But even more vibrant was another princess. Louis glanced across the room to Victoria and she turned with a gentle smile of deep reflection and looked directly at him, searching his face. *Olalla!* Again, it hammered upon him! She *was* Olalla. He was transfixed. Her loveliness struck to his heart. They looked deeply into each other. There was no one else—nothing else—there in that long moment. She glowed in the deep shadow of the palms, a jewel of color. Her eyes took hold and clung to him, binding them together like the joining of hands. This moment, drinking each other in, was sacramental, the wedding of souls—all that he desired and had not dared to imagine was united. In the hushed room, the lingering notes of Queen Kapiolani's *Ma Lanai Anu Kamakanai* softly faded away into silence.

> *Place your lei of fragrance round our dreaming,*
> *Dancing breeze, come touch my love and me.*

King Kalakaua rose, leading the applause for the singers, and moved toward the platform. "And now, not to disturb your reverie too much, I shall respond to a request from our little Princess." He held an ukulele up for the guests to see. "When I am alone, this is my comforter. Our hostess has asked me to play my favorite song for you, a song of tribute. *Koni Au!* I love life and, my dear friends, here is the song of the happy life: big, bright, happy! *Aloha!*"

The King positioned the *koa* instrument, tiny against his broad chest, and began to strum a pleasant series of vamping chords. His voice was husky, but true and melodic. He paused to note the expressions of pleasant surprise among the guests. "As Lydia has noted, it isn't possible to put English words to the song, but if we could, this is what we would say:"

> *I have gone and tasted of thee,*
> *Oh cool refreshing water,*

At this, the king laughed, "Or other substances more spirited ..."

> *Thy merits we will ever praise*
> *And of thee our song shall ever be.*

Kalakaua faced the doors leading out past the vine-covered verandah, came to attention, clicked his heels, and raised his glass in a salute: "*Koni Au!*"

With this, there arose from the shadows of the garden a crescendo of rolling drums. Then, in full voice, the Royal Hawaiian Band blared forth with *Koni Au*, the Hawaiian Drinking Song. Electrified by such stirring musical vitality, the guests leaped to their feet, danced, clapped, and waved their arms rhythmically to the exhilarating melody. Victoria spun the Merrie Monarch about and propelled him into the lead of a snake dance. All joined in, dancing gaily through the room, onto the verandah, around the band and back, finally collapsing breathless about the dining table. Louis looked at the king and nodded his head admiringly: "The Merrie Monarch! "

♦   ♦   ♦

Victoria and Archie stood, arm in arm, waving farewell to their departing guests. The carriages wound their way down the torchlit drive, with Bandmaster Berger and his men in the lead. From the colorful bandwagon, the sweet strains of a departing *"Aloha O'e"* welled up softly from the shadows, the melody drifting and riffling among the palms, waning in the distance. Overhead in the night sky, Orion's belt and the Seven Sisters of the Pleiades sparkled and glistened. Victoria snuggled against Archie, her heart bursting with the joy of the evening.

This was not a night to relinquish. Victoria strolled the beach, reviewing each moment, sealing every detail in her memory. Her peacocks accompanied her, curious but hushed, a group of attendants waiting patiently in her service. Sleep would not come easily tonight, and at this moment it was an opponent to resist by any means. Victoria seized upon those delicious seconds when she and Louis had exchanged glances. Volumes of feelings had been exchanged in a flash that took her breath away.

Sitting at the edge of the beach, beneath the blanket of bright stars, she sought calm in the steady rhythm of the surf. The evening had aroused a torrent of passions that erased any sense of time. Indeed, Victoria no longer existed in time as she huddled there in the darkness, hugging her knees, folded in the embrace of a floating sphere of delicate, rhythmic sound,

Slowly, the hum of the sea changed. A sounded intruded—perhaps the cry of a seabird, but different. It ebbed and flowed in the gentle night breeze. Victoria rose and looked into the darkness along the beach. She began to move, hesitantly, listening intently. The sound became an unmistakable melody. She moved toward it with eager steps. Then she gathered up her skirt and ran through the dark until she discerned a figure against the night sky and the blackness of the mountains.

Louis was perched on the prow of an outrigger, pensively playing his flageolet. Exhausted by the day's activities, his thoughts were, if not agreeable, even more resounding than Victoria's. Sleep for him also was out of the question. At the sudden approach of a figure out of the night, he dropped the flageolet, alarmed. Remembrance of the attack at the pier flashed through his mind. But every ounce of his being told him it was Victoria. She called out to him. He recoiled and began to walk hurriedly back toward Manuia Lanai.

"Louis!" Her voice in the distance was urgent, cutting into him. "Louis!" Insistent, closer.

"Louis! Wait. Wait—it's Victoria!"

Louis stopped. His back turned to her.

She caught up with him, breathless, fragrant in the darkness. "Didn't you hear me?" She came in front of him, staring at him wide-eyed. "Are you all right?" Still, he would not meet her gaze. "Louis! You were running away from me! Why?" She took him by the arm, drew him back to the canoe and pushed him down to look at him. Hair blown askew, Louis bent forward, his only response a groan audible above the sea sounds. He remained silent, then, restlessly, he rose and paced, kicking the sand. "I knew I shouldn't have come out here." He turned to her in exasperation, "I should have *known*—surely, you would be here."

Victoria pulled him down beside her, wrapped her arm about his shoulders and drew him to her. "Such unhappiness, Louis! When I feel such joy!" She peered around at him, her fingers on his chin, and turned his face toward her. "But it isn't joy if I can't share it with you. Tonight was magic! That moment when we looked at each other—we were soaring, you and I! I know it!" She gestured upward at the stars. "We were up there—beyond this world together, weren't we?"

Louis straightened, took her hands, kissed them, and held them to his cheeks. "Yes, we *were* soaring together." He hesitated, turned away, his voice husky, studying his words. "I want you to remember this—for always: never have I seen such perfection—such beauty—as I saw in you at that moment—"

"—in *us*, Louis!"

"—In *you*, dear one." Louis rose and moved away from her. Desolate, he looked out into the gloom beyond the surf.

"Victoria, Victoria. In *your* life—in this tormented world, full of imperfect people, where would I fit in?"

Victoria suddenly found herself incensed. "Fit in! Fit in to my life? Where *don't* you fit in?   And *I* in *yours*? Louis! I am—great God in heaven! I am very angry! What's been going on inside you in all the hours we've spent together?"

Louis withered under her blistering attack. "I've been thinking I'm a middle-aged, overburdened, unhealthy wretch—with the emotions of an adolescent! Married—besides!"

Victoria shook her head, bristling. "Poor, dear Louis! Well! That shows you've made some progress, but you miss the point completely! All of that has nothing to do with us!" She whirled upon him. "So! Am I Modestine again? Will you walk off and leave me? Walk out on yourself? Or am I Alison—that you simply forget where you left me? I'll haunt you, Louis! I warn you!'"

"Dear God, Victoria, you already do! Don't look at me like that!"

Victoria slipped down onto the sand and crouched before Louis, the glowing softness of her eyes radiant in his face, searing into his heart. She reached up and brushed back his hair.

"Victoria! What have I done?"

Suddenly she burst into tears, rose and turned away. " I don't know why this is happening!"

Louis rose and went to her, but as he placed his arms about her, she twisted away, her eyes blazing in the night.

"We'd come so far, hadn't we? *Kupanaha.* Remember? Leave me, Louis! Go live in your wasteland! Wander around in your forest! Wallow in your horror stories!"

Louis, utterly bewildered, approached her along a razor's edge, a man staggering under a suit of armor. But Victoria, a torrent of passion, was already moving swiftly away toward Ainahau.

◆ ◆ ◆

Climbing wearily into bed at Ainahau, a desolate Victoria struggled to draw from her memory that moment with Louis at dinner. It was all that was left. Joy, disappointment, outrage, and sleep? How could they possibly intermingle? But at last, the heaviness of a cloud of sheer exhaustion flowed through her bedroom, extinguished the day's activities, and buried her deeply.

Dreams were common companions of sleep for Victoria. She welcomed them, studied them. Under Uncle's tutelage, she used her dreams as a textbook to guide her; to contact and explore her soul. Although her dreams were often vivid, she had never experienced any like the one that visited her that night. Victoria found herself in a large chamber, cold and stern, despite a fire smoldering on the hearth. The floor and walls were naked. Ancient books of all sorts—devotional, historical, scientific—lay about. She sat on an uncushioned chair near a window, overlooking a wild mountainous view to the north. Beside her was a table on which she was writing.... It was so real! A sense of pressure on her fingers as she wrote, the coldness of the room, and the hissing of the fire.... Then a deeper level of sleep intervened and the hours passed peacefully until morning.

A hazy sun peeped over Diamond Head as Victoria awoke. She opened her eyes to a room scented with the evening's flower leis. Palm fronds rustled in the wind outside her window. Her thoughts drifted randomly, slowly converging on the new day. Gently, languorously, she swung her feet onto the floor and wrapped herself in her robe. There was a note—a scrap of paper—lying on the floor at her feet.

Surprised, Victoria picked it up. It contained a poem, written in pencil, *in her own handwriting:*

> *Pleasure approached—with pain and shame,*
> *Grief with a wreath of lilies came.*
> *Pleasure showed the lovely sun!*
> *But grief, with worn hand—pointed on.*

Stunned, Victoria only then recalled her dream. She had written this, surely. But poetry? The phrasing, the words—it could only have been Louis!

Out of last night's turmoil, had they entered the long-sought, overwhelming mystery? Why now, when all seemed lost? Louis had communicated this directly to her, and she had written it down! The dream—the bleak coldness of the chamber made her shudder. 'Pleasure,' 'grief.' Why such words? What did they mean? Those previously impenetrable channels Uncle spoke of: Victoria shook with an excitement that ranged from rapture to dread. Had Louis? Had she? Opened the spirit channel she longed for?

♦   ♦   ♦

Chapter VII

HIBISCUS AND THISTLE

Ballantrae was finally complete! Victoria's vigorous intervention had freed Louis from the onerous snag that had entangled him. The brothers were buried. The tomb at last was closed over the Master's body. His soul, if Louis had given him any, was gone to hell. Louis sighed. The cursed end of the Master had hung over him like the arm of the gallows.

And now? Louis ventured forth as usual on his beach excursions, only to find Victoria away from home. He wasn't the same, approaching Ainahau now with a heavy set of emotions: excitement, caution, then loneliness. From Manuia Lanai, his senses were ever attuned down the beach toward Victoria. His life was a mixture of uneasiness alternating with emptiness.

Surely, Victoria would avoid him. Their good-byes would be soon enough—in two short weeks. Bidding farewell to each other: that was a moment he crowded from his thoughts. He asked himself if, in truth, it was he who was avoiding her—and he knew the answer. After the emotional slashing of the evening at Ainahau, he dove into a frenzy of activity. First, there was Lloyd's project, *The Wrong Box,* which they finished in short order. Louis also consumed hours studying the Hawaiian language with a tutor. Then there were frequent visits with the king and countless champagne parties. In his quieter moments, Louis fired off additional letters to the London *Times,* defending the wobbly Hawaiian attempt to intervene among the three great world powers. His letters cried out for international respect. The royal crowd loved his advocacy of the primacy of the Pacific. Yet always a restlessness, an urgency to be elsewhere, besieged him. He deliberately escaped from a number of social events, while longing for another of Victoria's "ambushes". There had been one visit with Archie and Victoria late one afternoon at Ainahau—brief, superficial, pleasant. There had also been a riotous time aboard Dr. Trousseau's gas launch, an afternoon party cruise chasing whales off Diamond Head. Victoria was gay, lighthearted, and close to him. She touched him a number of times, attentive to his reactions. There was a deliberate, unspoken quality about her that day which Louis found indescribable. He tried to find it reassuring.

◆　◆　◆

Spring was in full regalia in Waikiki. The trade winds were gentle, and the passing storms of winter were now in northern waters. Gay colors mocked the uncompromising march of the days. The aromatic sweetness of plumeria was everywhere. Golden shower trees beamed like sunbursts, plover skittered about the lawns, their hard-edged plumage brightening for the long flight north. The fiery blossoms of the African tulip flared upon the fresh green of the pali. *Lanai-alii,* the "Heavenly Chief" sent its velvety golden blossoms sprawling over shrubs, muting the brilliant sprays of pink, lavender and crimson Bougainvillea. Only the shaggy heads of red poinsettia clung bravely to memories of Christmas and cooler days.

One Friday in April, in a confusion of emotions, Louis boarded the inter-island steamer *W.G. Hall,* bound for the Kona coast. It was a quiet departure, but not without the usual floral leis. One among them was from Victoria, bestowed with a bear hug and a vigorous kiss on both cheeks by Kumulipa. Long-haired Louis boarded the *Hall* barefoot, a blur in the flurry of passengers in his calico shirt, cotton trousers and yachting cap.

This passage to Kona was so different from those long, hungry, January days becalmed off leeward Hawai'i Island. This time he was leaving a humming city, with shops, palaces, tramcars, telephones, and even a railway under construction. He sailed past desolate shores, guided in the night by sea and harbor lights, to be set down at last in a village uninhabited by any white. Ho'okena stood on the same coast that he had wondered at before from the tossing *Casco*—the same coast on which Cook had ended a noble career in tragedy.

The King and Louis's tutor had excited his interest in this district of Kona, one most illustrious in the history of Hawai'i. It was the center of the dominion of the great Kamehameha. There, in an unknown sepulcher, his bones are still hidden. There, too, his reputed treasures lie in one of the thousand caverns of the lava.

The great volcanoes of Hawai'i interested Louis, but he rejected viewing the fiery work of goddess Pele. Instead, he favored a stay among the people of remote Ho'okena. The structure of the island fascinated him, so different from the sparkling beaches and shoreside forests of the typical South Sea island. On Hawai'i Island he would find rude prehistoric structures, black, barren, sloping sheer into the sea. Here would be black mouths of caves, bristling corrugated cliffs, scarcely anywhere a beach, nowhere a harbor.

The coast frowned upon the *Hall* as it drew near under a gigantic cowl of cloud. The island face was one of desolation. By mid-afternoon, in misty rain, the steamer lay to off Ho'okena. Louis boarded a whaleboat brimming with intermingled barrels, passengers, and oarsmen. Rain fell, blotting the somber colors of the scene. The coast rose but a little way, then was intercepted by cloud. There was a deceptive feeling of landing on an isle of some two hundred feet in elevation instead of the true fourteen thousand.

On the shore, under a low cliff, stood a score of houses painted gaudily in green and white, trellised and verandaed, with little gardens. The village was shaded by a grove of coco palms and fruit trees, springing miraculously from bare lava. In front, the population of the neighborhood, sixty to eighty strong, was gathered for the weekly event, the arrival of the steamer. The gathering was augmented by a generous scattering of horses, mules, and donkeys. The green trees, the painted houses, the gay dresses of the women, were in marked contrast to the uncompromising blackness of the lava. The rain, unheeded by the sightseers, blended and beautified the counterpoint.

The whaleboat ran in upon a breaker, and the passengers were deposited on a flat rock, where the next wave submerged them knee-deep. Louis looked up, savored the warm rain, and smiled at being drenched from the heavens above and the sea below. Here he was in this assembly, all decked out with the green garlands of departure. They must look like a shipwrecked picnic.

They picked their way to shore where the ship's purser introduced Louis to his host. Nahinu, a retired judge, also was the storekeeper at

Hoʻokena. He was a cordial man, limited in English but, dressed in pearl-gray tweed, resembling a self-respecting Englishman. Nahinu bustled about the business of organizing his shipments, while Louis inspected the combination store and storage shed that was the focal point and lounging place of Hoʻokena society. There was little notice of him. It was a commentary on the striking changes he had seen in the nineteenth-century Pacific. On other islands he had been the center of attention. Here, no one observed his presence. One hundred and ten years before, the ancestors of these people had looked at Cook and his seamen with admiration and alarm. They had called them gods, even volcanoes. They thought their clothes were loose skin, and their hats amazing portions of their heads. The pockets of these fantastic mariners were a treasure door: they plunged their hands into their bodies and brought forth cutlery, necklaces, cloth, and nails.

Louis's host led him down the shore, through the donkeys and mules, and made him quite comfortable in his home. He found a snug bedroom, a Bible on the table, and portraits of Kamehameha III, Lunalilo, Kalakaua, and even Queen Victoria. With Nahinu's wife, grown daughters, younger children, and good plentiful food, it was a setting that would have been familiar and exemplary in Europe.

That evening, Louis walked along the shore, reflecting on his nearness to sleepy Kealakekua Bay, where Fanny's ancestor, Captain Cook, had been massacred more than a century earlier. He scanned the trim lamp-lit houses that shone quietly, each in its narrow garden. Some ten miles from where he walked, Cook had been adored as a deity. His bones, after he was killed, were cleansed for worship. His entrails, by a grisly twist of fate, had been devoured by wandering children.

The surf surged against the rocky shore in muted sounds and the soft spatter of spray. Louis thought about Victoria, tried to visualize her, the dazzle of her against the lava-strewn darkness of this landscape. In the unfolding nightfall, he passed a wooden house, solitary on a bleak field of lava. A man and a woman sat in the shadows inside, watching him. The silent, somber dwelling was for lepers awaiting shipment to Molokai. Louis shuddered, for a moment grateful that Victoria was not sharing this scene. A chilling gust, dispiriting and penetrating, swept down off the mountain, rustling the vegetation, flattening the crests of the incoming swells. In the stillness of the ebbing surf, the sounds of an engine suddenly gripped Louis, eddying and thundering about his head. Distinct voices intermingled. He stood transfixed in amazement.

Suddenly, Victoria's voice surged out of the clamor, calling: "Louis! Louis!"

Immersed in this cloud of sound, he fought to recapture and assemble the moment, his heart striking like an eight-day clock. Just as abruptly, Victoria's voice, the noise, and the vortex dispersed with the swirling wind. The rude hut and the silent occupants receded into the gloom.

Louis was not a stranger to such experiences, nor did he fear them. In Tahiti, during one of his desperate fevers, a doctor medicated him with coca. For days and nights, his mind journeyed far and wide. He re-experienced friends and places now so distant, and found himself plunged into wild and spectacular storybook settings too plentiful to catalog. At other times, he had sensed the nearness of departed friends. Here in the gathering night, on this sculptured field of barren, undulating lava, were these sounds the agitated, whining spirits of the dead? His thoughts drifted to King Kalakaua, who was perpetually engaged in a treasure hunt. Kalakaua sought the treasure of Kamehameha the Great, guarded somewhere by ghosts and hidden in the caves at Ho'okena. The king had prevailed on Louis to consider this treasure during his visit. It was proceeds from whiskey that Kamehameha had sold to the pirates, which his female chamberlains had buried in the cliffs.

Engrossed, Louis lingered on the furrowed lava, gathering his jacket about him against the cool. At last he turned slowly toward the village. The comforting lights of distant cottages reflected soft disjointed lines upon the black mirror of the Ho'okena shore.

Welcoming the warmth of the Nahinu home, Louis turned in to bed at an early hour. This was the custom of the villagers, who used the sun as their timepiece. The air of mystery about Kona set him on edge—not from fear but a sense of the unexpected. He wriggled into his nightshirt. The leis of early morning had an unsettling funereal quality. He draped them over a chair by the window. The many events of the day preoccupied him, but, too fatigued, he managed only a few notes before the pencil fell from his fingers and his head dropped back on the pillow. As sleep enveloped him, Louis suddenly sat bolt upright.

Again he heard: "Louis!"

Victoria's voice—soft, next to his ear, comforting.

♦　　♦　　♦

In the early morning hours, in the surf-caressed hush of Hoʻokena, a sudden sound like a body crashing to the floor startled Louis from sleep. He opened his eyes in time to see a figure grope for the window sill, clamber out, and disappear. Half-awake, Louis stumbled to the window and peered out into the blackness. Nahinu and the rest of the family, roused by the clamor, flocked into his bedroom. Accustomed to earthquakes, they tried to reassure him, discounting Louis's sighting of an intruder at the window. Louis scanned the room: his leis lay crushed under the chair by the window; his calico shirt was missing! Yet, his billfold and some coins lay undisturbed on the dresser!

The judge in Nahinu was persuaded by the evidence: it appeared someone wanted something personal, not monetary, from Louis. Nahinu apologetically stated what Louis had heard many times before: one needed to know white men well before trusting them, but one need not hesitate to trust Hawaiians. True, they thieved from Cook— but because they believed him to be a god, they sought his mana.

"I think maybe that your answer. Somebody think you special," pronounced Nahinu. "They say you very close to Queen Victoria." Louis managed an ironic smile. "Still, no way to treat guests. We call police!"

That was the end of sleep for that night. At dawn, Louis and Nahinu went off to summon a police officer. They soon discovered that the officer, Kualii by name, already possessed intelligence bearing on the matter.

"Last night, one leper in the house out on the field—he escape. Somebody gave him knife, he cut a hole in the floor and ran off to the mountains. The other, the woman, she scared, she stay."

Kualii turned to Louis to explain. "Lot of lepers stay in the mountains. Bands of ʻem. Their families, friends—they think they help— keep ʻem supplied with food and guns. *Auwe!* Some of ʻem very sick, look terrible, but dangerous! Officer Kalani wounded last month when he try arrest ʻem. It's terrible, Judge! We just try to help ʻem. Not criminals. They get help on Molokai!"

The officer methodically formed a posse, hurried the men through hasty breakfasts of papaya and rice, then led them off on horseback into the mountains. For Louis, in a peak of excitement, the adventure was well worth the price of his shirt.

Nahinu explained to Louis the path they would follow. It led up the steep slope from the seaboard region, called *Ilima* for the flowering shrub, upward to *Apa'a*, named for the wind, to *Ma'u*, the place of the mist. In the massive, shrouded heights beyond, Louis saw *Wao Akua*, the region of the gods and goblins.

As the posse clattered over the lava, the officer ventured another theory to explain the night's event, cautiously echoed and entertained by Nahinu. That had to do with Kaona—after twenty years, still a frightening name on the island. Across the resonant lava slabs, Louis rode close beside Nahinu and Kualii as they recounted that story.

Kaona was a native who had achieved some prominence both in the legislature and as a district judge in Honolulu. He began to have visions during a time when the volcanoes on Hawai'i were erupting and the earth was shaking endlessly—worse than any elder could remember. Believing that the world was coming to an end, Kaona gathered a group of followers at South Kona, set up his own church, and began preaching.

"It was mebbe twenty years ago," said Kualii. "Kaona and his people would come around here wearing their white robes, tell us get ready for the end. Well, there was a missionary church here. Kaona made such a nuisance, the minister and some other white folks had him arrested. They sent him Honolulu, said he was insane, put him in asylum. A few months later he was back here, and the volcanoes they were still going very strong. Kaona was still hearing the voices, said the whole island gonna be swallowed up—except for South Kona! He try lease that land. The owner refuse. That was when the trouble started. Kaona folks wouldn't get off the land. Couple hundred people camped there. So the sheriff here, R.B. Neville, form one big posse to get them out. They got into a brawl, dragged one constable off his horse, and Kaona ordered his head split open with an ax. Then Neville got knocked off his horse. They tied him up and left him. Some time go by, then they beat his brains out with a club and stuck his head on one pole. Well, then Governor Dominis come over from Oahu, and he and Sheriff Coney put together one big force of natives and whites.

They surrounded Kaona's camp, and they arrested him. No resistance that time."

Nahinu shrugged ruefully. "Kaona, he put on one big show at the Hilo Court House—was his own lawyer. But they found him guilty, sentenced him ten years hard labor."

The riders continued through the region of misty rain. Bushes gave way to trees. Pheasants and quail rose in startled flight. Soon they plunged into forest groves where spring growth had silvered the new leaves of the candlenut trees, and bronzed the breadfruit and huge mangos. Officer Kualii resumed the saga of Kaona.

"Kaona—he was a prophet. He look around him and he see time runnin' out for his people. He try for title to only land that'd be left in the world. They say he was madman, and him using the Bible the way he did—that made him dangerous."

Nahinu added, "You see, Mr. Stevenson, some of Kaona's followers, they still around. Word is they be meeting up in the mountains soon. Mebbe the leper took your shirt, but mebbe Kaona folks. Why they want your shirt? Either way, same thing—power for healing, or for talkin' people into doing crazy things."

The officer now was very alert, studying the forest, looking for signs of habitation. It was evident he had made many such forays and knew the likeliest locations. Louis suspected that Kualii knew his destination exactly. Deep in the forest, they came upon a glade and a small stream. The officer spurred his horse into the clearing with loud shouts to announce his coming. A very elderly Hawaiian woman slowly picked her way out of the dense foliage. She had once been tall. Now she stooped and was very heavy, with a face wrinkled with age. She covered herself in a white gown and hood. Louis realized that informers, even in remote Ho'okena, had their place and usefulness.

"*Aloha*, Auntie," said the officer. "You stay good?"

Auntie offered a broad, toothless grin and scrutinized the members of the posse, especially Louis.

"You come buy coffee? Too early—not pick yet," Auntie informed. "Got papaya."

The officer smiled. "No, Auntie. Somethin' else. A man from the leper house in the village escaped. An' someone went steal this *haole* gentleman's shirt last night."

The old woman threw up her hands and cackled in amusement.

"Oh, Offisah! Mo' bettah! We got robes, nice white ones for the gentleman, okay?"

"No, Auntie. No laugh! This man famous Englishman. Write good books. Friend of Queen Victoria. Somebody steal his shirt. An' too, in Honolulu somebody went grab a fistful of his hair! What you know?"

Auntie hobbled lamely over to Louis, eyes squinting in the glare filtering through the trees. She devoted the next few minutes to studying him as everyone waited respectfully.

At last she sighed, crossed her arms on her broad breast, looked at the ground, and twisted about for another penetrating stare. Louis, stifling a grin, spoke in pidgin: "My shirt, no big thing! But why somebody do this? You know, Auntie?"

Auntie smacked her lips and paced about in the circle of riders. She turned again to Louis: "You read Bible?"

"Yes, Auntie. I know it very well."

"What you think happen to Hawai'i?"

"I think you can be very happy here for many years. The volcanoes—they make the island bigger and more beautiful."

Auntie frowned. "But why all this sickness? How we be happy when folks dyin' or bein' shipped from home an' family?"

Louis, the outcast from the lochs, crags, and braes of Scotland, recoiled, stunned.

"I'm afraid I don't know, Auntie. I think God wants us to be well and happy, to treat each other good. He shows our doctors things so they can do His work and cure us."

Auntie turned to the officer and pointed back at Louis: "That man there, he so skinny! How come he got so much *mana*?" Before the officer could answer, she made an imperious gesture. "I get his shirt for him. I send it down to you. No worry." She jerked her head toward the higher slopes. "One leper man, he want it for his girl up there. She very sick since police take him away. He very *kaumaha*—unhappy."

Louis had slipped off his jacket and was peeling off his shirt. "Please, Auntie. Give her this. But ask the man if they will please come back to the village. We want to help. Tell them I will go to Molokai. I will talk to the doctor."

This arrangement was a bit too informal for the officer. "Auntie, you do this? All right? You promise? We don't want no trouble with them! You tell them what Mr. Stevenson here said?"

The old woman surveyed them all slowly, nodded solemnly, watched them as they wheeled their horses to ride away. Louis paused, then brought his horse back: "Auntie!" He took off his cap and fingered the still sensitive back of his scalp. "My hair somebody took— what you think happen to it?"

Auntie looked at him thoughtfully and gathered her robe about her. "You go Molokai, you find! *Aloha!*"

◆　　◆　　◆

The riders turned southward through the tall trees toward the scrubland. They passed an abandoned house standing in a papaya orchard, then skirted the margin of the forest and headed downhill. The vast blue sea below them stretched to infinity. They passed Nahinu's coffee plantation, set among giant tree ferns, then continued on to a village—a Catholic church and several houses, some made of grass. One house in particular caught Louis's eye: two storied, painted white, with double balconies and many windows. Louis found the quality of the house remarkable.

Nahinu shrugged: "Look good on the outside. That the way with the local people—they spend all their money on the outside. Come, we visit. You see. They live on the verandah. No furniture."

The owner made them welcome at the "Great house." On entry, Louis found no chairs or tables, only lithographs of the British royal family decorating the walls. There was also one of General Garfield and, to Louis's amusement, Lord Nelson's portrait from a newspaper supplement. Only mats softened the floors. The setting intrigued Louis. There was a story here; what would a poor Polynesian man do with the power of sudden wealth?

The rest of the way home was downhill along the black lava bordering the sea. They traversed a wasteland of shattered lava twisted into spires and gouged into ravines. Here and there, well-holes hinted at vast subterranean vaults upon which their horses' hooves echoed beneath them. The stone work was fantastically fashioned, intricate in detail, like debris from the workshop of some brutal sculptor: dogs' heads, devils, stone trees, and gargoyles broken in the making by a ferocious artist. Amid this naked, jumbled wreckage, plants found root, rose apples bore their pink flowers, and an occasional bush achieved substantial height.

Armed with instructions from Nahinu and Kualii, Louis took leave of them. He turned his horse northward up the coast along the rude King's Highway toward Pu'uhonua, the City of Refuge. The strong smell of the open ocean and the bursting surges of surf along the rocky coves were a refreshing feast. At length he rounded a point onto a flat of lava that was bordered by an amphitheater of cliffs. The village of Honaunau was scattered under the cliffs within a gaunt, lofty grove of palms. Beyond the surf, near the point, a schooner rode silently at anchor, due soon at Ho'okena to load lepers.

The ruins of the City of Refuge presented to Louis a massive figure of thick walls fashioned of huge, smooth-faced, unmortared stone. It was earthquake-damaged here and there, and rose twelve to fifteen feet. The walls enclosed several acres devoted a century before to *heiaus* or temples. Some were a sanctuary for hunted men. The site contained a series of platforms for hula dancing, wrestling and boxing. There was a temple for storage of the royal bones of the House of Great Chief Keawe. Outside the entrance to Pu'uhonua, Louis found the towering remains of huge carved figures standing guard, frightful, glaring down in grim array. Louis dismounted and entered the sanctuary.

The enclosure was paved with lava. Everywhere tall coco palms jutted from the fissures and drew shadows on the floor. The sea nearby was loud and continuous. The rude monumental ruins, memorials of life and death, threw Louis into a muse. For him, there were places where the past became more vivid than the present and dominated his senses. He had found it so in the vestiges of Rome. Now it was so again in the city of refuge at Honaunau. The perilous existence of the old Hawaiian, the grinning idols of the heiau, the priestly murderers and the fleeing victims—all these rose before him and mastered his imagination.

Louis moved about, deeply absorbed. He found himself close to the towering wall and a low sea rock platform. On the bright horizon, soft, billowing clouds cast their opalescent shadows on the water and framed a woman in a simple lilac dress. She sat on the far ledge, gazing out to sea. A garland of deep red hibiscus encircled the crown of her hair. A covey of doves fed at her feet. Louis moved closer, and she turned toward him, brushing bread crumbs from her fingers. She smiled.

"*Aloha*, Louis!"

Victoria examined him dreamily, then smiled broadly. "You've lost your shirt!"

Louis, dumbstruck, moved away from the sunlight, turned and studied her. At his wits' end, he struggled to compose himself. "My shirt? Ha! Never mind that! It's my mind I think I've lost. My God, Victoria! Is this really you?"

A sly smile curled her lips. There was a brightness in her like a coal of fire.

"Dear Louis. Such surprise! We seem to have a way of startling each other. Well, you see, I'm simply returning a call."

Louis squinted at her cautiously. "Friends?"

"Always. Have I treated you *that* badly?"

"What you did was to someone who belongs to you." Louis's words were mindless, erupting within him like a cooling spring.

Victoria produced a sheet of paper from the folds of her dress and handed it to him. "I'm reciprocating your visit."

Louis studied the paper, showed a faint nod of recognition, and looked at her, puzzled. "Where did you find this? It's something from 'Olalla.' A poem in the story. Something I wrote back at Skerryvore one winter." Again, he looked at her in great perplexity. "This story, practically the whole thing, was given to me by—" He shrugged, embarrassed. "—By my brownies, the little people in my dreams. Where did you find this?"

"That night, after the party at Ainahau. In my sleep—oh, Louis, I went to bed so upset! Somehow I wrote this. It's in my own hand! I knew at once it was from you. I rushed out and found it in Dr. Trousseau's collection. Then I read the story of *Olalla*—for the first time—but never before that night! Am I *Olalla* to you, Louis? Is that who I am to you? You came to me that night. It was you who broke through the barrier. You did something I've been trying so hard to do."

Louis felt a fist grind into his stomach. He sat down quickly beside Victoria, his head in his hands. Slowly he reassembled his thoughts.

"Yes, it was that marvelous moment at the party, Victoria." He sucked in his breath. "You were magical! I looked across the room at you. Do you have even the remotest notion how beautiful you were? No, dearest one, you aren't Olalla. You are much more! Alive, real,

Victoria! But you set off the same soaring emotions in me—God! I sound like the young Commander in the story. It's the way he felt when he first met Olalla."

"But the poem. It's a goodbye poem, Louis, isn't it? Olalla and the Commander, they wanted each other so deeply. She cared for him so much. But in the poem Olalla turned—not to the soldier—but to a life of the spirit. Is that what you wanted to say to me?"

Louis's wits were slowly returning. He rose and paced slowly on the stone pavement.

"Dearest child, you and I are trying to put into words the inexpressible. I can't explain how these words formed in your mind or how they became so real! 'Goodby?' Heaven forbid! And how did we find each other in this bizarre place? What's happening to us on this peaceful afternoon? Are you real? Am I dreaming?" Louis spun about in bewilderment. "Last night, I heard your voice calling to me—several times!"

Victoria clasped her hands and exulted. "You did! Oh, I hoped you did! How wonderful!"

A feeling of agitation was mounting in Louis.

"I've missed you so the past few weeks? I've hardly seen you! You've avoided me!"

"We both needed time to think. I've been with Uncle. His instruction, I think—I hope—it's all finally coming together! You *are* dreaming. We're *both* dreaming—well, sort of, I think. It was you—your poem, especially your feeling—that sent the words and formed them in my mind. You made it all possible." Victoria rose and walked over to Louis, stood close before him, and put her arms on his shoulders. "You see, you're mistaken, Louis. There *are* words for what has happened to us. I can't express them the way Uncle does. But it isn't the words that are vital. It has to do with *mana*—spirit—and *aloha*—love. That was what you were feeling that night across the room. Oh, how wonderful!" She looked up at him with an expression that plunged down into him deeper than any anchor. "Louis, there's a part of the soul—it can picture something, something it wants so very much, and then make it happen. For a long time, I've known that up here." She tapped the dark curls shading her brow, "But finally, with you, Louis, this spirit has come to life! And, please! What about you?"

Louis shook his head quizzically, looking about at the ruins where they stood.

"Dickens said this sort of thing could be due to a fragment of an underdone potato. Look about you, Victoria: this crumbling ruin beside the beautiful sea, the spirits of all kinds surrounding us. Dreaming? But I feel the touch of your hands. And yet I have the feeling that my little people are scurrying about, building this scenario."

Victoria's fingers crawled gently up Louis's cheeks and caressed him affectionately. She made a wry expression and turned away.

"Sometimes you call me 'child.' I've been wanting to tell you how intensely I dislike that."

Louis braced himself for what he thought was coming.

Victoria gestured, drawing his attention to the stone platform on which they had been sitting. "Do you know what this place is?"

Louis studied the palm-shadowed terrace, the exacting design of its borders, the smooth, rounded, sea stone surface. He shook his head.

"This was once Hale o Papa, the women's temple. It was a refuge for my women ancestors at times when their religion required them to avoid men's company. It isn't by chance that I came to you here, Louis. I want you to be certain of two things about me. First, that I am a woman—not a child. The other has to do with another word of Uncle's, *kuleana*—responsibility. I respect your *kuleana*, as I know you do mine. I hoped this old *heiau*—what's left of it—would give me strength. Heaven help me, Louis, because I want you very much!"

Louis took Victoria in his arms, and they sat on the temple terrace looking out to sea. At length he chuckled: "You know, in Tahiti women sometimes claim to have a *kane o ka po*, or a man has a *wahine o ka po*, a spirit lover. These lovers visit each other only at night, and they have great adventures together. What outrageous fun!"

Victoria rose, stood looking down at Louis, and lifted the garland of hibiscus from her hair. She placed it gently on his head and kissed him, first on one cheek, then the other—and disappeared.

"Olalla!" Louis shivered and moved out into the sunlight for warmth. Now she, too, knew the story's ending.

> "*....behold the face of the Man of Sorrows. We are all such as He was—the inheritors of sin; we must all bear and expiate a past which was not ours; there is in all of us—ay, even in me—a sparkle of the divine. Like Him, we must endure for a*

little while, until morning returns, bringing peace. I looked at
the face of the crucifix, and, though I was no friend to images,
an emblem of sad and noble truths; that pleasure is not an
end, but an accident; that pain is the choice of the magnani-
mous; that it is best to suffer all things and do well."

♦   ♦   ♦

Louis wandered aimlessly among the ruins for a time. Then, drawn to the shore, he waded into the ebb and flow of a tide pool. It was cool and fresh, quite real and normal. He removed the hibiscus garland and buried his face in its fragrant coolness. Then his eye caught a silvery sparkle within the clustered blossoms. His fingers shook with excitement as he drew forth a silver talisman from its hiding place among the petals: a gleaming miniature hibiscus blossom— and intertwined with it, a tiny thistle.

Louis sat with the gentle waves lapping over him. Out to sea, beyond the schooner, a sunset was building below delicate pink streaks of cloud.

♦   ♦   ♦

Aboard the steamer once more, Louis mingled among the passengers, blending comfortably into their company. Leaning against the deck rail, he looked fondly at the momentary bustle in Hoʻokena.

He had spent a lovely week among God's best and sweetest works, the Polynesians. He thought of the unrelenting pressure upon him to write. If only he could stay here, he could get his work done and be happy. But the care of a large, costly family mandated his presence in Honolulu, where he always felt out of sorts amid heat, cold, cesspools, and beastly haoles. If only he could live as the only white in a Polynesian village, drink their warm wine of human affection, and enjoy the simple dignity of everything about him.

As the ship set out to sea, Louis looked back at a dreadful scene along the shore: the departure of the lepers, surrounded by wailing loved ones who clung to them, waving their arms, crying out in anguish. The lepers, silent, hidden under their robes, moved slowly toward the waiting whaleboat.

Kalaupapa, Molokai

Chapter VIII

GRAY MOLOKAI

May! Departure time. A shedding of tears. Victoria stood on the deck of the SS *Umatilla*, gazing at her throng of loved ones below along the wharf. She had completed all the good-byes and formalities. In those final days, Victoria had been a frequent sight about Honolulu in the Cleghorn carriage, with its sleek pair of bay horses, the footman standing on a box at the back. Her good-bye to Fairy was unthinkable, but done. Good-byes to Mama and Papa Moi at Iolani Palace, to Aunt Lydia at Washington Place, and to so many others—all seemed imaginary, as did the unreality of distant Britain halfway around the world. Papa Moi had authorized her absence for one year—such a long time!

Biting her lip, Victoria clung to the wooden railing in front of her. As the ship edged away from the wharf, the colorful multitude waved hands and handkerchiefs, calling out blessings and farewells. The sea of loved and familiar faces began to blur as her ship headed into the channel. The Royal Hawaiian band's closing strains of the national anthem, *Hawai'i Ponoi,* wafted unevenly across the water as the *Umatilla* nosed into the first ocean swells. There was a bit of solace for Victoria's oppressive loneliness: Maggie—Mother Stevenson—would be traveling to England with her. Archie would accompany her to San Francisco.

The one good-bye Victoria rejected totally was her parting from Louis. All the Stevensons were at the wharf. Louis wore his velveteen jacket and waved the Stewart tartan to catch her eye. He stood out clearly enough for Victoria to agonize over the strain and seriousness of his expression. Yesterday he had written a poem in her autograph album:

"Forth from her land to mine she goes,
The island maid, the island rose,
Light of heart and bright of face:
The daughter of a double race.
Her islands here, in Southern sun,
Shall mourn their Kaiulani gone,
And I, in her dear banyan shade,
Look vainly for my little maid.

But our Scots islands far away
Shall glitter with unwonted day,
And cast for once their tempests by
To smile in Kaiulani's eye."

"Written in the April of her age; and at Waikiki, within easy walk of Kaiulani's banyan. When she comes to my land and her father's, and the rain beats upon the window (as I fear it will), let her look at this page; it will be like a weed gathered and pressed at home; and she will remember her own islands, and the shadow of the mighty tree; and she will hear the peacocks screaming in the dusk and the wind blowing in the palms; and she will think of her father sitting there alone."—RLS

There had been one private moment during a farewell gathering. Louis was stiff and awkward, very unlike himself. When there was a moment, he had whispered to her: "I hope you liked my poem. I wasn't pleased with it—it's just silly window-dressing." He looked at her with a pleading expression.

"There's so much—so much more."

Quickly she had responded, "It's beautiful, Louis. And did you notice that you called me 'maid'? Not 'child'—I liked that." She looked intensely into his eyes, a quick, piercing keenness: "But, *of course* it's just the beginning. Say you *know* that!"

Louis attempted a smile, and felt himself flow out to her in a happy weakness. It was hard for him to speak. A certain lilt in her voice knocked directly at the door of his deepest tears. But in the midst of the occasion, looking about him, he saw the world like an undesirable desert, duty-bound, like soldiers on a march, and Victoria alone there to offer him some pleasure of his days. Ashamed, and on the verge of tears, he could only nod uncertainly and move away.

♦   ♦   ♦

Louis, hemmed in by the crowd on the wharf, welcomed the noise and confusion to conceal his surging emotions. Victoria was leaving him entangled in unfathomable mystery; neither would ever be the same. She was departing for his homeland. His deepest fear, indeed conviction, was that he would never see Victoria or Scotland again. 'Child-woman'—she was no longer that to him. He loved her and there was no shame in him to admit this. She came between him and the sun. For days the image of Victoria had been mixed in all his meditations. His solitary moments were unbearable without a glint of her in the corner of his mind. He had such a sense of her presence, that he seemed to bear her in his arms. The shattering waves of feeling inside him were the realization that he more than loved her—he was fervently, romantically in love with her. Their first meeting, the hours and days spent together, were stunning in their impact. He remembered as a youth his first awareness of love for a woman, and his search from that time on to find the love of his life. He knew now this unseeing quest never lay outside. Lovers do not finally meet somewhere in the world. They are within each other from the beginning.

Nearby, Fanny and Belle waved to the departing *Umatilla* and talked happily. Louis was never far from Fanny's watchful eye, and he was conscious of an occasional penetrating glance as they stood in the press of the crowd. Louis knew that too much had happened for him to conceal it entirely from Fanny. After all, she was his watch dog, his caretaker. Bless her heart! True, she had a suspicious nature, but that had been a valuable, if not always welcome, protection. Just then she looked across at him and smiled, and he remembered again the deep love, the rich harvest of years of adventure together from the beginning days at Grez. In loving Victoria, he believed he did not love Fanny less. In recent days he'd felt filled with love for Fanny and all the world. Why, then, did he wage this struggle with guilt? Guilt couldn't describe it. Why did he feel such remorse? What *had* happened to him?

In whatever scheme life had in store, Louis had stepped through a door into a vast new dimension that made the little people of his dreams insignificant. He'd been thinking much more about God than he had in those early irreverent, rebellious days. He needed approval, affirmation for what he was feeling. God could be real, meaningful to him, if He were a loving God. If so, wasn't loving a part of God's will? An energy to be shared? How much shared? Where did it lead? Louis was in that state of subjection to the thought of Victoria that it mattered not what he did, nor scarce whether he was in her presence or out of it. He had caught her like some noble fever that lived continually in his bosom, by night and by day, and whether he was waking or asleep. If one's state of mind were loving, how could one inflict or suffer such pain?

◆　◆　◆

The Royal Hawaiian band, drums rattling, swung into formation and marched up Hotel Street. The crowd slowly dispersed, saddened by the departure of their beloved Princess. *Umatilla* reached the lighthouse, cutting through the turquoise water inside the reef, reaching toward the deep blue of the outer ocean. Louis, lost in turbulent thought, suddenly found himself standing alone at the edge of the wharf. He turned back toward Fanny and Belle, shook his head with a wry smile, slung the tartan over his shoulder, and shrugged a dramatic gesture of despair.

◆　◆　◆

Molokai akina — gray Molokai — had long beckoned Louis. With Victoria departed, that island of banished souls seemed designed for Louis's mood. Leprosy: scientists had isolated a bacterium named *Mycobacterium leprae*, first cousin to Louis's own affliction, *Mycobacterium tuberculosis*. This was the bond to Molokai. Louis at Ho'okena had been painfully quick to identify himself with the leper. On May 21 he departed Honolulu aboard *Kilauea Hou* in the care of Captain Cameron and Purser Mr. Gilfillan. The latter was a lowland Scot whose seaman's expressions, amusingly nostalgic to Louis, embarrassed two Franciscan sisters bound for Molokai to join the ministry of Mother Marianne. Their fellow passengers on the steamer included a dozen patients, one a poor child in horrid condition, and a

Caucasian man who left behind a large grown family in Honolulu.

Louis brought aboard with him the same muddled, far from diminishing feelings that swirled in the wake of Victoria's sailing. Hunger and emptiness had stalked him in recent weeks. Now he felt a painful, gnawing, physical longing. It recalled the strenuous days in Tahiti when he was recovering from a fever. He had gone through a weaning process from the doctor's coca medication. That had been a bodily upheaval, but without any admixture of this persistent sense of penitence. Why this? He had felt love, and he had unselfishly shared an enriching, fulfilling experience. Evil! That frightening thought kept surfacing. The ship's disfigured passengers permeated Louis, surrounded him with an inexpressible cloud, powerful, uncontrolled, threatening, demonic. He *felt* like a leper.

Victoria's talisman was Louis's one comfort. He guarded it, revealed it to no one. It was at the heart of the mystery. It was real; he fingered it constantly, and at times, he allowed himself to return to the reverie of Honaunau and Victoria. His fingers burned. Was that guilt? Evil? Memory of a verse from the past kept intruding:

"That rare and fair romantic strain
That whoso hears must hear again."

Louis, his stomach grinding, retreated heavily to the palpable, to the discipline that enabled him to trudge through the tedium of law school. It wasn't enough. He felt himself teetering on the edge, losing control, looking at insanity.

Aboard the little steamer that night, rest was impossible. The churning in Louis's mind resonated with the nuns in the neighboring cabin, seasick from the heavy rolling of the ship. By first light Louis was on deck. *Kilauea Hou* was wallowing under stupendous cliffs, as far as the eye could see along the windward north coast of Molokai. At dawn a tiny, bare tongue of land came into view, a harsh stony shelf extending seaward from the gloomy, abrupt cliffs. This was the "leaf of land", the four square mile Kalaupapa peninsula, trifled in between cliff and ocean, now lying athwart a hazy rising sun. The shelf of Kalaupapa formed long after the main mountains of Molokai. A small volcano, *Kauhako*, erupted from the cliff side and spewed its lava to form this plain. The remnant of its crater was visible through the morning haze, a minor swelling upon the flush landscape. Kauhako, by legend, had a bottomless lake within its crater that connected to the sea. Some of the deepest soundings in the Pacific fell away beneath them. To Louis, the peninsula seemed a mere buttress in air and water of the vast cathedral front of the island.

While on Oahu, Louis had inquired extensively about the history of the lazaretto. Molokai teemed with healthy Hawaiians in ancient times as evidenced by the remnants of heiaus and hundreds of acres of terraces for taro cultivation. By the mid-nineteenth century, Liholiho, Kamehameha IV, and brother Lot, Kamehameha V became greatly alarmed by the spread of leprosy. On Maui, in 1845, a high chief and his cohorts were the first to fall victims. In January 1865, Kamehameha V signed a segregation act. In succeeding years a receiving hospital was built in lower Kalihi on Oahu. Segregation of lepers to Kalaupapa began soon after. The government administration, confused in the management of this complex medical problem, was unprepared, and handled matters in a blundering fashion.

Lepers were expected to be self-supporting. Local Molokai farmers agreed to sell their land, but the government dallied for months. Houses were not maintained, the fields went untilled. The setting deteriorated badly by the time the "clean" inhabitants departed. The first shipment of lepers landed without food or money, to find roofs fallen from the houses, and taro rotting in the ground.

They were deposited on the peninsula, strangers to each other, victims of a shared calamity, disfigured, mortally sick, and banished without sin from home and friends. To Louis, it seemed that in the chronicle of man, there had been no more melancholy landing than this: the leper immigrants among the ruined houses and dead harvests of Molokai.

The first outcasts divided the bleak territory among themselves. They went to work repairing and farming, and industry began to revive. Then came a second and a third deportation. Sharing and subdividing broke down. The first two companies showed promise of subsisting on their farms, but the third, and all others afterward, became paupers fed by the government. A swift process of decivilization set in: cards, dancing and debauch. Women served as prostitutes, children as drudges, the dying were callously uncared for. Heathenism revived, okolehau [potato liquor] was brewed. In their orgies, the disfigured sick ran naked by the sea. Curiously, there was a general lack of crime. Disputes centered on food, for example a meat-rationing squabble. There had been but one chief luna from the first, a Mr. Meyer, who was more of a visiting inspector since he lived at the top of the pali and visited only at intervals or in emergency. Louis learned of ten sublunas—lepers—who had "governed" over the preceding 20 years. Some disputes had a comic opera touch with rumbles of threatened violence, then peaceful resolution.

Joseph DeVeuster, Father Damien, arrived in May 1873. Louis had keenly anticipated visiting Father Damien, only to be cheated by his death five weeks earlier on the first Monday of Holy Week. Damien brought a unique array of energetic talents to his chosen life's work. He was a natural leader, an organizer of choirs and sports, a nurse to the afflicted. He spoke Hawaiian, ate and drank from common receptacles with his parishioners, and—sealing his fate—in all ways avoided shunning them. He was a skilled carpenter who could lay water pipes, build churches as well as coffins, console the dying, and preside over their burial. Father Damien recruited and organized the kokuas, the healthy helpers, the working bees of the sad hive, the laborers, butchers, storekeepers, nurses and gravediggers. Damien was also a stubborn thorn in the side of the government, and a perennial pest pleading for better care. With an inward sharing of his own dark side, Louis heard fully of Damien, whose weaknesses and worse made him admire him even more. This was a European peasant: dirty, bigoted, untruthful, unwise, tricky, but superb with generosity, residual candor and fundamental good humor: convince him he had done wrong, which might take hours of insult, and he would undo what he had done and like his corrector better. To Louis, he was a man, with all the grime and paltriness of mankind, but a saint and hero all the more.

Kilauea Hou was now off-shore in the lee of Kalaupapa and ready to discharge its human cargo. The first whaleboat bore the dozen patients ashore, and Louis and the two nuns followed. As they approached the rocky shoreline and the landing stairs, Louis came face-to-face with the legion of the lazaretto.

Here was a throng of the dishonored images of God, a population of gorgons, fantastic and monstrous. Horror and cowardice worked in the marrow of Louis's bones to witness this great crowd. They were pantomime masks by the hundreds, in poor human flesh, waiting to receive the sisters and the new patients.

Louis had protective gloves for this visit, but decided not to extend his hand—that seemed less offensive than gloves. A sense of embarrassment stunned him, to be there among this multitude of the suffering. In his thoughts of Damien and his own trivial preoccupation, Louis condemned himself as a useless spy. Any design of writing would be gross intrusion, and he felt ashamed to be there, among the many suffering and the few helpers. The cold, persistent tread of evil reverberated inside him. Once onshore, quickly, unobtrusively, he set forth on foot with his bundles, his wrap and camera to find the guest house on the distant windward coast at Kalawao.

Kalaupapa was a long, bleak, irregular, ungardened village. There were three churches, a Y.M.C.A., a graveyard, a jail, a butcher shop, the Superintendent's office and the Bishop Home for Girls. As he passed through the village, Louis exchanged greetings here and there; at one point he found an attractive woman who beckoned to him from her porch. She was gentle and sympathetic—she thought he was the new white leper—but her manner shifted abruptly when she realized her error. Each was startled by the sudden change of focus, and Louis wandered away wondering if, perhaps, this was where he belonged.

Beyond the village, houses became rare. Louis stopped occasionally to talk with people sitting in their doorways. It was a dreary country, dry stone walls, grassy, rocky land, one sick pandanus tree to challenge the flatness. Once out upon the grassy, boulder-strewn plain, a semblance of peace returned to him. On the towering cliffs above, woody growth clustered like ivy. Steep waterfalls plummeted into deeply shaded valleys from the cloud-crested pali above. The cry of wind in the grass and the beat of the sea soothed him. His spirits lifted to the chirping of the birds from the cliff side forest. In this naturally fortified prison of disease, several hundred horses, cows and donkeys grazed serenely.

As he trudged through a passing rain shower, Louis met many lepers, noisy, excited, riding their horses hard toward the landing to greet the new sisters. At length, he met the Superintendent, a leper, who brought him a dogged, cranky brute of a horse. It was still early morning as Louis followed the curving road past Kauhako crater, its spiny lava tail trailing off toward the sea. He prodded his horse down a slight incline, past the Kalawao store, the Siloama Church, St.

Philomena's, Damien's Boys Home, the prison, and a graveyard.

The village of Kalawao was beautiful. Pleasant houses nestled in flower gardens, and the surf broke brilliantly against the islets off the shore. Here, too, the village cowered beneath the monstrous green face of the pali. The guest house adjoined the dispensary and the hospital, with the doctor's residence close by. Exhausted, Louis opened the gate, turned his horse loose, did a quick exploration, and found the bedroom. The first day passed in restless, agitated sleep. His sense of isolation was oppressive. No patients were allowed to approach the cottage. Nightmares frequently jolted him out of sleep, and he awoke to massive silence broken only by the drone of the surf, and the forlorn chirp of crickets. From the hospital a mournful bell tolled at intervals.

Louis's week within the lazaretto was one of mounting strain. Observing the lepers was an unsparing test of his composure. They coped in remarkable ways with individual and collective suffering. This only intensified Louis's groping efforts to re-establish some balance in his own turbulent state of mind. He exerted every effort to thrust his own physical malady into the background. Still, his uncertainty, yet persistent hope, kept merging into the conviction with which the lepers confronted their own mortality. Early on, Louis had planned to visit the lazaretto briefly, then return to Oahu by climbing topside to the crest of the pali on a recently built cobblestone trail. The doctor scrutinized Louis, reviewed his medical history, and emphatically barred that strenuous path. There would be no early escape from the lazaretto, this place of malady and folded hands. Louis would remain longer in this setting of ugliness, disease, disfigurement and living decay. He would witness the intimate knitting of fortitude, kindness, and moral beauty with physical horror. Could he endure living longer among these maimed, disfigured people seated by open graves?

With growing agony, Louis endured the marred, moribund community, with its idleness, its furnished table with rations and no work, its horse-riding, music, and gallantries under the shadow of death. He found here that disease no longer stirred pity, nor did deformities create shame in the patient, or disgust in the beholder. It seemed there was nothing in their bodies of which they might be deprived, yet still they retained the gusto of living. Horror, sorrow, all idea of resistance, all bitterness of regret, had passed from the minds of these sufferers.

The sick colony smiled bravely upon its bed of death.

Late one afternoon, riding back from Kalaupapa, Louis heard in the distance the strains of song and laughter, and soon met a group of lepers returning from a junket. They wore their many-colored Sundays' best, bright wreaths of flowers about their necks, gamboling along the way, men and women chasing and changing places with each other. From the distance, it was indeed an engaging scene. As he drew within recognition, two were unhumanly defaced. He remembered a leper girl from Ho'okena, darkly cloaked, head held down. At Kalaupapa she might adorn herself, and be applauded in a play or historical tableaux. Love laughed at leprosy. Couples married until the last stage of decay, the last gasp of life. Within this huge hospital, patients were rarely in pain, often capable of violent exertion, all bent on pleasure. The leper set aside the habits of the healthy world, and harvested each moment claimed from this slow, ugly, and incurable disease.

With the passing days, Louis found only fleeting relief from the initial and enduring shock of the lazaretto. He visited the hospital and watched the doctor and the lay brother dress patients. The scene was one of incongruous nonchalance. Louis sat and spun yarns with old, blind, leper beachcombers. One was a former luna, who had accidentally cut off his disease-numbed ear. Now he was elderly, blind, a composer of doggerel poems. Louis located Limu's parents, brought them letters and gifts, and reassured them of the health of their stalwart son. It was the youth of the lazaretto who were the greatest hope of strength for Louis. He spent time at the Boys' Home, watched them at play with football, marbles and kites. Concerts were on a regular schedule. Damien, with his fine singing voice, had imbued them with music: fiddles, drums, guitars and penny whistles abounded.

To better cope with his struggle, Louis patched together a routine of a daily three-mile ride to Kalaupapa to play croquet, or go guava-hunting with the seven leper girls at the sisters' Bishop Home. Mother Marianne, a woman of exceptional love and courage, now carried on the early accomplishments of Damien. Under her administration, Bishop Home became a place of love and care rather than the neglect, loneliness and abuse of earlier days. The Home was cheerful, clean, comfortable, and airy. Christmas cards, pictures, photos and dolls were at each girl's bedside, and dressmaking and plays occupied them daily. Mother Marianne's ministry drew Louis momentarily out of his melancholy and inspired his poem dedicated to her:

To see the infinite pity of this place,
The mangled limb, the devastated face,
The innocent sufferers smiling at the rod,
A fool were tempted to deny his God.

He sees, and shrinks; but if he look again,
Lo, beauty springing from the breast of pain!—
He marks the sisters on the painful shores,
And even a fool is silent and adores."

KALAWAO, MAY 22ND, 1889

Such distractions would, for a time, sustain Louis. But the solitary times were increasingly agonizing. Restless and jumpy, his appetite flagging, he remained in his cottage at night, distracted himself playing the flageolet, or writing letters. He dreaded sleep and the resurgence of a flood of nightmares not experienced since childhood. He was feverish, then chilled in the cool nights. Outside, it was pitch dark, damp with fine rain, the only sounds were the distant, despondent bell, and the humming of the sea, an unpleasant civilized sound to him like telegraph wires.

It was on such a night, moving on toward dawn, that Louis found himself plunged into and swept away by a dream of Victoria. He came upon her in a verdant glade, her face sunlit. The deep brown of her eyes was magnetizing. He approached her, his head pounding, his chest exploding. He seized her, embraced her hungrily, laid her upon the grassy carpet and cast himself upon her. He clawed at her garments, kissing her violently. Victoria remained motionless, soft, yielding, drawing him deeper into the bottomless pool of her eyes. . . .

Louis awoke shuddering, inflamed, horrified, gasping, beating at the air, hurling his bedclothes about, raging in the blackness of the bedroom. His bones were grinding, his teeth gnashing with pain. He felt sick to death, nauseated, consumed by a sense of abject shame and despair.

And then, with breath-taking suddenness, a strange sense of

strength and lightness, a wild recklessness, poured through him. He felt his agony swiftly transformed into an incredible sensation of boundless evil and wickedness. Springing from his bed exultantly, Louis moved with startling agility about the bedroom, hurling impediments out of his way. His hands explored his body and his face, sensing a newness, boldness, sharpness of his faculties, a violently surging power in that moment. He felt light as a feather, with the coiled steel of a murderous fury. He threw on his clothes, and burst through the door into the yard. His horse, startled, shied away as he flipped the saddle on its back. In a flame of anger, Louis seized a whip, belabored the horse savagely, hurled the saddle full at its head and ran out through the gate, a strange haunted figure of deformity. He set off headlong up the slope through the village, waving his fists with malevolent glee, strung to the pitch of murder, lusting to inflict pain. Uphill, he spied a saddled horse in a neighboring yard. With raging strength, he kicked down the gate, seized the horse by its bridle, and dragged it into the road. A leper boy ran out of the cottage in consternation. Louis wheeled, and hissed at the disfigured child. He cursed him. He no longer recognized his harsh, snarling voice. He mauled the boy, and threw him violently to the ground. Leaping on the horse, with the wild laugh of a madman, he jerked the reins fiercely toward Kauhaku. He whipped the horse viciously, and roared up the road with the fury of a tornado. In the dimness of early morning, Louis gloated at the sinews, the knuckled hairiness of his hands, gripped the reins ferociously and kicked the horse into a breakneck gallop.

◆　　◆　　◆

New York City was an overwhelming scene of bustle and confusion for Victoria. As the railroad train spanned the vastness of the United States, she found the towering range of the Rocky Mountains, the boundless prairie, the overflowing energy of the new nation, and the diversity of its people, to be an amazing experience. She was too excited for any restful sleep along the way, but in moments of meditation, she experimented with her newfound, transcending bond to Louis. Her Wise One had not failed her: distance was not a barrier. The love she bore—the essential ingredient—was full and deep. Their bond was secure.

Louis had appeared so troubled the day she sailed from Honolulu that Victoria had carried an unsettled mood with her throughout the voyage to San Francisco. Then in an exhausted sleep in the hotel, she had received a reassuring poem that she faithfully recorded:

> *"I have dreamed a golden vision,*
> *I have not lived in vain. . . .*
> *I swear had we been drowned that day*
> *We had been drowned in love."*

Victoria had lain quietly in her bed reliving the afternoon on the shore at Honaunau, daydreaming of ways she might have prolonged that moment. She sent her own thought waves of love into the air, prayerfully addressing them to Louis, picturing him as she saw him dozing peacefully, that very first evening on the beach. Later, in a fitful sleep, another poem came to her:

> *Swallows travel to and fro . . .*
> *Towered clouds forever ply,*
> *And at noonday you and I*
> *See the same sunshine above . . . .*
> *So at scent or sound or sight,*
> *Severed souls by day and night*
> *Tremble with the same delight—*
> *Tremble half the world apart.*

Louis's love poems visited Victoria at intervals across the United States. She had learned something very early about Louis: those things that really mattered to him—the deepest feelings—he expressed in poetry. Prose was fine for *Treasure Island, Kidnapped* or *The Black Arrow*. That was his sport. It was in poetry that his heart poured out; and those intense emotions had carved their way into Victoria's very being. Another night...

> *"All things on earth and sea,*
> *All that the white stars see,*
> *Turns about you and me.*
>
> . . . .

> *The earth through all her bowers*
> *Carols and breathes and flowers*
> *About this love of ours."*

On shipboard, leaving New York harbor, an ominous, chilling sense of foreboding descended on Victoria...

> *I have left all upon the shameful field,*
> *Honor and Hope, my God, and all but life;*
> *Spurless, with sword reversed and dinted shield,*
> *Degraded and disgraced, I leave the strife.*
>
>   . . . .
>
> *I fling my soul and body down*
> *For God to plough them under.*

Victoria was beside herself with apprehension. She struggled to banish her fear, and place herself in a state of mind to cope with this alarming message. The harbor, Manhattan, and the vast city lights of New York were disappearing in the distance, the waning twilight profiling massive clouds, framing the play of lightning within them. Victoria channeled her thoughts into the power of that scene in the western sky.

◆   ◆   ◆

Louis drove his beleaguered animal as far up the side of Kauhako crater as the exhausted horse could manage. As it stumbled and lurched in the loose lava, Louis bellowed with rage, leaped to the ground and heaved his way upward on foot toward the rim of the crater. In a frenzy, he dug his way in the yielding surface, still shadowy in the pre-dawn light. Once across the rim he plunged into the sea of dense vegetation, leaping, sliding, and thrusting, ripping vines and branches out of his path. Far below shimmered the pool, the bottomless lake. Louis hurled himself downward, tearing his way, scratched and bleeding, screaming hoarsely. He had a sense of flight, weightlessness, violence of utter release, as he thrust himself through the underbrush. He staggered, fell and rolled his way downward. In a final lunge, he threw himself hoarsely to the ground at the edge of the lake.

He reached his grimy hands into the brackish water, doused himself, and glimpsed his contorted face in the rippling surface. It was a countenance of unbridled evil, completely divorced from any hint of humanity. As the ripples subsided, Louis studied himself. With agonizing slowness, his blurred and fleeting features gradually became recognizable as himself. Then, in a kaleidoscopic swirl of images, he saw Victoria's face. Louis rolled over, screaming in despair, clutching at his face.

Above him, a slender figure stood, looking down at him, motioning with a calming gesture.

♦ ♦ ♦

Victoria knelt beside Louis and placed his head in her lap. Neither spoke. In the gentle unfolding of the morning, she stroked his brow, hummed softly to him, and with the caress of her glance, she calmed him into a deep sleep. The sun, heralded by waking forest birds, rose over the eastern rim of the crater and peeked down upon them through the forest. Louis slept on, a sleep too deep and blessed for dreaming.

Slowly, in the warmth and brightening of the day, Louis roused. Victoria gently peeled away his clothes and washed his wounds. Then she shed her own garments, took him by the hand, and led him into the lake. They clung to each other in the coolness of the water, still without a word.

At length, Victoria broke their silence. "Kalaupapa. Did you know this strange piece of the island, according to the legend, is where the ancient chiefs gathered to marry?"

Louis's smile was otherworldly. His eyebrows rose questioningly.

Victoria continued, "In those days, this seemed to be the only neutral ground away from their furious battles."

Louis grimaced, muttering, "Neutral ground! No neutral ground for me last night. Not in this past week of unmitigated hell! Last night I visited the real hell." He shuddered. "Horrible! I think it started with a dream." He paused and pressed his hands against his temples. "Victoria! You were there! Oh, my God, yes!"

Louis immersed himself in the cool lake and came up slowly, looking at Victoria. He recalled that lustful dream, and the wild events that followed. She nodded knowingly and led him back to the shore to recline in a sunny glade. "It wasn't just *your* dream, Louis. *I was here*! Waiting for you."

Louis studied her and felt again the stabbing in his gut. "At the City of Refuge," he paused a long pause . . . "Victoria, you said you wanted me so badly. God, *help* me! I want you, too. Oh, God *help* me, I do want you! Selfishly! In every way!"

Victoria, glowing, turned softly to him. "Louis, I want to have your child."

Louis looked down at his hands, his slender fingers again those of a cultured gentleman. He looked at her tenderly and nodded a confused agreement.

She smiled at his bewilderment, hunched her knees up under her chin and looked squarely at him. "If you really love me, you'll make love to me, won't you?"

Louis avoided her intent expression and fumbled with the black sand on which they sat.

Victoria was unrelenting. "I know you've worried, wondering when it would come to this. Dearest Louis, rest your troubled heart. I know already that you love me—*really* love me. We *shall* have a child together. I know that. I carry so much of you inside me already. Love of my life, when that wonderful moment comes that we are together—and only then—you will have been freed of such nightmare hells as you had last night."

They passed the day together in Kauhako—'*journey into space*'. Then, slowly they climbed through the crater forest, Victoria nestled against him, her head on his shoulder. A gentle mist drifted and glistened about them, the drops standing upon Victoria's bright cheeks like tears, and playing about her smiling mouth. Strength, like a giant's, seemed to come upon Louis with this sight. He could have caught her up and run with her to the uttermost places in the earth. The words they spoke were beyond belief for freedom and sweetness. Hand in hand, each empowered the other in this forbidding land of the lazaretto.

♦   ♦   ♦

Chapter IX

ESCAPE FROM GREAT HARROWDEN

Hawai'i quickly lost its gusto for Louis. The excitement, the zest had departed with Victoria. He became restless, anxious to resume his travels in the South Seas. He would forever be attached to these islands, and to the friendships he had forged in the winter and spring of 1889. As the time of leave-taking approached, the superficial gaiety of the royal scene could not dispel a heavy sense of foreboding nor premonitions of a crisis for the kingdom.

Fanny, the reluctant sailor, swung into action and arranged passage for them on the *Equator,* a two-masted, eighty ton trading schooner bound for the Gilberts and beyond. With some reluctance, they decided that Joe Strong would accompany them. Louis's somewhat more than faint hope was that errant Joe's artistic and photographic abilities would enable them to prepare a diorama and materials for speaking engagements. Perhaps it could keep Joe out of trouble with opium, and would certainly shore up the family's economic base, both of which were Louis's ever-present worries.

Kalakaua gathered the Stevensons' closest friends for dinner in the bungalow at Iolani Palace the night before their departure. Through the evening, Louis and Fanny made valiant efforts to maintain a lighthearted tone, but that seemed largely to fall flat. With a hesitant smile, Fanny had said, "Well, we're all packed up now. Would you like to know what we're taking?" She unrolled a long list. "A barrel of sauerkraut, a barrel of salt onions, a bag of coconuts, native garments, tobacco, fishhooks, red combs, Turkey red calicoes—all the latter for trading purposes—a hand organ, photograph and painting materials, magic lantern, fiddle, guitar, taro patch fiddle, and a lot of songbooks. Shall I continue?"

It was in their hearts to keep trying, but the pensiveness of this small gathering would not budge. Fanny finally drifted off to sit somewhat apart in the salon, silent, observing them keenly, but in her silence expressing even more deeply than the others a sense of departure dreariness.

In the conversation that ensued, Louis fretted over Hawai'i's susceptibility to the encroaching world outside. That and the collective heaviness of their feelings launched David Kalakaua on a series of unhappy reflections.

"Susceptibility?" He recalled the late 1830's, when Kauikeauoli was king. "The French were the troublemakers. They sent a frigate, the *Artemise*, under orders to bombard the city because of persecution of the Catholics. The Chiefs and some of the foreign community scraped together $20,000 as a bond to guarantee compliance. I was just a keiki then," the king recalled. "Everyone was petrified. The missionaries thought their women would be subjected to the unbridled lust of the French."

Kalakaua's mood lifted momentarily. He grinned a bit sheepishly: "It wasn't totally bad. It overturned our national policy of total abstinence, and opened up Hawai'i to French wines and brandies. And, another change for the better: the religious community achieved more of a balance."

Current happenings on Oahu preoccupied them all. Robert Wilcox was stirring things up with his group of armed local men, the Kamehameha Rifles. The King shook his head in a half-admiring grimace: "Such a hot-head, that Wilcox. I sent him to Italy to the Royal Military Academy. I needed someone like him to help me strengthen our military; but he came back thinking he was a second Garibaldi, even to the fancy Italian uniform. Reformers—look out!"

Archie Cleghorn passed the brandy decanter about. "Wilcox's Liberal Patriotic Association—what a rag tag bunch! But they're stockpiling guns, I know!"

Louis blew a smoke ring. "An old-fashioned bloodbath? Ask the Scots about that, eh, Archie? I wish Wilcox *could* turn the clock back. But not a bloodbath! It's the wrong choice and the wrong time. He's headed for nothing but trouble, that young Don Quixote." Louis smiled, remembering those electric moments at Punchbowl. "But he makes a marvelous, dramatic picture."

The king glanced across the room at his sister. His eyes seemed to well up with tears. He appeared to lose his composure, turned away and downed his brandy. "While Wilcox was away, and you, Lydia, were in Britain at the Queen's golden jubilee—that's when the Reformists jammed their bayonet constitution down my throat."

Lydia shifted resolutely in her chair. "Now, David, please don't dwell on that. It's all talked out and settled." She turned to the others. "Wilcox tried to place David and me at odds with one another. He claimed I'd have kept David from giving in on the new constitution." She looked searchingly at the king, uncertain whether to continue. "I? Stop him? They planned to dethrone my beloved *kunane*—to kill him!"

Kalakaua, his palms pressed tightly against his cheeks, moved to Lydia's chair, reached down and pressed her shoulder. "You had every reason to doubt me when you returned. Perhaps, after all, it would have been better had I chosen death."

John Dominis reacted vehemently. "I was here! I saw it happen! David was betrayed by his advisors." He jerked his head toward the palace. "That hall over there was lined with soldiers. Fixed bayonets! His own soldiers were supposed to protect him, not coerce him!"

The king turned to Louis as the originator of this sad discussion. His smile was perplexed, downcast. "Yes, Stevenson, you see how vulnerable Hawai'i is! In the '40's another warship, the British *Carysfort*, sailed in to guard their interests. The Hawaiians were frightened, sure. The foreigners panicked, piled their things together at the waterfront to stow on shipboard. British sailors were brawling with the natives. It was chaos."

"King Kauikeaouli was desperate. He knew the British had set out to annex the islands to Great Britain. And the British *succeeded!* They took over the Fort, hauled down our flag and raised the Union Jack. We were dumb struck! I was a pupil at the Chief's Children's School. They invited us to the Fort. We heard the king's voice ceding our islands to Great Britain. There was a deafening gun salute. When I opened my eyes, our flag was gone! I ripped the gold insignia from my cap and trampled it in the dust! All of the boys did. We were no longer chiefs. *Auwe, auwe!* We were British subjects."

"People accuse me of being such a supporter of the British. For good reason! It was their basic fairness that saved us. On the other side of the world, months earlier, the British Foreign Office had issued a policy statement. The *Carysfort* hadn't heard about this!" Kalakaua, animated, rose from his chair and paced the room, waving his cigar. "The Foreign Office—listen to this!— announced that native governments in the Pacific islands should be treated with great respect, with forbearance and courtesy, and their laws and customs should be respected. Well, the word got here four months later. So much for British reign!"

Kalakaua sat down heavily, exhaling audibly in a long deep breath. He paused and looked about the room, distracted. "Odd. I was missing our little princess Victoria just then. She is our future." He gestured toward the newly installed telephone equipment in the corner of the salon. "Just like that amazing contraption. It's going to connect us all—not just Honolulu—so that we can talk, communicate, understand each other. Our Kaiulani will have such things."

Father Archie joined in the reminiscences. "Our vulnerability is coming from all sides. There was the 'Great *Mahele*,' when I was fifteen. Everything changed! American sugar planters kept pressuring the king and the chiefs for private land tenure. Finally, he gave in, kept some crown lands for himself, and gave huge tracts to the chiefs. Oh, the chiefs had been pressuring him, too. And then, naive, greedy; the chiefs sold, leased or gave it away! You know who picked up the land: it wasn't the Hawaiians. They ended up with less than one percent of the available land in the islands."

"So here I am," said Kalakaua in exasperation. "The Hawaiian League—the Reform Party—is running the show. In the last two years they've turned out all my appointees, voted down my best programs, and turned my armed forces over to the Minister of Foreign Affairs. Worst of all, now America has exclusive rights to Pearl River Harbor. Yes, France and Britain have had their day with us. Now it will be the Americans."

David gave them a faint smile and a wink. "But I still have the royal veto! Those reformers—Thurston, Ashford—they have no sense of humor." He chuckled. "I hear Thurston's so scared of me he carries a gun when he's around the palace."

♦　♦　♦

Louis secretly accomplished one final mission before sailing. This fulfilled his craving to meet with Victoria's "Uncle." Victoria had never suggested this and he felt some apprehension that their relationship might be jeopardized by such a meeting. Still, in his loneliness after her departure, Louis's need to meet Uncle became overpowering. He clung desperately to the slender thread suspended between him and his princess.

Limu was Louis's contact to seek out Uncle. Louis had also been mulling over another mission, this in regard to Limu. Now was an opportune time to accomplish both. When he proposed the visit to Uncle, Limu was matter of fact; Louis thought he even seemed to be expecting it. They left Manuia Lanai on horseback before sun-up and rode through the hills back of Diamond Head toward Windward Oahu. At sunrise, they descended from the pali into a lustrous green land stretching out to a shimmering, cerulean sea. They followed the coast northward, the sheer, glossy ribs of the Koolau range to their left, and passed occasional coastal villages. By noon they arrived at Waimanalo. Limu led the way to a cluster of grass houses scattered about beneath the coco palms along the margins of a stream. Limu nodded toward a canoe shed on the beach. Louis dismounted and made his way to the shed, while Limu led the horses into the cooling stream.

The canoe shed was a towering, deeply shaded, grass-covered A-frame structure. As Louis approached, he detected a man chiseling away at a long dug-out canoe. The man was huge of frame. He turned toward Louis as he approached. Louis was dumb struck! It was *Kalamake!*

In the quiet coolness of the canoe shed, Kalamake greeted him with warmth and friendliness. But here was a different Kalamake from the man Louis had seen so frequently in Honolulu. In this setting, this remarkable human appeared to grow out of the earth about him, much as did the grass and the palms. There was a deliberateness, a gravity about him previously unnoticed. His gaze was penetrating. Looking into Kalamake's eyes was like plunging into the vastness of Polynesian history. Even in the shade of the canoe shed, there was a luster about his face, a bright, shifting play of color, that held Louis spellbound, almost blinding him.

The two men visited beside the canoe for what seemed a timeless interval for Louis. Kalamake understood totally the evolution of Victoria's world. Louis felt his way cautiously through Kalamake's statements and beliefs. Could he hope for some glimmer of fore-knowledge? But it was to no avail. In awe, Louis steeled himself to accept the realization that much more would remain unspoken. It shook him to wonderment. Was this extraordinary man, like that ancient druid, King Arthur's Merlin, approaching life in the present along a mysterious path from the historical future? There were tanta-lizing hints—but only that. The focal point for both men was deep concern for Victoria. How lasting was this ability to communicate with her through vast distances? Kalamake appeared secure, Louis not at all, with this new-found ability.

At the end of the day, Louis and Limu rode back through the palm-strewn shadows of the setting sun. In a deep state of wonder, he reviewed Kalamake's words. It all reduced itself to love. Love generates spirit—*mana*. *Mana* reaches out—even through the vastness of time and space—and touches the loved one. *Mana*: this is the vehicle! It all was so simple. But how in this life, this world, this breed of humani-ty? Louis knew and rejoiced in one thing: for Victoria and for him there was Kalamake.

At Manuia Lanai, as he took leave of Limu, Louis handed him a little pouch. "Here, Limu. This is for you. Something special, I think."

Limu unfastened the pouch and drew out a necklace of *puka* shells. He turned it over in his fingers admiringly, and looked ques-tioningly at Louis.

"It's from a girl named Loke. *Loke*—remember that name. She made it. She's very *momona*. You will like her. Ask for her at Queen's Hospital."

◆　　◆　　◆

Kalakaua saw the Stevensons off with final festivities: champagne, leis, an exquisite model of a schooner, and his heartfelt wish that the winds and waves would be favorable. It pained the King to see his slender, animated friend depart from his kingdom. The Band played a last "*Aloha Oʻe*" and the *Equator* disappeared over the horizon to southern seas.

The *Equator* stopped at the Gilberts, then went on to cruise the

Tokelau and Ellice groups. The family survived a Fourth of July riot at Butaritari on the island of Great Makin. Louis reveled in recording such events and continued, as his family described it, to go off half-cocked with letters and articles for the British press about the plight of Polynesia.

Adventure followed Louis like a shadow: on one voyage they picked up King Tembenok, an absolute despot of the Gilberts, accompanied by his court, harem and bodyguards. If such a passenger list did not offer sufficient writing material, a store of fireworks accidentally exploded. Only quick-thinking Fanny prevented a seaman from throwing Louis's flaming manuscript trunk overboard during the holocaust.

In September of 1890 the Stevensons landed at Apemama, dominion of King Tembenok, and remained for several unsettling weeks amid rumors that the ship had been lost. The Gilberts were the independent dumping ground of white riffraff of the Pacific. Out of this setting of thieves, murderers, turncoats, and escaped criminals, Louis wrote *The Beach at Falesa*. The story came into focus when he first saw Uma:

One afternoon, Louis was sitting on the shore. There was a crowd of girls about, a handsome lot, all dressed up for the arrival of the ship. He saw one coming on the other side, alone. She had been fishing; all she wore was a chemise, and it was wet through. She was young and very slender for an island maid, with a long face, a high forehead, and a strange, shy, distant look. She was *Victoria*! She invaded his dreams. Together they plotted a tale of a murderous trader who exploited natives' superstitions for his own gain. In one intensely vivid dream, Victoria and Louis spent a wild night in the jungle amid singing trees, devils, and gunfire. At dawn, she left him, he half-awake, she giggling, disappearing into the bush. The dream set off too many echoes of Victoria. With the completion of the story, Louis sank into a spell of listless, morbid depression.

All was not well between Louis and Fanny as their extended cruise progressed. There were a number of things: by the time the *Equator* returned to Apemama, they were all suffering from sores and malnutrition. They were quarreling openly about Louis's expressed determination to write a magnum opus about the South Seas.

"Don't you see, Fanny? Nobody has had such stuff; such wild

stories, such beautiful scenes. No one has been so close to such singular manners and traditions. What an incredible mixture of the beautiful and horrible, the savage and civilized! The main theme would be the unjust—yet I can see inevitable—extinction of the Polynesian Islanders by our shabby civilization."

Fanny's mind was made up. "Louis, you alarm me! You're forsaking your true genius. You're mired in linguistics and archeology. You—who have such ability to portray living, breathing human beings."

"All right! You want a masterpiece—that's what you want me to write! Well, where is it? I can't get hold of it, Fanny! My God! I hope I'm not dried up! But in the meantime, there's all this Pacific material. How can I ignore it?"

"You're not 'dried up.' You've taken it into your Scotch Stevenson head that you have a stern duty to these islanders! What a thing it is for me to deal with a 'man of genius!' You're like an overbred horse! —No, mule!"

Tensions of this kind between Louis and Fanny were not new. It might take time but they had always been manageable. But Louis, on one unfortunate day, made the blunder of saying Fanny had the soul of a peasant. It wounded her deeply. As his consort through artistic thick and thin, she deserved better, and for one as creative as she, it was a cut that did not heal.

The year 1891 was critical in two ways: Louis visited Sydney, Australia twice during that year. In that cooler climate on each occasion he became desperately ill. The first bout, with Louis hemorrhaging and near death, Fanny strong-armed the sea captain of the *Janet Nicoll* to allow them on board and away to the tropics. In three and one half months they visited thirty-three low islands. Louis rallied amazingly, but the same circumstances repeated in Sydney later that year.

The positive side of 1891 was the Stevenson's discovery of Samoa. The climate was right, and regular mail ships called at Apia. The decision was agonizing: Louis would never again see Scotland. With great sadness, he accepted this verdict and plunged ahead on new ventures. Three hundred and fourteen acres of land above Apia on the slopes of Mount Vaea would be the setting for the great house at Vailima.

◆ ◆ ◆

A chill rain spattered the window panes of Great Harrowden Hall. Victoria found England in the winter of 1892 to be a reminder of the cloud-scudding, rainswept upland of Waimea. At Harrowden, she was attending classes for the first time ever. Two years had passed in this land on the other side of the world from Hawai'i. The Hall was a gloomy pile near the village of Wellingborough in Northamptonshire, a few hours by carriage north of London. A private school for girls now, the Barons Vaux had built it in the Fifteenth Century. An ivy-covered facade did little to soften a forbidding main gate with heavy pillars and a wrought iron fence. Like a grim whirlpool, Harrowden sucked Victoria in and closeted her from the world.

On the day she arrived, Victoria saw two angelic figures adorning the main gate. She looked at the Hall, then at the two angels, and shuddered. In a surge of melancholy, she absorbed them in her heart, and appointed them her guardians. How to put her time in England in a happy frame? She tried valiantly. It began well, with visits to London, the West End theaters, the art galleries and the Crystal Palace. The Tower of London impressed her deeply and smoldered in her thoughts. The mysterious, governing presence of the baleful ravens, and the sad stories of imprisoned, condemned royalty. Young lives, and so many lives, had ended in the Tower. Great Harrowden felt like the Tower to Victoria. She tried to live those stories of spirit and courage: Sir Walter Raleigh writing his history of the world, while awaiting death within its battlements. Raleigh, Mary Queen of Scots, and their like, and the angels of Great Harrowden Hall, were bits of encouragement to the 'child of air,' shut away now from glowing tropical vistas. The heady, exciting freedom of riding Fairy about Oahu! Victoria ached longingly for this and for the gracious flow and color of the islands. The pretty things she liked to surround herself with seemed out of place in England, where ladies were wearing dresses made like men's clothing

The angels at Harrowden gate were a support. Sir Walter Raleigh's indomitable will was an inspiration. Archie's occasional visits to England were a renewal. But in the world of Victoria's spirit, there was only Louis. Their communications flourished in dreams and poems, and in this way, Victoria could feel his enduring presence. She rushed out to purchase his books and stories whenever they became available, and scanned the London *Times* for his letters. Her favorite stories were those in which Louis cast women in principle roles. Kate in *Catriona*, and Joanna in *The Black Arrow* were not just her favorites; Victoria recognized herself in these women. She delighted to see how clearly her influence emerged in Louis's writing. It was another way in which he spoke to her. The stories appeared in her dreams at times, and were another link between them. But there were unsettling times. Inevitably, in reaching through the shadows for each other, when her mood was at low ebb, a wall seemed to rise between them. At other times she was certain it was Louis whose spirits were sagging. Then, in the night, a poem would literally grow within her, warmly filling her heart, yet wrenching it in painful joy:

> *Love—what is love? A great and aching heart;*
> *Wrung hands; and silence; and a long despair.*
> *Life—what is life? Upon a moorland bare*
> *To see love coming and see love depart.*

One night Victoria dreamed of a voyage on a gaily colored ship, its sails of Stewart tartan. They probed a nighttime sky, tacking their way among towering clouds. Beneath them flowed cities, mountain ranges, and the vastness of oceans bathed in moonlight. In the distance, a gentle hue of rosy dawn peeked at their vessel, tinting the billowing sails. Louis's words were waiting for her as she awoke to the gray sullenness of Great Harrowden Hall:

> *My love was warm; for that I crossed*
> *The mountains and the sea,*
> *Nor counted that endeavor lost*
> *That gave my love to me.*

♦ ♦ ♦

From her 'tower' on the other side of the world, Victoria hungrily, apprehensively, followed the turmoil in Hawai'i during these years that, for her, moved so ponderously. Wilcox's secret maneuverings had erupted in the July 30 1889 uprising. It had the trappings of a comic opera, but seven men were killed and several wounded in the futile storming of Iolani Palace. No lasting punishments were meted out, and Wilcox, the hero of the moment, with a solid native vote, was able to get himself elected to the legislature.

A burgeoning National Reform Party favored independence and defeat of the bayonet constitution. Another insurrection seemed probable. The legislature voted no confidence in the ministers and Kalakaua appointed a new cabinet. Wilcox waited in vain for an appointment, firing off incendiary speeches. The king sought a constitutional convention but couldn't move this through the divided legislature. In the Spring of 1890 United States President Harrison signed the McKinley Tariff Act. The reciprocity treaty with the Hawaiian kingdom was thereby virtually wrecked. Pressure in Hawai'i for a favored place with the United States escalated, as the full impact of the Act bore down upon the islands. Hawai'i's crippled sugar industry found the Harrison administration unsympathetic.

In November, in poor health, Kalakaua appointed Princess Lili'uokalani regent and sailed for San Francisco, never to see his islands again. The news of Papa Moi's death in January shocked Victoria, and plunged her into grief.

January 30 1891 began the reign of Queen Lili'uokalani, ill-fated from the outset. Each day more powder was loaded into the Hawaiian cannon. Wilcox and the Native Sons of Hawai'i hammered at return of governing powers to the monarch. Again, Wilcox felt abandoned, this time by his Queen. He formed a new Liberal Party favoring fiery republicanism. The Reformists countered with their thrust for annexation.

Victoria shuddered, and paced about her apartment in frustration, as she read these agonizing letters from home. Early in 1892 the secret Annexation Club began meeting in attorney Lorrin Thurston's office. Their goal: a territorial government—not a State within the United States. The "backward" nature of the electorate would threaten their control. Perhaps a coup d'état and a provisional government would bring their plans to fruition? The Club found President Harrison's secretary of State, James Blaine, exceedingly sympathetic.

Government spies infiltrated Wilcox's Hawaiian Patriotic League. In May 1892, Wilcox and several others were arrested and charged with conspiracy. It had come down to this: Royalists versus the Annexation Club. The outcry in the islands was that traitorous sugar barons would overthrow the monarchy for their own gain. The editor of the *Honolulu Bulletin* was arrested for libel and silenced by pressure from American Minister Stevens, a dedicated annexationist. Queen Lili'uokalani spoke out against her enemies in harsh, even rash tones. A group of loyal young Hawaiians appointed themselves round the clock guardians of the Queen and took up posts at Iolani Palace. The Hawaiian cannon by this time needed only a spark.

♦   ♦   ♦

On a gray, misty evening, Victoria peered through the leaded window panes, dreamily reflecting on the drifting patterns of moisture on Great Harrowden's broad lawn. The light from the fireplace played upon her face, and made it glow and darken through a spectrum of delicate hues. Her fine features were more beautiful than ever, now deeply underpainted by the gift of her inner world. Outside, occasional carriage wheels had streaked the first falling of snow on the road leading up from the gate. She thought of Louis's farewell poem and—how true!—its reference to rain beating upon the window.

The news from home was commingled gloom, very rare bright spots, and never sufficient. Papa Moi's sudden death: how deeply it had shaken her! Not since Mother Likelike had she been so bereaved. A few months earlier, Kalakaua had written mysteriously, warning her against certain enemies. This remained unfathomed, but letters from Archie and Aunt Lydia underscored the increasingly volatile political scene. Pleasant news? Archie was building a new house at Ainahau! From a distance, her Scottish blood rising to the surface, she worried about his finances. Aunt Lydia had named Archie governor of Oahu, and in her letters to the new queen, she hoped his rising government responsibilities would not deprive him of more lucrative appointments.

Archie's visits to England were warm moments to interrupt Victoria's loneliness. His business affairs were generously weighted with time for sharing, and that was always entertaining. He might come home from all-night observations of police operations in the London slums to regale his daughter with suspenseful stories. Their holidays at Menton on the French Riviera were highlights, but still only momentary breaks.

A wintry chill held Great Harrowden Hall in its clutches. The uncertain afternoon drizzle had become a fine snow that blew in gusty, powdery clouds as nighttime advanced. One by one, lights in the apartments glowed spectrally. Victoria spent an hour re-reading a portion of *The Black Arrow*. It was a diverting way to fit together the background of English history, the Wars of the Roses, and the shifting loyalties to Lancaster and York that she struggled to understand for school examinations. Whenever she read the story, the pages always seemed to open to the exciting scene where Dick Shelton rescued Joanna. It was hardly bedtime reading, but it left her feeling warm and hopeful inside. At last, she set her books aside, turned down her lamp, sighed deeply and began preparing herself for sleep. Snuggled under her comforters in a deep feather bed, perhaps at last she might find a bit of warmth. The wind whistled against the windows, plastering them with swirling bundles of wet snowflakes. Between the gusts, the silence within Great Harrowden and on the dismal plain outside, was oppressive.

The wind outside strengthened, slashed at her windows and took on a whistling intensity. Victoria descended swiftly into sleep along a spiral staircase of swirling snow that enfolded her like a warm blanket. From a distance, and mingled in the gusts, there emerged a voice! Someone was singing in the winter gale! Victoria felt her body rise from her covers and drift to the windows. Deep in her dream, she wiped away the frost, and peered out. There was nothing to be seen in the ghostly shadow of the parapet, but the singing continued and the voice became forceful:

> *I had four black arrows under my belt,*
> *Four for the griefs that I have felt,*
> *Four for the number of ill men*
> *That have oppressed me now and then.*
> *One is for Sir Oliver Oates,*
> *That cut Sir Harry Shelton's throat.*
> *A black arrow in each black heart.*
> *Get ye to your knees to pray:*
> *Ye are dead thieves, by yea and nay!*

What? A familiar ring to this voice out of the darkness?. Victoria beckoned to the casements and, as they flung open, she leaned out into the swirling snow.

"Louis! Great merciful heaven! Come in here! Quickly! You'll catch your death! What in the world are you doing out there?"

Victoria clutched excitedly at a figure swathed in a snow-covered surplice and black robe. She grasped him, pulling at him vigorously. In the excitement a chain about his neck broke loose, a talisman fell to the sill and disappeared over the parapet.

"Oh! Oh! Oh!" He lurched away from her grasp, clutched his throat, and looked down into the darkness. "Oh! Oh! Oh!"

The slender, hooded apparition clambered into the room, shaking off the snow, muttering in breathless excitement: "I've looked high and low in the Greenwood for you! Tell me all is well with you!"

Victoria gasped, incredulous, then, her hands to her face in a wide grin, "Oh! Louis! Louis!" Delighted, she grasped his shoulders in the dimness of the room.

"Mark you," he pronounced, drawing himself up. "This house is full of spies; I heard their feet follow me in the corridors. They breathe behind the arras. We are safe for this while, if there be safety anywhere within these walls." He clapped Victoria on the shoulder. "By the mass, my heart is glad to see you. I thought ye were gone! Where hid ye? "

Victoria was convulsed with a combination of laughter and amazement. Was Louis in utter seriousness? Was that a sly smile lurking in the shadow of his cowl?

"Louis—really! Are your eyes open?"

Louis plunged on, breathless. "Have they told you of tomorrow's doings?"

Victoria collapsed into a chair and rocked with laughter. "Tomorrow? Examinations! Tests!" she cried.

"Tomorrow or tonight, I know not," he said, "but one time or other, they do intend upon your life. I had the proof of it; I have heard them whisper; nay, they as good as told me. Sir Daniel schemes to marry you off to Lord Shoreby." Louis groaned in frustration. "More ill-gotten gain for Sir Daniel!"

He began to search about the room. "No," he said, "there is no escape visible, yet 'tis a pure certainty there is one." In the corner of the room he found an open chink through which some light glittered. He tested the unyielding boards with his fingers.

Victoria ran to Louis, seized him by the shoulders and scrutinized his face. Determined he was, like a knight upon a quest!

Victoria shrugged, her arms akimbo, and shook her head with a perplexed smile. "Well, then—a quest?" thought Victoria. "If adventure this be, then let us make the most of it." She slapped him forcefully, both hands upon his chest, and stood off from him resolutely. "I will stay by you. If you are to die, I will die with you. And I can help—look!" A weapon materialized in her grasp. "I have stolen a dagger—I will do my best! I will most joyfully face any jeopardy to flee with you."

"I swear," he said, "upon the cross of Holywood, y'are the best soul, and the truest, and the bravest in all England! Give me your hand."

Louis continued to examine the room. The far end of the apartment, where they stood, was in complete darkness.

"Brave knight," she cried, "I am lost; we are both lost! Let us flee if there be yet time. They will not rest till they have found me. Or see!" She made for the door. "Let me go forth; when they have found me, ye may flee."

"Dearest lady," he said, "in the Greenwood, y'ave saved my life, and I have saved your's; and we have seen blood flow. By St. Banbury! 'Twas another of Sir Daniel's tricks to hide you and keep us at a distance. He hath been a foul lord to both of us. But now death has me, and my time's out, and before I die I must say this: y'are the best maid and the bravest under heaven, and, if only I could live, I would marry you blithely; and, live or die, I love you."

Victoria answered nothing.

"Come," he said, "speak up, my lady! Be a good maid, and say ye love me!"

Victoria, misty-eyed, cast off her role. "Why else, Louis," she murmured, "would I be here?"

Obsessed, Louis ran to the door, listening. "Hark! Heavy feet upon the corridor! He seized the great old bedstead with both hands and bent himself in vain to move it.

"Help me, for your life's sake, help me stoutly!" he cried.

Between them, with a huge effort, they dragged the big frame of oak across the room, and thrust it endwise to the chamber door.

Drawing a stout sword, Louis lunged to the corner of the room. He thrust the blade deep into the seam of the trapdoor, and weighed strenuously on the hilt. The trap moved, gaped a little, and at length came widely open. Seizing it with their hands, they threw it back. It disclosed a few steps descending, and at the foot of them, where sure-ly a would-be murderer had left it, a burning lamp.

They followed the narrow, dirty passage to a door which stood partly open. Heavy cobwebs hung from the roof; and the paved floor-ing echoed hollow under the lightest tread. Louis threw off the friar's robe revealing a jacket of deer's leather, with a black velvet collar. The green hood upon his head and the steel crossbow at his back were the habit of the Black Arrow Band of the Greenwood! He twirled about in the dim light, smiling, inviting her admiration.

"Now," he whispered, "we are here in the midst of open snow, and compassed about with enemies. Go, a-Mary's name! Run 'ye for yon-der windmill and the granary with the open doors. Mind ye' the word is 'England and Edward,' and the counter, 'England and York.'"

Victoria paused, viewed the broad darkness of the snow-covered lawn, turned toward him and melted into his arms. "You are truly beautiful, dear knight! I do indeed love you with all my heart."

Thus they set forth together along the road to Brighton, the moon silvering the frozen snow. They kept near the margin of the forest, coming forth, from time to time, in open country, and passing poor folks' houses and small farms. They ran on, holding each other by both hands, exchanging smiles and loving looks, and melting minutes into seconds. They passed through open leafless groves and down snow-clad alleys, under the white face of the winter moon; Louis and Victoria walking hand in hand in a heavenly dream of pleasure. And so they continued all night long, leaving in the distance the battle of Shoreby and the loneliness of Great Harrowden Hall....

◆　◆　◆

In the winter of 1892 there were other alternatives for travel from Northamptonshire to Brighton. By far, Victoria preferred her excur-sion with Louis. At Number Seven Cambridge Road, in the home of Mrs. Rooke, she found a happier setting. Here she was broadly, sensi-tively tutored in literature, history, French, German, and English. There was the fun part: music, singing, and dancing. General deport-ment at Mrs. Rooke's was a time of riotous laughter, but Victoria did demonstrate that—by British standards—she could learn how to walk into a room gracefully.

Mrs. Rooke had a little house, LaChaire, at Rozel, St. Helier on the island of Jersey. Visits to Rozel, even in mid-winter, were a welcome diversion for Victoria who discovered, indeed, puzzled over her preference now for cold weather. The long, rough boat rides from Southampton, especially between Guernsey and Jersey were a lark for a sea-going Princess.

Always there was Louis. One evening, standing on the lawn looking out across the Gulf of Saint Malo toward the lights of Brittany, she caught a song murmuring among the lonely pines of winter:

Fair Isle at sea—thy lovely name
Soft on my ear like music came,
That sea I loved, and once or twice
I touched at Isles of Paradise.

♦　♦　♦

Princess Victoria Kaiulani

Chapter X

CHRISTMAS IN HAWAI'I: OVERTHROWN YET EVERGREEN!

Atlantic Ocean Liner *Teutonic* docked in New York harbor on March 1 1893. She was met by reporters and hordes of people who swarmed onto the pier for a glimpse of Princess Victoria Kaiulani. She did not disappoint them. An arresting and dramatic figure, Victoria was groomed in a dark traveling costume and a broad blue hat. Around her neck she wore a garland of La France roses and smilax reaching to her waist. The newspapers raved about a tall, beautiful young woman of sweet face and slender figure, with decidedly good eyes of soft brown, and dark, wavy hair. Reporters found her complexion not more dark than many girls whom one might meet on Broadway.

Victoria looked out at the sea of friendly and reassuring faces on the pier, always with an underlying wonder if she might see Louis. This, wherever she found herself, had become a habit with her. Standing beside her guardian, Theophilus H. Davies, she read a statement, and now it was clear why she had come to America:

> *"Unbidden I stand upon your shores today where I had thought so soon to receive a royal welcome. I come unattended except for the loving hearts that come with me over the winter seas. I hear the Commissioners from my land have been for many days asking this great nation to take away my little vineyard. They speak no word to me, and leave me to find out as I can from the rumors of the air that they would leave me without a home or a name or a nation.*
>
> *Seventy years ago, Christian America sent over Christian men and women to give religion and civilization to Hawai'i.*

Today, three of the sons of those missionaries are at your capitol asking you to undo their fathers' work. Who sent them? Who gave them the authority to break the constitution which they swore they would uphold?

Today, I, a poor weak girl, with not one of my people near me and all these statesmen against me, have strength to stand up for the rights of my people. Even now I can hear their wail in my heart, and it gives me strength and courage and I am strong...strong in the faith of God, strong in the knowledge that I am right, strong in the strength of seventy million people who in this free land will hear my cry and will refuse to let their flag cover dishonour to mine!"

On January 30, Victoria had received three staggering telegrams brought to her in rapid succession by Theo Davies: "Queen deposed;" "Monarchy abrogated;" "Break news to princess." Davies proposed an immediate trip to Washington and Victoria quickly agreed:

"Perhaps someday the Hawaiians will say that Kaiulani could have saved us but she didn't even try! I will go with you."

Wherever she went, Victoria was a personal success on her mission. An adulating press followed her: "....Whenever Kaiulani passed through hotel dining rooms, comments of admiration were heard on all sides....delicate beauty, with exquisitely small, well shaped hands, an accomplished musician, an artist, a linguist with the genteel manners of a born aristocrat...."

In Washington President Grover Cleveland and his wife received Victoria at the White House. She found Mrs. Cleveland to be a greatly loved, beautiful young first lady. The President was warmly positive; he intended to see justice done. Victoria, in word and appearance, forcefully contradicted the vicious propaganda of the Provisional Government: Hawai'i's rulers were *not* "undisciplined savages."

Hawai'i, as viewed from Washington, was a battleground of bitter charges and countercharges among the parties concerned. The commissioners from Hawai'i's provisional government were there pushing hard for an annexation bill. Victoria's cousin, Prince David Kawananakoa, had arrived in Washington with Paul Neumann, the deposed queen's lawyer. There was tension in their corner. Theo Davies was accused of working against the interests of the queen and of displaying extraordinary zeal on behalf of Victoria. There were hints of estrangement within the royal family: prior to the overthrow of the monarchy, Judge Sanford Ballard Dole had suggested that Queen Lili'uokalani retire in favor of Victoria, and act as advisor to the throne with a regency of other prominent Hawaiians. The Queen wrote to Victoria that she would be offered the throne, but—wait! The provisional government was weakening. People all over the islands were petitioning to restore the Queen. Aunt Lydia admonished her: "Be guarded, don't accept any overtures, or be put in an awkward light. Practice self-possession, think before you speak or act, keep cool at all times. No blood has been shed; everything around us is in commotion."

The press in Hawai'i continued its campaign of constant harassment. Archie wrote that for the present it was better that Victoria not be in Hawai'i. The newspapers in Honolulu were publishing nasty articles, especially the *Star* which began publication under the auspices of the Annexation Club. As for Victoria, she never received overtures to the throne. She returned to England and lived for the day that would end her four year exile. Always, always, there was comfort from Louis:

I will make a palace fit for you and me
Of green days in forests and blue days at sea.

♦ ♦ ♦

The overthrow of the Hawaiian monarchy: how did it happen? Anyone who was more than casually interested in the Hawaiian scene could not have been surprised. For years, explosive powder had been ladled into the cannon. Honolulu, at all levels of government and citizenry, was a scene of growing unrest, of jockeying for power. It had become United States policy to station a warship continually in Hawaiian waters to support the queen, and to aid her government in preserving internal order. In this way, the United States also emphasized its "hands-off" warning to European powers, especially Great Britain and Germany. All that was needed was the combination of events which took place in January 1893.

Upon her succession, Queen Lili'uokalani had promptly named Victoria Kaiulani the heir apparent. Living up to her reputation for being tough when necessary, Lili'uokalani informed the existing cabinet ministers that she would accept their resignations, a move which the Supreme Court eventually supported. Tensions escalated through 1892 over her control of her cabinet. This forced Lili'uokalani into an enduring, never satisfactory compromise over its membership. There were rumors of the cabinet's involvement in a coup attempt against the throne. The cabinet also opposed bills the queen pushed through the legislature providing for a lottery and controlled opium use. Ultimately, she attempted to oust the cabinet, and announced her intention to form a new constitution which would restore full power to the Monarchy and rights to the Hawaiian people. Her ministers, asunder in their loyalties, scurried downtown to warn a newly-formed "Committee of Safety," a group of foreign businessmen, most-ly American, secretly organized to overthrow the monarchy and annex Hawai'i to the United States.

The Committee was well prepared to employ an historical model already over-used in the diminutive Sandwich Islands: build up ten-sion and agitate for outside help. American Minister John L. Stevens, strongly sympathetic to the Reform party, informed the revolutionists that he would recognize their provisional government as the true gov-ernment of Hawai'i as soon as they occupied Ali'iolani Hale, the prin-cipal government building. He would land marines from the *USS Boston* upon call. The queen's government could have managed a smaller number of revolutionaries from within. But the United States marines? That would not be a contest: huge cannon, and well-trained troops against police, palace guards, and trained volunteers? Now the annexationists needed a pretext, a riot.

American troops, followed by their artillery, came ashore on the afternoon of January 16. They paraded down King Street past Iolani Palace with the U.S. Navy band in the lead. The band greeted the queen, watching from her balcony, with a royal salute, a drooping of the colors and four ruffles of the drums. They proceeded to encamp at Arion Hall, ready at arms, artillery in readiness only seventy-six yards from Ali'iolani Hale—far from the American property the queen assumed they had come to protect. The queen, now aware of the Committee of Safety, met hurriedly with her cabinet and Governor Cleghorn of Oahu and proclaimed, through circulars and an extra edition of the Hawaiian language newspaper, that the consti-tution would be changed only by methods provided within the existing constitution. The paper reported that ministers of England, France, Japan and Portugal, but not of the United States, had met that morning and would support the queen. The two banks in town stood ready to help the Hawaiian government with money if needed, and many merchants stood with the queen. The people were cautioned against any acts of violence.

The "Annexation Club", a thousand or more, met at the skating rink. Inflaming speeches depicted the islands' danger of a bloody revolution. It was incumbent upon them to devise ways and means to maintain law and order, and protect the life, liberty, and property in Hawai'i. Lorrin Thurston, blaming Lili'uokalani said, "Now is the time to act and overthrow this disgusting monarchy."

In the mid-afternoon of January 17 it happened; the pretext for which the revolutionaries were waiting: a shot from a revolver in downtown Honolulu; a wounded policeman. Chaos reigned, and diverted Lili'uokalani's guard from the palace. In the confusion, a delegation of a newly formed Provisional government called on the unprotected queen at Iolani Palace to demand her abdication.

While the queen's ministers were in the police station drafting a letter to Stevens requesting his assistance [Stevens stipulated that this must be in writing], the Committee of Safety took over the government building without resistance. Once in control, with a strong armed force surrounding the government building, the Provisional Government declared martial law and issued a long proclamation. It denounced the excesses and unkept promises of Kalakaua's regime, and the attempts of his successor, Queen Lili'uokalani, to follow the tactics of her late brother in attempting to restore royal prerogatives and reduce popular rights.

Lili'uokalani immediately protested to the United States. She realized the actions of the U.S. Minister, and the landing of troops were illegal. She yielded to superior force, to prevent loss of life until such time as the United States Government should undo this action and reinstate her as constitutional sovereign of the Hawaiian Islands.

In March President Cleveland kept his promise to Victoria. He announced he would send a special investigator, Congressman James H. Blount of Georgia, with authority over any other American official in Hawai'i, to report on the situation in Hawai'i. The Provisional government commissioners were furious, but they had succeeded in having Lorrin Thurston recognized as their minister to Washington.

In August, Blount completed his study and left Hawai'i to submit his report. He found that a great wrong had been done. The Hawaiians were overwhelmingly opposed to annexation. He suggested that their legitimate government should be restored. Cleveland subsequently responded by asking congress to "devise a solution consistent with American honour, integrity and morality."

◆   ◆   ◆

The *S.S.Mariposa* slipped quietly into Honolulu harbor early one morning in December 1893. Aboard were Louis and his cousin [and later biographer], Graham Balfour, on a short pleasure trip. That was the public version of this visit. The truth was that Louis couldn't stay away; he had to see for himself the results of the tragic events of the past year. Rising early, Louis leaned over the rail to watch the pilot boat as it chugged out to meet the *Mariposa*. As it drew closer, Louis recognized a conspicuous figure waving from the bow. He was a very tall, powerfully-formed man who dwarfed the seaman beside him. It was Kalamake. Once on board, the big Hawaiian gathered Louis in a smothering embrace, then scrutinized him with a fondly serious gaze.

Kalamake was the Honolulu version that morning, masked for public observation.

Louis was the first to speak. "Well, Kalamake, you, at least, have not changed." Louis nodded toward the harbor and sniffed the land breeze, "Even from here I can smell a difference in Hawai'i."

Kalamake shrugged fatalistically. For a moment Louis caught a glimpse into the depth of the man's eyes and he recalled once more the Tahitian proverb: "The coral waxes, the palm grows, but man departs."

Kalamake gestured toward the shore, not unhappily. "The seasons, Mister Stevenson, they come and they go. It's like my canoes: every year my canoes are better, faster. But the sea they ride on, the sea is in command. The Cleghorns—many people—are very sad. We miss the king. And Queen Lydia, she lost her husband. Mr. Dominis is dead. Now she lives very quietly in Washington Place, although at least she's no longer a prisoner. Yes, many things have changed, but the sea: the sea is always in command."

The *Mariposa* was at the wharf now, and Kalamake began assembling Louis's luggage. Louis knew he had more to say, and he felt Kalamake's uncomfortable suspense. He interrupted his busyness.

"Kalamake, what about our princess? I don't feel I'm in touch with her. What can you tell me? Where is she? Is she all right?"

Kalamake raised his hands in reassurance. "She was sick for a time. What happened to the queen really upset her. But she's better." He smiled approvingly." She says *you* make her very strong!"

Louis breathed a relieved sigh.

Kalamake reached down into his trousers and drew forth a small package. "She told me to return this to you. You lost it—" Kalamake grinned. "—in England!"

Louis, his fingers clumsy with excitement, undid the soft bundle. Wrapped in a silk of Stewart tartan was the silver talisman, gleaming warmly at him.

Kalamake took the little silver piece and turned it over in his big hands. "These two pieces—these little flowers—they're stuck together, aren't they? Strong!"

Louis stared at Kalamake in amazement! "Good heavens! I thought I'd never see it again. It just disappeared one night. I thought the help at Vailima had stolen it!"

Kalamake looked at him quizzically, amused. "You don't recall a snowy night? A gloomy old place called Great Harrowden?"

Louis sucked in his breath, looked at Kalamake, and slowly smiled. "Ah! Yes—yes I do!"

Waiting at the wharf were Archie Cleghorn and George Trousseau with warm greetings for Louis. They too, bore an air of change, a sadness under their heartfelt welcome. A carriage was waiting, and they accompanied Louis and Graham to the San Souci Hotel in Waikiki. At least one thing hadn't changed: the hotel and the small thatched cottages still displayed the panel decorations done a few years ago by Belle and Joe Strong.

In the days that followed, Louis spent much time with Archie and the Doctor, reminiscing about old times, and assessing the new. The tone of the city was strikingly different, but the Royal Hawaiian Hotel and the Pacific Club clung tenaciously to a gracious, colorful past. In these settings the three friends had much news to share.

One afternoon, sipping wine on the porch of the Royal Hawaiian, Louis inquired about that young firebrand, Wilcox. Trousseau, bursting into a broad smile, slapped his knee and described Wilcox's raid on the palace a month after Louis had left for the Gilberts.

"Wilcox and one hundred and fifty armed men, all in red Garibaldi shirts—that was the Liberal Patriotic Association uniform—invaded the Palace grounds and government office buildings across King Street. Oh! Stevenson, you surely missed it! What a day! The Royal Guard refused them entrance to the Palace. Then, in dread and dismay, they watched Wilcox move cannon onto the grounds and demand King Kalakaua's signature to their constitution."

Archie interjected: "Then our militia got into it! Early the next morning, with ten thousand rounds of ammunition borrowed from the USS Adams the volunteers took positions atop the Opera House and Kawaiahao Church looking down into the palace grounds."

"It started this way," Trousseau said. "Wilcox made his move on the palace at 3:00 a.m. on July 30. He went looking for the King at the palace. He thought he'd planned a secret operation! We all knew they'd been shipping guns to the island for months. How they thought they could keep a secret in Honolulu is beyond me! Well, the King was spending the night with Queen Kapiolani at her residence. When he was told of the Red Shirt invasion, he went with the royal guardsmen to the boathouse. Then he talked back and forth with Wilcox over the telephone."

Archie nodded. "Wilcox—the well-intentioned patriot—kept sending the King messages. He wanted him to come back to the palace and sign his new constitution. Well, of course, Kalakaua stayed where he was. Ah! But Wilcox was determined."

Trousseau tapped the ash from his cigar and filled his champagne glass. "What happened was inevitable. From somewhere, somebody fired a rifle, and all at once everybody was shooting. Their cannon! Well, Wilcox scored a few hits on the Opera House before our riflemen drove them away. Oh, but our militia maneuvered bravely: they rushed Ali'iolani Hale and forced the Red Shirts out."

Archie chuckled, "Then, what did Wilcox and his men do, but run off and hide in the king's bungalow. Then our boys got a little over-enthusiastic. Two from the baseball team—actually it was the pitchers, Wodehouse and Turton—began lobbing dynamite sticks over the palace walls onto the roof of the bungalow. Wilcox's men finally came out with a white sheet tied to a pole, but the roof, the second story—

all torn to pieces! As for Wilcox's constitution: that fool should have known. The King had no power on his own to change it."

Trousseau nodded. "Ah, poor Wilcox! Well, as it turns out, they weren't too hard on him. He was out of jail and running for the legislature in no time."

The conversation turned to Kalakaua's death in San Francisco. Trousseau noted that he'd suffered a stroke and kidney failure.

"Strange," the doctor mused, "you know, Stevenson, the way many of his friends called him 'Taffy'. Somehow, I never could do that. It didn't fit the man or his stature. I loved him like a brother, but ...." Trousseau broke off sadly and fumbled with his cigar.

"His funeral procession was something you should have witnessed. It shocked the missionary-minded folk. The Hawaiian Societies all attended, of course. The members of Kalakaua's secret *Hale Naua* society created a dramatic scene. In the procession they were very heathenish in their appearance, and they howled in the most unearthly manner. Leading them was their high priest, a huge Hawaiian in a warrior's helmet, carrying the king's feather helmet, a kapu stick, and a secret gourd."

Inevitably their conversation turned to the overthrow of the monarchy. Archie had been badly shaken by this, and was inclined to blame the queen for all their troubles.

Archie poured forth his unhappiness. "If she'd abdicated on the night of the 16th or early on the 17th, I think the throne could have been saved. I kept telling her a provisional government was bearing down on her."

Trousseau pounded the table. "It was a comedy of errors—no, not a comedy! It might never have happened if it weren't for that skirmish on Fort Street."

Archie leaned across toward Louis. "You see, what happened was that one of our policeman came across a wagon loaded with arms. He grabbed the horse's reins and tried to arrest this squad of revolutionaries who'd been going from store to store buying arms. John Good, the man who was their leader—he's now Captain of the Army of the Provisional Government—he shot the policeman in the shoulder. They raced up Fort Street with the police in pursuit, but that shot was heard all over Honolulu. It drew the police away from Ali'iolani Hale. It also drew off the men who were assigned to stop the revolutionist riflemen, and to arrest any conspirators who approached the government building. They all rushed pell-mell down Merchant Street to see what happened."

"It so happened," Trousseau added, "that the Committee of Safety at the same time had split up and headed for Aliʻiolani Hale by different routes. In the confusion, with just one rifleman around, the few clerks on duty surrendered to them without a protest."

"Lydia was led away from the Palace as a prisoner." Archie shuddered at the recollection. "I'm a skeptic, Stevenson, but what do you make of this? The night of the overthrow, Honolulu was rocked by the worst earthquake ever recorded in the islands! The Hawaiians, of course, said that goddess Pele was outraged."

Their attention turned to Victoria and Louis listened intently as Archie told of his visits with her in England. Trousseau produced a newspaper clipping from his pocket to share with Louis:

"This was Victoria's statement of farewell to American Press. I thought you might like to have it:

> "Before I leave this land, I want to thank all whose kindnesses have made my visit such a happy one. Not only the hundreds of hands I have clasped nor the kind smiles I have seen, but the written words of sympathy that have been sent to me from so many homes, have made me feel that whatever happens to me I shall never be a stranger to you again. It was to all the American people I spoke, and they heard me as I knew they would. And now God bless you for it—from the beautiful home where your fair First Lady reigns, to the little crippled boy who sent his loving letter and prayer."

Trousseau clearly was worried about the overthrow's impact on Victoria. He confided his fear that she might have suffered a shock from which she would never fully recover.

Thus passed a gloomy December for Louis which the warmth of his friends could not dispel. He tried to keep busy, and in every way he avoided officials of the provisional government. Amid the unrest he made one unobtrusive call on Liliʻuokalani, well aware that attempts were still being made to restore her to the throne, and that her life was repeatedly threatened.

Louis sat for Allen Hutchinson, the English sculptor, who did a casting for a bronze bust. A happy moment was the renewal of his acquaintance with the Honolulu Scottish Thistle Club, when Louis was invited to address them one evening. He was tired and drawn, but the newspapers described him as dashing in a suit of brown corduroy brightened with his favorite red sash. It was another occasion of warmth and sentiment. The members designated Louis an honorary chieftain and bestowed a bronze thistle as a lapel emblem. Louis cherished it, but against the blue loneliness of separation from Scotland, he felt that he had lost something that had been his due—his native, predestinate, and forfeited grave among honest Scots.

Louis spent much time writing at night, but he couldn't bring himself to write about Oahu. He did write about the perpetual ringing of the reprehensible *kelepono* outside his hotel room. Honolulu didn't agree with him; he felt headachy and always out of sorts. He was getting sick again, and he knew it. Perhaps it would only be a slight cold, but he was feverish, and Dr. Trousseau ordered him to bed.

◆   ◆   ◆

Through bright moments in shadowy days, December inched its way toward Christmas Eve. Along Waikiki beach, the lights of the cottages nestled among the palms were muted. Distant Honolulu huddled against the cloud-banked mountains, dismal beneath a pale, diminished sunset. At Sans Souci, Louis, too, was huddled in his bed, too disconsolate to write, lonely, feverish, a picture of weariness in a darkened room. A roach journeyed across the floor, and in the stillness seemed to scrape its way along.

Louis mused: "How fitting a companion for this Christmas!" He wished he hadn't come to Hawai'i. He felt completely demolished by the experiences of the past month. He was too depressed even to recapture vital memories of days in the pristine, primitive islands of the south seas. Now, indeed, he was certain of their ultimate fate.... At least, for the moment, the hotel *kelepono* wasn't ringing off the wall....

He didn't hear the tapping at first; he'd drifted off. A soft tapping at his door, and then the door opened slowly. A slender figure in a flowing white costume shimmered in the doorway. A crimson band was about her waist, and a wreath of ohia lehua, the fiery volcano blossom, framed her dark curls. Victoria! Ever more beautiful, more appealing! She flashed a smile, and the room was suddenly bright, electric!

"Aloha, Louis! Merry Christmas! I've brought you a present!"

Victoria crossed the room to his bedside, sat beside him and kissed him. She held her clasped hands out, her fingers bunched together.

"Take a guess! What do I have? Just for you!"

Louis sat up, grasped her hands and opened them. Coils of wire!

Victoria laughed at his perplexity and whispered in his ear. "It's the wires to the telephone outside in the hall! There will be no disturbances tonight!"

She took his hands and drew him out of his bed. "It's Christmas Eve, Louis! We're spending Christmas together!"

Louis, his nightshirt drooping, his long hair in disarray, stood befuddled before her. He felt mute, dumb struck, helpless to describe the gloomy prospects for a Honolulu Christmas in 1893. At last, words came to him:

"Victoria, beloved child—"

Victoria's eyes flashed. "Now, Louis, don't start with 'child' talk again!"

He began again. "Dearest Princess—"

"Well, Louis, I don't suppose you can call me that, either!"

"Dear heart! Not Honolulu. You can't believe what things are like now. Use your magic. Take us somewhere else. Let's go back to the Gilberts—"

Victoria taunted him with a sly smile: "Or Scotland? Would you like that?"

Louis's retreated. His eyes took on a faraway look. "No. Not just now. I don't think I could—"

Victoria swirled her long gown and struck a pose: "Louis, you and I are going to celebrate Christmas right here in Honolulu—but not Christmas 1893. This will be the very first official Hawaiian Christmas in 1862!"

As swift as the swirling of her gown, Victoria transported them into downtown Honolulu. It was early evening. People laden with greenery were wending their way down from the mountains. Hand in hand, Victoria and Louis mingled with the lighthearted, laughing crowds and browsed along lawns where colorful outdoor suppers were in full sway. The torchlit streets were a rhythm of prancing pa'u riders swathed in the red and green of Christmas. Merry passengers in brightly decorated carriages careened down the streets, waving, and tossing flower leis to passersby. Music and singing filled an air fragrant with the scent of flowers, roasting turkeys, pigs, geese and beef.

In unison each thought of the banyan tree, and the peacocks at Ainahau, and remembered with a sudden shudder that there was no Ainahau on Waikiki beach that Christmas eve. Nor were there the troubled hearts, the strife and bitterness. In the spinning Pacific world of the mid-nineteenth century, here was a momentary scene of carefree merriment.

In their festive stroll, Victoria and Louis came to Kawaiahao Church. From a distance in the deepening evening, the church glowed with myriad candles. Inside, with much hugging and kissing, the congregation gathered, rejoicing in the blazing scene, the decorated altar, and the resplendent Christmas robes of the choir. The church service, solemn and dignified, lasted until after midnight without a single nodding head. When they left the church he learned the reason: as the congregation emerged from the sanctuary, guns began firing from atop Punchbowl, and flaming tar barrels came tumbling down the slopes.

The climax of the evening was the procession through the streets of the city from the church to the palace, led by the Anglican bishop and King Alexander Liholiho. Behind them, the robed choir followed, and men bearing kukui-nut torches to light the way. Louis and Victoria drifted with the procession, singing the Christmas hymns, Victoria in Hawaiian, Louis haltingly recalling this lyrical language he had studied.

At the gates of the palace, the procession paused to watch the brilliant fireworks, the screaming rockets erupting from the hills. Then everyone joined in singing a final carol and the national anthem to end the memorable night ... the first Christmas officially celebrated in Hawai'i. For Victoria and Louis, that day would be timeless; they had celebrated it together.

◆ ◆ ◆

The magnetism of Ainahau was too strong for Victoria and Louis to resist. In the darkness of that Christmas morning, they made a torch-lit pilgrimage to the place where the banyan would one day stand. They stood looking in wonderment at the sprawling beach grass where this miracle would take place. Louis led Victoria to the beach, and they sat gazing up at the brilliant stars of the Hawaiian sky.

Louis expressed surprise. "Strange! Honu—I miss your turtle! I wonder if she's here somewhere?"

Victoria laughed. "Of course! Honu's here, all right, as sure as the sea. She was well over a hundred years old when she came into my life. And Modestine is here, too! But let's not look for them now. This evening is too precious. They'll understand."

The night drew on, so fleeting it was frightening, and they clung to each other. Victoria shook in his arms.

In the darkness of the starry night, in the slow, muffled rumble of the rolling surf, she shifted her position and searched his expression. "Louis, that day in the crater on Molokai. Do you remember what I said? About having something very special of yours? I know you and I have given birth to stories, to beautiful poems—but can't I claim something more? My body aches for you. Can't I claim something for loving you so passionately, so completely?"

Louis cradled her, his face close to hers and took a long breath.

"We can claim a love of the highest order, you and I. I know that I have lost all reason in my love for you. The goods of this world, my place in it, fame, social position and the rest, they mean nothing to me now. If you are a flame, dearest one, and I vow that you are, I can only compare myself to a moth. You swirl about me and the duties of my life like an overpowering whirlpool."

Victoria embraced him fiercely, melting into him. "I yearn, Louis, I can't describe my hunger for you in any other way. How is it wrong? If we loved God in this way, if we would sacrifice everything for the vision of His face, wouldn't He love us in return? He would have to respond, wouldn't He?"

"He would love us, and insist that we do good and not harm. He's even said something about us, something like this: if the vital spark in a mustard seed can pass unchanged through countless deaths and resurrections, then surely the spirit of a loved one will pass from his body into the one he loves."

Victoria sat up and crouched beside him. She held his face in her hands.

"Damnation, Louis. What a way you have with words! You're not even close to what I'm talking about. Do I have to act like the Hawaiian women back in the whaling days, chasing the sailors around Honolulu? Do I have to swim naked out to your ship?"

"Some day," Louis said, "when we're both gone from this world, both of us forgotten, I'd like there to be a lasting reminder of what we've had. Of this wonderful love that flows between us—and that so few experience."

"Something you want to write, isn't it? Of course! It would be your masterpiece! Well—."

Louis groaned in frustration. "*Our* masterpiece! But it eludes me. I feel I almost have it, at times. But it's always just out of reach!"

In silence they strolled in the wash of the surf down the beach to the Sans Souci. As they parted, Victoria embraced him, and gave him a last, guileful glance: "One day you'll find me in Scotland. Then we'll see ...."

♦ ♦ ♦

Dr. Trousseau pondered Louis's slow recovery, kept him in bed and notified Fanny. The *R.M.S.S.Monowa* arrived from Apia several days later and Fanny took charge. They departed on the *S.S.Mariposa* bound for Samoa and Vailima a week later. It was a quiet departure, only a last chat in the stateroom with Archie Cleghorn. The king was dead, the monarchy overthrown; there was no band to serenade the departing ship.

♦ ♦ ♦

Chapter XI

A PERFECT FRIEND

The Stevensons settled at Vailima and met head-on the myriad conflicting elements in Samoa. First, there was the usual shortage of money. Louis had to find funds to build a house, and this led to Fanny's decision to sell her beloved Skerryvore, the home in Bournemouth that was a gift from Father Stevenson. Then, Vailima was *The Silverado Squatters* re-lived. A temporary cottage with virtually no furniture or cooking facilities! Livestock was a necessity, and shelter for pigs and chickens competed with their own basic needs. Pigs kept escaping, haunting the forest, and chickens mysteriously disappeared.

The property itself was everything Louis had dreamed of. Clearing the land revealed huge orchid-adorned banyans with trunks thicker than the height of a tall man. The forest swarmed with song birds. The primeval forest rose up behind them to Mount Vaea, 1300 feet high. Out in the sea were the violet mountainous contours of distant Atua. Vailima would be built facing the sea, between two streams, one of which had a waterfall and a clear, deep pool.

Louis sweated in the hot Samoan mornings, wielding his long bush knife mightily. Fanny planted seeds brought from Sydney to supplement the forgotten taro and papayas, the lemon and lime trees that lived undiscovered until the clearing process. In time, Fanny and Louis would create a bountiful Vailima Plantation that would yield a wide variety of foods including cantaloupe, mangos and pineapples. Fanny kept an assiduous watch on the native boys who were inclined toward stealing this provender to sell in Apia. *Tamaitai* (Madam), was her formal name but her vigilance earned her the nickname, *Aolele* (Flying Cloud), from the native help. The help also thought of her as witch woman of the mountain because of her sudden movements and strange piercing glance. In the early days, the Stevensons were not, even by South Seas standards, a handsome society couple. Henry Adams, a visiting historian and friend of Henry James, found these toiling pioneers living in a clearing dotted with burned stumps in a squalid, two-story Irish shanty. Louis was so emaciated he looked like a bundle of sticks in a bag. He went about in dirty striped pajamas, the baggy legs tucked into coarse woolen stockings. Fanny's mission-ary nightgown was no cleaner than her husband's shirt and drawers. Though Adams could not overlook the dirt and squalor, he did con-cede that Louis was extremely entertaining. There were no dinner invitations to Vailima in those days. Louis wrote later to Henry James: "we have almost nothing to eat; a guest would simply break the bank....What would you do with a guest at such narrow seasons?—Eat him? Or serve up a labor boy fricasseed?"

Settling in at Vailima had a steadily erosive effect on Fanny. She suffered from the heat, and had spells of almost paralytic exhaustion. Historian Adams observed that Louis seemed to gloat over discom-forts. The household was forever in a state of turmoil with bewilder-ing changes of servants. Finally the Stevensons found a Samoan chiefling who turned out to be a reliable overseer. Then, one day a stal-wart gardener appeared, a "huge mutton-headed Hercules who paint-ed his face to frighten away ghosts, of which he was desperately afraid."

Other things drained Fanny's previously abundant resources. Louis's statement that she had the soul of a peasant became some-thing over which she brooded. For him to denigrate her creativity, the driving force of her life, hurt her more than he ever realized. She shouldered a burden of pain, depression and shame. Louis, ever harassed by the need for money, thought to soften his tactlessness by whipping himself: a man who is supporting his family by his work insults his creativity and is not an artist either. Fanny was injured as well by the physical demands of creating a home. Arthritis hobbled her, at times, so badly that she could not go up and down stairs. She would have to sit on the back veranda in a shouting supervision of the help; a sort of pidgin dialect no one else could understand.

When at last, the new house was begun, always the problem of money surfaced. They worked for months to devise plans that still went beyond their means. To dry Louis's papers, they required a chimney, the only one in Samoa. Every item of building material had to be imported from America or 'the Colonies', as Australia and New Zealand were called.

During his trip to England, Lloyd successfully sold Skerryvore, and he and Mother Stevenson were on their way to Samoa. Louis sailed for Sydney to meet them but Fanny was too incapacitated to accompany him. This left her to contend with the builders. At home, she was vulnerable to the exhausting demands of the help with their personal problems, drunken behavior, even the practice of cannibalism in the neighborhood. Servants reported the activities of ghosts of persons killed and eaten. At night the kitchen and the stable seemed haunted. Noises were heard in the earth under the garden, and there were earthquakes. For several days a hurricane raged; the temporary cottage was so unstable that Fanny had to move bedding, candles, mosquito nets and other necessities into the newly completed stable. She lived in the stalls, constantly sweeping out the water and lying in a wet bed, devoured by mosquitoes.

When Louis returned with Mother Stevenson, he was still quite ill from another hemorrhage setback in Sydney. The scene was too much for Maggie. She left a sofa she had brought, and stayed only until the *Lubeck* sailed back to New Zealand. She would wait for the completion of the Great House.

There were other stresses bearing down upon Louis and Fanny. They lived with constant rumors of war in Samoa. Apia was a neutral municipality, jointly but not harmoniously administered by the United States, Britain and Germany. After a recent native war the three powers appointed Commissioners and a Chief Justice to deal with the island of Upolu. The three nations backed the former king, Malietoa Laupepa, but most of the islanders preferred the high chief, Mata'afa, the rival claimant. Missionaries and traders took sides and the Stevensons championed the romantic Mata'afa. Soon Louis was writing impassioned letters to the London *Times* and getting embroiled in ways that appeared certain to guarantee his deportation.

The three Strongs, Belle, Joe, and little Austen arrived upon this feverish scene with a maid, a cat and a cockatoo. The Stevensons met them at the jetty as they came in from the *Lubeck* in a small whaleboat. There were horses waiting for them and Belle was delighted by the ride up the mountain to Vailima between the coco palms and bananas, along a steep trail through dense jungle, great trees joining over their heads. A sharp turn in the way revealed the new Great House. Peacock-blue, and red-roofed, under enormous ironwood trees, it rose on a wide sweep of lawn beyond the gate. It was a scene of greenery, starry blossoms of jasmine vines, and hedges of brilliant hibiscus.

Belle assumed charge of the kitchen and the house, and Louis rose at dawn to write. As for Joe Strong, the family's worst fears soon happened. Joe had responsibility for the chickens and many died from improper feeding. Soon he was scrounging drinks, and finding excuses to sneak down to Apia. He became an object of gossip, and greatly added to the numerous other strains on the family. Fanny seethed with anger and resentment.

Vailima came together with the arrival of the furniture from Skerryvore. Husky Samoans carried the piano up the rocky trail swung on poles from their shoulders. Vailima became an impressive estate for the viewing of local society: mahogany, silver, crystal, china, family portraits, hundreds of books, delicious food and wines. Fanny's vegetable garden, the only one in Samoa, produced artichokes, aubergines, sweet corn, tomatoes, melons, and yard-long beans. Islanders looked in awe upon the possessions, the pomp and style of the new white chief's household.

With the exception of Maggie Stevenson, everyone went barefoot at Vailima in the daytime They chain-smoked Virginia cigarettes they rolled themselves. A bowl of mildly alcoholic *kava* was on the sideboard from mid-afternoon on, and everyone gathered for a dip in the swimming pool under the waterfall. The broad lawn provided informal cricket matches played with oranges from the trees. Evening was an occasion for dress in tropical white, the men with cummerbunds; cocktails on the veranda before dinner. A close friend described Louis, the Laird of Vailima, as a sick man, indeed a workhorse supporting with difficulty the whole expense of a large household of idle adults. The women of the household gave elaborate affairs, but the continual entertaining seemed to originate more from Louis than Fanny. Louis had a way of inviting friends up to Vailima for dinner, and the family, when he rode into town, never knew how many he would bring home.

Joe Strong's misdeeds multiplied. They discovered he'd been robbing the storeroom at night, and when they confronted him, he went the rounds of their friends slandering Belle. He heaped even further insult upon Belle: Joe had been living with a native woman of Apia ever since his arrival. This was an old affair begun on an earlier visit in Samoa. Belle, Fanny and Louis reached the inevitable decision and rushed a divorce through the court in Apia.

Fanny finally collapsed from the accumulation of these stresses in her life in Samoa. Still, the one most critical item was the fundamental change that had been taking place in Louis. His insistence on writing a heavy, factual book was an on-going but comparatively minor source of dispute; more significant, Louis's mature work had outgrown Fanny; he no longer needed her advice on potential masterpieces. Word from London described his recent novel *Catriona* as a resounding success. After the years of struggle against tuberculosis and poverty, it appeared that her role in the fight to give him health and success was no longer indispensable. Even more, in those times Louis's thoughts and creative energies were turning back to Scotland, and she found herself unable to share or be helpful in this. She was unaware of a desperation Louis felt, a sense of being creatively dried up, a longing for the roots that would enable him to move forward in his literary ventures.

Fanny became subject to intense moods and tantrums. She occupied herself as usual in the garden, she was there at her place at dinner, but slowly she became a stranger. Through many weeks in which the family lived with heartbreaking anxiety, Fanny was odd in her thinking and behavior, suspicious, irritable, and utterly unpredictable. Louis and the children worked as a team smoothing over unpleasant scenes and making excuses to outsiders. At times Fanny raged out of physical control requiring restraint to keep her from running away. She was lost in strange and threatening fixations of thought, and terrifying hallucinations welled up from her chaotic inner world.

On a night of severe agitation, Fanny ran off into the forest above Vailima. The children were attending a social function in Apia, and Louis had been unable to persuade or restrain her. She rushed out of the house screaming, holding her head, cursing. Louis grabbed a lantern and followed her, hoping to calm her. Stumbling through the forest, at last he found her on the ground sobbing. At length, she became calm, but totally within herself, oblivious to him, her lips moving silently. It was an unearthly quiet, only the toll of the cathedral bell from town, and the dim sound of the distant surf below.

Suddenly there was a rush of air and a high-pitched sound. Perhaps it was agitation of the wind in the forest about them. The lantern flared up and Louis and Fanny found themselves in a circle of bright light. Beside them a finely textured mat appeared, and then very slowly two figures formed out of a mist welling up from the mat. At their feet was a flaming tray and as the fragrant smoke cleared, Louis recognized Victoria. Standing opposite her on the mat was the giant figure of Kalamake.

Victoria stepped off the mat and gestured urgently to Louis.

"Quickly, Louis. Get on the mat. There's no time. Uncle will tell you what to do."

Louis, bewildered, clung to Fanny.

Victoria was insistent. "Hurry, Louis. I'll look after Fanny. Go!"

Kalamake guided Louis onto the opposite corner of the mat and placed a shell necklace about his neck. Steadying him with one hand, quickly he rekindled the fire at their feet with herbs and leaves. Kalamake began to mutter and wave the branch of a palm. The fire blazed up and the smoke made Louis's head swim and his eyes darken. The sound of Kalamake's muttering rang in his ears. Suddenly, to the mat on which they were standing, came a sudden thrust, that seemed to be more swift than lightning. In a flash, the forest disappeared, and the breath was beaten from Louis's body. A brilliant light rolled upon his eyes and head, and he found himself transported to a beach by the sea, under a strong sun, with a great surf roaring. He was speechless, gasping.

"In the name of God, where are we?" cried Louis.

"That is not the question." replied Kalamake. "We have matters at hand that we must attend to. Go, while I recover my breath, into the borders of the wood, and bring me leaves of an herb and a tree which you will find growing there plentifully—three handfuls of each. And be speedy." Kalamake sat on the sand and panted.

Louis went up the beach, which was of shining sand and coral, strewn with singular shells. He puzzled over the beach and the line of golden palms against the sky, tall, fresh and beautiful. The more he thought, the less he was able to conceive what quarter of the islands he had come to. In a border of the grove where it met the beach the herb was growing, but the tree was farther back. As he went toward the tree he was aware of a young woman who had nothing on her body but a belt of leaves. She seemed not to notice him so he stood and hummed aloud. Up she leaped at the sound. Her face was ashen; she looked this way and that, and her mouth gaped with the terror of her soul. It was a strange thing that her eyes did not rest upon Louis. He greeted her reassuringly, but he had hardly opened his mouth before the young woman fled into the bush. She kept calling and warning others. Presently Louis saw more people running—men, women and children, all running and crying like people at a fire. He began to grow afraid himself, and returned to Kalamake bringing the leaves. He told him what he had seen.

"You must pay no heed." said Kalamake. "All this is like a dream and shadows. All will disappear and be forgotten."

"It seems none saw me," said Louis.

"And none did." replied the kahuna. "We walk here in the broad sun invisible by reason of these charms. Yet they hear us; and therefore it is well to speak softly, as I do."

With that, Kalamake made a circle round the mat with stones, and in the midst he set the leaves.

"It will be your part," he said, "to keep the leaves alight, and feed the fire slowly. While they blaze, which is but for a little moment, I must do my errand; and before the ashes blacken, the same power that brought us will carry us away. Be ready now with the match; and call me in good time, lest the flames burn out and I be left."

As soon as the leaves caught, the kahuna leaped like a deer out of the circle, and began to race along the beach. As he ran, he kept stooping to snatch shells; and it seemed to Louis that they glittered as he took them. The leaves blazed with a clear flame that consumed them swiftly. Presently, Louis had but a handful left, and Kalamake was far off, running and stopping.

"Back!" cried Louis. "Back! The leaves are near done."

At that Kalamake turned, and if he had run before, now he flew. Fast as he ran, the leaves burned faster. The flame was ready to expire when, with a great leap, he bounded on the mat and thrust the bag of shells into Louis's hands. The wind of his leaping blew out the flame; and with that the beach was gone, and the sun and the sea....

♦ ♦ ♦

As the whirlwind in Louis's mind slowly subsided, he found himself on a road running up the valley of a brook shaded by willows and birches. As he lurched along in wonder, Kalamake's bag of shells in his hands, he heard a gurgling of falls and pools. The road seemed unused, the land uninhabited except for an occasional gaunt farmhouse. Louis's puzzled scrutiny of the place grew into excitement and mounting joy. This was a scene from his boyhood! It was the moor lands of southern Scotland! Perhaps he was in the Lammermuirs, perhaps beside Glencoe in the Pentlands. The soft ring of a kirk bell came to him in the breeze.

Louis fingered the bag of shells; they were warm, vibrant in his hands. In the distance he saw the kirk standing beside the brook in a grassy green among gravestones, an ancient, dwarfish place. There was a manse close by, a mere cottage, surrounded by a bright flower garden, with a collection of beehives off to one side. The silence was profound except for the drone of the bees and the tinkle of the brook. *Hermiston!* He would call this place *Hermiston!*

It must be Sunday! There was no doubt that spring had come at last. It was warm, with a latent shiver in the air that made the warmth only more welcome. The shallows of the stream glittered and tinkled among bunches of primrose. Vagrant scents of the earth were intoxicating. The gray sobriety of the winter setting was awakened only in patches of color; Louis wondered at its beauty; an essential beauty of the old earth breathing to him. He lingered for a time in the kirk-yard. A tuft of primroses bloomed in the cold earth beside an old, black tombstone, and he stopped to contemplate the contrast. He was struck also, with a sense of contrast in the day, the season, and the beauty that surrounded him—the chill within the warmth, the gross black clods about the opening primroses, the damp earthy smell that was everywhere intermingled with the scents.

Louis entered the little kirk, and went up the aisle reverently, with lowered eyes, taking his place in a pew. He would call this the Hermiston pew: a little square box, dwarfish in proportion with the kirk itself, and enclosing a table not much bigger than a footstool. There he sat, feeling himself to be an apparent prince, the only undeniable gentleman and the only great heritor in the parish, taking his ease in the only pew, for no other in the kirk had doors. His position commanded an undisturbed view of a congregation of solid men in plaid, strapping wives and daughters, oppressed children and uneasy sheep-dogs. There was no one present with the least claim to gentility. The rest of the congregation, like so many sheep, oppressed him with a sense of hob-nailed routine, day following day—of physical labor in the open air, oatmeal porridge, peas bannock, the somnolent fireside in the evening, and the night-long nasal slumbers in a box-bed. Yet surely, many of them were shrewd and humorous, men of character, notable women, making a bustle in the world and radiating an influence from their low-browed doors. He knew besides that they were like other men; below the crust of custom, rapture found a way; he could hear them beat the timbrel before Bacchus—could hear them shout and carouse over their whisky-toddy; and not the most severe faces among them all, not even the solemn elders themselves, but were capable of singular gambols at the voice of love. Men drawing near to an end of life's adventurous journey—maids thrilling with fear and curiosity on the threshold of entrance—women who had borne and perhaps buried children, who could remember the clinging of the small dead hands and the patter of the little feet now silent.

Louis marveled that among all those faces in the kirk, there should be no face of expectation, none that was mobile, none into which the rhythm and poetry of life had entered. "O for a live face," he thought. He studied the living gallery with despair. One would be at risk of wasting his days in such a joyless, pastoral place, with death coming to him, and his grave dug under the willows. Then the Spirit of the Earth would laugh in a thunder-peal at the huge fiasco.

And yet, the nasal hymn singing, full of turns and trills and graceless graces, seemed the essential voice of the kirk itself upraised in thanksgiving. "Everything's alive," he said; and again cried it aloud. "Thank God, everything's alive!"

♦   ♦   ♦

A distant whir, then a mounting, gyrating sound, and a brilliant flash of light: Louis found himself breathless, in his bedroom, panting, clutching the arms of his chair. He peered about him in the meager light. It was Vailima. The house was silent; was it dawn or dusk?

"My God! Kalamake took me to Scotland!" he muttered to himself. He rose and paced the room in excitement, absent-mindedly fingering a string of shells about his neck. He rushed to the upstairs gallery, and looked out over the railing into the half-light. Through the ironwoods, a misty calm lay over the ocean and a trace of brightness tinged the eastern sky.

"Hermiston! Hermiston!" He repeated excitedly. "That tiny kirk! Kalamake—the bag of bright shells—good Lord! He was feeding my little people! And the girl! There was a girl in the kirk—dark, like a gypsy. She had a bouquet of roses! She turned and looked at me!"

Louis rushed into his bedroom, lit a lamp and searched frantically for his pad and pen.

"Scotland! Hermiston! Oh! I've got to get this down!"

Running his fingers feverishly through his hair, he began to reassemble and record that moment in the kirk. "The prayer had ended and I had leaned back in the pew under a tablet on the wall. It was the only ornament,—" he paused to recapture the scene, "—in the roughly masoned chapel, and appeared to commemorate the long descent and local greatness of the—."

Louis looked at the lamplight flickering on the ceiling, deep in thought—"I'll call the family *Weir*. The girl: a name! A name! She was smiling, just the shadow of a smile, something between playful and sad."

"Kirstie! What last? —Elliott—I like that!" Then he was off again: "In her new Glasgow finery, she chose that moment to observe the young laird. She was aware of the stir of his entrance, but she kept her eyes fastened and her face prettily composed during the prayer." Louis scribbled frantically. "It was not hypocrisy. There was no one further from a hypocrite. The girl had been taught to behave and in every circumstance to look her best. That was the game of female life, and she played it frankly. He—what's his name?—*Archie*! Ha! Victoria would like that! I'll call him Archie Weir! Archie was the one person in church who was of interest, who was somebody new, reputed to be eccentric, known to be young, and a laird, and still unseen by Kirstie."

Louis got up and paced about the room, gesturing to himself. Thoughts rekindled, he sat down to resume his writing.

"Small wonder, there in her attitude of pretty decency, that her mind should run upon him! If he spared a glance in her direction, he should know she was a well-behaved young lady who had been to Glasgow. He would admire her clothes, and it was possible that he should think her pretty. At that her heart raced—just a trifle."

Louis laughed to himself, and shook his head as he wrote. "She proceeded, by way of a corrective, to call up and dismiss a series of pictures of the young man who should now, by rights, be looking at her. She settled on the plainest of them,—a pink, short young man with a dish face and no figure, at whose admiration she could afford to smile; but for all that, the consciousness of his gaze kept her in something of a flutter till the word 'Amen.' Even then, she was far too well-bred to gratify her curiosity with any impatience. She resumed her seat languidly—this was a Glasgow touch—she composed her dress, rearranged her nosegay of primroses, looked first in front, then behind upon the other side, and at last allowed her eyes to move, without hurry, in the direction of the Hermiston pew. For a moment they were riveted."

Louis put his pen down and rubbed his hands together. "And now what—?"

Again he was pacing the room, muttering: "Next she had plucked her gaze home again like a tame bird meditating flight. Possibilities crowded upon her; she hung over the future and grew dizzy. The image of this young man, slim, graceful, dark, with the inscrutable half-smile, attracted and repelled her like a chasm. 'I wonder, will I have met my fate?' she thought, and her heart swelled."

Louis rubbed his chin in contemplation. "Let's give her some kind of a family. A brother—no several brothers, rustic, tough. Some in the kirk with her. One she stays with in Glasgow. Clem, we'll call him. He's sitting beside her."

"Clem: prosperous, looking at the minister in a patronising way. He was leaning forward when Archie first saw him. Presently he leaned nonchalantly back; and that deadly instrument, the maiden, was suddenly unmasked in profile. Her accoutrement was, indeed, a cause of heart-burning, and almost of scandal, in that infinitesmal kirk company. The dress was drawn up so as to mould the contour of both breasts, and in the cleavage between trembled a brooch and the nosegay of primroses. About her face clustered a disorder of dark ringlets and a little garland of yellow French roses surmounted her brow. Among all the rosy and all the weathered faces that surrounded her in church, she glowed like an open blossom."

Again, Louis paced, rubbing his hands together, reaching for words. Once more at his desk: "Archie knew she must be Kirstie, his housekeeper's niece—and he found in her the answers to his wishes. Archie continued to drink her in with his eyes, like a wayfarer with an unquenchable thirst. In the cleft of her little breasts the fiery eye of the brooch and the pale primroses fascinated him. He saw the breasts heave, and the flowers shake. And Kirstie was conscious of his gaze, conscious of changing color, conscious of her unsteady breath."

Louis paused in his inspired scribbling, rose again, and walked about the room rubbing his chin. Suddenly he gripped his temples in wild consternation. "Good God! It wasn't just Kalamake—Victoria was there! In the forest! Victoria—and Fanny!"

Only then did the full impact of the previous evening strike him. "Oh, my God! Fanny! What's happened to Fanny?"

Louis grabbed the lamp, and rushed down the dim stairway into the great hall. A pleasant fire flamed on the hearth; Fanny was lying back in her leather armchair beside the hearth, sound asleep.

Belle tiptoed in from the dining room, a tray of tea things in her hands. She shook her head, crinkled her eyes to caution him.

"Mother's been sleeping there all night—like a baby," she whispered. "She's hardly moved. Lloyd and I found her here when we came home. Don't wake her—she looks so peaceful."

Louis went over to Fanny and studied her face, her quiet breathing. One thumb was hooked inside a shell necklace hanging about her neck.

Louis whispered softly to her, "Fanny?"

Fanny stirred slightly, sighed and opened her eyes. She smiled up at him mistily, reached out and fingered Louis's necklace. There was a long, thoughtful pause of remembrance, then a bright, reassuring smile.

"Louis, dear, you and I have a perfect friend!"

◆ ◆ ◆

In a cottage in faraway Kettering, England, Victoria recounted the thoughts of a tropical dream. She remembered Fanny, solitary, trapped in a jungle thicket, lost, frightened. She had calmed her, nourished her, and led her to safety. As these images resurfaced in her thoughts, Victoria felt the blood rise to her head in a warm, fulfilling way. The distance between herself and Louis—and Fanny—for a moment seemed to disappear.

Louis's response came to her a few nights later:

Since Thou hast given me this good hope, O God,
My life shall nowise lack the light of love,
My hands not lack the loving touch of hands,
But day by day while yet I draw my breath,
And day by day until my last of years,
I shall be one that has a perfect friend,
Her heart shall taste my laughter and my tears,
And her kind eyes shall lead me to the end.

♦   ♦   ♦

Princess Victoria Kaiulani

Chapter XII

SCOTLAND AT LAST!

Kettering was one more trial, another way-station in Victoria's exile. True, there were friends, indeed, some good ones. Male suitors were part of the scene both there and on the continent. In that regard, Aunt Lydia wrote to encourage her interest in a Japanese prince who was being educated in England. Fun and flirtation might be appropriate terms for her social activities where men were concerned; as for Aunt Lydia's suggestion, she quickly dismissed it. She could not marry someone she didn't love.

Victoria traveled extensively throughout Europe. It injected a measure of gaiety into her life, and she enjoyed the big city excitement of Berlin and Paris. But neither metropolis could reach deep into her like her fair islands. The scenes of western Europe were not what her heart longed for. The nearest substitute was her vacations with Archie on the French Riviera, and he often was able to make the long sea voyage to be with her.

On one such vacation in Mentone, in 1894, Victoria and Archie were breakfasting on their patio. Below them, the Mediterranean coastline swept away in hazy cliffs and bays, edging a bright blue sea. It was a commanding view, but command, control of events—that was an attribute oppressively absent for both of them. There was a repetitiousness about their times together which Victoria keenly regretted: Archie felt such a commitment to bolster her spirits, to encourage her, and Victoria saw little basis for this, not where the future of the Hawaiian monarchy was concerned.

Archie cleared his throat, and wiped his mustache with his napkin. "You know, the foreigners who thought the provisional government was such a good thing: they are falling away, Victoria. Nobody—

except those scoundrels running the government—likes the atmosphere of suspicion they've created. There's a strong feeling everywhere that trouble might break out at any time."

Victoria listened attentively, but there was something about her that was missing. There wasn't the vivacity, the animation of former times. A sadness clung about her; her cheeks were flushed, and her dark eyes had taken on a prominence that made her beauty more haunting than ever. She stirred, and tried to appear more cheerful. "Aunt Lydia did write recently that she feels some encouragement about restoration of the throne."

Archie planted his big fists on the breakfast table. "It's true! Well, why not? With the mess they've made? I tell you, Victoria, the PG's are frightened, on the run. People aren't going to stand for this! They've planted spies all over the islands. They've banned all large meetings."

Victoria nodded. "Yes, Aunt Lydia said people can't even have a lu'au without being suspected of holding a royalist meeting! Honestly, Father! They say the PG's are now calling themselves the Republic of Hawai'i! Can you imagine?"

Victoria paused to fiddle with her spoon, then she gave her father a pointed look. "Speaking of coercion, has Aunt Lydia said anything to you about arranging a marriage?"

Archie wriggled in his chair, and seemed to concentrate on carving up his melon. "Well, dear, she has said a few things to me about that."

Victoria flared, looked off into the distance, then at her father. "And who, pray, would it be? A Japanese prince? Or Prince David? She says she wants a prince, and children to make the throne more permanent. Believe me! I haven't seen any prince with whom I would want to make anything permanent!"

Archie was ready for a cautious pursuit of the matter. "Have you been looking?"

"If it's someone I love, I'll know it, Father. Otherwise, it would be totally wrong."

Archie sighed, but he looked relieved, and brightened a bit. He could tell Lydia he'd tried. "I've brought you something—it's, well, it's a bequest."

"Oh?" Victoria flushed. Something else bittersweet. "A bequest? What? Where is it?"

"Well, it's back at Kettering—a bit much to carry! It's from a very dear friend of yours."

"Oh, of course! Dr. Trousseau?" Victoria's expression saddened. She was suddenly close to tears. "That dear, dear man."

"He died with his boots on," Archie recounted, "as I always knew he would. Ah! There was a fighter! And he didn't make any distinctions among his opponents, either—Kings, Queens, the Board of Health—," Archie shook his head admiringly. "Mostly the Board of Health! He would tear into them like a tiger; always fighting to make the islands the world's healthiest place!"

Thoughts of Trousseau brought a wistful smile to Victoria's face. "Oh, Father, remember the day we rounded up his runaway ostriches in Waikiki?"

They shared a quiet smile, a nostalgic moment recalling a dear friend, and resumed their breakfast, as the warm sun climbed high over the blue Mediterranean.

"Well," Victoria recalled with a start, "What did Dr. Trousseau bequeath to me?"

Archie looked at her thoughtfully, his head turned a bit to one side. "Surely, you must know?....He left you his collection of Louis Stevenson's work! He thought he had some selections you would want."

"How sweet of him. He introduced us, Father. He presented Louis to me—" Victoria drifted off to faraway images, musing softly. "—in a way—" Victoria hesitated, lost in thought. "—in a way that might never have happened. If it weren't for Dr. Trousseau—."

"Happened?" Archie leaned toward her in puzzlement.

"Yes, 'happened,' Father." She gazed off vacantly into the distance. The raucous cry of a seabird caught her glance, and distracted, she followed its flight, alone in her thoughts.

"He was very generous with his time while you were at home. Was there—?" Archie began, and then thought better. "Do you hear from him? Does he ever write?"

Victoria looked down at her long, slender fingers and shook her head. She looked slowly at Archie from beneath her raised brows. Then she smiled. "He doesn't *have* to write to *me*, Father." Archie's daughter always had a way of dazzling and mystifying him.

Archie fumbled with his napkin and laid it on the tabletop. "I suppose not. A very busy man, I'm sure."

"But his books, Father. You brought them all the way from home?"

"I wanted to surprise you—"

"Father, dear—!" Victoria was suddenly impatient, pleading. "Why couldn't you have surprised me by *sending* for *me*? How much longer must I remain a captive here?"

And so it went, with the devoted father, and the daughter of whom he was so proud, and for whom he held so much hope.

♦   ♦   ♦

From the vast distance between them, Louis's excitement about the Weirs, and Hermiston, seemed to crackle in the air about Victoria. The impact of his experience with Kalamake had been more profound, more productive than she dared hope.

And Fanny, who gave Louis so much that Victoria could only long to give: Victoria yearned for some hopeful word. Had her healing ministry that night in the jungle led to recovery? When Victoria and Kalamake had burst upon that dreadful scene, Fanny was writhing on the jungle floor, screaming, tearing at the ground, tearing her hair, striking out at Louis.

When Louis and Kalamake departed in the explosive flash of light, Victoria knelt beside Fanny and spoke to her. "Fanny!" Softly, "Fanny! It's Victoria. Dear Fanny, you're *safe!*"

Victoria took her shell necklace and placed it on Fanny. "These are *lima ikaika*, Fanny," she whispered soothingly. She took Fanny's hands, and began to rub them gently against the shells. Fanny began to weep; twisting back and forth, she screamed hysterically.

"He's gone! He's gone! The witches have taken him! He doesn't want me! I'm filled with poison! I'm rotting away!" Fanny's shrieking was agonizing. She lifted herself up, then threw herself back on the ground. Suddenly, she rolled over, deathly silent, and regarded Victoria suspiciously. There was a glimmer of recognition.

"*You*! Why are *you* here?" Fanny raised up on one elbow. "Are you here to poison me? Destroy the peasant—is that why you've come?" Fanny leaped to her feet, ran behind the trunk of a huge banyan, and cowered from her. "The Scottish princess?" she screamed out of the darkness. "Here to steal my husband? Poison us all? *You!* You're a witch! You steal his thoughts, you dry him up! You poison him! I know what you're up to!"

Victoria picked up the lantern, and slowly walked to the place of Kalamake's flaming tray. Methodically, she fashioned a smooth circle in the jungle floor, and sat down. Fanny's eyes, burning with fear, followed her, seething with mistrust.

"You are not poisoned, Fanny. Nor is Louis. Tonight, we have brought you power. At this very moment, Louis is away with Kalamake gathering power—power to do his very best work. And you will—you *must* share in that."

Fanny approached a few steps, cautiously groping, desperate for safe and orderly thought.

"Come, sit down, Fanny. Keep your fingers on the shells, feel their strength flowing into you, filling you." Victoria beckoned to her warmly. "You are such a grand lady! You, who have given Louis so much strength! Tonight, Kalamake and I have brought you just a bit more—for you, and for Louis."

Victoria reached out to Fanny, put her arms about her, and lowered her so that she lay within the circle. Fanny began to cry, and her body shook convulsively. "Keep stroking the *mana* shells, Fanny. Feel the calmness of the great sea flowing into your body, bringing peace to your thoughts. Feel the great storehouse of your love being replenished. Dear Fanny, feel peace and rest."

Fanny looked up at Victoria. Bedraggled, utterly exhausted, it was the old, shrewd, scrutinizing look she'd always been noted for. "It's very strange to *see* you," she burst out. "You're always around us! Every day, I feel if I turn around suddenly—you'll be there! Why are you trying to help me? Can't you leave us alone?"

Victoria guided Fanny's hands back to the shells. Fanny sobbed insistently. "You love my husband! You have, from the very first! You're waiting to take him away from me! Take him. I'm dying! I'm poisoned!"

Victoria's manner, and the gentleness of her words, slowly disarmed Fanny. "I come in love, dear Fanny. For you and for Louis. Take him away? It would be like pulling a great tree out by its roots—a tree you've nourished through so many harsh seasons." Victoria stroked Fanny's brow, and pressed her eyelids shut. "Now rest, dear one. Feel the power build inside you."

All of Victoria's vitality passed from her to Fanny in that tortured jungle setting. In the days that followed, Victoria barely found strength to move. Depleted physically, she was even more drained in her spirit. Her hopes and dreams with Louis seemed shredded, blown away. As for Fanny, except for this dramatic moment of psychotic confusion, she never consciously knew the extent of Louis's other life, nor of Victoria's role in it. But Fanny, the 'flying cloud', could sense such matters at a deeper level. More than most, if this had ever penetrated her rational consciousness, she would have found it believable, this sharing which continued through the years after the banyan days at Ainahau. That night in the jungle, Victoria sacrificed the hope she had nurtured for so long. She would never have something alive, something enduring, a tangible product of her love for Louis.

The awareness of Victoria's desolation echoed and re-echoed in Louis, as he embraced a new-found, dynamic source of energy. Perplexed, he longed to share it—to live it—with Victoria. After the mystical sojourn at Hermiston, he sent her a poem wrapped in a dream.

> *God gave to me a child in part*
> *Yet wholly gave the father's heart:—*
> *Child of my soul. O whither now,*
> *Unborn, unmothered, goest thou?*
>
> . . .
>
> *Alas! alone he sits who then*
> *Immortal among mortal men,*
> *Sat hand in hand with love, and all day through*
> *With your dear mother wondered over you.*

♦ ♦ ♦

A series of dreams flooded Victoria's sleep in the weeks that followed. One scene was repeated each time: Victoria was certain that she found herself in the moorland of Scotland; a wild scene, far out of sight of any house. From far off Samoa, Louis's dreams carried him to her in this lonely, marshy place he would call the Devil's Hags. They found each other in a hollow among heather-strewn hills. Nearby stood a mossy gravestone and, a bit down the slope, a rocky monument. The lonely beauty of the place, among cries of curlew and plover, was haunted by a feeling of past violence. Louis, in his waking hours, had been busily sketching in this moorland scene which appeared repeatedly in Victoria's dreams. It was a place of conflict, a site where he might recreate, in a new form, the strife of an earlier period in Scottish history. This had been the setting of the death of the Praying Weaver of Balweary; slain by 'Bloody Claverhouse', the man commissioned by King Charles the First to act against the Covenanters, the Scottish opponents of his popish tendencies.

The Devil's Hags, became for Louis the center stage for Hermiston. He began to trace events which seemed to him like the bones of a giant, buried there and half dug up, naked and imperfect, dwelling in the memory of scattered neighbors. His would be a story told on winter nights, when sleet was on the windows and the cattle were quiet in the byre; a tale of the Justice-Clerk and of his son, young Archie Weir of Hermiston; of the two Kirsties and the Four Black Brothers of Cauldstaneslap; and of Frank Innes, the young fool advocate that came into these moor land parts to find his destiny.

Defying the stark history of this isolated spot, Victoria and Louis spent enchanted hours here, their love fulfilled and blooming in the heather. Victoria's hair was perfumed silk ruffling against his cheek; he thrilled at her head buried against his breast, her arms wound tightly about him. Ever so slowly, she would lift her face to his, and, bending, he kissed her. Her mouth was incredibly sweet, soft as a melting berry, a fragrant blossom. Her body, under the thinness of her dress, was all of the ripeness of spring time, stirring, quivering, unfolding, shower-softened, sun-drenched. Louis plunged into that softness, utterly lost, enfolded in it for eternity. They shared an exquisite, harmonious flow, an ever-rising tide of joy, pulsing its way finally to a great cry of rapture. They would lie together, clasped in each other's arms, one with each other. Suddenly, each dream would end in a sudden reversal, a sensation of wrenching, agonizing pain. With each new dream, Victoria helplessly weighed her enduring, increasing ache against the joy of their time together.

At Vailima, Louis, bursting with vitality, at the peak of his creative power, pursued what he was certain would be his masterpiece. Belle had become tremendously helpful in serving as his amanuensis, and his upstairs study for several hours each morning was a spirited setting in which Louis dictated rapidly and excitedly, pacing up and down, acting out each part. Belle, equally enthused, rushed to record the torrent of his thoughts.

Victoria, during the time of this intense build-up of Louis's inspired writing, suffered from severe headaches and was desperate for relief. After one particularly difficult day, she retired early; almost immediately she fell asleep and, through the tunnels and passages of her mind, she found herself climbing up the moor toward Cauldstaneslap, the pass between two hillocks. The pass opened like a doorway to Hermiston in the distance. Immediately on the other side, Victoria descended to the Devil's Hags. Here was total seclusion in the marshy hollow, full of springs, crouching junipers, and pools where the black peat-water slumbered. At the farther end of the hollow, beside a sluggish stream, began the downward path to Hermiston. A wide view lay before her of the braes on the other side, still sallow and rusty with winter, the path marked by tufts of birches. The windows of Hermiston glittered in the western sun. Here Victoria sat and waited, and looked for a long time at these far-away bright panes of glass.

By the time the sun was low, and all the easterly braes lay plunged in shadow, she was aware of a figure coming up the path, half running, now pausing and seeming to hesitate. She watched at first with a total suspension of thought. There began to grow upon her a subdued choking suspense. *He* was coming; his hesitations had ceased, his steps grew firm and swift; no doubt remained; and the question loomed before her: the aching pain—what was she to do?

Victoria stood up and showed herself an instant in the gap against the sky line; then she fled, trembling, and sat glowing with excitement on the Weaver's stone. She shut her eyes, seeking, praying for composure. Her hands shook in her lap, and her mind was full of futile speeches. Gradually the wheels of her nature ceased to go round so madly, and she sat in passive expectation, a quiet, solitary figure in the midst of the gray moss.

In the meantime, Louis was rapidly drawing near. As he mounted the slope and came into the hollow of the Devil's Hags, he saw her womanly figure in a gray dress and pink kerchief: Victoria, leaning low, and lost, and acutely solitary, in these desolate surroundings, on the weather-beaten stone of the dead weaver.

Victoria turned the back of her kerchief up over her head. It framed her vivacious, yet pensive face. Her feet were gathered under her, and she leaned on her bare arm, shimmering in the fading light. Louis, was struck with a certain chill, a reminder that he now dealt in matters of life and death. This was a grown woman he was approaching, endowed with her mysterious potencies and attractions, the treasury of the continued race, and he was neither better nor worse than the average of his sex and age. His throat was dry as he came near; but the appealing sweetness of her smile stood between them like a guardian angel. He took his seat at the other end of the tombstone and studied her for the thousandth time, wondering: what was she?

Victoria looked upon him with a subdued, twilight expression that suited the hour of the day. Her eyes were gently suffused and shining. His heart went out to her with boundless compassion and warmth. His question was answered, again and again: here was a human being tuned to a sense of the tragedy of life; there were pathos and music and a great heart in her. He should behold Victoria in his mind's eye for ever, perched on the same tomb, in the gray colors of the evening, gracious, dainty, perfect as a flower.

Victoria drew herself together slowly and stood before him, expectant; she was all languor; her arms ached for him, her soul was on tip-toes.

Tears, in that hour of sensibility, came into his eyes; and the girl, from being something merely bright and shapely, was caught up into that zone of things that echoed of life and death. Fate was playing his game artfully with this poor pair of children. The generations were prepared, the pangs were again made ready, before the curtain rose on the dark drama.

Louis rose to her and held her face in his hands. "Kirstie—dearest Kirstie—"

Victoria's expression radiated, sending back to him the intensity of his passion. Then she looked away and, within his arms, she reached up to fix his gaze squarely upon her. Tears slowly welled up in the corners of her eyes and her expression turned to one of pleading.

"Not Kirstie, Louis," Victoria entreated him softly, seeking desperately to recapture him. "Please, Louis. This time, call me who I really am. I'm Victoria. Please, Louis, hold me. Don't lose me!"

Victoria crumbled, sobbing in his arms. "I know what will happen to Kirstie and Archie—"

The Hags were in shadow, but still through the gate of the pass, the sun shot a last arrow. The emptiness and solitude of the great moors seemed to be concentrated here. Victoria's face was excruciatingly sad, a glimpse of a world from which all light and comfort were on the point of vanishing.

Louis drew back from her. The tormenting sacrificial moment they both dreaded had come: would it be the emergence of the masterpiece, and with this the downfall of the girl?

In far off Samoa, Louis suddenly broke off his pacing and the flood of his words. Belle looked up at him in alarm, as he dropped heavily into his chair. He leaned forward, head in hands, and rocked back and forth. "Oh, God! Oh, God!"

"Louis!" Belle cried. She dropped her notepad and leaped to her feet. "Are you all right? Can I get you something?"

Louis fended her off with an outstretched arm, shook his head, and rose wearily to his feet. "No, no! Let's keep going," he muttered. Once more, he was standing in the shadows of the Hags, about to set foot on the barren, unyielding path he had set for his masterpiece. He was a laird, she was a country girl. Already there was talk. What would his father say?

"No, Kirstie, not today," he said. "Today I have to talk to you seriously. Sit ye down, please, there where you were. Please!" he repeated.

"Louis! I beg you! Don't do this! I'm *not* Kirstie! I'm *not* Alison!" Victoria, the trap closing in on her, writhed in agony. I'm *not* Modestine! In heaven's name, I beg you!"

Poor Louis stood dumbfounded. She had moved some steps away from him before he recovered his speech.

"Kirstie!" he cried. "O, Kirstie woman!"

Resigned, defeated, Victoria felt herself sucked relentlessly into the overpowering whirlpool of Louis's creative drive. She turned round on him. "What do ye 'Kirstie' me for?" she retorted. "What have ye to do with me? Go to your own friends and deafen them. If I canna get love, I'll have respect, Mr. Weir. I'm come of decent people, and I'll have respect. What have I done that ye should deal with me lightly? What have I done? O, what have I done?" And her voice rose in the third repetition. "I thought—I thought—I thought I was so happy!" and the first sob broke from her like the paroxysm of some mortal sickness.

Louis ran to her. He took her in his arms, and she nestled to his breast as to a mother's, and clasped him in hands that were as strong as vices. "I have nothing left to give or keep back," she sobbed. "I was all yours from the first day, if you would have had a gift of me." He felt her whole body shaken by the throes of distress, and had pity upon her beyond speech. Pity, and at the same time a bewildered fear of this explosive engine in his arms, whose works he did not understand, and yet had been tampering with. There arose before him the curtains of earlier years, and he saw for the first time the ambiguous face of woman as she is. In vain he looked back over their conversation; he saw not where he had offended. It seemed unprovoked, a willful convulsion of brute nature....

Victoria watched in terror as Louis, very slowly, silently, inch by inch, began to fade, to contort, until, at the last there was only a faint trace of a tortured face, and that receding into the gloaming.

The horror of Victoria's dream left her drenched in fever and totally exhausted. She sank into dreamless unconsciousness. The following day, weak and depleted, she had recorded a poem:

> *Whene'er this mortal journey ends*
> *Death like a host, comes smiling to the door;*
> *Smiling, he greets us, on that tranquil shore*
> *Where neither piping bird nor peeping dawn*
> *Disturbs the eternal sleep.*
> *But in the stillness far withdrawn*
> *Our dreamless rest for evermore we keep,*
> *And our sad spirits turn toward the dead*
> *And the tired child, the body, longs for bed.*

♦ ♦ ♦

Louis paused in his dictation to Belle. He felt crushed, and torn apart by the morning's writing, unable to stop, yet struggling with profound weariness and a sense of being utterly consumed. He was so deeply enmeshed in Hermiston; he often had noticed Belle looking at him strangely, wondering, excited by the work, but apprehensive about his intensity. If Louis pulled himself back a distance, he could exult in the caliber of this work. But the last encounter of Kirstie and Archie: that had beaten him. He was spent. He flung himself back into his chair. No more today.

For the past few days, Fanny had been feeling low and upset. Why not go downstairs, help her with supper and perhaps each could distract the other? Fanny had been preoccupied, telling the family that she knew something dreadful was going to happen to someone they cared for. These odd premonitions were nothing new for Fanny. The family was accustomed to the strange insights which would well up from inside her, but this was taking a toll. Her fear seemed to point to some friend of the family, possibly Graham Balfour, who was away on a cruise. Louis laughed and teased about it, minimizing what appeared to be building up to sheer terror on Fanny's part.

Louis, dog-tired, made his way downstairs and flopped into a chair in the kitchen.

"You know, Fanny. I've been thinking a lot more about that offer—you know, the lecture tour." He sighed and leaned on his hand. "You could visit your sister in California again. It would be a good change for us."

"I think I'd like that Louis. Perhaps in the summer when the weather warms up over there."

Fanny rummaged about in the utensils and busied herself with preparations for a salad and Louis suggested a dressing he had devised.

Louis, stretched out in his chair, looked up at her between his fingers. "Let's make that special mayonnaise dressing. Will we eat soon? I feel starved."

Louis slowly inched his way out of his chair and disappeared into the cellar for a bottle of fine old burgundy. Then they repaired to the verandah, Louis trying hard to summon the energy to chat amiably, as he helped Fanny stir the oil and lime juice. The surging emotions of that morning were unrelenting and kept crashing in upon him. He couldn't drive from his thoughts the lovely, gentle face on the moor, pleading, clinging to him, sobbing in her unhappiness.

Suddenly Louis put his hands to his head. "What? What's that?" he exclaimed. "Oh, my God! What pain!" He stared helplessly at Fanny, "Do I look strange?"

The gentle face on the moor, the dark, gypsy curls against the pink kerchief, became a softly colored mist that twisted wildly about his head, swirled and slowly faded in a receding rush of sound.

Louis staggered and fell to his knees. Quickly Fanny and Sosimo, his butler, helped him through the doorway into the great hall and into his grandfather's armchair. Louis instantly lost consciousness, lying back, breathing harshly, his face very red, his eyes wide open. Lloyd was called and rode downhill at breakneck speed for the doctor; the minister was summoned. Nothing more could be done. At ten minutes past eight on December 3 1894, Louis's breathing faded away. By the foot of the great redwood staircase, Fanny's small figure stood alone and apart, rigid with shock.

Louis's body was covered with the big Union Jack that flew over Vailima. The family sat stricken as chiefs began to arrive with fine mats and flowers which they laid over Louis, bowing and saying, "*Talofa* [farewell], Tusitala." The Roman Catholic boys asked to 'make a church,' and they chanted prayers and hymns for a long time.

The doctor said that burial must be by three o'clock the next afternoon. Louis had chosen as his final resting place the top of Mount Vaea. In this short time a path had to be cut, and all through the night could be heard the sounds of chopping of trees on the hillside, the low murmur of native voices, and Sosimo reciting the Catholic prayers for the dead in mingled Latin and Samoan.

The new day was sunny and beautiful. All morning, Samoans came, and the great hall glowed with flowers. Fanny helped to dress her husband in a white linen shirt, dark trousers, and a blue sash in the tropical custom. His plain silver wedding ring was on his finger—the mate of the one she always wore, from the days of their marriage when they could not afford gold.

By early afternoon, the superhuman task of clearing a path to the peak was completed. At about one o'clock the first relay of strong Samoan pallbearers began the steep and rugged ascent—made the more difficult as they carried shoulder-high the coffin with its pitifully light burden.

Half an hour later, the family and friends, nineteen white people and sixty Samoans, toiled up the rocky slope. At the top, the coffin waited under the frayed British flag. The coffin was lowered into place and almost hidden with wreaths and crosses of flowers. The Reverend Mr. Clarke read parts of the Church of England burial service and a new prayer written by Louis for family worship the night before his death:

....suffer us a while longer to endure, and (if it may be) help us to do better...if the day come when these must be taken, have us play the man under affliction. Be with our friends; be with ourselves....

♦ ♦ ♦

Victoria knew the contents of her father's December letter without opening it. The London papers were quickly informed of Louis's death, but she, in her dream—and Fanny—had been eye witnesses. Increasingly, over many months, she agitated about her senseless exile. If there were danger for her, it was of no matter. She wanted to go home, to be with her people. The turmoil of the months before Louis's death still dogged her. She had lost weight, was chronically fatigued and, at times was so depleted that she had fainting spells.

Louis's death could not in any way assume real proportions for Victoria, much as that dreadful dream on the moor had seared itself into her brain. In the years since Hawai'i, there had been gaps in their sharing; but she always lived with hope and assurance of their unbreakable tie; she could not accept death as an end to this. Nevertheless, her sleep was fitful and, although she continued to dream of Louis, these were distant dreams, and in hazy settings that seemed to draw upon times they had shared in Hawai'i.

While she remained in England, Victoria sought opportunities to visit Scotland. For all the painful reminders the moors of the border countryside held for her, nevertheless she felt closer to Louis, more alive, even more expectant.

It was after Victoria's twenty-first birthday, during a visit to Scotland, that she awoke from a very deep and restful sleep to find, joy of joys—a poem wafted to her from Louis:

> *And last, O Lord, I pray*
> *For hearts resigned and bold*
> *To trudge the dusty way—*
> *Hearts stored with song and joke*
> *And warmer than a cloak*
> *Against the cold.*

If nothing else he had,
He, who has this, has all.
This comforts under pain;
This, through the stinging rain,
Keeps ragamuffin glad
Behind the wall.

Yes, Louis was behind the wall. But he was able to exhort her to hang on and keep trying, to keep humor and hope alive. How very like Louis! What was it like in this cosmic state to which he had gone? He'd been on the edge of it in life so many times, perhaps to him it might not seem that different. Victoria's mind was filled with questions. Death had never been truly frightening to Victoria; she'd seen much of it, and that very close. The idea of losing someone permanently through death was foreign to her. She felt Mother Likelike's presence enduringly in the years away from Hawai'i. And dear Kalamake felt like a physical attachment to which she was warmly bonded in the most difficult of times. Louis was the bright rising star in her firmament—the guiding star. Now, she'd been instructed, if she had 'a heart stored with song and joke', she had everything she needed. Filled with hope, she claimed Louis's offer gladly.

Victoria and Archie had booked reservations at the Johnston Lodge at Anstruther in Fife. Fife was a compromise. Archie hoped the weather would permit him to play golf at nearby St. Andrews. Victoria's delight was the view from the lodge across the Firth of Forth to the battlements of Edinburgh Castle. She could see the smoke of the Old Town, the city lying in waves around Castle Rock, and washing up to the Pentland Hills beyond. The hills had scattered patches of snow from what, thus far, had been a mild winter. Mild, but for Victoria, who reveled in cool weather, it was bracing. She felt strong and healthy, in touch with something revitalizing. It was New Year's Day! That, especially seemed to crown it all!

Archie was off to St. Andrews, and Victoria hired a coach and driver to go to Edinburgh. She would do something that, since Louis's death, had become irresistible for her. She would visit 17 Heriot Row where Louis had grown up!

Her coach and driver were prompt, and they were off at a brisk trot along the North side of the Firth. In the distance she could see the whole black length of Edinburgh, tailing down from the castle upon its crags above the loch in a long line of spires, gables, and smoking chimneys. Victoria snuggled under her robes and smiled to herself as she dreamily watched the little villages drift by her window: Elie, Leven, Buckhaven, Kirkcaldy. The air was bracing, fragrant with the scent of resting pastures.

The ferry brought them to the South shore and Victoria, standing at the rail, studied their two fine horses, longing to leap on the back of the taller one and ride off at a gallop into the city.

Edinburgh surprised her. It seemed so much smaller than she'd expected. Perhaps it was the Castle that dwarfed and dominated its surroundings. They approached the Old Town, grim and sooty, where the growth of the city had forced the buildings into high and dense arrangements, and thoroughfares had been compressed down to lanes. The spire of St. Giles Cathedral and the Parliament Buildings looked down on them.

There was an animation, a bustle about the city this day, which clearly marked it as New Year's Day, the great national festival. The wind whistling in the streets was cool and the air brisk, but the faces, the manner and the lively step of the people, were robust and warm. Music emanated from street corners and upstairs rooms. Stores were closed, but not the taverns or the toyshops. Bakers and confectioners appeared to be working overtime. Victoria recalled that Louis had once said that at this season, on the threshold of another year of calamity and stubborn conflict, people felt a need to draw closer the links that united them. He said they'd reckon the number of their friends at the New Year, like allies before a war.

They crossed High Street along North Bridge and turned down Princes Street toward Queen Street Gardens. The driver drew his horses to a halt on the North side of the Gardens and looked down at Victoria.

"Here we are, Miss." He gestured toward a tall gray stone house. That'un there—that's Number Seventeen."

Victoria, flushed with excitement, stepped down from the carriage and moved slowly along the garden walk opposite Number 17. At last, she could picture that 'Child of Air' playing in the garden, giving life to blades of grass, to unseen things. In the upstairs windows, she imagined Louis as a small boy looking out from a sick bed, sailing boats upon the counterpane, and assembling armies for great battles.

There were few people visible on Heriot Row. The city and family gatherings had called them away. As Victoria strolled the Garden walk, a figure approached from among the trees in the distance. As he drew closer, he—for it was a man—presented a colorful picture. He was brightly kilted in flashes of red, walking sturdily towards her, the silver buttons of his dark jacket glistening in the winter sun. The kilt, as he drew closer, was the Royal Stewart tartan. The man's long hair framed a smoothly chiseled, firm, yet smiling face. The nose was strong, but his eyes brought Victoria to a halt.

Louis came up to her, his smile broader with each step. He bowed deeply and ceremoniously, then stepped back for her to appreciate him more fully.

"And, who, pray, did you think it was? Robert the Bruce?"

Victoria studied him in amused delight. His face was glowing with a vitality she'd never seen before.

"Well, lass. Are ye no' going to say something?"

Victoria beamed with delight. "What is there to say? Here you are! Of course! I came looking for you."

"That you did, and as I knew you would."

Victoria reached out and touched him. Reassured to that extent, she said, "Can I—can I ask you how you are? Would that make any sense?"

Louis grinned, reached down and flipped the highly ornamented leather sporran he wore in front of his kilt.

"Look! I have a purse!" He threw his empty hands apart. "It's empty—but it doesn't matter! And, notice—no notebooks!"

Louis threw up his hands in pleasure. "Victoria! Finally, I'm finished writing!"

Victoria frowned and looked at him quizzically. "Will you still need me?"

Louis gripped her enthusiastically. "Ay, lass. Mar thin tongue kin tell!"

Quickly Louis hooked his arm into Victoria's, vigorously swung her about, and propelled her toward the waiting carriage.

"Come on, my lady! It's a New Year for you, a very new something or other for me. We have much to talk about, and our carriage awaits!"

Louis ordered the top rolled back from their carriage, and they rode swiftly into the Old Town through the Gardens below the Castle. Louis stood in the carriage as they went, waving to passersby, and halted their driver at the fountains to watch the children playing winter games, and sliding on the ice.

Victoria looked up at him, laughing. "Would you like to join them?"

"I did. While I was waiting for you!" He turned to the driver and gestured broadly: "Coachman! Drive on! To the Castle!"

Swiftly they turned up the spacious Esplanade, the scene of military parades and, in earlier days, executions. They rattled over the drawbridge entrance to the Castle and on to the Citadel. Here Louis ordered the driver to stop, and led Victoria to a magnificent viewing point overlooking the city, the Firth, and the Pentland Hills.

Louis looked at her fondly, reminiscing. "Do you know, ever since the day we landed in the *Casco;* you were there at the wharf, riding Fairy, wearing your Stewart tartan .... I've wanted to bring you to this spot. Somehow, I thought that then, you would immediately know me—really know me."

Louis seemed so self-assured, strong, vibrant that he took Victoria's breath away. He put her at a loss for words. To relate to him had always been so effortless, but in this meeting she was touched by a sense of awe. All she wished to do was enjoy this man she loved.

Haltingly, she found words. "Louis, this bond between us. It's like steel. I've never stopped feeling it. Will it always be there? Will you come to me, just as you have today?"

"I'm in a state I can't describe. Its dimensions are vast, breath-taking. Far beyond anything I ever imagined in life—and, you know, I was known for my imagination. I know this, Victoria, you are the one bond in this life that I haven't been able to release."

Victoria turned to look off over the battlements. "I absolutely refuse to release you. I cannot conceive of such a thing!"

Louis put his arm about her waist, and turned her toward him. "This 'letting go'—I was led to understand—afterwards, that is—after I died, that letting go would be easy. In life I never really believed any of this. I remember how the Marquesans were so preoccupied with the spirits of the dead. I just thought it made good fiction.

Victoria looked up at him with an expression that would have melted a statue. "Then, what are we to do?"

Louis sighed, smiled and stroked her chin. "You're unfinished business, Victoria. That appears to be why I'm still here."

He recalled the talisman and fished it out from under his shirt. He held it up between them and twisted it about in his fingers. "Hibiscus and thistle. All wrapped around each other ...."

Victoria was delighted. "Splendid! Then you're coming home with me! Will you come like that? Or, do I need to pack you in a chest? I'd like to know where you are!"

"This state—is that the right word?—that I'm in. Have you noticed? I'm really most agreeable. I never, ever, felt better in the other life. Imagine the best day in your whole life, Victoria: that's what this is like!"

The evanescent day was beginning to dim, and in the sub-arctic Scotland sunset, the city took on an indigo shade beneath a sky of luminous green.

Louis took Victoria by both hands and drew her to him. His face was a ruddy glow under the sparkling eyes. "Before you pack me away, there are a few more things in Edinburgh that I want to show you."

He led her to their carriage, and they sped out of the Castle and down the Royal Mile to Holyrood Palace where they tarried for a moment.

"Here's a palace for you, Princess. Would you like to live in Queen Mary's apartments?" Louis pointed to a little building with a pyramidal roof. "How about Queen Mary's Bath over there? You could bathe in wine, as she did to preserve her beauty."

Victoria wrinkled up her nose. "Louis, this space you're in—or whatever you call it—can you see into the future? Will I ever be Queen of the Hawaiian Islands?"

"Your mother, in her dying moments, wasn't very encouraging."

"Well, do you know?"

"I have only one certainty. I know that I love you beyond words. I cannot imagine ever—ever—being separated from you."

The carriage moved on in the gathering dusk to Arthur's Seat. Again they left the carriage and climbed the ancient volcano to look down upon Duddingstone Loch. The loch was filled with skaters, clusters of swiftly moving figures, opening, closing, and moving through each other like intermingling streams of water. As night drew on, figures melted into the dusk, until only an obscure stir, a coming and going of black clusters, was visible upon the loch. A little longer, and the first torch was kindled, and flitted rapidly across the ice in a ring of yellow reflection. This was followed by another and another, until the whole loch was full of skimming lights.

Louis embraced Victoria and she nestled against him. "You asked me what it's like on the other side. You know, Victoria, I was never at a loss for words. But about that—I am. But, look—down there—it's like that."

"It makes me feel like I could float out over all those lights. I—we—could soar and swoop like birds," Victoria murmured. "I'd never be cold, never too hot, never away from you."

"And all the books, in all the world, in every language, would be written, and read, and put aside." Louis breathed in deeply and, in the velvet darkness, basked in the warmth of his princess. "But, come," he said. "there's more."

They followed a torchlit path down the slope toward their carriage. The celebrating of the holiday crowd continued unabated, and at the foot of Arthur's Seat, a large number of kilted fun-seekers were gathered, laughing and drinking, sharing Scotch buns, currant-loaf and shortbread.

As Louis and Victoria made their way through the happy crowd, he recalled something, and reached into his sporran to bring out a sheaf of paper. He handed it to Victoria.

"It's for you. Don't read it now. Save it for another time."

Down the road, in the distance, a cluster of torches could be seen proceeding slowly toward them. Suddenly, there was a hush in the crowd as the group of marchers came closer. In the stronger light of the gathering, they were seen to wear gowns of gray, with a white St. Andrew's Cross on back and breast. These were menacing figures, each carrying a long staff, from which dangled a white cloth.

Louis and Victoria stared at them, transfixed.

"Oh, my God! Oh, God! Louis exclaimed. "It's the plague officials."

They were now quite near and closing directly on Louis.

"My God, Victoria. They've come for me!"

Abruptly, they seized him, and the silent crowd parted as the baleful figures dragged Louis away within their torch-lit cluster.

Victoria screamed in rage. "Stop! Stop!" She turned to the crowd. "Don't let them do this! Stop them!"

The holiday crowd turned aside, unmoved, and returned to its revelry.

In desperation, Victoria looked about her for some action to take. Her carriage stood close by. She raced to it, leaped into the driver's seat, pushed the coachman aside. At her crack of the whip, the horse tore down the road after the plague-hunters, lunged into the group of robed men, and scattered them. She yanked the horse to a stop, reached down, pulled Louis up beside her, and they dashed off into the night .

As they went, Louis took the talisman from around his neck and placed it over Victoria's head. They slowed to a trot, then a walk, as they approached Queen Street Gardens, and Heriot Row just beyond. Victoria felt a long, vice-like embrace, a whisper in her ear, "Look for me—the child in the garden—." And then that loving pressure—and Louis—were gone.

♦ ♦ ♦

Hence I not fear to yield my breath
Since all is still unchanged by death;
Since in some pleasant valley I may be,
Clod beside clod, or tree by tree,
In ages hence, with her I love this hour.

I hear the signal, Lord,—I understand.
The night at Thy command
Comes. I will eat and sleep and will not
Question more.

♦ ♦ ♦

Queen Lili'uokalani

Chapter XIII

INTO THE MISTS OF MANA

A contemplative Princess sailed from Southampton on October 9 1897. Victoria would enter her twenty-second year in just seven days. Archie had booked their passage by way of New York, destination, heaven be praised: Hawai'i! Her long exile was drawing to a close. As Victoria departed, she cast a fond, bittersweet eye through the drifting mists of the Celtic Sea toward the coastline of Britain. Amid the cry of sea birds, England was fading away, a muted silhouette beneath an autumn sky.

Victoria's reflective mood dominated all else during the days at sea. She searched incessantly through the spaces, the shrouded corners, and the fertile gardens of her mind. She was preoccupied with sorting out the uncompromising sweep of world events. She felt a keen sense of urgency. How might Hawai'i fit into all of this? What did the future hold for her? What would be her role? What were her strengths? How could she apply them? Where were the handles, the knobs, the wheels one might reach out and seize to set a course toward everything she valued?

In Victoria's endless inner conferences, the unanswered questions were always the same: what was unique about her Hawai'i? In what ways would the world be diminished without Victoria's little garden? How might the essence, the spirit of Hawai'i be preserved for all time? A constant strength, a guiding light in her deliberations was her marvel over one ultimate, towering fact. This made all things possible: of all that was meaningful within her, the bond she had shared with Louis remained the most secure, and she lived by its nourishing strength.

Victoria's arrival in New York City was largely unnoticed, unlike her pilgrimage of a few years earlier. Victoria and Archie stayed briefly in New York, then boarded a train for a special trip to the District of Columbia to see—and this stuck in Victoria's throat—*ex-Queen* Lili'uokalani! It had been eight long years since she had seen her aunt—the last survivor of *Na Lani Eha*. Over the years they had exchanged many letters, the troubled contents of which would now be historical; but to be with her again, this dear, heroic, superbly talented lady; this had Victoria on the edge of her seat.

The train pulled out of New York and chugged its way through the marshlands of northern New Jersey. "New" Jersey! Victoria smiled at that and thought about Rozel and the old—the real—Jersey, that wooded isle where she'd spent so many pleasant times. The word 'new' seemed to preface everything in the United States, and that brought her back to the nagging core of her deliberations. The world order was changing: how might she cultivate her little garden?

Archie was much in tune with her thinking as they sped through the rolling pasture land of eastern Pennsylvania. Wooded stretches were already heralding the approach of autumn; maples were turning brilliant orange and yellow, the oaks a somber deep red. Mounds of faded corn shocks huddled in the fields. The outskirts of Philadelphia loomed ahead: "City of Brotherly Love!"

Victoria gave Archie a pensive, pleading look. "Brotherly love, Father. That's 'aloha'—what's going to happen to that in this whirlpool we're living in?"

Archie shook his head. "I used to think that the islands were my whole world. Now it feels like another huge world has moved in with us."

Archie brushed the condensation from the window of their Pullman compartment and studied the racing landscape.

"But, you know, dear, nothing remains the same. If we keep our wits about us, there's always room for improvement." Archie smiled to himself and puffed on his pipe. "Your grandfather, for example: he planted some of the finest trees in Honolulu, brought them from New Zealand. The island was really quite barren then."

Archie brightened with an enthusiastic smile, "And now! Oh, Victoria! Wait 'til you see our new house at Ainahau!"

"New things don't have to be bad, do they?"

Archie stroked his beard ruefully. "No, they don't. But the change from old to new can be pretty grim. Your Aunt Lydia can tell you some things about that. George Trousseau had a favorite saying, 'Never get in the path of an invading army.'"

Victoria shuddered. "The Royalist uprising some months ago must have been a terrible experience for her."

Archie nodded. "She was smack in the middle of it. Finding that munitions dump buried in her garden at Washington Place! She denied knowledge of it, but that gave the government all the evidence it needed to imprison her in the palace, and throw her retainers in jail."

"What about the forced abdication she signed?" Victoria frowned, her eyebrows knitted. "I wonder what I would have done?"

"Actually, the government didn't know what to do with the queen after the uprising. When they found that ammunition supply, the press screamed for vengeance. They were all in favor of hunting the rebels down and killing them, and sentencing the leaders to death under martial law."

"Abdicate? I wonder if I would have done that?"

Archie's voice raised. "They told her she was in no position to abdicate. Told her she'd ceased to be queen on January 14 1893 when she tried to abrogate the constitution. Imagine! They brought her to trial, too, before a military commission. Five years at hard labor and five thousand dollars fine. Robert Wilcox, you know, was one of five leaders sentenced to death."

"Did her abdication do any good?"

"Perhaps. In the end, no one died for their royalist principles. The sentences were commuted, and practically everyone's been freed. In fact, Lydia has full citizenship now. She's free to go wherever she wishes."

Victoria flushed with pride in her aunt. "So, now she's back in Washington fighting for restoration. What a woman!"

Their train had passed Baltimore, left its city smoke, its long houserows fading in the distance. Now they were on the upper reaches of Chesapeake Bay nearing the United States capital. A pale October sun was setting beyond little towns and villages that rose up suddenly outside their compartment window, and rushed past them in the daylight's ebb.

♦　♦　♦

It was a homesick Aunt Lydia whom Victoria and Archie called upon at Ebbett House. Lili'uokalani suffered from the extreme climate in Washington and longed for the freedom to return to Hawai'i. It had been a long, sticky summer and now the unpleasant climatic prospect was for frosts, cold weather and wet snow.

Victoria's presence greatly warmed this proud and stately lady. She carried her age well at fifty, but hers had been a lonely vigil, made much more difficult by the loss of the husband she so greatly missed, John Dominis.

Lili'uokalani at this strange, dislocated time in her life had become an even more arresting, impressive figure. Her face and manner retained the beauty, the stature, and the graciousness of earlier days. The years had superimposed upon this lyrical, poetic lady a greater solemnity, and a quiet, unshakable firmness. How much her strengths reminded Victoria of King David, Victoria's beloved Papa Moi!

At their meeting, all three were choked with emotion. It was a time for tears of happiness, mingled with tears of sadness for loved ones no longer with them, and for things that would never be the same.

Victoria was greatly impressed with Lydia's grasp of Washington and world politics. She had the eye of a keen and discerning analyst in sorting out so many questions which had been stirring inside Victoria.

Over tea, and later at dinner, Lili'uokalani outlined the current picture for them.

"It has not helped us at all that Grover Cleveland lost the election last fall to William McKinley. It certainly heartened the hopes of those eager annexationists. All the gossip around Washington was that McKinley would support annexation, and indeed he has. The Annexation Treaty has been before the Senate since June."

What do you think the chances are?" asked Archie.

"The Senate—the whole United States, in fact—is a curious place. Living here has been quite an education for me in democratic government. The treaty? Well, it has had an agonizing zigzag progression. Simply exasperating! Encouraging one day, not so the next. The House has already passed it, although the Speaker opposed it and did quite a remarkable job of delaying it, as long as he could. In the Senate—well, you've seen the newspapers—it's being filibustered by the anti-annexationists. The Southern Senators don't want us because of the racial issue; and they don't want competition with their sugar industry.

"What about the others?" Victoria asked.

Lili'uokalani raised her hands approvingly. "Well, they have a point of view that I like. They're opposing the Treaty as unconstitutional. They contend that the United States can't annex a country by joint congressional resolution."

Archie sat back, pleased. "Well, that really sounds quite good, doesn't it?"

Lili'uokalani shook her head. "No, Archie. You see, in Washington these things muddle about on different levels. Whatever looks like it's on top and winning may simply be window-dressing. The annexationist strategy, I'm told, has been to keep the Senate in session, and let their opponents wear themselves out in the summer heat. They want people to get tired of the filibuster, to think of it as an unreasonable obstructionism.

"Then there's another big issue," Lili'uokalani continued, "involving another island—Cuba. Things are in chaos over there. The United States and Spain have been in strong disagreement about Cuban government for a long time. Most Cubans—so they say—want to break away from Spain, and the Spanish government's mismanagement has certainly given them ample cause to want independence."

"Do you think there'll be war between the United States and Spain?" Victoria asked.

"Frankly, I do. And that will mean a naval war in the Pacific. War in the Philippines. And unfortunately, that's where Hawai'i comes into the picture."

"Ah, yes, I see," nodded Victoria, "a war in the Pacific means the United States will need Hawai'i as a base."

Lili'uokalani smiled at her approvingly. "Very perceptive, young lady." She grinned proudly at Archie. "There. You see? This one will make a fine queen. Excellent! And another curious development: the British in recent times seem to be sympathetic toward the United States' annexation of Hawai'i. It would bolster the British position against Germany in the Pacific."

Victoria shrugged. "It certainly doesn't sound like there will be much chance for the monarchy."

Lili'uokalani raised her hands in dissent. "Not so fast! Now I want you both to listen very carefully. Failing annexation, the Republican government in Hawai'i will ask you, Victoria, to take the throne as a figurehead."

Victoria's face became deeply serious. She leaned forward in her chair to hear Lili'uokalani's words.

"If you accept, you would of course have followers—but you would have embraced a very unpopular government. The opposition to Sanford Dole's government is forty-to-one. Even now it can hardly maintain itself."

Lili'uokalani looked intently at her niece. "Now, Victoria—what would you do?"

Victoria sat back in her chair thoughtfully. "If what you say is true, Auntie, then I would decline. I think I'm following your thought. Oh, yes! I see!" Victoria pressed her hands to her lips deliberately. "You're looking for the Republic to collapse! Yes, indeed! And what will replace it?"

Lili'uokalani thumped the dinner table emphatically. "Exactly. That will mean a call for a plebiscite and then, Victoria, accept the throne! For yours will be a government sustained by the love of your people."

Archie's Scottish pessimism could be restrained no longer. "But, if we *are* annexed by the United States?"

Lili'uokalani shrugged, took a deep breath and set her chin.

"Failing the throne, I would have to fight for the Crown Lands. This is the traditional inheritance of the monarchy and I'll wage war with the United States tooth and nail for it."

The three fell into reflective silence as the dinner table was cleared. This had been a joyous, nostalgic, and instructive meeting with Auntie Lydia. It was clear to Victoria that her own urgent inner debate was just beginning.

Lili'uokalani rose from the table and led them into the living room. "Enough of affairs of state for one night. Now we're going to spend the rest of the evening with some Hawaiian friends who want to see you."

Indeed there proved to be a sizable number of friends, her Washington staff, native islanders and well-wishers who called that evening. For Victoria, a visit with Aunt Lydia would not have been complete without morsels of those happy times that had been remote from her for so very long: reminiscing, laughter, 'talking story', getting out the ukuleles to sing the old songs, the songs of wind and wave, of waterfalls, sunsets at sea and fragrant flowers.

A few days later, Victoria and Liliʻuokalani bid farewell to each other with tears in their eyes. When would they see each other again? And what would be the circumstances?

♦   ♦   ♦

Victoria was a smash hit in San Francisco. Archie had grabbed an armful of newspapers before they sailed on the SS. *Australia* in early November. Over dinner they chuckled and exclaimed over the reports printed about Victoria in the San Francisco newspapers. While there, she had been inundated by reporters who vied for the most descriptive terms to apply to the Hawaiian Princess: 'She was a flower—an exotic—of civilization....charming, fascinating, individual.... She had the taste and style of a French woman, the admirable repose and soft voice of an English woman....tall, willowy slenderness, erect and graceful, a pale face, full red lips, soft expression, dark eyes, a very good nose, and a cloud of crimpy black hair knotted high.' One reporter wrote: 'She is beautiful. There is no portrait that does justice to her expressive, small, proud face. She is exquisitely slender and graceful, holds herself like a Princess, like a Hawaiian—and I know of no simile more descriptive of grace and dignity than this last. Her accent says London, her figure says New York; her heart says Hawaiʻi. But she is more than a beautiful pretender to an abdicated throne; she has been made a woman of the world by the life she has led.'

♦   ♦   ♦

Victoria arrived in Honolulu harbor on November 9 1897 to be greeted by the greatest welcoming crowd ever seen at the Oceanic Wharf. A joyous time of receiving friends followed, then she descended to the wharf where a landau awaited them. Kalamake's powerful figure stood out from the crowd as he waited for her, holding the reins of the horses. Dismounting from the back of the coach, grinning broadly, was a tall, slimmer, handsome Limu to assist them. Victoria made her first act a visit to the Royal Mausoleum to Mother Miriam's resting place, then on to the new house at Ainahau.

Looking out from the landau, Victoria studied the Honolulu

scene. There were many changes, some rather striking, some subtle, but her dominant observation was that so many of the Hawaiians looked so poor, and that so many people seemed almost destitute.

The landau's matched team traveled smoothly across the Waikiki rice fields, plunged into the greenery bordering the beach, and turned into the long lane leading to Ainahau. Victoria leaped eagerly from the carriage to survey the handsome house built upon the old Ainahau. Archie had designed a large, open structure, beautifully symmetrical, its broad porch supported by handsome pillars. Directly in front, the proud giant banyan awaited her.

Victoria, whirling and dancing with delight, rushed over to the banyan, caressed the long filaments of its aerial roots and embraced as many of its multiple trunks as her arms would reach. She sat down beneath it, and with an exuberance she had not felt for a long time, scanned the new house, the lush landscape and the sea beyond. Cautiously, as the excitement abated, her peacocks emerged from the vegetation and clustered about her. The final touch was waiting for her in the distance, in a grazing spot back of the beach: Fairy!

From her seat at the base of the banyan, Victoria spread her arms joyously, and looked toward Archie, beaming at her from the porch.

"Oh, Father! I'm *home*!"

◆　◆　◆

Victoria's soaring joy at being home was a sand castle, steadily challenged by the waves. Many things contributed to her troubled state of mind and it was extremely difficult to sort out and deal with these multiple sources of her distress. Being home heightened her questions and uncertainties about the kingdom's future. The United States Senate crept along in its annexation deliberations, treating Hawai'i like a minor spectator on the sidelines of the world arena. That winter, the US Battleship *Maine* was blown up in Havana Harbor, and the impact on world-watchers was electrifying. For those hopeful for the Hawaiian monarchy, the effect was added discouragement.

Political uncertainties were in the forefront of Victoria's thoughts. Unrest in the islands about annexation and the monarchy was constantly in the air. Win or lose, what would be her role when the political outcome was accomplished fact? No matter what Hawai'i's political fate might be, what could she do to preserve her treasure—her unique island garden?

Victoria made the best of things in day-to-day life, plunged into local affairs, picked up where she had left off with her charities, and became active in the Red Cross Society and the Hawaiian Relief Society. Aunt Lydia loaned her the use of her span and splendid horses, and Victoria systematically restored them to good condition. Fairy by now was eighteen years old, but still capable of a gentle canter in the cool Manoa breezes and this, always, remained one of Victoria's greatest pleasures. In short order she was eating poi and raw fish as though she had never left home. She was relieved to find that she hadn't forgotten her Hawaiian. She exercised her well-regarded hostess skills that winter with a lu'au for Prince David under the banyan at Ainahau to celebrate his thirtieth birthday. That event produced some flashbacks to the happy evening years ago with the Stevensons and Papa Moi.

But it wasn't the same, hard as she tried to pump up her own spirits. She couldn't feel settled; many of the old natives were missing. There were a hundred guests at David's lu'au, mostly Hawaiian, and they sang long and lustily to the accompaniment of—it was now called the Hawaiian National Band.

It became a matter of some importance to Oahu society to find a mate for Victoria. Local gossip focused on her admirers and rumors buzzed about of possible husbands. Prince David Kawananakoa was always under consideration on the local scene, and Victoria was also linked with two dashing young haoles. One, a Captain Putnam Bradley Strong from the troopship *Peru,* was a companion for horseback riding and swimming in Waikiki surf. Another was Andrew Adams, a New Englander and writer for the *Honolulu Advertiser.* Archie particularly liked Andrew, even steered him into an overseer position with one of the plantations. Victoria also liked Andrew, felt a kind of attraction to him, but she couldn't shake her preoccupation with other, more demanding matters. They quarreled frequently and eventually decided friendship was a more comfortable ground. A beautiful, single young woman: the social pressures annoyed her, the smiling people who, behind their fans were wondering—wasn't there anyone good enough for her to marry?

Then there was her state of health. Victoria hadn't reckoned on a problem adjusting physically to her return to Hawai'i. She found herself in an on-going struggle. She suffered terribly in this tropical climate that she had always loved. She felt the heat strongly and couldn't shake off the continual headaches, fatigue and tension. Tired as she was, she couldn't relax, she seemed to be on an unending vigil.

But most of all, Victoria missed Louis. The simple, enduring, irrevocable truth was that she had long ago given him her heart and soul. It seemed, indeed, that their mystical bond had always existed, only waiting for a setting in which to become active. There was nothing left over for anyone else. That private chamber in her emotional life had been filled—was now filled—to overflowing.

Although Victoria could feel Louis's abiding presence, it wasn't the same as reaching out and touching him, embracing him, looking deep into those dancing, magnetic eyes, laughing with him, daydreaming, creating. Louis had never left her without hope. The things that passed between them, the times spent together—she never abandoned her conviction that this would continue. She always wore the silver talisman about her neck, next to her heart. The packet Louis handed to her that last night in Edinburgh had contained a prophetic poem which she read, re-read and sealed in her mind:

> *Though he that, ever kind and true,*
> *Kept stoutly step by step with you,*
> *Your whole long, gusty lifetime through,*
> *Be gone a while before—*
> *Be now a moment gone before—*
> *Yet doubt not; soon the season shall restore*
> *Your friend to you.*

> *He has but turned the corner—still*
> *He pushes on with right good will*
> *Through mire and marsh, by heugh and hill*
> *That selfsame arduous way—*
> *That selfsame, upland, hopeful way,*
> *That you and he, through many a doubtful day*
> *Attempted still.*

> *He is not dead—this friend—not dead,*
> *But in the path we mortals tread*

Got some few trifling steps ahead,
And nearer to the end;
So that you, too, once past the bend,
Shall meet again, as face to face, this friend
You fancy dead.

Push gaily on, brave heart, the while
You travel forward mile by mile,
He loiters, with a backward smile,
Till you can overtake;
And strains his eyes to search his wake,
Or, whistling as he sees you through the brake,
Waits on a stile.

It was to these words that Victoria clung, as the winter of 1898 marched on toward spring. A dream kept recurring of Louis beckoning to her across a moorland scene. She ached for new times to spend with him, and in her mind they held near-constant dialogue.

Victoria found herself looking for excuses to leave Oahu, and favored spending time with Eva Parker in the cool hills of Waimea, on the Big Island of Hawai'i. The Fourth of July celebration in Honolulu, with the fourth anniversary of the founding of the Hawaiian Republic, gave her ample reason to want to escape. Victoria had little to do with the people involved in the government of the Republic, and realized that her presence embarrassed them and made them uncomfortable.

In April the hammer blows became heavier and more frequent. The United States went to war against Spain. On July 6 1898 the Senate passed Annexation by a simple majority: 42 votes for and 21 against. Twenty-six senators refrained from voting—enough, had they joined with the 21 "no" votes, to have defeated annexation. President McKinley signed the resolution into law the next day, and word reached Honolulu by ship on July 13.

Was there relief for Victoria in this? Her vision was focused first on her islands, not on the throne. Annexation would force her to achieve her goals for Hawai'i by a different path, but achieve them? She vowed that somehow, she would!

♦   ♦   ♦

At midnight on August 1, ex-Queen Lili'uokalani returned on the *SS Gaelic* from the United States. Awaiting her at the wharf was a sea of silent faces, streaked with tears. Lili'uokalani appeared at the head of the gangplank, dressed in black from head to foot. She looked down at her greeters and called out in a strong voice, "Aloha!" The peals of "aloha" rang out in response. Lili'uokalani walked straight and proud down the gangplank on the arm of Prince David. Across the wharf, men, women, and children, weeping openly, stepped back respectfully to make a path. In the moonlight Victoria left the Cleghorn carriage and moved forward quickly through the crowd to embrace her Aunt. The carriage took them straight to Washington Place where the driveway blazed with torches. The night air filled with ancient chants of greeting as hundreds gathered on the lawn, offering their gifts and support.

The government celebrated Annexation Day on August 12 with a ceremony lacking in any joy. It was too sad a time; bitter and heartbreaking for too many. There were frequent rain showers throughout the day as Sanford Ballard Dole lowered the Hawaiian flag and offered the sovereignty of the Hawaiian Islands to United States Minister Harold M. Sewall. *Hawai'i Ponoi* was played for the last time as the flag was lowered. Before it ended, the native musicians threw down their instruments and ran around the corner of the palace to weep in private.

Editor Edmund Norrie of the *Independent* wrote: "Farewell, dear flag, farewell, dear emblem of love and hospitality...of a trusting, confiding and childlike people with hearts that know no guile."

No Hawaiians attended the ceremonies. The tension of that day had the aura of an execution. Victoria, Prince David, and loyal Royalists gathered about their queen at Washington Place. In November, having lost the throne irretrievably, Lili'uokalani left once again for Washington to begin her fight to regain the crown lands. It was a depressing moment for Victoria when the *SS Coptic* sailed away. Neither she nor the Queen knew that they had embraced for the last time.

◆　◆　◆

The questions were the same. The approach to the answers would have to be different. The history books may say that Victoria's heart had been broken; that the telegrams she received in England announcing the overthrow were an initial blow, and that she never recovered from the loss of the monarchy. But, the historians could not have known Victoria Kaiulani!

Immediately after annexation, Victoria summoned two people whose advice and counsel she valued. Her prime concern—Hawai'i—was clearly in her sights. Now, she must formulate a strategy to insure the integrity of her garden.

"I must find a way," she thought. "I know it will need—not just vision, political clout, money—I have to find a way to reach deep into the heart of every man, woman and child who lives or will live in our garden. I'm going to emblazon a shared identity—a faith, a transcending conviction, something magical and beyond words—seal it in the heart of every Hawaiian, Oriental, Caucasian, Hispanic, or Black who lives here. Oh, Louis, help me! I must find something to weld us together."

In her mind's eye, Victoria pictured the people of the Islands joining hands, brothers and sisters, bonded in making themselves and their garden flourish.

On a bright autumn morning at Ainahau, with the sea sparkling like a million mirrors behind them, Victoria met under the banyan with Kalamake and Robert Wilcox. They couldn't be more different from each other, these two men, and Victoria sought to draw every positive thought she could out of their minds.

Wilcox had undergone an obvious change since the days when she and Louis had known him, prior to the raid on the palace. He was still the animated, fiery, expressive man she remembered, but older, more settled, more deliberate.

Uncle—Kalamake—never seemed to change. He carried his magic about him quietly, unobtrusively, but Victoria could not have been less conscious of this than if there had been telegraph wires buzzing nearby. His was a radically different power from Wilcox's, and she needed them both.

For a time they reminisced, and clearly Wilcox still relished the old days of warfare. Kalamake, to Victoria's amusement, led him on, encouraging him to tell of the Royalist strike against the Republic in January 1895.

Wilcox couldn't sit still and tell about such matters. He rose and paced before them, occasionally pausing to gaze out to sea and reflect.

"We really were encouraged by the Queen, you see. The success of the overthrow was actually a freak. It was accomplished by such a puny bunch. We figured if they could get away with it, so could we. By '85, we really thought we could pull it off. We brought guns ashore at Waikiki under cover of darkness, we even made bombs in downtown Honolulu. I tell you, we had caches of guns planted all over the place."

Wilcox rubbed his chin thoughtfully. "It's odd about such things. The night before we planned to launch our attack, one of our people fired on a squad of police out looking for hidden guns. A helluva mistake—excuse me, Princess—just like the fluke that gave the overthrow its opportunity. That sounded the alarm. It gave the government time to call out its regulars and volunteers. They pinned us down on the slopes of Diamond Head, and used their field artillery on us from Kapiolani Park. They couldn't aim worth a damn, but we took a few casualties."

"I remember some they chased up into the valleys behind town," Kalamake said. "No food or water; a pretty hard time."

Wilcox shrugged. "Well, that's all over. It's a good thing, I guess." He turned to face them quizzically, "How did you get me off on this subject?" he asked.

Victoria laughed. "Before you arrived, Uncle and I were wondering if you were the same old Robert Wilcox!"

Wilcox gave her a sly grin. "Well. I'm happily married, a family man now."

Victoria smiled, "I know. Princess Theresa Cartwright. She's a dear. I'm so happy for you."

"—And," Wilcox grinned proudly, "we have two healthy keikis!"

Wilcox sat down beside them, stretched out his legs and gazed at the surf. "Am I the same Robert Wilcox? Before I can tell you that, Princess, I think you'll have to tell me why you asked me here."

Victoria was well-prepared. "You don't need to call me 'Princess' anymore, Robert. Victoria's fine."

"I asked you and Uncle to come because I believe we have something to offer to Hawai'i—something we *have* to offer—at a time when we all could otherwise feel utterly dispossessed."

Victoria warmed to the thoughts she'd been carrying inside these many months.

"Hawaiians—we've been going around hanging our heads, feeling like we have no reason for living. We've lost our leaders, we've lost our independence. And the hard, cold truth is, there really aren't many Hawaiians left anymore. Look at you, Robert. Your father was a haole sea captain. Mine—me—ex-heir to the throne—my father is a Scotsman."

"Yeah, okay, Princess! And I'll call you that if I want to. But don't tell me I'm not Hawaiian!"

Victoria stood and smiled triumphantly at Kalamake. "There, you see, Uncle? He's not a full-blooded Hawaiian like you. But listen to him! I tell you: being Hawaiian—it's a state of mind!"

"What would you have us do, Princess?" Kalamake asked.

"We must take that state of mind, that feeling that's so strong in Robert, and we've got to infect everyone who comes near us. We have the makings of a whole new world society—right here!"

Wilcox sat up enthusiastically. "I like that!" Then, deliberately, "So, what are we going to do? Put 'em all in uniform and issue orders?"

Victoria turned to Kalamake. "Uncle?"

Kalamake leaned back and closed his eyes. "We've always had the answer. It's 'aloha'. And I will confess something. The word aloha—love, mercy, compassion—is Hawaiian. But the meaning of aloha, it never started here."

"That's right, Uncle," Victoria added, "it's an ideal the world over, and—believe me—neglected, given lip-service. We've got to make the word 'Hawaiian' spell out an attitude, not something racial or religious that separates people. And we must give our people who live here an identity. We're going to produce a people filled with aloha—but smart, aware, alert, drawing from the best the world has to offer and making something greater from it "

Wilcox remained skeptical. "Oh, come on, Princess! People exploit each other. They set up barriers, there's no trust. Even in the same family, they fight. Sorry, Princess. It's just the nature of the beast."

Carefully, Victoria reviewed her thoughts with them until, at last, Wilcox looked at his watch and excused himself.

As he stood, Wilcox gave Victoria a long, compassionate look, smiled in admiration and shook his head slowly. "I wish you could convince me, Princess. I wish I could see a way—"

"Well, Robert, for yourself—just you alone—do you believe in what I've been saying?"

"I would love to see it!" He gave a warped smile. "I almost said—'fight' for it!"

Undaunted, Victoria smiled. "Well, that's *one*. I make *two*. And Uncle, I know how you feel about it."

"I wish you well in what you seek to do, Princess."

"I'm counting on you, Robert—you '*Hawaiian!*' And what will be your plan of action?"

Wilcox faced Victoria with a broad smile and saluted her. "I wondered when you might ask. Haven't you heard? I'm announcing for the United States Congress!"

With that, Wilcox, the Garibaldi warrior, turned and strode off toward the stables.

This was Victoria's first opportunity since returning home to spend a leisurely time with Uncle, and they shared much as the afternoon passed. The soft beat of the surf and the stillness of Ainahau did nothing to diminish Victoria's resolve. Kalamake sat facing out to sea, and as Victoria studied his eyes she had the same feeling Louis had once described. It was as though she were looking down the corridors of history.

"And you, dear Princess," Kalamake asked at length, "are you ready for the tasks you have set for yourself?"

"I am. It all comes down to spirit, doesn't it? You know the future, Uncle. I can see it in your eyes. You know I haven't much more time, don't you?"

"Yes, child. I do know that."

Victoria smiled pensively. "It used to rankle me when Louis called me 'child'. But with you, my spiritual father, dear Kalamake, it has a nice feeling."

"My task," Victoria began, "will need everything you have taught me. Please, Uncle, stay close beside me, always. What I cannot do in this life, I shall—I must somehow do in the spirit!"

Victoria looked up at the giant banyan and marveled at the prolific spread of its branches, the richness of its leaves, the cathedral-like buttresses of its huge trunk.

"The banyan tree," she said, her voice dropping to a reverent whisper, "The oldest tree in the world. Evergreen, Uncle. Think of that! *Ever* green! A sacred tree. Buddha meditated under a banyan. How powerful it is—bold, dauntless, indestructible! It spreads its roots into thin air and makes contact with the nourishment of Mother Earth. And it grows and shelters, and the fiercest storms can't uproot it. Oh, how wonderful, how beautiful it is!"

Victoria turned to Kalamake, her eyes glowing. "When I am gone, I want everyone, when they see a banyan, to think of Kaiulani, and her love for her people, and for these islands. I'm going to haunt them, Uncle, in a loving way, in the spirit of 'aloha'. Whenever they see a banyan, they will feel kinder, more compassionate toward their fellow man, and, in wisdom, they will tear down the barriers."

♦   ♦   ♦

On October 1 1898, Victoria gave a lavish dinner in honor of the five Annexation Commissioners appointed by President McKinley. It was a gala affair. Victoria was radiant in a white gown, her bright eyes flashing, and she was the admired center of the large number of distinguished guests.

In early December, along with several friends, Victoria made arrangements to sail on the inter-island steamer *Kinau* to the Big Island. Her dear friend, Eva Parker, was to be married, and Victoria looked forward eagerly to this social event. The forthcoming wedding would be at Mana, seat of the Parker Ranch, and known for its grand way of life.

As Victoria was preparing her departure from Ainahau, she brought out a strongbox from her bedroom, took the talisman from around her neck, with a long last look at the intertwined blossoms of silver, she placed it in the box and locked it. It would be turned over to Limu who would accompany her as far as Hilo. The strongbox had been for several years the receptacle for Victoria's earthly reminders of Louis, the poems she had received in her dreams, her notes and mementos of their times together. Limu was waiting for her below with the carriage.

"Limu, there is something I need you to do for me while you are in Hilo visiting your family."

Limu began storing her luggage in the back of the landau. Victoria held the strongbox close to her as he reached for it.

"This box," Victoria said, "is something I want you to take up to the volcano. I won't be going there, and I want you to give it to Madame Pele for me."

Limu took the box from her, examined it admiringly, for it was a handsomely tooled container, and looked at her questioningly.

"This is a beautiful box, Miss Victoria. Are you sure? You really want me to do that?"

"Yes, I'm sure, Limu."

"Wait! I've got an old box in the stable." He grinned like a co-conspirator. "How about giving that one, instead?"

Victoria smiled patiently. "No, Limu, that's the one I want to send—well, in a way, I'm giving it back—"

"You really want me to throw it? Into the fire pit?"

"If you can. As close as you can. I don't want you to take any risks, Limu. I don't want you to get hurt."

"You know, Miss Victoria, over there on the Big Island, folks throw Pele a bottle of gin sometimes. Wouldn't that do?"

Limu, utterly mystified, acknowledged Victoria's determination and reluctantly agreed. After all, such an offering to the volcano goddess might be reasonable. But there was something about the princess's manner that puzzled him, and raised doubts. Still, lava flows were weaving a destructive course down the windward side of the island. It would be like the princess to want to do something good....

The trip to Hilo in December was a rough one and the *Kinau* was battered by strong northeast trade winds all the way. Victoria spent much time on deck, thrilling to the cool gusts and watching for the first signs of Hawai'i, with its overhanging clouds, and deep clefts in the windward mountains on the Hamakua coast.

From Hilo, Victoria and her friends traveled to the cool, elevated mountain region of Waimea. Her buggy had hardly any springs, and the road was one to be encountered only in a bad dream. It rained all that day and the next and, typical of Waimea at such times, they couldn't see twenty yards away through the dense fog. Still, it was a merry group, the wedding and the Christmas holidays were on the way, and, for Victoria: it was cool!

Waimea had always occupied a special place for Victoria second only to Ainahau. The sweep of the broad mountain valley between towering Mauna Kea [white mountain] and the soft, green, billowing

Kohala Mountains to the north made her heart sing. A few days after their arrival, the trade winds returned and swept away the clouds from Mauna Kea to reveal a dense snow cap reaching down to the eight thousand foot level. Victoria reveled in this breezy, invigorating mountain locale. Alas! Louis had never seen this sight. The clouds had denied him that. How he would have loved it! It was so much like the southern borders of Scotland; the air was sweet with evergreen scents and she had never felt more alive, more in love with her islands.

Eva Parker had planned an enormous wedding with holiday festivities to follow. The supply of liquor would be unlimited, more than sufficient for her guests to float on for days and nights on end. There were rides and picnics planned, and Victoria joined the group in a ride into deep, mysterious, secluded Waipio Valley. That evening the natives called, to serenade and dance for the merry pleasure-seekers, and on return from the valley, Victoria had the kind of exciting ride she missed on Oahu, jumping her horse over logs and pig holes.

As Christmas approached, Victoria was reluctant to leave the Big Island. Overall she had been feeling so much better, but headaches still nagged at her and made her unwilling to return to the warmth of Honolulu.

Christmas and New Years passed. In the cool, windswept Waimea nights Victoria dreamed of another New Years spent in Edinburgh with Louis. By day she plunged into the activities of her Mana Ranch friends, who filled the hours with games, laughter and excitement.

The Parkers scheduled a picnic ride one January morning. Victoria had slept deeply during the night, and felt, as she looked out across the pasture land, as though she were still in a dream. It was as though she were everywhere at once—that she was here at Mana Ranch, and also looking down upon them from the top of snowy Mauna Kea. She felt herself floating far out on the distant blue ocean. And yet, with it all, and at the same time, she found herself in distant lands and a part of many people. 'Child of Air'! That old thought—that mysterious something she first felt with Louis—returned to her: never so strongly, never with such a purity and intensity as at this moment!

The air was chill as they mounted their horses and cantered off into the soft, green hills. Victoria spurred her horse into the lead, coaxing the others into a race. As they descended from Mana toward the lower pastures of Ahualoa, abruptly, the brisk trade winds sweeping across Waipio Valley brought a sudden, saturating downpour. It drenched Victoria and blew through her like an icy knife.

The chill rain enhanced the ineffable feeling that had greeted Victoria on her awakening that morning. The effect was magical. Suddenly she felt free, and light as a feather; her horse beneath her seemed, like Pegasus, to be sailing on wings. She threw off her cape, shook her long curls loose and, with a cry of delight, galloped off into the storm. The mists which hung over the mountains descended like a blanket about her, comforting, soft, buoyant, and silent.

In the distance, through the driving rain, Victoria saw a shadow fading in and out of the misty gusts; she spurred her horse, driving toward it eagerly.

Across the rain swept hills toward Mana, beyond the mist, Victoria heard her friends' faint voices fading in a last call to her.

The shadow became a figure—a man on horseback. He waved, wheeled his horse and beckoned to her. He was wearing a kilt, the Stewart tartan, and he called her by name.

"Victoria! Hurry, woman! We've waited long enough!"

♦ ♦ ♦

> *Well hast thou sailed: now die,*
> *To die is not to sleep.*
> *Still your true course you keep,*
> *O sailor soul, still sailing for the sky;*
> *And fifty fathom deep*
> *Your colors still shall fly.*

♦ ♦ ♦

EPILOGUE

Victoria's friends, drenched and shaken to the core, carried her, limp and unconscious, back through the driving rain to Mana Ranch. But this wasn't Victoria; not the dark-eyed, vivacious young beauty who had graced their company these past few weeks. The 'Child of Air' had flown far away.

On January 24, the Honolulu papers reported that Victoria was quite ill at Mana, and that Governor Cleghorn had left on the *Kinau* with Dr. Walters, the family physician. Victoria was quickly taken on a litter down the long verdant slope from Waimea to Kawaihae harbor, then onto the steamer *Mauna Loa* for return to Honolulu.

In the days that followed, the family stood by at Ainahau, helplessly watching, as Victoria slowly, steadily slipped away from them. Late one night, the family was summoned to assemble in the sick room, a semi-circle of stricken faces beside her bed. On Monday, March 6 1899 at 2:00 a.m. her breathing stopped and suddenly all was still. The physical body of Victoria Kaiulani had died at twenty-three years and five months.

At that hour, below in the shadows of the garden, the peacocks of Ainahau began to scream wildly. Loud and long, their cries pierced the darkness.

Pale rider to the convent gate.
Come, O rough bridegroom, Death,
Where, bashful bride, I wait you, veiled,
Flush-faced, with shaken breath;

I do not fear your kiss. I dream

New days, secure from strife,
And, bride-like, in the future hope—
A quiet household life.

Princess Victoria Kaiulani lay in state at Kawaiahao Church surrounded by fragrant maile and floral crowns of carnations and ilima. The following day Honolulu reverberated profoundly with the tolling of bells, the booming of cannon, the funeral dirge, and the wailing and chanting of the natives. The long, mournful procession slowly wound its way up Nuuanu hill, to the Royal Mausoleum where Kaiulani was laid beside her mother, Princess Miriam Likelike.

♦   ♦   ♦

Victoria Kaiulani contracted a Streptococcal upper respiratory infection at Mana Ranch. Over a few weeks her body reacted to the infection with a complicating rheumatic fever which attacked her heart, already weakened during the previous few years, by the development of hyperthyroidism. This latter condition fatigued her heart, made her lovely eyes more prominent, and rendered her intolerant of tropical heat. A curious, remarkable element in Victoria's medical history is this development of a thyroid disease. The thyroid gland enlarges and increases its activity during pregnancy, and, indeed physicians sometimes see this phenomenon in women who deeply desire pregnancy but have not conceived, pseudocyesis, or so-called "false pregnancy." Victoria longed for such a consummation of her love for Louis. Not having a child was one of Louis's deepest regrets. Between them they gave birth, among other things, to his greatest masterpiece, *Weir of Hermiston*, but it wasn't the child they both desired.

Robert Louis Stevenson died of a cerebral hemorrhage. How ironic! After being hounded and shackled—physically, but not in his indomitable spirit—by tuberculosis, for so many years of his life, he fell victim to an unrelated catastrophe. When one studies the last chapter of unfinished *Weir*, and the intensity Louis injected into Archie Weir's scene with Kirstie, it is not difficult to imagine that, for Stevenson, that creative moment came too close to what was totally unacceptable to him: ultimate separation from Victoria. His poetry pervasively denies separation from the loved one by death.

At the summit of Mount Vaea a large tomb was built of blocks of cement over Stevenson's grave. Upon the base are two bronze plaques. One, in Samoan, bears the words, 'The Tomb of Tusitala', followed by the biblical speech of Ruth to Naomi: '...thy people shall be my people, and thy God my God; where thou diest, will I die...'. At the right and left are portrayed a thistle and a hibiscus flower. On the other side, in English, is Stevenson's 'Requiem'

Under the wide and starry sky,
Dig the grave and let me lie,
Glad did I live and gladly die,
And I laid me down with a will.

This be the verse you grave for me;
Here he lies where he longed to be;
Home is the sailor, home from the sea,
And the hunter home from the hill.

♦   ♦   ♦

Queen Lili'uokalani, Lydia Dominis, died at her home in Washington Place in 1917 at the age of 79. To her people this great lady left the memory of a remarkable monarch, but more than that, she left them a song as well—the haunting and beautiful *Aloha O'e*.

Archibald S. Cleghorn died on November 1 1910. Ainahau, and the banyan tree he planted, were willed to the Territory of Hawai'i to be used as a park in Kaiulani's name. The offer was never accepted, and in 1917, the land was sold and subdivided. Tusitala Street is located in this section and commemorates Stevenson. It was on this short street that the banyan stood. In time the lot on which the tree stood was deeded to the Daughters of Hawai'i to be used as a park. On October 16 1930 a bronze plaque was attached to the tree. A banyan tree, in low relief, dominated the plaque, and a single peacock graced the lower left-hand corner. On it was inscribed Stevenson's famous poem to Kaiulani, written in "the April of her Age." In time the huge tree began to endanger nearby homes as the residential district of Waikiki expanded, and it was cut down in 1949. Plans were then made for a memorial in the form of a large rock, "Chief's Rock" to which the plaque would be attached. For those who wish to appreciate the banyan tree to the fullest, a tour of Hilo's Banyan Drive will remind them of the wisdom of Victoria Kaiulani's choice of this magnificent work of nature as her life statement.

Robert Kalanihiapo Wilcox married Princess Theresa Cartwright who bore him two children. In 1900 he was elected Hawai'i's first representative to the US. Congress. In 1903, at age forty-eight, while running for the office of sheriff of Honolulu, Wilcox suffered a series of hemorrhages and died. There was an unresolved contention that he had been poisoned.

Vailima was sold for 1,750 Pounds to a retired German fur merchant from Vladivostok. When the Germans annexed Samoa in 1900, Vailima was used as their Governor's residence. In the First World War the New Zealand occupation turned the place into the British Government House. Later, with the island of Upolu under the mandate of the United States, the estate was the residence of the American Administrator. In 1961 Western Samoa became the first republic in Polynesia. Vailima was partly wrecked by a hurricane in 1966, but was rebuilt as a permanent home for the Head of State.

Frances Mathilda Van de Grift Osbourne Stevenson (Fanny) lived as a sort of Dowager Queen of Samoa for a time. After Louis's death, Fanny devoted her energies to the protection and publication of his letters and his biography. The squabble over the biography, mainly the question of who would complete the lagging work, gave rise to literary gossip for years. Fanny traveled widely in America and Europe, enshrined as the widow of an acclaimed genius. She died suddenly on February 18 1914 at Stonehedge, her estate in Montecito, near Santa Barbara in California. The cause of her death, as with Louis, was a brain hemorrhage a few weeks before her seventy-fourth birthday. According to her wish, her body was cremated and the ashes taken to Samoa to lie on the mountain top beside Louis's grave.

Margaret Stevenson (Maggie) died of pneumonia in Edinburgh at the age of sixty-eight. Fanny was called to Scotland to help settle the Thomas Stevenson estate, and this became Fanny's main inheritance for life.

Lloyd Osbourne was appointed American vice-consul in Apia in 1896. In that same year he married Katherine Durham in Honolulu. Fanny had in mind a dutiful daughter-in-law, but Katherine in time seemed to become a caricature of Fanny's darker side. Two sons were born of the marriage, but things went badly. There was a long separation, during which Katherine was forced to live with Fanny while the two barely spoke. Much of this time, Lloyd was pursuing a literary career in New York and London, and furthering the creeping progress of Stevenson's biography. In later years Katherine, after her divorce from Lloyd, went public with her bitter feelings toward Fanny. In 1916 Lloyd finally found marital happiness with Ethel Head, Fanny's chosen successor to Katherine.

Joseph Dwight Strong, Jr. moved frequently in childhood, as his father was a Congregational minister, at one time pastor of the Fort Street Church in Honolulu. Joseph's artistic ability attracted so much attention that he was sent abroad to study. In November 1879 he married Isobel Stuart Osbourne ("Belle") and one child, Austen, was born to them. While living in Samoa the Strongs became estranged and were divorced. Joe remarried, and died in San Francisco in 1899.

Isobel Stuart Osbourne Strong ("Belle") was remarried at age fifty-six to playwright Edward Salisbury Field. Mr. Field was several years younger and their marriage took place on August 29 1914, six months after Fanny's death. Field had long been a protege and companion of Fanny's. Field and Austen Strong, more than once, had plays running simultaneously on Broadway. In later years, oil was struck on some of Field's California land. Belle died in 1953, her ninety-fifth year, a millionairess, surviving Lloyd and Austen, having lived on in an aura of memories, memoirs and interviews.

Austen Strong, the son of Belle and Joe, was born in 1881, and trained as a landscape architect. He gave up this profession in 1905 for play writing. Austen was happily married in 1906 to Mary Wilson in Providence, Rhode Island. Austen became a Broadway success, one of the best known playwrights of his generation in New York and London. His hits of stage and screen include *Three Wise Fools* and *Seventh Heaven*.

Limu buried Victoria's strongbox not far from a lava flow on the slopes of Kilauea. Madame Pele did not, however, see fit to claim it, for which the author is extremely grateful. One can only interpret Pele's restraint as a wish on the part of the volcano goddess that Victoria Kaiulani's story would be told, remembered and remain alive in all who are Hawaiian in their hearts. Limu graduated from technical school on Oahu and found a rich companionship with Loke, thanks to Louis. In 1910, they moved to the plantation village of Pepeekeo, where Limu served as a harvesting superintendent. They lived out a happy life on the Big Island, and raised seven children. One grandson became an outstanding sumo wrestler in Japan.

Kalamake will live forever. Stevenson illustrated Kalamake's magical abilities in his short story *Isle of Voices*. In Hawaiian his name means, among other things, riches, freedom from want, unending vitality. He is the Merlin of our story, the spirit who approaches the present from the future. Kalamake, the enabler, is the swift prow of the Hawaiian canoe as it cuts the wave. He is the cry of Kaiulani's peacocks, the spreading energy of the banyan tree, and the model for all who strive to fulfill the challenging potential of Kaiulani's garden.

♦ ♦ ♦

Bright is the ring of words
When the right man rings them,
Fair is the fall of songs
When the singer sings them.
Still they are caroled and said—
On wings they are carried—
After the singer is dead
And the maker buried.

Low as the singer lies
In the field of heather,
Songs of his fashion bring
The swains together.
And when the west is red
With the sunset embers,
The lover lingers and sings
And the maid remembers.
– R.L.S.

♦ ♦ ♦

GLOSSARY OF NAMES
AND TERMS

'a'ala: Fragrant, sweet-smelling. *Fig.*, of high rank, royal.

'aha inu: Drinking party.

Ainahau: Land of the hau tree.

aloha: Love (used as a greeting or farewell).

'auli'i: Pleasant.

aumakua: Spiritual ancestor.

auwe: A term to express wonder, fear, scorn, pity, affection; to
    groan, moan, grieve.

haggis: Chiefly Scot, a dish made of the heart, liver, etc. of a sheep
    or calf, minced with suet and oatmeal, seasoned, and boiled
    in the stomach of the animal.

haku mo'olelo: Author, story writer.

hamo: To fondle, caress.

hana aloha: Love magic.

haole: White person; formerly any foreigner.

hapa haole: Part-white person; part white and part Hawaiian.

hau: 1. A lowland tree (Hibiscus tiliaceus). 2. Cool, iced; ice, dew,
    snow; to blow, a cool breeze.

hawawa: Unskilled, awkward.

heiau: Temple. Place of worship.

hiamoe iki: A little sleep; nap.

hinuhinu: Bright, glittering.

holoku: A long, loose gown flowing waistless from a yoke.

hone: Sweet and soft, as music; sweetly appealing, as perfume or a memory of love; to tease, mischievous.

hoʻokipa: To entertain.

hoʻopalemo: To drown.

kahili: Feather standard, symbolic of royalty.

kahu maʻi: A nurse.

kahuna: Priest, minister, sorcerer, expert in any profession.

kahuna nui: High priest; highest rank of the ancient order of craftsmen-priests.

kanaka: Human being, man, human, mankind, person, individual, subject.

kane: Man.

kapa: Tapa (q.v.), as made from *wauke* or *mamaki* bark; formerly quilt or clothes of any kind, or bedclothes.

kapu: Taboo, prohibition; special privilege or exemption from ordinary taboo; sacredness; forbidden; sacred; holy, consecrated.

kaukau: Food.

Keawe: (Kiawe) A picturesque tree, also Algaroba or Mesquite, brought to Hawaiʻi from Paris in 1828.

keiki: Child

kelepono: Telephone.

koa: An endemic forest tree (*Acacia koa*), the largest and most valued of the native trees; its fine wood is used for canoes, surfboards, calabashes, ukuleles.

kokua: Helper

Koni Au: Hawaiian song, Kalakaua's favorite. Pangs of love for the flow of spirits

kukui: The candlenut tree.

kunane: Brother, or male cousin of a female. A term of affection.

kupanaha: Surprising, strange, wonderful, extraordinary, marvelous.

kupuna: Grandparent.

lanai: Porch, veranda; temporary open-sided roofed structure near a house.

lauhala: The pandanus tree.

lava-lava: A rectangular cloth of cotton print worn like a kilt or skirt.

lei: A wreath or necklace, usually of flowers or leaves.

lepo'ae'ae: Edible mud.

likelike: Alike, like, similar, resembling, similar.

lima ikaika: Power.

limu: Seaweed.

loke: Rose, rosy.

luau: Hawaiian feast.

mahalo: Thanks, gratitude; to thank. Admiration, praise.

mahele: Portion, division. The Great Mahele; land division of 1848.

maile: A native twining shrub (*Alyxia olivaeformis*), with shiny, fragrant leaves, a favorite for decorations and leis.

Mai poina 'oe ia'u: Don't forget me.

malo: Loincloth.

Mama Likelike: Princess Miriam Likelike, wife to Archibald Cleghorn, mother to Victoria Kaiulani, sister to King David Kalakaua. Descended from the High Chief Kepookalani, first cousin to Kamehameha I.

mana: Life force.

mauka: Inland.

moi: King, sovereign, ruler, queen.

momona: Sweet.

muumuu: A straight, full chemise with a flounce around the hem.

Na Lani Eha: The Four Sacred Ones.

nui: Big, large, great, important.

ohia: A tree native to Hawai'i; it is the first tree to grow on a new lava flow.

Pali-uli: A legendary land of plenty and joy, said to be on Hawai'i.

pa-u: a woman's skirt or sarong, especially as worn by female horseback riders.

Papa Moi: Victoria Kaiulani's nickname for King David Kalakaua.

pikake: 1. Arabian jasmine (*Jasminum sambac*), a shrub with fragrant, small white flowers used for leis. 2. Peacock.

pohaku makamae: A gem.

poi: The Hawaiian staff of life, made from cooked taro corms, or rarely breadfruit, pounded until smooth and thinned with water.

puka: Hole or perforation; door, gate, opening.

tapa: See *kapa*.

wahine: woman.

◆   ◆   ◆

BIBLIOGRAPHY

HAWAI'I

Apple, Russ: Mo'olelo na Apu Columns In: *Hawai'i Tribune-Herald*, Hilo HI, 1993.

Beamer, Billie: *The Royal Torch.* San Jose, CA: Billie and Billie Publishing, Inc., 1989.

Cahill, Emmett: *Yesterday at Kalaupapa.* Honolulu HI: Mutual Publishing & Editions Limited, 1990.

Cameron, Robert: *Above Hawai'i. A Collection of Nostalgic and Contemporary Aerial Photographs of the Hawaiian Islands.* San Francisco CA: Cameron and Co., 1977.

Daws, Gavan: *Shoal of Time: A History of the Hawaiian Islands.* Honolulu HI: University of Hawai'i Press, 1968.

Day, A. Grove and Kirtley, Bacil F.: *Horror in Paradise.* Honolulu HI: Mutual Publishing Co., 1986.

DeMello, Jack: *Music of Hawai'i. From the Missionaries Through Statehood; The Golden Years of the Monarchy; The Twentieth Century.* Recordings commissioned by Hawaiian Land Co. and Dillingham Corp. Honolulu HI, 1966-68.

Dougherty, Michael: *To Steal a Kingdom, Probing Hawaiian History.* Waimanalo, HI: Island Style Press, 1992.

Feher, Joseph: *Hawai'i: A Pictorial History.* Honolulu HI: Bishop Museum Press, 1969.

Goonan, Kathleen Ann: *Kamehameha's Bones.* In: Asimov's Science Fiction Magazine, 1993.

Kaʻanoʻi, Patrick: *The Need for Hawaiʻi: A Guide to Hawaiian Cultural and Kahuna Values.* Honolulu HI: Kaʻanoʻi Productions, 1991.

Kahananui, Dorothy: *Influences on Hawaiian Music.* Lecture at Kamehameha School's 75th Anniversary, 1965. Honolulu HI: Kamehameha Schools Press.

Katsuki, Betty: *Medical Men Who Helped to Shape Hawaiʻi.* Hawaiʻi Med. J.: 40:10(279-286) September 1981.

McBride, L.P.: *The Kahuna: Versatile Mystics of Old Hawaiʻi.* Hilo HI: Petroglyph Press, 1972.

Mebane, Midge Hill: *Hives in Paradise.* Hilo, HI: Windward Publishing Co., 1983.

Mills, George H., M.D.: *Hawaiians and Medicine.* Hawaiʻi Med. J.:40:10 (272-276), September 1981.

Morris, Aldyth V.: *Damien.* Honolulu: University of Hawaiʻi Press, 1980.

Morris, Aldyth V.: *Liliʻuokalani.* Honolulu: University of Hawaiʻi Press, 1990.

Noyes, Martha H.: "We Will Eat Stones." *Honolulu Magazine,* January 1993.

Orozco, David J.: *Hawaiian Reflections*-Stories and Observations of Mark Twain, Jack London, Robert Louis Stevenson and Charles Warren Stoddard. Honolulu HI: Mauna Loa Publishing Co., 1989.

Paltin, Samuel J., M.D.: *Huna of Hawaiʻi: A System of Psychological Theory and Practice.* Hawaiʻi Med. J. 45:6 (July 1986).

Pukui, Mary Kawena, Elbert, Samuel H. & Mookini, Esther T.: *The Pocket Hawaiian Dictionary.* Honolulu: The University Press of Hawaiʻi (1975)

Seiden, Allan: "Robert Kalanihiapo Wilcox, the Quixotic Warrior." *Aloha Magazine, September-October 1992 (38-45).*

Stokes, John F.G.: *Heiau of the Island of Hawaiʻi: A Historic Survey of Native Hawaiian Temple Sites.* Ed. by Tom

Dye. Honolulu HI: Bishop Museum Press, 1991.

Stone, Margaret: *Supernatural Hawai'i.* Honolulu HI: Tongg
Publishing Co., 1979.

Thompson, Vivian L.: *Hawaiian Legends of Tricksters and
Riddlers.* Honolulu HI: University of Hawai'i Press, 1969.

Westervelt, W.D.: *Myths and Legends of Hawai'i.* Honolulu HI:
Mutual Publishing Co., 1987.

Hawaiian Legends of Old Honolulu. Rutland VT: Chas. E. Tuttle
Co., 1963.

Wisniewski, Richard A.: *The Rise and Fall of the Hawaiian
Kingdom.* Honolulu HI: Pacific Basin Enterprises, 1979.

Yardley, Maili: The Island Way: How Christmas first came to the
Islands. *The Honolulu Advertizer,* Honolulu HI: December
23, 1993.

Zambucka, Kristin: *Princess Kaiulani: The Last Hope of
Hawai'i's Monarchy.* Honolulu HI: Mana Publishing
Company, 1982.

Zambucka, Kristin: A Cry of Peacocks. Videotape. Honolulu:
Green Glass Productions, 1993.

ROBERT LOUIS STEVENSON

NOVELS AND TALES

New Arabian Nights (1882)

Treasure Island (1883)

More New Arabian Nights: The Dynamiter (with Fanny
Osbourne Stevenson, 1884)

Prince Otto (1885)

Memoir of Fleeming Jenkin (1887)

The Black Arrow: A Tale of Two Roses (1888)

The Master of Ballantrae (1889)

The Wrong Box (with Lloyd Osbourne, 1889)

The Wrecker (with Lloyd Osbourne, 1892)

David Balfour (also called *Catriona,* 1893)

Island Nights' Entertainments (1893)

The Ebb-Tide: A Trio and Quartette (with Lloyd Osbourne, 1894)

Weir of Hermiston (unfinished, 1896)

St. Ives (completed by Arthur Quiller-Couch, 1897)

SHORTER FICTION

An Old Song (1877)

A Lodging for the Night: A Story of Francis Villon (1877)

Will o' the Mill (1878)

The Sire de Maletroit's Door (1878)

The Suicide Club (1878)

The Rajah's Diamond (1878)

Providence and the Guitar (1878)

The Story of a Lie (1879)

The Pavilion on the Links (1880)

Thrawn Janet (1881)

The Treasure of Franchard (1882)

The Body Snatcher (1884)

Olalla (1985)

The Strange Case of Dr. Jekyll and Mr. Hyde (1886)

Markheim (1886)

The Merry Men and Other Tales and Fables (1887)

The Misadventures of John Nicholson (1887)

The Bottle Imp (1891)

The Beach of Falesa (1892)

The Isle of Voices (1893)

POETRY

> *A Child's Garden of Verses* (1885)
>
> *Underwoods* (1887)
>
> *Ballads* (1891)
>
> *Songs of Travel and Other Verses* (1896)

ESSAYS AND TRAVEL BOOKS

> *An Inland Voyage* (1878)
>
> *Picturesque Notes on Edinburgh* (1878)
>
> *Travels with a Donkey in the Cevennes* (1879)
>
> *Virginibus Puerisque* (1881)
>
> *Familiar Studies of Men and Books* (1882)
>
> *The Silverado Squatters* (1883)
>
> *Memories and Portraits* (1887)
>
> *In the South Seas: A Record of Three Cruises* (1890)
>
> *Across the Plains* (1892)
>
> *A Footnote to History: Essays on Samoa* (1892)
>
> *Vailima Letters* (to Sidney Colvin, 1895)

COLLECTED EDITIONS

> The Edinburgh Edition, ed. Sidney Colvin (1894-98).
>
> The Pentland Edition, with biographical notes by Edmund Gosse (1906-07).
>
> The Swanston Edition, with an Introduction by Andrew Lang (1911-12).
>
> The Vailima Edition, ed. Lloyd Osbourne, with Prefatory Notes by Fanny van de Grift Stevenson (1922-23).
>
> The Tusitala Edition (1923-24).
>
> Robert Louis Stevenson: The Complete Shorter Fiction. Peter Stoneley, ed. New York: Carroll & Graf, Inc. 1991.

COLLECTIONS, BIOGRAPHIES, CRITICISMS

Aldington, Richard. *Portrait of a Rebel: The Life and Work of Robert Louis Stevenson.* London: Evans, 1957.

Baildon, Henry B. *Robert Louis Stevenson: A Life Study in Criticism.* London: Chatto & Windus, 1901.

Poems, edited with introduction and notes, by George Sidney Hellman, The Bibliophile Society, 1916.

Poems, with introduction and notes by George S. Hellman and William P. Trent, The Bibliophile Society, 1921.

Prose Writings, edited with introduction and notes by Henry H. Harper, The Bibliophile Society, 1921.

Letters to Charles Baxter, ed. De Lancey Ferguson and Marshall Waingrow. New Haven: Yale University Press, 1956.

Five Poems and Letters to Charles Warren Stoddard, Privately Printed, 1924.

Balfour, Graham: *The Life of Robert Louis Stevenson*, two volumes, Charles Scribner's Sons, 1901.

Bermann, Richard A.: *Home from the Sea*, translated by Elizabeth Reynolds Hapgood, Bobbs-Merrill, 1939.

Boodle, Adelaide A.: *R.L.S. and His Sine Qua Non*, Scribner's, 1926.

Brown, George E.: *A Book of R.L.S.*, Scribner's, 1919.

Calder, Jenni: *RLS: A Life Study. London:* 1980.

(ed.) *Stevenson and Victorian Scotland.* Edinburgh: 1981.

Caldwell, Elsie Noble: *Last Witness for Robert Louis Stevenson.* Norman, OK: 1960.

Candler, B.P.: "Stevenson and Henley," *Putnam's Magazine*, 1909.

Carre, Jean Marie: *The Frail Warrior*, translated by Eleanor Hard, Coward-McCann, 1930.

Chesterton, G.K.: *Robert Louis Stevenson.* New York: Dodd, Mead & Co., 1928

Colvin, Sir Sidney: Introductions and Notes to *Vailima Letters,* Scribner's, 1896.
Letters to His Family and Friends, 2nd ed.
New York: Scribner, 1911.
Letters, South Seas Edition, Scribner's, 1925.

Cooper, Lettice: *Robert Louis Stevenson.* London: Home & Van Thal, 1947.

Cornford, L. Cope: *Robert Louis Stevenson,* Dodd, Mead & Co., 1900.

Daiches, David: *Robert Louis Stevenson.* Norfolk, CT: New Directions, 1947; and Glasgow 1947.
Stevenson and the Art of Fiction. New York: 1951.
Robert Louis Stevenson and His World. London: Thames and Hudson, 1973.
Literature and Gentility in Scotland. Edinburgh: 1982.

Dalglish, Doris N.: *Presbyterian Pirate,* Oxford University Press, 1937.

Eigner, Edwin M.: *Robert Louis Stevenson and Romantic Tradition.* Princeton: Princeton University Press, 1966.

Elliott, Nathaniel: "Robert Louis Stevenson and Scottish Literature." *English Literature in Transition* (1880-1920) 12 (1969): 79-85.

Elwin, Malcolm: *The Strange Case of Robert Louis Stevenson.* London: Macdonald, 1950.

Field, Isobel (formerly Strong, nee Osbourne): *Memories of Vailima,* (with Lloyd Osbourne) Charles Scribner's Sons, 1902.
Robert Louis Stevenson, Scribner's, 1911.
This Life I've Loved, Longmans, Green & Co., 1937.

Fisher, Anne B.: *No More a Stranger,* Stanford University Press, 1946.

Fowler, Alistair: "Parables of Adventure: The Debatable Novels of Robert Louis Stevenson." *Nineteenth-Century Scottish Fiction: Critical Essays,* ed. Ian Campbell. Totowa, NJ: Barnes & Noble, 1979.

Furnas, J.C.: *Voyage to Windward: The Life of Robert Louis Stevenson*, New York: Sloane, 1951.

Gosse, Edmund W. : *Biographical Notes on the Writings of Robert Louis Stevenson*, Privately Printed, 1908.
"Robert Louis Stevenson" in *Critical Kit-Kats*. Dodd, Mead & Co., 1896.
The Pentland Edition of *Collected Writings, 20 vols., 1906-07.*

Guthrie, Charles John (Lord): *Robert Louis Stevenson, Some Personal Recollections*, W. Green & Son, 1924.

Gwynn, Stephen: *Robert Louis Stevenson*, English Man of Letters Series, The McMillan Co., 1939.

Hamilton, Clayton: *On the Trail of Stevenson*, Doubleday, Page & Co., 1915.

Hellman, George S.: *The True Stevenson, A Study in Clarification.* Boston: Little Brown & Co., 1925.

Henley, W.E.: "R.L.S.," *The Pall Mall Magazine*, December, 1901.
Poems, Scribner's, 1906.

Hennessy, James Pope: *Robert Louis Stevenson* (1974)

Issler, Anne Roller: *Stevenson at Silverado*, The Caxton Printers, 1939.
Happier for His Presence, Stanford University Press, 1949.

James, Henry: "Robert Louis Stevenson" in *Partial Portraits.* London: 1888, pp.137-174.

Jefford, Andrew: 'Dr. Jekyll and Professor Nabokov: Reading a Reading' in Noble.

Kelman, John, Jr.: *The Faith of Robert Louis Stevenson.* New York: Revell, 1903.

Kiely, Robert: *Robert Louis Stevenson and the Fiction of Adventure.* Cambridge: Harvard University Press, 1964.

Knight, Alanna: *Robert Louis Stevenson Treasury* (1985)

Low, Will H.: *A Chronicle of Friendships*, Scribner's, 1908.

Lucas, E.V.: *The Colvins and Their Friends,* Methuen & Co., 1928.

Lyell, W.D.: 'The Real Weir of Hermiston'; an address delivered to the Glasgow Juridical Society (Edinburgh, 1903).

MacCulloch, J.A.: *R.L. Stevenson and the Bridge of Allan, with Other Stevenson Essays*, John Smith & Son, 1927.

Mackay, Margaret: *The Violent Friend: The Story of Mrs. Robert Louis Stevenson 1840-1914*. Garden City, NY: Doubleday, 1968.

MacPherson, Harriet Dorothea: *R.L. Stevenson, A Study in French Influence*, Institute of French Studies, 1930.

Maixner, Paul (ed.): *Robert Louis Stevenson: The Critical Heritage* (1981).

Masson, Rosaline: *The Life of Robert Louis Stevenson*. Edinburgh: W. & R. Chambers, 1923.

McGaw, Sister Martha Mary: *Stevenson in Hawai'i*. Honolulu HI: University of Hawai'i Press, 1950.

Miller, Karl: *Cockburn's Millennium* (1975).
Doubles (1985).

Miyoshi, Misao: The Divided Self. New York: 1969.

Moffett, Cleveland: "Will H. Low and His Work," *McClure's Magazine*, September, 1985.

Moors, J.H.: *With Stevenson in Samoa*, Small, Maynard Co., 1910.

Morley, Christopher: "An American Gentleman," *Saturday Review of Literature*, September 20, 1947.

Noble, Andrew (ed.): *Robert Louis Stevenson* (1983) [Noble]

Osbourne, Katherine D.: *Robert Louis Stevenson in California*, McClure, 1911.

Osbourne, Lloyd: *An Intimate Portrait of R.L.S. New York:* Scribner's, 1924.
Introduction to Works in South Seas Edition, Scribner's, 1923 and 1925.
Collected Works, Vailima Edition, ed. with Fanny Van de Grift Stevenson (26 vols., 1922-23.)

Pinero, Arthur Wing: *Robert Louis Stevenson as a Dramatist*, with introduction by Clayton Hamilton, Columbia University, 1914.

Pope-Hennessy, James: *Robert Louis Stevenson*. Edinburgh: Chambers, 1923; London: 1974.

Prideaux, W.F.: *Bibliography of Robert Louis Stevenson* (1903); revised edition, 1917).

Raleigh, Walter: *Robert Louis Stevenson*, Edward Arnold, 1910.

Rice, Edward: *Journey to Upolu: Robert Louis Stevenson, Victorian Rebel*. New York: Dodd, Mead, 1974.

Sanchez, Nellie Van de Grift: *The Life of Mrs. Robert Louis Stevenson*, Scribner's, 1922.

Saposnik, Irving S.: *Robert Louis Stevenson*. New York: Twayne, 1974.

Scott, J.D.: 'Novelist-Philosophers: R.L. Stevenson and G.D. Brown: The Myth of Lord Braxfield', *Horizon*, XIII, 298-310 (May 1946)

Simpson, E. Blantyre: *Robert Louis Stevenson's Edinburgh Days*, Hoder & Stoughton, 1914.

Simpson, K.G.: 'Author and Narrator in *Weir of Hermiston*' in Noble.

Smith, Janet Adam: *R.L. Stevenson*. London: Duckworth, 1937.

Stern, G.B.: *No Son of Mine*, The McMillan Co., 1948.

Steuart, John A.: *Robert Louis Stevenson, A Critical Biography*, two vols., Little, Brown & Co., 1924.
The Cap of Youth, Being the Love Romance of Robert Louis Stevenson, Lippincott, 1927.

Stevenson, Fanny Van de Grift, *The Cruise of the Janet Nicholl, A Diary*, Scribner's, 1914.
Introduction to Works in Biographical and South Seas Editions, Scribner's, 1905 and 1923-25.

Stevenson, Margaret Isabella: *From Saranac to the Marquesas and Beyond*, edited and arranged by Marie Clothilde Balfour, Scribner's, 1903.

Letters from Samoa, edited and arranged by Marie Clothilde Balfour, Scribner's, 1906.

Strong, Austin: "The Most Unforgettable Character I've Met," *The Reader's Digest*, March, 1946.

Strong, Isobel and Osbourne, Lloyd : *Memories of Vailima*. New York: Scribner, 1902.

Swearingen, Roger G.: *The Prose Writings of Robert Louis Stevenson: a Guide* (1980)

Swinnerton, Frank: *R.L. Stevenson, A Critical Study*. London: Secker, 1914.

Trent, William P.: *Stevenson's Workshop*, The Bibliophile Society, 1921.

Watt, Francis: *R.L.S.*, Methuen, 1913.

Williamson, Kennedy: *W.E. Henley*, Harold Shaylor, 1930.

MISCELLANEOUS

Campbell, Joseph: *Myths to Live By*. New York, Bantam Books, 1973.

From Scotland to Silverado, ed. James D. Hart. Cambridge: Harvard University Press, 1966.

From the Clyde to California: Robert Louis Stevenson's Emigrant Journey. ed. Andrew Noble. Aberdeen University Press, 1985.

du Maurier, George: Peter Ibbetson, (1891).

George L. McKay: *The Stevenson Library of Edwin J. Beinecke*, 6 vols. (New Haven, 1958).

Our Samoan Adventure, ed. Charles Neider. New York: Harper, 1955.

Smith, Janet Adam, Ed. *Henry James and Robert Louis Stevenson: A Record of Friendship and Criticism*. London: Hart-Davis, 1948.
Collected Poems, 2nd ed. New York: Viking, 1971.

Stevensoniana, An Anecdotal Life and Appreciation of Robert Louis Stevenson, edited by J.A. Hammerton. Edinburgh: John Grant, 1910.

I Can Remember Robert Louis Stevenson, edited by Rosaline Masson, Stokes, 1922.

Autograph Letters, Original Manuscripts, Books, Portraits and Curios, consigned by Mrs. Isobel Strong (Later Mrs. Salisbury Field), November, 1914, January, 1915, February, 1916.

Letters to the Colvins, offered by Edward Verrall Lucas, 1928.

The McCutcheon Collection, American Art Museum, 1925.

◆ ◆ ◆